REBELLION
—ON THE—
Chesapeake

AMERICA'S FIRST REVOLUTION IN 1676

A NOVEL

CAROLIN A. CRABBE

GFG Press

≫ TABLE OF CONTENTS ≪

Part III

⋙ ACKNOWLEDGEMENTS ⋘

When I began research on the Virginia uprising in 1675-1676, I was not sure where it would lead. I soon decided a historical novel could bring the first steps that shaped the destiny of America to more readers and promote interest in exploring history to better understand the choices of our future. Until this point, my career has been technical with little scope to spread my wings in a more artistic milieu. Writing historical fiction has been challenging, but great fun as well. I am especially indebted to my writers' critique group who provided so many helpful comments on creative writing, and plot and character development. In particular, I would like to recognize George Vercessi and Michael Williams for reading the entire book more than once and each time, sharing with me their thoughtful insights. Cinda Crabbe MacKinnon made excellent recommendations on characters and the story arc. Marvin Wooten, who has hiked the Great Warrior Path, gave me terrific suggestions on what to expect when walking these trails in the seventeenth century. Barbara Eustace Miller and Margo Thorning helped me improve the early chapters. Melanie Stephens my illustration and graphic designer produced elegant maps and illustrations, and formatted the book. Thank you wonderful colleagues and friends for your encouragement and support.

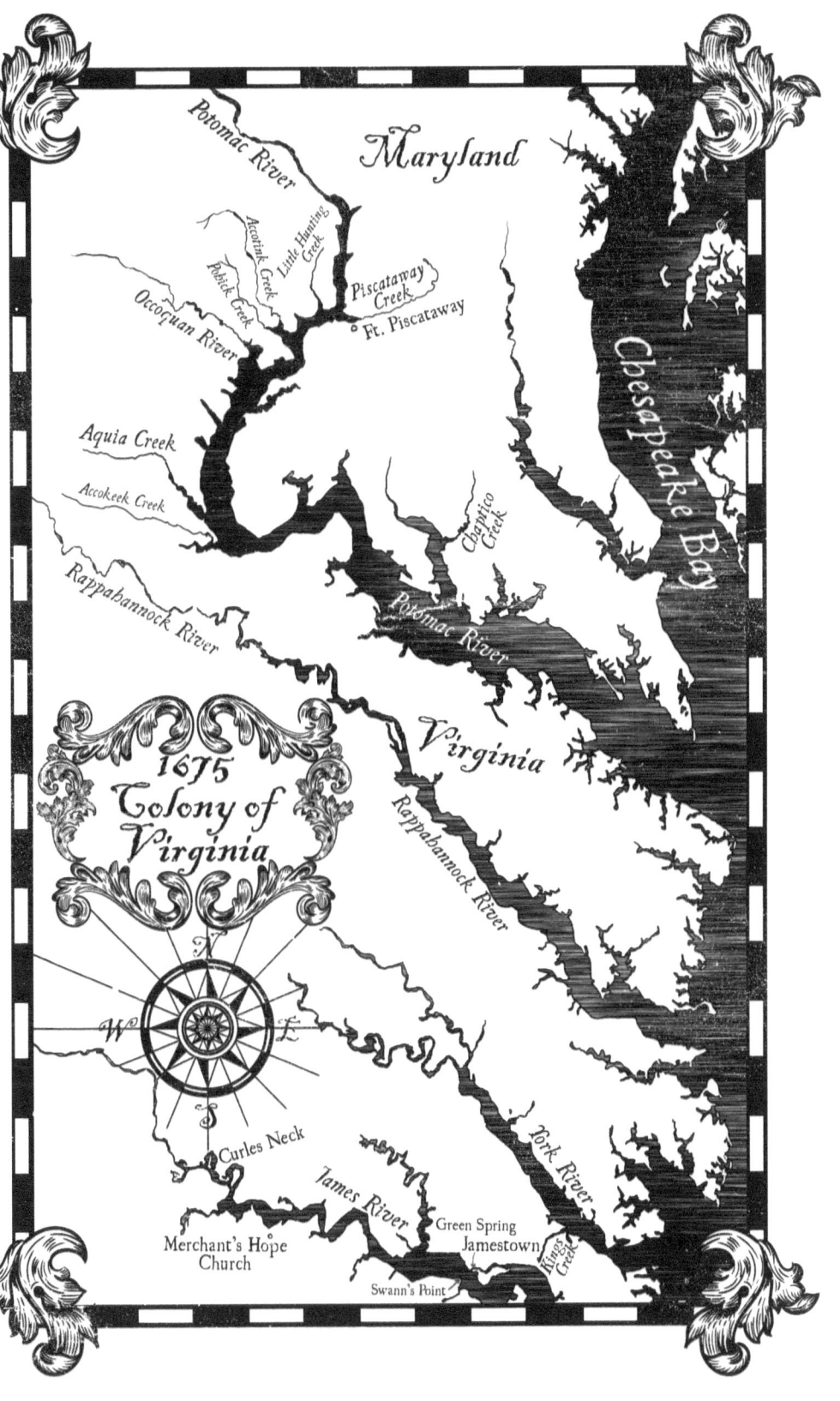

Potomac River

Maryland

Accotink Creek

Little Hunting Creek

Piscataway Creek

Ft. Piscataway

Pohick Creek

Occoquan River

Chesapeake Bay

Aquia Creek

Accokeek Creek

Chaptico Creek

Rappahannock River

Potomac River

Virginia

1675
Colony of
Virginia

Rappahannock River

N

W · E

S

York River

Curles Neck

James River

Green Spring
Jamestown

Kings Creek

Merchant's Hope
Church

Swann's Point

PART I

CHAPTER 1

THE DOGUE ATTACK

Potomac River and Stafford County
Season of the Full Buck Moon —Early July 1675

THE SURFACE OF THE WATER SHONE LIKE OBSIDIAN IN THE moon's light as the eight warriors propelled the war canoe down the river. The outgoing tide pushed them southward making their paddling almost effortless. They had not spoken since boarding, and Wannis sensed their tension as they drew closer to their destination—what the English called Stafford County where Virginia's isolated, northernmost plantations were located.

Wannis had turned fourteen two summers ago, marking his passage into manhood, gaining him entry into the sweat lodge, and now, the right to participate in his first raid. He tried hard to emulate the others and carve his paddle smoothly but the high pitch of a mosquito kept whining in his ear. He shook his head vigorously causing the canoe to shudder.

His uncle Uwanno, who sat in front of him, growled at him over his shoulder. "Keep steady or I'll leave you home next time."

His uncle was their *cockarouse* or war captain—a man you did not cross. His face had a twisted, cruel look caused by the deep scar running from his missing ear to his chin. While Dogue warriors shaved the right side of the head to allow a clean shot with bow and arrow, Uwanno shaved it all, leaving only a short, bristly ridge from forehead to neck. This, he coated with animal fat, so it spiked. He adorned the cockscomb with one of his trophies of war—a dried human hand. He looked fearsome—no bad thing for a war chief.

Maybe he could look as ferocious. Wannis scowled at the thought, but at the same time, a mosquito bit him. He slapped at it. This time, the canoe rocked and his brother Nicotagsen, sitting behind him, punched him in the back.

"Stop it," Nicotagsen hissed, "or I'll toss you overboard."

"Sorry. It bit me." Wannis turned to see his brother glaring at him, his face and body glistening blood red in the moonlight.

"Use the puccoon grease next time." Nicotagsen and the others generously applied a concoction to ward off insects. Wannis hated its smell, but next time he would use the mixture made from rancid bear grease and the crimson puccoon flower.

He settled back into paddling and clenched his teeth, determined to ignore the mosquitoes.

Half a moon ago, he had crossed the river with his three brothers. He and Nansemond, the youngest, had visited his mother's Piscataway sister Mary, who married the Englishman, Giles Brent. His older brothers, Nicotagsen and Chinkotook, continued south in their canoe to Thomas Matthews' place in Stafford. They had trapped all summer and hoped to trade their pelts for one of the English containers made of this strange substance called *metal*. It would be a gift for their mother, to make watering her vegetable garden easier.

Wannis had hardly settled on the riverbank with Nansemond and Mary, trailing their lines in shallow water to attract crabs, when their brothers' canoe returned early. They paddled as though pursued by devils.

Before the canoe even reached the beach, Chinkotook vaulted into the water and raced up the oyster-strewn shore toward them. His angular face contorted in fury as he flung his gear on the ground, snarling, "Matthews cheated us."

"His man, Robert Hen, did. Matthews wasn't there," Nicotagsen, corrected him.

Chinkotook scowled at him. "Hen told us Virginia's governor prohibited fur trade. I told him we'd traded up and down the river long before he arrived. He took my furs but then threw a handful of blue glass beads at me."

"And when I tried to explain Matthews promised us metal containers for our beaver pelts," Nicotagsen said, "he called us liars and savages."

"You mean the man kept your furs?" Wannis looked shocked, for they were valuable.

"Yes." Chinkotook hissed. "Then he pulled out a gun and ordered us off the property."

Hen cheated and humiliated his brothers. Tonight, Wannis thought with a smile, they would even the score with this man by taking his pigs as payment for their furs. That would teach him.

Uwanno raised his right arm and pointed. Without missing a beat, they changed course, leaving the Maryland shoreline behind and heading across the river. As they followed the bright, silvery path the moon cast, the only sound they made came from the water's gentle rippling around the paddles.

By the time they reached Robert Hen's house, the moon would be plunging over the edge of the western sky, just as planned. Wannis asked his uncle why they did not attack the day after Hen cheated them. Uwanno explained, "The time of the full buck moon, when a deer's new, velvety soft antlers push through his forehead is best. The full buck moon makes warriors invincible."

They stilled their paddles and glided onto the sandy beach. When the canoe grounded, Uwanno eased his leg over the side, stepping into ankle-deep water. The others followed.

Wannis tread softly across the sand behind his uncle, trying not to crunch on the oyster shells. Overhead, the cicadas droned, masking much of the small noise he made. The cicadas appeared only three or four times in a lifetime, but when they arrived, their incessant cacophony made up for the years they missed. That summer, his grandmother complained she lost her hearing because of them.

At the top of the slope, his uncle took his arm and motioned him to head west, skirting the cabin to reach the sheds in back. The preceding week, in their council house, Chinkotook had sketched a rough diagram in the earth depicting the pigpen and other outbuildings in relationship to the house.

He raised his knees, placing his feet with care to avoid making noise. When he reached the three-sided shed, Wannis opened the pouch secured at his waist and scattered chestnuts in front of the nearest pig. "Come little fellow." The animal stood up and rooted, moving closer and grunting contentedly. He moved backward slowly, scattering more nuts. Other pigs joined in. He was amazed at how loud their snorting sounded. Pigs, like most domesticated animals, did not normally eat in the middle of the night, and their rooting was audible whenever the cicadas stopped whining.

Wannis squatted and stroked the ear of the piglet that followed him. "Why don't you come and live with us," he whispered, gently tucking it under his arm. He continued to feed it as he walked back to the canoes. Nicotagsen reached out to take it and he started back up the slope, but his uncle grabbed his shoulder and pointed. In the dim light, he saw Chinkotook approaching Robert Hen's house. Uwanno shook his head in disgust and motioned Wannis to accompany him.

They hugged the wall of the house and from inside, Wannis heard a voice whisper, "Shhh. Stay hidden until I call you." So, Hen and his family were awake. Reaching the corner, Wannis heard the gentle jiggling of the wooden bolt on the front door and peered around in time to see Chinkotook crash through the door. A musket discharged with a roar, followed by a loud crash and the sound of something metal clattering to the floorboards.

"Aiiyeeay!" Uwanno let out a bloodcurdling war cry and lunged forward. Wannis saw his uncle struggling with a man who must be Hen. Their breathing and scrapping rang out in the stillness. Suddenly, his uncle grasped the man's gun and jerked him through the doorway. He raised his war hammer—three feet of hard wood and jagged stones—and smashed Hen's head. The man collapsed, and his uncle bludgeoned him repeatedly, each time throwing the full weight of his body behind the blows. At last, Uwanno bent over Hen, and using his hunting knife slashed into the man's scalp, pulling away a bloody chunk of skin and hair.

Wannis tried to enter the cabin but his uncle shoved him back. "No time. Chinkotook is dead. Idiot went in to steal that metal container for your mother."

6

They dashed down the slope and splashed out to the canoes. Uwanno held up the dripping hair lock, before flinging it into the canoe along with Hen's musket.

Again, they paddled in silence, but this time for a different reason. Wannis's mind raced. This was supposed to be a raid, no more. Instead, Chinkotook lay dead. Wannis sat slumped forward, tasting the saltiness of sweat and tears running down his face. With his head down, he paid less attention to whether his paddle moved in concert with the others. The sun had disappeared long ago, but the evening brought no respite from the heat, which now hung over him like a damp, unwanted blanket.

⫸⫷

The next day, Robert Rawlings and his wife emerged from the wooded trail into the bright sunlight and crossed the clearing nestled between the small house and the Potomac River. They took this path almost every Sunday, on their way to the parish church. The field was a riot of yellow and blue wildflowers and the six-foot high plant called gravel root, with its huge mops of dark pink clusters. Their two young daughters skipped in front, arms outstretched.

"Bet you can't catch me," one yelled, as she navigated through the flowers.

"Girls, come back," their mother called.

Usually, Robert Hen, the herdsman, would be tending his pigs, and Rawlings stopped and chatted with him. It was always a brief exchange because Rawlings's wife kept walking with the girls, for they disliked the smell emanating from the pigsty.

This Sunday, the yard was vacant of both the herdsman and his pigs. The only sounds came from the ever-present droning of cicadas and two mockingbirds, tossing their melody back and forth across the meadow. The front door of the cabin stood open and lumps of clothing covered the stoop. Rawlings called out, "Good morning, Mr. Hen."

No one answered. Then, a muffled cry came from inside the house. He grabbed his wife by the elbow and muttered, "I don't like this. You and the girls go back into the woods. I'll holler if it's all right. If I don't, run home and bolt the door."

His wife started to protest, but his grim, homely face showed he was not making a request.

He unsheathed his long hunting knife and scanned the house and the surrounding area before moving forward. When he reached the edge of the untidy yard with its weedy vegetable patch, he drew in a breath. Hen's body blocked the doorway. His head twisted in an unnatural way showed his face was a pulp of raw flesh. The top portion of his head had been hacked away.

Rawlings backed away, his eyes sweeping the scene around him. From the cabin, the sound came again. Someone sobbed softly.

"Help," a small voice cried.

"Is that you, Tobey?"

He moved back toward the door, stepped over the herdsman's body and peered into the cabin. On the floor, an all-but-naked Indian lay in a pool of blood, his head and shoulders draped on the trundle. Nine year-old Tobey Hen's small face, wet with tears, peered at him from the space between the two beds.

"Come on out, boy. They're gone," Rawlings said. Tobey tried to crawl out but the Indian's body blocked him. Rawlings grabbed the man's legs and pulled him off the trundle to make space.

"What happened?" Rawlings asked.

"We was attacked by Dogues," Tobey said, skirting the dead man carefully. "The pigs started snorting in the middle of the night, waking Papa and me. He told me to hide under the bed. He killed the first one." Tobey regarded the body sprawled face down. "I knew it was an Indian. I smell't animal fat. I was scairt to come out lest he wasn't dead and I could see more of them outside. Papa fought them but he never came back."

Tobey reached the front door and saw his father. "Papa," he cried, dropping to his knees.

Rawlings heard his wife call him. "Stay there, Emma." Rawlings reached down and pulled Tobey up, hugging him close. "Come on, boy." He turned and walked toward his wife. "They were attacked by Indians."

8

Emma's mouth opened and her face seemed to whiten.

"I'm taking you back home and then going to Mason's for help."

When he put his arm around Emma's shoulders to steer her back toward their home, Tobey tugged at his other arm. "Mr. Rawlings, please don't leave me here."

"Of course we won't. Come, you poor child," Emma said, taking him by the hand. "You stay with us and protect us." Tobey nodded his head, straightening his spare frame. Emma hurried them back along the path that crossed through the meadow.

After arriving home and making sure they bolted the door, Rawlings headed toward Pohick Creek and the home of the head of Stafford County's militia, Colonel George Mason.

≫ CHAPTER 2 ≪
VIRGINIA'S REVENGE

Pohick Creek, Virginia
Early July 1675

O N THE FIFTH OF JULY, THIRTY-EIGHT MEN FROM neighboring plantations answered Colonel George Mason's summons of the militia. Most of them had come by boat for each plantation had a dock where they loaded tobacco for shipment down the Chesapeake Bay to England. No roads existed this far from Virginia's only town, Jamestown.

He stood on the bank of Pohick Creek surveying them with his second in command, Captain George Brent. Next to them were his houseguests, John and Tom Lucas. The latter were the nephew and son of his friend Thomas Lucas, former Burgess and a founder of Rappahannock County. His friend passed away two years earlier and he tried to guide the young men and offer advice in managing their plantations.

"I reckon these are all we can expect," Mason said. "You don't have to join us." He looked at John and Tom.

"We wouldn't miss it." John Lucas brushed his dark curly hair from his forehead, revealing a pronounced widow's peak. He was a captain in the Westmoreland County militia.

"Let's get going then." Brent kneaded his cheekbone with his knuckles. He and his men had left his property on Aquia Creek the day before. "We have more transport than we need to get us to the Maryland side."

Mason faced the militia and raised his arms, shouting "Men! We're heading to the Maryland side to pursue the Dogues. We don't need all of the boats, so some of you go with neighbors and let's take the fastest ones." He turned back to Brent. "I gather from your cousin, that our destination should be about twenty miles upstream from here."

"Yep. There are two Indian settlements there," Brent replied.

At daybreak several days earlier, his cousin Giles Brent sailed downstream on the Virginia side near Accokeek Creek and spotted war canoes across the river. The canoes rushed up from the south and he might have missed them except they were making an ungodly racket—like animals being slaughtered. One of the braves stood up and howled, waving his arms in the air, as though he was the one making the noise, but this did not fool Giles. He knew they carried something in the bottom of the canoe that was alive and squealing. When Giles got to his cousin's house, he learned about the Dogue raid, and he and George agreed the canoes held the stolen pigs.

"I haven't heard of the Dogues before," Tom Lucas said.

"They're an Algonquian-speaking tribe," his older cousin answered, holding the rowboat steady for Mason, before pushing it from shore. "They used to live on the Virginia side of the Potomac." He grabbed the oars and pulled toward Mason's shallop, which bobbed in the current. "They moved away when planters settled Stafford. I think they pay tribute to the Piscataway king."

"Speaking of the Piscataway," Mason said, "Brent is related by marriage to Mary Brent, the daughter of the Piscataway king, Kittamaqund. Doesn't speak much about it, but he knows a lot about them."

John Lucas could understand why the man kept quiet. So many people judged the tribes as primitive. He thought they had much to learn from them. They were good farmers, hunters, tended to be tall and well-shaped, had gleaming white teeth and looked healthier than most of the English.

They reached Mason's double-masted shallop, the largest ship in their motley flotilla. Half of the men boarded it. The rest went in Brent's eight-oared pinnace and several smaller boats. They headed up the Potomac and when they reached the Maryland shore, they dropped the fore and aft sails, letting them flap in the breeze.

Lucas scanned the landing. Huge trees, which came almost to the water, shaded the sandy beach, while a squirrel chattered, and a glossy, black crow answered with harsh caws. Except for the crow's menacing cries, it was a peaceful place.

Under the umbrella of an immense sycamore tree, the hull of a broken canoe protruded from the sand. The site had been used as a landing, but now there were no canoes and no paths leading away from shore. Puzzled, he surveyed the beach again, noting that its exposure to waves and tides would not make it a good harbor. It curved around to the south. There might be an anchorage on the other side.

The crow's shrieks caused him to look up just in time to see a mockingbird fold back its wings and dive straight at the predator. The plucky bird continued to harass the crow as it flew out over the water to escape. Lucas chuckled.

With the crow gone, silence returned, and the chirps from the woodland resumed, punctuated by the mockingbird's melodic songs. He whispered, "All that tweeting and clucking is a good sign, Colonel Mason. If the Dogues were waiting to cut us down, the woods would be silent."

"My thoughts exactly," Mason murmured.

Brent cupped his hands around his mouth and said quietly, "There could be a harbor hidden behind the weeds to the south. I'll go see."

He inched along the shoreline in his pinnace. There did not appear to be any footprints in the sand along the shore. No one had landed here since the last rain. The beach extended south for about fifty feet, then curved east and the strip of sand and gravel became overgrown with reeds and catkins. Paddling on the edge of the growth, Brent found what he was looking for—a path cut through the reeds that ran through the water southeast to northwest. Because of its angle, it was undetectable as they sailed past. From the foredeck, he could just make out six canoes beached beyond the natural barrier of reeds on the leeward side of the cove.

He returned to the waiting ships and motioned to the others to disembark. They followed him up the sloping bank. At the crest, they peered down into the neatly concealed harbor. The sun filtered through the trees glinting off the water as scores of tiny mayflies flitted across its surface.

"Too tight for us to squeeze in," Mason observed, swatting at a flying insect trying to land on his sweaty face.

"Yep. We should anchor along the shore," Brent said. Mason nodded in agreement and ordered the men to secure the boats and set a watch.

He turned to two of his men and pointed at the canoes. "Make sure those canoes never sail again. Sink them. The rest of you, come with me." He skirted the cove and on the far side easily picked up a well-worn track that led away from the water. After following it a short distance, it split. The path leading north followed along the embankment of a creek.

Mason stopped and pointed at it. "I'll follow it. You take the other trail." He turned and gestured, "You men, with me."

Lucas and his cousin followed Brent and his men as they headed down the path that angled southeast. Lucas noted the evidence of civilization: footprints and a partially-eaten crabapple.

The scouts ranged ahead, returning to report that there was a small settlement over the hill. Lucas and the others followed them up a rise, dropping to their bellies as they neared the top. The cicadas whined, their high-pitched droning rising and falling, almost masking the sounds of laughter drifting toward them. In the clearing, children played.

"I wonder where their warriors are." Lucas whispered.

"Probably out hunting." Brent backed down the slope carefully. He sent his men to surround the settlement and readied himself by drawing his sword from the baldric that hung over his shoulder.

His Nanjemoy interpreter shook his head. "Big knife is not friendly. Dogues may attack." Brent sheathed it and waited a few more minutes for his men to get into position.

"Let's go," Brent said.

They walked down the incline, stopping short of the clearing. Lucas could see six *yehakins*—rectangular, barrel-roofed houses made of wooden frames. The walls were made from reed mats that hung from the frame. Many were rolled up because of the heat. He wondered what they did in the winter, for mats would not keep the cold out.

A group of young children stopped playing and stared at them. Several women, stretching animal skins over sapling frames or tending their vegetable gardens also stopped their work.

"I don't see the pigs," the man on his right muttered.

"Maybe they're hidden in the woods," Brent said.

A tall, muscular warrior ducked under the reed mat of the largest yehakin and headed toward them. He wore a deerskin loincloth, which hung to his knees. The right side of his scalp was shaved but he had a long plaited lock of dark brown hair that dropped almost to his waist on the left side. It boasted an adornment of something black and shiny. As he stopped in front of them, Lucas saw it was the wing of a raven.

The warrior smiled, flashing even, white teeth. Lucas who had some Algonquian thought he said, "I am Nicotagsen, George Brent. How is our cousin Mary Brent?"

The string of small bones and glass beads hanging from Nicotagsen's neck jingled as he extended his hand to Brent. To Lucas's surprise, Brent ignored the outstretched hand and scowled.

"He thinks he's related to me through my cousin's wife, Mary Brent," Brent spat. "But these savages all look the same. He could be Mattawoman, Choptico, Portobacco, Nanjemoy, Anacostan or Dogue, for all I care." He turned to the Nanjemoy interpreter. "Tell him I want to speak with his chief."

The interpreter repeated the message in Algonquian while Brent glowered at Nicotagsen, his arms crossed over his chest with the fingers of one hand resting on his sword.

Nicotagsen cocked his head to one side studying Brent, finally saying, "I shall call my father, Weghucasso. He is our *werowance*." Turning, he walked back toward the same large dwelling he had exited.

Lucas imagined what he would tell the chief. Nicotagsen treated them with courtesy, but Brent answered with surliness.

14

A frail old man, who must be Weghucasso, emerged from the *yehakin*. Nicotagsen did not join him but slipped out the back.

The first thing Lucas noticed about Weghucasso was that he was shorter than most of the women. That was unusual as the men of the tribes were taller than the average Englishman. Weghucasso appeared at least seventy years old. Still, he had a regal presence. He opened his arms wide in greeting, but Brent cut him off.

"You Dogues killed Robert Hen and stole his pigs. I demand you give them back and turn over the men who did this thing." Brent stared at his Nanjemoy interpreter, giving his head a jerk to prompt the translation.

Weghucasso listened to it. "Why is it that the English are fully able to speak for themselves when they want to barter, but lack idiom at other times?"

The Nanjemoy lowered his head to hide his smile.

Weghucasso stared at Brent. "I'm surprised, George Brent, that you don't observe the most minimal courtesies. The man you speak of cheated our people. We took his pigs because he didn't pay us. No one would have died if Hen had not killed my son Chinkotook. Now, I ask you to leave our land."

The Nanjemoy paused, not eager to translate this to the mercurial Brent, but finally did so. He tried to soften it, but without success, for Brent's face darkened.

Weghucasso turned to the Nanjemoy and said in a slow measured voice, "These white people are discourteous. They make astonishing demands, but this is the first time I'm accosted by a kinsman demanding my men be turned over for punishment. Usually, we're the ones complaining because the English animals run over our fields and devour our crops. When I complained to Governor Calvert and asked he pay us for damage, do you know what he told me?"

The interpreter had trouble maintaining a neutral expression.

"He told us to build fences," Weghucasso said, raising his eyebrows, "to deter their livestock from nibbling their way through our fields. I suggested tactfully that he should instruct his people to build the fences." Weghucasso chuckled and the interpreter did too.

"What the hell is he saying?" Brent glowered at the interpreter, his grim features even darker.

Lucas said, "Sir, the *werowance* says that Hen cheated the Dogues and they took the pigs as payment."

"Bah," Brent growled, revealing stained teeth.

"Maybe we should listen to the whole story," he persisted.

Shut up," Brent said. "Tell him to stop prattling and give us the men who killed Hen."

After hearing this translated, Weghucasso frowned. "We have lived in peace with the pale men for many passages of the sun and moon. If my people have done anything, I will judge them, but they will never be turned over to you for punishment.

Brent shifted from one foot to the other as the interpreter translated. Suddenly, he lunged forward, grabbing the short, frail man by the twisted lock of his graying hair. Weghucasso, stronger than he looked, tried to wrench free, startling and unbalancing Brent who had unsheathed his sword and swung it wildly. It sliced through the *werowance's* skull. As Weghucasso crumpled to the earth, Lucas tried to suppress the sour gorge that rose in his throat.

Pandemonium broke loose as men raced into the clearing, firing their guns and slashing with their swords. From between the houses the Dogues launched arrows. One struck the man standing next to him, and Lucas dove for cover, pulling his cousin with him.

He watched in horror as women and children screamed and ran for the woods but were butchered before they could reach safety. Then he noticed a small boy, no older than nine or ten, darting back and forth and moving in his direction. The lad reached Weghucasso and threw himself over the body crying what sounded like, "Father."

One of the men raised his musket to smash the lad's head in when Lucas lurched forward and grabbed the weapon. The man spun around and was about to hit Lucas when he recognized him.

"Leave this one. We need a hostage and the governor may

want to question him," he said. He did not give the man time to answer but picked the boy up and threw him, struggling over his shoulder.

⫸⫷

Darkness approached, so they marched out of the settlement and hurried back to the boats. They did not have to wait long for Mason and his men emerged from the woods a short time later.

Brent greeted them. "You should have seen what we did." He grinned showing his bad teeth. "Killed all of them, mostly with the stocks of our muskets. Saved the powder. They won't be stealing any more pigs."

Mason and his men did not react.

"Why the long face, Colonel? We heard gunfire, and thought you might have killed some too."

"We attacked the wrong Indians. May God assoil us."

"What do you mean?" Brent asked, staring hard at Mason.

"We killed Susquehannocks, not Dogues." Mason grimaced, shaking his head. "They didn't look like the Algonquian tribes on the Virginia side. They were very tall and the men wore long breeches. Their hair flowed down from top knots and the entire lower parts of their heads—from ear to ear—was clean-shaven. I should have known. Once we opened fire on them, one of them ran at me shouting *"Agaendeero, agaendeero.* We're Susquehannocks, we're friends."

"What does it matter if they're Dogues or Susquehannocks?" Brent said.

"The Susquehannocks are among the most ferocious of warriors," Lucas said. "John Smith wrote about them seventy years ago. He said they were giants with greater prowess than the Dogues, fiercer than Virginia's Algonquians, and with a thirst for vengeance."

"That's right," Mason said. "We're lucky they've always lived far north on the Susquehanna River."

"Hmf," Brent snorted. "Look what I have," he said, changing the subject and hauling the young Indian boy up by a braided rope that encircled his neck.

"Who is he?" Mason said. The boy stared vacantly and for the first time, Lucas noticed his eyes. They were not brown, but were the color of the ocean at its deepest.

"I killed the chief myself," Brent boasted, "and this boy's his son. Lucas saved him. That Dogue was old enough to be his great-grandfather. I'm keeping him as a slave."

Mason scrutinized the boy, and to Lucas' relief, said, "I think not. I'll take the boy. The governor may want to ask him about their raid on Matthews' place." Brent squinted at him, but finally turned his back and issued orders for his men to board and cast off.

Mason's men tugged his shallop close, and he waded out to it.

All the way back across the Potomac, Lucas turned over the day's events. Brent, thankfully, was in his own boat. He did not want to listen to the man brag about his prowess in clubbing the Dogue women and children to death. He shook his mane of dark hair as if to clear his head of their sorry achievements: annihilating two Indian communities—men, women and children. They might be the guilty Dogues. They might not be. Heaven knows what they had unleashed.

※》》《《

As they neared Mason's plantation on Pohick Creek, Lucas glanced at the boy, who sat huddled to starboard. He had not spoken and, in fact, had not moved, staring fixedly into the distance. "Will you raise him to serve on your plantation?"

Mason shook his head slowly. "Nope. The Indians don't make good indentured servants or slaves. Many say they're indolent, but I reckon they think working for someone else is demeaning. They're good farmers. God knows, they raise crops to feed themselves with greater skill than we do."

When they landed, Mason turned the Indian boy over to his wife. After supper, they visited him.

"How's he doing?" Mason asked his wife.

"He refuses to eat, speak or open his eyes. It's as though we weren't here," she said. "Small wonder, poor little fellow, seeing his father murdered before his eyes."

"What's your name, boy?" Lucas said in Algonquian. "What should we call you?" Nansemond lay on the pallet as if asleep and did not open his eyes.

He did not move for days. He lay on the pallet immobile, eating and drinking nothing. The loss of family and home would be trauma for anyone, but being superstitious people, they thought he might be possessed by demons that lived in the woods with the savages. What they did not know was that the lad, Nansemond, had just begun his training to be a medicine man, and his sleepy state was a self-induced trance.

Finally, Mason's wife suggested baptizing him to ward off any evil.

Mason agreed. "Why not? Baptism never hurt anyone."

Miraculously, once baptized, the boy finally opened his extraordinary blue eyes. With relief, Mrs. Mason propped his head on the pillow to feed him warm beef and barley soup. "There now, that's more like it. Tell me what your name is?" she asked him kindly, holding the spoon to his mouth.

⋙✖⋘

After Lucas returned to his small plantation, he had trouble sleeping. One evening, well past midnight, he awoke with a start, sitting up so quickly that he almost fell off the bed. He gasped for air, clutching at his chest.

He had thrashed about for the covers encased his body like a shroud. God! What a nightmare. He took deep breaths of air, finally slowing his heartbeat and managing to pull the sheets loose.

It was a horrifying dream. The Susquehannocks swept across the river to his plantation—hundreds of them.

For many years, they had peace with the Susquehannocks, but Mason's ill-advised murder of their people gave them cause to seek revenge.

He awoke the next morning, tired and unsettled, but with no

19

remembrance of having dreamt. As he went about his work, that day and those that followed, he felt edgy. The unease over what they may have started continued to gnaw at him.

⟫⟫ CHAPTER 3 ⟪⟪

EAGLETON AND GREEN SPRING PLANTATIONS

Charles County, Maryland
July 1675

THOMAS SWANN HEAVED THE RUDDER TOWARD HIM AND his men pulled on their oars, turning the shallop into the inlet at Eagleton. Three days ago, they left Swann's Point, his plantation on the James River. They raised the jib sheet and glided downstream. Once they exited the estuary and entered the Chesapeake Bay, the wind died and they ended up rowing most of the way. He felt exhausted and looked forward to sleeping in a bed tonight and getting out of his perspiration-drenched clothes.

Sweat trickled from his hair down his neck and he wiped it. "Damn!" he grumbled, quickly retracting his hand.

"Still hurts?" his helmsman said.

"Like fire," Thomas said. To stay cool, they took turns pouring buckets of bay water over their heads. Just his luck that yesterday a jellyfish lurked in the pail he used. It had been a hot, dry spring and summer and they proliferated in drought; the lack of rain elevated the saline level and enabled the creatures to swim into normally fresh water creeks and rivers. He could see dozens of the white blobs in Eagleton's cove.

Eagleton belonged to his friend, Edward Swann. They met in England years ago; both men found it intriguing that they shared the same last name, a love for writing, and lived in America. They had corresponded ever since and Edward repeatedly invited him to see his Oronoco—the special strain of tobacco he grew.

The pier extended forty feet, with ships moored on both sides and a dinghy secured at the end. "Guess we must anchor out," Thomas said.

The helmsman glanced at the crowded dock. "Yes, sir."

Edward's house nestled among huge elm trees. To the left, workers transplanted tobacco into a parched brown field. Several men stared back at him, and oddly, they were heavily armed as though guarding the workers.

He recognized Edward who waved at him before motioning to one of his men. Soon they were rowing out to the shallop. Reaching it, Edward tossed up a mooring line, then hurried up the rope ladder and emerged on deck. Thomas threw his arms around Edward in a crushing embrace.

"I'm glad you finally came for a visit." Edward stepped back and punched him on the shoulder.

"I wanted to see this Oronoco you keep raving about." Thomas' bright blue eyes twinkled.

Edward took off his hat and wiped his forehead. "We're just transplanting the seedlings." He pointed at the dry, hard-packed earth. "It's only rained twice since the end of April, so I've lost half of it."

"I doubt I'll make much of a crop of the sweet tobacco, myself. The heat this summer is abominable and the cicadas are driving everyone crazy." He gestured at Edward's musket. "Are you having trouble with the indentures again?"

"No. I guess you haven't heard. John and Tom Lucas," Edward pointed at the men on shore, "sailed over yesterday to warn us that the Dogues massacred a settler in Stafford."

"Massacred?" Thomas exclaimed, clearly startled.

Edward told him about the attack and Virginia's retaliation.

"I knew Thomas Lucas from Rappahannock," Thomas said. "He founded the county, but he died several years back. Are those boys any relation?"

"His son and nephew," Edward said. "Come. I'll introduce you and they can tell you about it. They took part in the attack on the Dogues, although George Mason and his men managed to attack the Susquehannocks in error."

Thomas gave his men orders before descending into the rowboat with Edward.

Edward looked up at Thomas' crew. "We'll send it back for you. Joe," he jerked his thumb at the man in the dinghy, "will show you where you can get something to eat."

When they reached the pier, Edward's two visitors, John and Tom Lucas, held the sides of the boat while they climbed out. Edward introduced them. As they walked up to the house, John Lucas filled Thomas in on the salient points of the raid against the Dogues that resulted in the massacre of a Susquehannock village.

"If the Dogues had waited to take the issue up with the governor instead of stealing the pigs," Thomas said, "he might have sided with them."

John chuckled. "You're right. The governor's making so much money off his fur monopoly that he might even have compensated them himself."

"Why did Mason attack the Susquehannocks?" Thomas asked.

"He mistook them for Dogues. By the time he realized they weren't, his men had murdered them—men, women and children."

Thomas knew most colonists were prejudiced and did not see the Indians as human. They all looked alike. If one wore breechcloth and the other long trousers, or one shaved one side of his head, they did not notice the distinctions—not to mention that the languages sounded different.

As if reading his thoughts, John said, "I don't know how they could make that mistake. The Indians around here wear breechcloths. The Susquehannocks are different; they wear long leather trousers and shirts."

When they reached the house, Edward's wife, came out to greet them. "You're just in time to join us for supper," she said with a smile.

"And what are we having, dear?" Edward placed his arm around her shoulders.

"Your favorite, fish in oyster sauce." She led them into the dining room.

The first course included corn fritters, cabbage, a leafy green vegetable and several puddings. They ate in total silence until John broke it, saying, "Everything is delicious. I can't remember when we've eaten so well. Right, Tom?" He glanced at his cousin.

"Our manners are bad, Mrs. Swann, but in part it's because you've provided us with such a feast."

She smiled, clearly pleased.

The second course arrived and the four men still ate with gusto but managed to talk in between the food. With the plates cleared, Edward's wife excused herself. They retired to the library, which also functioned as Edward's office, to sample the port Thomas brought.

Edward served the others and, with a sigh, settled himself in his chair. He held his goblet up to the light and took a sip. "Ah, nectar of the gods. Thank you for bringing this." He grinned at Thomas and then became serious. "I didn't want to discuss this Indian thing in front of my wife. I think we'll have trouble from the Susquehannocks."

"Not the Dogues?" Thomas said.

"No," Edward leaned forward. "The Dogues haven't threatened us. We outnumbered them years ago. The Susquehannocks are another matter altogether. Years back, they captured a group of Jesuits who came up the Susquehanna River to save their souls. They stripped them and drove stakes through their bodies just below the ribs. They tied each one's arms to their stake and goaded them toward home. Every step they took ripped flesh from their insides. It must have been excruciating. Only one of the priests survived. I think they let him live to tell the others not to venture into their territory."

Thomas tilted his goblet, swirling the port in slow circles. "What are the Susquehannocks doing this far south? I know they used to raid the Powhatans, but I thought they stayed in the Susquehanna Valley."

"Actually, Governor Calvert invited them back to Piscataway Creek a couple of years ago. He gave them guns, two barrels of powder and two-hundred weight of lead to help them defend us against the Seneca," Edward said.

Thomas's eyebrows shot up, and he let out a low whistle.

"The Seneca are dangerous," Edward continued. "The governor thought that having a fierce ally buffering the Maryland plantations would keep them in the north. For the most part, it's worked."

Thomas set his glass down. "I thought they were the same tribe."

"No," John replied, looking at him with eyes as dark as teak. "They're both Iroquois. Their languages are similar, but they hate each other. They've warred for at least twenty years. Several years ago, when those damned Frenchmen up by the lakes threw their support behind the Seneca, they pushed the Susquehannocks out of their main settlement on the Susquehanna River."

Edward finished his goblet and reached for the bottle. "I think we're in for trouble." He held the bottle out but Thomas shook his head.

"No, thanks. I think I need to get back and let the governor know of this. He'll want to convene the Council of Advisors and send a delegation to the Susquehannocks. Hopefully, we can negotiate a peace before all hell breaks loose."

⟫⟩⟨⟪

Several days later, Thomas sailed homeward. On the way, he stopped at Green Spring on the James River, the home of Sir William Berkeley, his Majesty's Governor of the Royal Colony of Virginia. As he walked up the oyster shell path, he admired the beautiful brick mansion at the end of the walkway. His own house had two stories, with six windows along the ground level and seven across the second floor, but the governor's house was far more spacious and elegant.

At the front door, a slender black man greeted Thomas. His black skin reminded him of the pithy shell that ripens around a walnut. The man took his hat and asked him to wait. He wondered what it would be like to be a slave, forced to work for cruel owners without hope for a better life. Slaves made up five percent of the workforce thanks to owners like Hartwell, Brent,

Claiborne, Ashton, Allerton and Beverley: lazy bastards.

He and his friend William Drummond argued vehemently against bringing non-English speaking workers into the colonies, especially since there was a large supply of indentured labor which was cheaper. England's constant clashes with Scotland, Ireland and Wales produced a stream of dissidents they could deport to the colony to work. They also expelled undesirables: orphans, thieves and prostitutes.

Indentured laborers worked hard. At the end of their seven years, they were freed, given fifty acres, a set of clothes and farm implements. Most of the well-to-do larger planters resented the new freedmen who represented an increasingly vocal and demanding middle class.

His thoughts were interrupted by the return of the black man who directed him toward the closed door of Sir William's official room. Thomas raked his fingers through his mane of white hair before he knocked.

"Enter," a voice called out, from the other side of the heavy oak door. The governor sat at a great mahogany table. "Forgive me for not rising, but I'm in agony." His shoe was off and his foot rested on a small stool, presumably to reduce swelling. He gestured at a chair with a well-manicured hand. "Please take a seat."

"Thank you." He shook his head sympathetically. "The gout again?"

The governor grimaced. Sir William was only slightly older than him, but how he had changed. Rich food and a sedentary life-style made him stout and probably contributed to his gouty foot. The man could no longer rise to his feet to greet others with a firm handclasp.

"I apologize for coming unannounced but there is something you should know." He told him about the Dogue attack, the Virginians' retaliation by invading Maryland, and slaughtering innocent Susquehannocks.

The governor's widely spaced, heavily lidded eyes, revealed no emotion. Thomas expected him to be outraged and call a meeting of his Council of Advisors. The fact Mason and Brent crossed into Maryland without authorization was serious.

"I don't think the Susquehannocks will pursue this because their economic interests are at stake," the governor said. When Thomas did not reply, Sir William continued as though instructing a small child. "You see, it's quite simple. They enjoy the fur trade with us as much as we do."

"But, we've broken the peace and killed their people. They are ferocious warriors and they will seek vengeance. We must send a delegation to them and offer compensation before it's too late."

The governor drummed his fingers on the table. His once luxurious, Cavalier mustache twitched. It used to sweep upward, but his sagging cheeks created deep wrinkles running past the corners of his mouth, causing it to droop. Finally, he regarded Thomas. "Frances and I shall dine shortly. Will you join us?"

"I'd like nothing better, but I've been gone for a week and need to get home." He gambled one last time. "Won't you consider convening the Council to discuss this matter?"

Sir William's straight resolute mouth frowned as he glanced back at his papers and shook his head. "Thank you for bringing me the news but it's not necessary. If there is nothing else..." He dismissed him with a limp wave of his hand.

It took all of Thomas's control to close the door quietly behind him.

⋙⋘

Thomas expected rumors of the massacres to sweep down the Chesapeake Bay like the outgoing tide. Ships delivered goods and picked up hogsheads of tobacco up and down the bay and along its Virginia Rivers, the Potomac, Rappahannock, York and James. Planters and their families were glad to see the merchantmen for that reason, but also because it gave them the opportunity to trade the latest gossip.

Several days after Thomas arrived back at Swann's Point, he saw what he had been waiting for—one of the large sea-going merchant ships dropping anchor in front of Jamestown's dock. He lost no time rowing across the river. Once on shore, he identified the captain and went over to ask him about the Dogue attack.

"I've just come from Westmoreland," the man said. "Innocent Virginians were murdered in their beds as they slept by the treacherous Dogues."

"That's not what I heard. I understand a colonist cheated them and they took his pigs in retaliation. No one was massacred in their sleep." Thomas watched the man's face go blank. By this time, people stopped to listen and as the crowd grew, so did the tale, bearing little resemblance to what John Lucas described at Eagleton. With his fears confirmed, he headed for the Snow Goose, a public house owned by his friend Richard Lawrence.

Lawrence had studied at Oxford and maintained an active interest in ideas and current events. He thought he was one of the most talented men in Virginia. He also served excellent food, which reminded Thomas he had not eaten since morning.

The Snow Goose was Thomas' favorite meeting place. In fact, the people who flowed into Jamestown—from the trading ships, to travelers on their way to New England or the West Indies, and burgesses and councilmen in Jamestown for the General Assembly—all chose this public house over any other.

It took up the entire basement—four steps below ground level—and also the attic which could sleep twenty or thirty people. A back staircase linked the basement and attic.

Thomas stepped down into the public room. He opened the door and the aroma of food greeted him. Across the room, Lawrence's immaculately groomed head leaned close to another darker one belonging to William Drummond. He walked over and pulled up a chair.

"You've heard what happened?" Drummond said, raising bushy eyebrows. He was a sober, heavy-set, Scotsman with black hair and eyes that could twinkle with mischief.

Thomas nodded. "If you mean the attacks, I learned about them several days ago from a friend in Maryland. The only thing is, the story being spread around town is a bit one-sided." He told them about Hen cheating the Dogues, and the exaggerated retaliation of the Virginians led by Mason that wiped out both Dogue and Susquehannock settlements.

"Not good," Drummond said. "We don't want to go to war again. We'd do well to parley with the Susquehannocks and try to appease them."

His friend, Drummond, constantly amazed him. The Scotsman came to Virginia in 1637, deported as an indentured servant after being captured in Scotland's Covenanter uprisings. Drummond found the conditions of indentured labor so deplorable—about half died in five years—that he led an uprising of escaped servants. They caught him, added three years to the seven of his servitude and flogged him in public. When he completed his indenture, he rose quickly and now owned over a thousand acres and was Thomas's business partner. Also, Thomas's eldest son, Samuel, married Drummond's daughter, Sarah.

"You're right," Thomas said. "Our governor isn't the least worried. I suggested we seek them out and he brushed me off."

Lawrence shook his head, drawing on his pipe as he held a flame to its bowl. "When I came to Virginia twenty years ago, our governor was a reasonable man. We shared political beliefs. We were both loyal subjects who fled England to escape Cromwell." He inhaled again and exhaled, allowing the smoke to spiral upward. "Now, he doesn't care a whit for anyone except himself."

Like Drummond, Lawrence did well in Virginia. In addition to the highly profitable Snow Goose, he owned hundreds of acres along the Rappahannock River and represented Jamestown in the House of Burgesses.

"There's Bland." Lawrence motioned to the sandy-haired young man to join them.

Giles Bland sat down, smiling mischievously.

"You look pleased with yourself," Lawrence said.

"I've been to see Sir William," he chuckled.

"That's scarcely a reason for joy." Drummond swirled his ale and smiled, his black eyes sparkling.

Bland laughed and leaned forward on his elbows. "The governor fined me five hundred pounds of tobacco for insulting his friend...Thomas Ludwell." He drew out the last two words derisively.

Drummond nodded and matched his sarcasm. "Sir Ludwell,

who arrived in Virginia as an indentured servant only ten years ago and became a nobleman? His grandmother's related to the governor in some way."

The others laughed.

Bland's saga of the "piercéd glove," as it came to be called, set the colony atwitter. His father sent him to Virginia to recover their plantation from the Ludwells, who seized it illegally when his uncle died. He argued with Thomas Ludwell, who insulted his family. Bland challenged him to a duel. The man failed to show up, so he nailed his glove to the door of the State House, a mark of cowardice. Everyone saw it, and Ludwell became the butt of jokes and much sniggering behind his back. The governor fined Bland, but sent Ludwell to England on a handsome salary to represent the colony.

"Well, I have good news," Bland continued, the grin never leaving his face. "My mother wrote the king about the unfairness of the fine, and His Majesty agreed with her and revoked it. I took his letter absolving me to the governor."

"He must have had an apoplectic fit." Drummond guffawed and slapped his thigh. His black eyes twinkled.

"No one has better contacts than you," Thomas said. "Your wife, the daughter of the king's Master of Requests; and, your mother related to his Secretary of State. Sir William doesn't have that type of connection through his high and mighty brother, John, the Lord Berkeley."

Shouting two tables over drew their attention. The group had been rowdy for some time, but now people in the tavern stopped and stared.

"He's one of the governor's servants," Lawrence said.

"I said the governor knew about the Indian attack weeks ago," the man slurred, his hands banging the table as his elbows slipped and his head fell forward. A second later, he jerked upright. "Ludwell heard it from a ship picking up cargo on the York River."

"Thomas Ludwell?" someone asked.

"No, you ninny! Thomas is in England living off our taxes. It's his brother, Phillip. More ale, girl," the inebriated servant said, slamming his mug down before continuing. "Ludwell took the shortcut over the peninsula by horseback to deliver the news to His Honor. So he knows about the massacre, all right."

Thomas turned back to the others and lowered his voice. "So, Sir William did know. He didn't react when I told him about it. He didn't appear worried or even interested in convening the Council. I wonder what he's up to."

"Nothing that could be good for us," Lawrence said.

⟫⟫CHAPTER 4⟪⟪
CURLES NECK PLANTATION

James River, Virginia
Season of the Green Corn Moon - August 1675

WANNIS KICKED, PROPELLING THE MAKESHIFT RAFT toward shore. When they started across, haze cloaked the Powhatan, the river the English called the James. Now, as the east lightened, the sky and water still appeared indistinguishable, both a milky opaline. The color reminded him of the inside of the bay's oysters. Ahead, he could just make out the shadowy shape of the trees. He felt the tingle of a jellyfish sting and scissored his legs vigorously to escape it.

As soon as his brother-in-law, Connawa, announced plans to take warriors south to buy gunpowder from a Siouan-speaking tribe called the Occoneechee, Wannis begged his father to let him go. Connawa was Susquehannock, not Dogue, and the *cockarouse*, or war captain of his tribe. Wannis' own tribe of Dogues was small and they seldom traveled, and certainly not on a trip taking him hundreds of miles south, along the Chesapeake Bay, and across four great rivers to reach the mighty Roanoke. He could hardly believe his good fortune that his father agreed.

He felt, more than heard, the slight crunch as they ground into the gravelly beach. He drew himself out of the water and joined the others to help unload their goods. They checked the powder and weapons first and then dried themselves and dressed. For him, the latter was simple: he put on the knee-length loincloth Dogue warriors favored, hung his knife at his hip and slipped into his moccasins.

Connawa laughed. "How is it that you wear those," he pointed at the footwear, "but otherwise are naked?"

The others laughed too and Shae-ee-kah lunged at Wannis grabbing at his loincloth. "Let's see what you're hiding under there." Wannis slapped his hand and dodged away.

Connawa's warriors wore trousers and long shirts. His brother-in-law reached for a pair of buckskin pants. Wannis noticed they were far too short and started to laugh as he saw stocky Shae-ee-kah trying to put on a pair that were clearly too long and tight for him.

Connawa grinned. "I'll trade, brother." He tossed the trousers to Shae-ee-kah, his black eyes flashing with amusement.

"My powerful equipment wouldn't fit into your skinny ones, anyway," Shae-ee-kah smirked in his low gravelly voice.

Connawa slipped into a tunic beaded by Chee-na-wan, his wife and Wannis's sister. Then he cinched a leather belt, holding his knife and a bag of powder. As he finished, he motioned to a warrior. "Tong-quas and I will scout ahead."

Wannis admired the Susquehannock's attire, but it promised to be a steamy day so he was glad to be bare-chested and in a loincloth. Shae-ee-kah might have read his thoughts for he threw an arm around his shoulder, gave him a squeeze and said, "You look as cool as the water, little brother."

Wannis got to know Shae-ee-kah during their journey and noticed he was devoted to Connawa. As they covered up their rafts with tree branches and debris, disguising them as best they could for the day when they would come this way again, Wannis asked him, "How did you and Connawa become such good friends?"

Shae-ee-kah flashed him a searching look before replying. "We grew up along the Susquehanna. When we passed eleven cycles of the seasons, the Seneca came, and Connawa saved my life." Shae-ee-kah spat into the water, then sat on a log, spreading his legs and adjusting the long knife at his waist into a more comfortable position. "Everything was blanketed in whiteness, just as it is today. We went beyond the gates of the palisade to the edge of the river to check our crab traps. Connawa's younger brothers came along, for they followed us everywhere. Our fathers left a week before to hunt game for the winter and our mothers went with them to cure the meat and tan the hides. Each year we hunt farther from our valley because the pale ones cut the forests and drive the game away."

"I know," Wannis nodded. "We've had the same destructive experience with the English."

"Connawa waded out to check the first trap; his little brothers followed. I stopped on the ridge to remove my shoes. We wore shoes made from cornhusks then. No good in water. Not as good as these." He held up his Algonquian-style moccasins before putting them on. Wannis knew that when Connawa became war captain, he insisted that his warriors wear leather moccasins. His wife introduced this innovation and he readily adopted it, when he realized moccasins were superior for stealth and traveling long distances.

"Connawa had just lifted the first trap, when shouts and cries peeled down the embankment from our town. We couldn't see too far in the mist, but from the screams and war howls, we knew our village was under attack. Connawa dropped the crab trap, wrenched the baskets from his two brothers and shoved both boys into the canes at the water's edge."

Shae-ee-kah leaned his head to the side and thumped it with his fist to drain the excess water from his ear. He pinched his nose and blew, flinging his hair back and exposing the fringe of crimson-dyed deer hair that encircled it. "I started after them but was grabbed from behind, jerked off my feet and dragged up the slope by the hair. Each time I struggled, it came out by the root. I got a glimpse of the man who held me and when I saw he wore a cap with one feather pointed skyward, I knew he was a Seneca. He had his back to the river. Either the fog prevented him from seeing Connawa and the boys, or he thought they were too small and insignificant to worry about."

"The next thing I knew, Connawa raced up the rise on bare, silent feet, and unsheathed the puny, little dagger his father had given him." He showed Wannis with his hands something half the size of a normal weapon. "He wasn't a match for a grown

34

man, but he came anyway. And do you know what he did?" Wannis leaned forward expectantly.

"He stabbed that Seneca in the one place he could reach that could do serious damage. He sliced the blade across the back of the knee, ham-stringing him." Shae-ee-kah stretched his leg out demonstrating.

Wannis wondered if he would have the nerve to go after a fully-grown man. "What happened next?"

"Well, the man bellowed with rage and dropped me. He tried to pivot on his left leg, but blood spurted out. I think Connawa cut more than tendons. The Seneca raised his war mace, a fearsome thing this long and spiked with slivers of stone." Shae-ee-kah widened his hands about three feet apart to indicate its length. "He swung it over his head intending to crush Connawa's skull into a bloody pulp, but Connawa stepped into him, angling that little knife of his under the ribcage. The man opened his mouth to howl, but his war cry became a gurgle as he fell forward, landing on Connawa and carrying him down the embankment."

"Connawa crawled out from under him and grasped my arm. He hauled me into the river, and shoved me down behind the reeds. We stayed like that, listening until the shouts and screams stopped. Late in the afternoon, when it was silent, we came out of hiding. Our village was decimated; the women and children taken captive, and the warriors left to protect us were dead. I didn't know what to do, but Connawa did. We began to dig shallow, oval graves for the bodies. It kept us busy."

Wannis let out a sigh, the suspense of the story leaving him drained. "The Seneca, are like all tribes. They take women and children young enough to become useful members of their tribe, and kill those who won't assimilate."

"It's the easiest way to replace those killed in battle or who die from the English diseases. Anyway, the very next day, Connawa hacked away the Seneca's scalp and ears. We were both green boys the morning the Seneca came to kidnap the women and children of our village. The ears still hang on a cord around his neck." He gestured at Connawa, who stepped back through the brush into the clearing.

Wannis stared at the grotesque thing he thought was a rawhide amulet. His brother-in-law was a formidable warrior with a commanding presence and a beak of a nose, set in an angular, sharp-planed face. He shaved the lower part of his head from ear to ear, allowing the crown to hang down his back in a braid holding two perfect turkey feathers. Their snow-white edges stood out against the blackness of his hair. Wannis wanted to be like him.

"We should get going," Connawa said. "I want to be across the little Pamunkey River before sunset tomorrow."

They started to collect their belongings when Shae-ee-kah let out a low hissing noise and raised his hand for silence, touching his nose. Then Wannis smelled the men too. They crouched back in the underbrush at the edge of the clearing. Beyond, men walked toward them, the fingers of mist lifting in spirals around them. They were Englishmen and unaware they were observed from the woods—an easy arrow strike. As he watched, the men set their bundles down and began working in the soil around small tobacco plants.

The world was still and the only sound came from the continuous droning of the cicadas until the workers began chatting.

Without moving a muscle, Wannis studied them and jumped when Connawa leaned close to his ear. "Can you understand them?"

Wannis nodded. "Yes, they're talking about how hot and dry it is this year. How the crops have failed," he whispered.

"Why do the English men do the work of their women?" Connawa asked.

"Because the men are the farmers. The women care for the home."

"Hmf," Connawa snorted. They watched for a few moments longer, and then Connawa motioned to them. Picking up their powder and guns, the eight warriors melted into the forest, and headed north.

Swann's Point on the James
August 1675

Thomas gazed out the window of his library and estate room at Swann's Point. The sloping, sun-dappled lawn and Jamestown across the gleaming water of the river made a peaceful scene, but its serenity could not erase his uneasiness since returning from Maryland. He waited several weeks hoping Sir William would send a delegation to the Susquehannocks to restore peace. When the governor eventually convened the Council of Advisors for the last day of August, his relief was short-lived, for he learned his fellow councilor, Nat Bacon of Curle's Neck, asked to be excused.

He set the book down and leaned forward to catch the slight breeze wafting through the windows. This summer, the heat was unrelenting, except here on the northeast side of the house, which sheltered under a stand of sycamores. Their peeling white bark and broad lime green leaves created a refuge from the high temperatures.

Drumming his fingers on the table, he stared at the bookshelves holding his precious imported books. Virginia had come a long way toward self-sufficiency he thought, but books and publications continued to be scarce, thanks to their governor. The man opposed every effort to set up local printing houses, as well as schools, so most people in Virginia were illiterate. Thomas could quote Sir William on this:

I thank God, there are neither free schools nor printing, and I hope we shall not have these for a hundred years; for learning has brought disobedience and heresy into the world. And printing has divulged them, and libels against the best government. God keep us from them both.

The governor made this statement in a report to the Lords of Foreign Plantations. He was proud of it and presented a copy to each of his councilors. Thomas shook his head in disgust. It kept people in ignorance and the reins of governance in Sir William's hands.

He benefited from his association with the governor. They

achieved many good things for the colony over the past twenty-six years, but giving its citizens a chance for a better life was not among the achievements. The governor and his adherents made it a point to suppress the emerging middle class by withholding the vote from freedmen, taxing them heavily and requiring they serve in the militia.

"Mr. Swann, the boat's ready," a voice said from the doorway.

"Thanks. Let's go." Thomas thrust the carved, ebony chair back from his desk and headed for the dock.

Curles Neck Plantation
August 1675

Just after daybreak, twenty-eight year-old Nat Bacon, joined his men in the field of his plantation. He dumped his gear and headed up a row of transplanted tobacco shoots. Last week, they removed the extra stalks and topped them; this week they would weed and remove caterpillars.

They worked in silence. Nat finished with a plant, and before moving to the next, straightened and groaned, pressing one hand against his lower back. Rob, his overseer, gave him a lopsided grin. "Standing and bending over the plant is hard on the back. Try squatting or sitting."

"Thanks," Nat mumbled. He found the work on his Virginia plantation hard, but to make a go of it, like many owners, he worked alongside his servants. Nat enjoyed this aspect of plantation life for both the camaraderie and the satisfaction of working his own land and watching it produce.

He glanced at Rob and noticed him shaking the dirt from the icicle-shaped root of a dandelion, before tossing it into a curved basket.

Nat grinned. "Don't tell me you'll eat those?"

"They're delicious," Rob grinned back. "Mildred will fix them for supper."

"Respectable Englishmen shouldn't eat weeds." Nat chuckled.

"I learned to eat these during the famine," his overseer said. "We would've starved without our vegetable gardens. The Powhatans taught me about greens. Have you ever noticed how healthy they look? Strong teeth, glossy black hair and well-developed bodies?"

Nat thought for a moment. He enjoyed physical activities, like swordsmanship and equitation. "They are pretty good-looking people. If they eat them, I'll try them. Too bad we can't eat all the weeds out here." He gazed around at the prickly and crawling plants shooting up around his tobacco. "It hasn't rained for weeks, and yet they grow faster than the tobacco."

The sun inched above the horizon, beating down on their hunched backs. At the edge of the clearing, Rob's seven-year-old son stepped out into a row and headed toward them.

"You have a visitor," the boy called out, giving his forelock a tug. "He says he's Mr. Swann."

Nat tossed the two-foot milkweed into a pile and straightened. "Thanks, Jamie." He turned to Rob. "Take a break, and then keep the men weeding."

Rob nodded and Nat headed several rows over where a water bucket was wedged into the soil. Grasping the ladle, he swept off his floppy hat, bent over and poured some over his head before taking a sip. Dropping it back into the pail, he replaced his hat and followed the furrow to its end. In front of him was the house he built under the spreading limbs of an ancient elm tree. He found Thomas lounging under his tree.

"What a pleasure," Nat said, removing his droopy hat with a flourish and executing a perfect bow over his dirt-caked boot.

Thomas stood and laughed. "Glad you dressed up to see me, Nat. Your tobacco looks better than you do, even with the drought." Nat wore a grimy and sweat-stained shirt and his jet-black hair, normally tidily gathered in a queue, hung wetly about his shoulders.

Nat surveyed the field he had just crossed. "Well, the lack of rain hasn't destroyed the crop entirely. Believe it or not, we weeded the lower part less than a week ago and picked the ripe leaves." He ran the back of his hand over his forehead, and then pointed at the yellowing leaves. "I wish it ripened all at once."

Thomas grinned. "Look at it this way; since the leaves ripen at different times, we can harvest the same field over, over, and

39

over again."

Nat gave a mirthless laugh. "I just hope when the autumn ships arrive, we have enough hogsheads to roll down to the dock.

"You should get another two years of good yields. After that, you might be able to raise corn for a couple of years. Then, there's nothing to be done but let nature reclaim it."

Nat's wife, Elizabeth walked up to them with a tray of drinks and they both accepted one. "Don't pay attention to him," she said. "He likes to gripe. We're glad you advised us to buy this property." The previous owners were killed in an Indian uprising so the land was not cultivated for thirty years.

"I heard you weren't coming to the council meeting," Thomas said, "so I came to persuade you. I need you to help me convince the governor we should send a peace delegation with gifts to the Susquehannocks before it's too late."

"I can't come. Elizabeth isn't well." He put his arm around his pregnant wife.

"Don't be silly," Elizabeth said, pushing his arm away. "I'm fine and this sounds important."

"It is," Thomas confirmed. "Perhaps you might come for the day. How we deal with this problem could be a matter of life or death. If we ignore it, we could end up in a situation like 1644. That started as a minor incident over land encroachment and turned into a full-blown war with the Powhatan. They descended on us like locusts. Killed four hundred colonists in less than an hour—shot with arrows or bludgeoned to death with war clubs. They wanted to wipe us out, and almost succeeded—killed about one-third of us.

Nat hesitated.

"It's settled then." She smiled. "You're going. Thomas, would you like another drink?"

"Thank you." Thomas held out his cup.

Nat leaned forward, swatting at a yellow jacket buzzing around his face. "Crewes told me you led the army that destroyed their chief, Opeechena, in the last uprising."

"Opechancanough," Thomas corrected him, shaking his head. He well-remembered the king of the Powhatan people and

Pocahontas' uncle. "He was a shrewd leader. He went to war against us twice to stop our invasion of his tribal territory. The first time, he killed over three hundred of us. The second time, we invaded land given back to him by the treaty that put an end to the first war."

"I guess we both crave land with the same characteristics: fertile, well-drained soil situated on a body of water for easy transport." Nat took a sip.

"Yes." Thomas shook his head in disgust. "Anyway, we didn't kill Opechancanough in battle. He was over ninety years old when I captured him, unable to walk and basically helpless. We carried him to jail on a litter. A couple days later, one of the guards shot him in the back. It wasn't an honorable moment for us. He was an old man; still dangerous, but not deserving of such a death."

They sat in silence. Thomas looked up. "But, on a happier note, I understand you have a new overseer."

"I don't know how we got along without him. I found Rob and his family in Jamestown, half-starved and looking for work. Rob's expertise has saved us."

Thomas took a sip from his cup. "Did you know his father was a Lord of the Realm and lost everything during England's civil wars? He came to America but couldn't pay the passage, so indentured his whole family for seven years. Luckily, the man who bought the indenture took all four of them."

"I didn't know that," Nat said. "He did tell me when his indenture ended, they moved to a plot on the Rappahannock River. After a couple of years, the tobacco depleted the soil and their yields declined to almost nothing."

Thomas nodded. "That's the problem with a single-crop economy, especially one like tobacco. We all borrow from London merchants to stay afloat, gambling on a better crop and higher prices. If that doesn't happen, you can lose everything."

"Did you know there are about forty thousand people in Virginia, and well over half of them are indentured servants," Nat said.

"That's probably about right. A handful of landowners have slaves, but over two-thirds of the labor force is indentured servants. Speaking of which, I'd better get back to my own and make sure they're all working."

Nat laughed, lifting his cup. "Well, here's to success tomorrow."

Thomas took a long swallow and pushed up from the chair, unfolding his tall, angular frame.

"I'll go to the dock with you," Nat said, matching his step to Thomas' slower one. Reaching down, Nat held the side of the craft as Thomas boarded.

"Farewell then," Thomas said, taking his seat. "See you tomorrow." Nat shoved the bow out into the estuary and his men began to row. When they reached the bend in the river, Thomas waved.

On the way home, Thomas' thoughts kept drifting back to the problem that concerned him, and for that matter, most planters on their isolated plantations—an uprising by the Indians. Although they enjoyed nearly thirty years of peace, the natives were always a subject of discussion when people came together—either to speak of them fearfully, disparagingly, or both.

In the second war of 1644, Thomas was a militia captain. He had an advantage other Englishmen did not: he spoke Algonquian. A Pamunkey girl with a broken leg staggered into their fields at Swann's Point one spring and they had set the leg as best they could. Afterwards, she limped badly, and although the Pamunkey vehemently resisted becoming servants to the English, they also viewed those with handicaps as a drain on the tribe's resources. She chose to stay with them and help in the kitchen, and at the same time, taught Thomas her language.

Thomas knew better than most how difficult it was to fight the tribes. They lived in dispersed settlements and would attack and then melt into the forests. It was frustrating until Thomas got the idea to mimic their tactics. He put together the first mobile units that could chase the Indians immediately after an attack. This in turn required excellent intelligence. He found the warring tribes, and sometimes the Powhatans themselves, would sell information. Thomas's language skills and his ability to acquire and decipher this intelligence proved invaluable. The new governor of the colony, Sir William, promoted him to colonel of the Surry County militia.

The sound of the boat gently bumping the dock as his men grabbed the lines to tie up, jarred him out of his thoughts. Well, he still held his title, colonel of the militia, but they would need a younger man if war came.

⋙ CHAPTER 5 ⋘
The Council of Advisors

Green Spring, Virginia
August 1675

THOMAS STEPPED OUT OF THE ROWBOAT ONTO THE LANDING and gazed up the path to the governor's house. His knees felt like they had been crammed into the boat for weeks, not the short time it had taken to cross the river. He shook out his blue juste-au-corps, a knee-length coat popularized by the king. It was welcome in the winter he reflected, draping it over his arm, but not in Virginia's summer.

"Thomas," a familiar voice called out.

Turning, he saw Nat and two men about thirty feet out dropping their sail and coasting into the landing.

"Fend off," the helmsman called out, as his companion pressed a long pole against the rowboat to prevent ramming it.

"I'll be in council most of the day," Thomas called out to his man. "They should feed you, but if not, there's food in the satchel. Don't stray far because when we're finished, I'd like to return to Swann's Point." By the time he turned back, Nat's crew had secured a line to the pier and his friend stepped onto the dock.

"I dressed for the occasion this time." Nat grinned, holding out his arms at shoulder height before slipping into his dove-grey waistcoat. He flung his juste-au-corps over his shoulder. They walked to the end of the pier and headed up the oyster shell path leading to the governor's house.

"Hopefully this will be short," Thomas said. "I can't tolerate these long drawn out meetings, where everyone feels the need to pontificate. Anyway, I told Mary I'd be back this evening. I decided I would rather sleep in my own bed than share a room with Bray or Bridger. They both snore and my wife doesn't."

Nat laughed. They climbed the steps to the front door. Thomas reached out to grasp the brass knocker. Before he made contact, the door swung open, held by the same black servant who had opened the door on his last visit. Across the entry hall, in front of the open doorway, Nat Bacon's older cousin stood mopping his neck with a handkerchief. They shared the name Nathaniel Bacon, which caused much confusion. When Nat arrived in the colony people begged him to call himself "Nat," to try to avoid confusion as they were already accustomed to calling his cousin "Nathaniel."

"Thomas." The older Bacon stepped forward to shake hands. Releasing Thomas' hand, he tugged his bright green waistcoat down over his belly and peered from under black eyebrows that gave much the same dark impression as Nat's, despite his bald head. "You look well. How is it I am younger than you, but you keep your youthful figure?"

Thomas chuckled. "Clean living, Nathaniel, clean living. That and I still take a hand in my fields now and again. In this heat, that trims the fat off."

Both Bacons laughed. "That's amazing. You have enough indentured servants to do the heavy lifting. You could manage the estate from your office."

"True," he said, "But a bit of field work helps keep my fingers on the pulse of the business."

They reached the open door of the dining room and Sir William motioned to them across the gleaming surface of the long table. "Come in, gentlemen." He gestured at the empty chairs.

The other councilors stood to greet them, except for Phillip Ludwell, an attractive man with an expensive wardrobe and extraordinary emerald eyes. He stayed in his seat next to the governor. He was impeccable in bright blue satin and the governor wore a silver silk ensemble. Thomas tried not to chortle as he envisioned the table covered their silk hose and shoes with square-toes, high heels and elaborate satin bows. They would be more comfortable in Charles II's court than in this Virginia Council meeting.

Once they took their seats, the governor nodded at Henry Hartwell, the council's clerk, who sat by the window at a small table. Hartwell bent his gaunt frame back to the task of dipping his quill in ink, poised to record Sir William's words.

"I was just briefing the council on the Indian attack in Stafford. We've received petitions from our northern counties expressing their concerns. In addition, the governor of Maryland, the Honorable Charles Calvert, protests the impudent conduct of Mason and Brent. He remonstrates me for allowing Virginia to invade Maryland territory, not that I blame him."

Joshua Bridger, who was hard of hearing, slapped the palm of his hand on the table. "Hear, hear."

Sir William ignored the outburst. "I need not remind you I've many years of experience with the Indians." He sat back, causing the curls of his luxuriant, brown periwig to sway around his shoulders. Thirty years ago, when he first met the governor, the wig was a status symbol popularized by bald King Louis XIII. He still insisted on wearing it, but it was an incongruity in Virginia's hot summers.

"In my opinion," the governor continued, his heavy lidded eyes sweeping around the table, "this Dogue incident is an isolated event and this man Hen was attacked for petty revenge." He cleared his throat and leaned back in his chair, pausing to admire the large ruby ring on his hand. "Whether or not he cheated the Dogues, we may never know. Fortunately, only he was killed. I'll write to Calvert, of course."

"Your Honor's assessment is flawless," Ludwell intoned. "Now we've retaliated and shown these Dogue savages they can't raid our plantations and kill our people, I'm sure this will be the last we hear of them."

Thomas suspected Ludwell arrived early to discuss what Sir William wanted from the meeting. He grimaced and glanced across the table at Nat, who nodded imperceptibly.

"Let's not overlook the facts, gentlemen," Nat said in his resonant baritone voice. "We need to keep in mind that Mason and Brent murdered not only an entire settlement of Dogues, but a village of Susquehannocks too, breaking our treaty with them. The Susquehannocks are a vengeful people and unlikely to forget this treachery."

"Nat's right," Thomas added. "Another person was killed on the Maryland side since the first Dogue attack. We need to send a delegation to the Susquehannock leaders and negotiate a settlement as soon as possible."

"We've no such news." Ludwell's luminescent green eyes, which the ladies found so attractive, flitted between Nat and Thomas. "Have we, Sir William?"

Nat cut in before he could answer. "I've heard this too. We need to take action now, before things get out of hand."

Thomas glanced around the table. Nat's cousin, Nathaniel Bacon, and William Coles dipped their heads in agreement, but he could see the others were not convinced. Ludwell was one of them and he glared at Nat, his handsome eyes clouding. Thomas knew Ludwell did not appreciate others disagreeing with him.

"We're trifling with a grave problem, gentlemen." Thomas stretched his arm and rested it on the table. The governor's hooded eyes stared at him. Thomas recounted his visit to Maryland and discussions with John and Tom Lucas of Rappahannock, ending with a warning the Susquehannocks would seek revenge.

Bridger, half listening with his elbows on the table, sat back scraping his chair. "I think Sir William is right. What is done, is done. We have more pressing business to consider."

Thomas frowned at Bridger and considered asking him what he thought was more important than the survival of the colony. Before he could, Nat barked, "For Christ's sake, man. We've attacked the Susquehannocks. They're more dangerous than the Algonquians, and if what Thomas says is correct, we may be in for another war."

Thomas detected the faintest lift of Sir William's mustache, which extended to the corners of his straight, resolute mouth. The governor liked to see Nat provoke others, as it provided him the opportunity to intervene and rescue them.

Finally, the governor asked, "What would you propose to do?"

"We should try to appease the Susquehannocks by offering an apology and acceptable recompense." Thomas tried to keep his voice even. "We learned in the last war with the Powhatans that they are motivated by vengeance. We need to make sure this doesn't happen again, for where the Powhatans failed, the Susquehannocks might succeed in destroying us."

Sir William glowered, drumming his well-manicured nails on the arm of his chair. His eyes flitted to Ludwell, who took his cue. "Sir William, while our fellow councilors express interesting views, you have far more experience than any of us in this matter. You put down the Powhatan attacks which led to a peace which has lasted for thirty years."

"Just so." The governor beamed. "I think the less we meddle with the Dogues and Susquehannocks, the better. They'll forget about it in time." A servant crossed the floor, bowed from the waist and whispered in his ear. Sir William nodded, dismissed him, and then studied the faces around the table.

"Since there are expressions of concern, if nothing more than to assure the masses we listen to them, I'll appoint a commission to investigate and consult with Maryland if necessary. I suggest we adjourn for an early supper in the garden and come back to draft the instructions after we've eaten." Sir William stood. "Oh, and I'll appoint the two justices of the peace from Stafford County to head this inquiry. What are their names?"

"Colonel John Washington and Major Isaac Allerton," Ludwell replied.

"That's not enough," Thomas protested.

"It's quite enough, Thomas." The governor gave him a warning stare. "Washington and Allerton have property where this trouble began. They can report and propose a course of action based on what they find. Supper is served. Shall we?"

Thomas was angry but tried hard to keep his face devoid of expression. Most of his fellow councilors preferred to ignore a dangerous situation in order to remain on good terms with the governor. For the past fifteen years, he was proud to be a member of the council, but recently, the governor had appointed men more interested in their personal gain and staying in his favor than legislating for the benefit of Virginia.

Nat came up to him and tapped his arm. "I need to let him know I'm leaving early as Elizabeth is unwell."

Thomas nodded. "Find me after you speak to him and I'll walk you to the dock. I'm getting something to drink." He headed for the doorway where refreshments were set up in the breezeway. He accepted a pewter cup of fruit juice before stepping off the back steps to join Nat's cousin, Nathaniel Bacon.

"You tried, Thomas." Nathaniel said. "Perhaps the governor's instincts are right on this."

"You don't believe that, do you?" Thomas took a sip. "He's begging for trouble."

"Good afternoon," a booming voice shouted in Thomas's ear. Someone slapped his back, shoving him forward and causing his drink to spill. Frowning in irritation, Thomas turned to see the pasty face and colorless eyes of Robert Beverley, a burgess who insinuated himself into the realm of the councilors. Beverley, short and stocky with liver-colored hair acted as Sir William's spy in the House of Burgesses. He threw himself wholeheartedly into persuading the members to support the governor's policies.

"Sorry, Thomas," Beverley said, as the older man glared at him.

Before he could respond, Sir William's servant stepped close to him. "Young Mr. Bacon said to tell you he's waiting, sir."

Impatient to get away from Beverley, Thomas abruptly excused himself. Nathaniel remembered he needed to consult with Ballard and made his escape too. Beverley found himself standing alone.

Thomas hurried through the center hallway and out the front door to catch up with Nat, who waited for him beside the path.

"I can't believe Sir William thinks a commission studying the murder in Stafford will help." Nat swung his juste-au-corps over his shoulder. "For God's sake, all the players are dead—Hen and the Dogues. There's no one to give a first-hand account, so they'll just be compiling a fat report of hearsay."

Thomas ground his teeth and cleared his throat. "Whenever others support a view different from our governor's, he calls for a commission to study the matter. His followers get paid a tidy sum, and when they report back, unsurprisingly, they recommend whatever he wanted. It ensures he gets his way, while giving the appearance of listening to those he governs. What I don't understand is he's always been the first to deal with troubles with the tribes. It's unlike him to dither."

"Maybe it has to do with his monopoly of the fur trade," Nat said. "There's a lot of gossip he's making a fortune and doesn't want to do anything that might jeopardize it."

Thomas stopped. "That's why his stand makes even less sense to me. If his fur trade concerns him, then why not appease the Susquehannocks? I'm thinking he's becoming senile."

Nat shrugged. "One thing: he's paying more and more attention to what men like Ludwell and Beverley say. They flatter him. Thank goodness, Beverley wasn't there. The governor seems to invite him everywhere."

"Oh, but he was. He came in time for drinks. Our leader always has him on hand whenever he wants to sound out the common man, not that Beverley gives a damn about the people he represents."

The two men reached the pier where Nat's men stood ready to cast off. Nat boarded and they pushed off, hoisted the sail, and headed upstream, Thomas watched them disappear before returning to the house.

The afternoon session passed slowly. They drafted the commission, with Bridger and Bray quibbling over the wording. At last it was completed and the governor signed it with a flourish.

Fort Piscataway, Maryland
Season of the Full Corn Moon – End of August

As they turned into Piscataway Creek, Wannis reflected that it would be good to return to his own village tomorrow. He could not wait to tell Nansemond and Nicotagsen about his exploits and pondered how he would embroider his tale about Occoneechee land. He learned much by observing the Occoneechee and the Susquehannock barter. Connawa was a master at obtaining the best deals. The Occoneechee seemed pleased with the Susquehannock furs, which were renowned up and down the east coast for their fine quality and great variety. Still, when the Occoneechee expressed hope they could trade in the future, there was something about their body language that rang false. It bothered Wannis that he could not pinpoint why and when he asked his brother-in-law, Connawa replied they could not be trusted.

His thoughts were interrupted as the canoe ground into the beach. Chee-na-wan, his sister threw herself at Connawa, who swung her around laughing. Wannis helped pull the canoe onto dry land and then headed up the bank to greet her. Then he noticed they were no longer smiling. His sister reached him and hugged him close, then pulled back, with her arms still around him. Tears streamed down her face.

"What's the matter?"

"Everyone's dead." She hugged him to her again. "Mother, father, grandmother and Nansemond. The English slaughtered them. Our uncle and Nicotagsen were the only survivors." She told him Uwanno was hunting the day of the attack. He returned to find bodies littering the ground. He set about burying the dead, but when he picked up Nicotagsen's body, it groaned. With their clan wiped out and not knowing what else to do, Uwanno brought Nicotagsen to Chee-na-wan. He did not find Nansemond's body.

Wannis took deep rasping breaths, feeling like he was suffocating. He tried hard not to let the tears spill down his face, but he could not stop himself. Connawa put his arms around both of them and they stood in a small huddle.

"Maybe Nansemond escaped." When he contemplated his ten year-old brother alone in the forest, struggling to survive, another rush of tears filled his eyes.

"That's what Uwanno thinks," she said. "He's done well in his training as *werowance*. Uwanno says his god eyes will protect him."

Legend among their people was that long ago gods came from across the sea and intermarried with the Dogues. Now every couple of generations, a child would be born with the god's blue eyes.

"Tears are the rivers carrying our loved ones away from us. But they are never completely gone because we never have enough tears to wash them away." His brother-in-law leaned his head down and brushed his forehead gently against Wannis's.

He did not trust himself to meet his brother-in-law's gaze.

"Now, you'll become my brother and a member of my tribe," Connawa said, squeezing him.

That night, Wannis dreamt. Nansemond stood in the sunlight. His god's eyes seemed to gleam with blue fire in the bright light. In one hand, he held a squirrel who cocked his head looking back with curiosity. Wannis moved toward him, but his brother and the animal evaporated, and he fell headlong into an immense hole. Down, down, down he fell. At last, he hit the bottom and crawled to his knees. This time, Nansemond lay before him on a slab, cold and covered in something white. His eyes were closed. Wannis reached out to touch him, but this time a voice echoed in his head. "Don't mourn me, brother. All is well." He awoke with a start. He felt he should remember something, but he could not. He pulled the sleep fur up to his chin and rolled over in its warmth, falling back to sleep easily.

The next day, he shaved his head from ear-to-ear. He left the crown long in the Susquehannock manner. He asked his sister to make him trousers and a tunic. When Connawa adopted him, it turned the saddest day of his life into one of hope. In the days that followed, he tackled his assigned chores with zeal, both to fit in and to numb his thoughts. It was challenging because of the traditional rivalry between their peoples. Occasionally, Connawa would stand beside him and let the others know whose hearth he belonged to, but for the most part, he stayed away. Wannis understood why his brother-in-law did not intervene when the Susquehannock women teased him, and the young men ribbed him; he needed to learn to defend himself. Nicotagsen improved slowly and it was wonderful to have him and Uwanno close. But the one he missed the most was Nansemond, his little brother, who had shadowed him everywhere.

⋙ CHAPTER 6 ⋘
LITTLE HUNTING AND PISCATAWAY CREEKS

Stafford County, Virginia
Early September 1675

The two men stood side-by-side on the bank of Little Hunting Creek where it flowed into the Potomac. The first bright colors of autumn touched the trees on both shores, although the vivid reds and bright yellows were a month away.

Colonel John Washington bent his lanky, narrow-shouldered frame to catch his fellow commissioner's comment. "Is that where the fort is?" Major Isaac Allerton pointed at the Maryland coastline and entrance to Piscataway's bay.

"Yep." Washington ran his hand over his straight auburn hair. His home was in Westmoreland County, but a year earlier, he acquired a thousand virgin acres along the Little Hunting. Not long after, to his dismay, he learned the fierce Susquehannocks had a fort just across the river from his new property.

"How many do you reckon there are?" Allerton said.

"Several hundred, I hear."

Allerton let out a low whistle. "I thought they lived in settlements of thirty or so."

"Generally they do, but Governor Calvert invited several tribes here." Washington pressed his lips together. "He signed a treaty with them eighteen months ago and gave them property on Piscataway Creek, to buffer Maryland from the Seneca to the north. I've seen them entering and exiting the cove, but for the most part, they avoid this side of the river. Thank goodness, my family is still in Westmoreland. If they lived here, the

Susquehannocks need only send a couple of war canoes. Damn Mason for killing their tribesmen."

"I heard they don't kill their prisoners right away. They assemble the whole tribe to watch them being tortured to death." Allerton shuddered. "It's some sort of sadistic entertainment. It's unchristian."

"Well, they're no Christians. They're pagans. They worship a pantheon of gods. They make offerings to them before they eat, harvest, and do battle." Washington shook his head, seeing no parallels between those ministrations and those of his own Anglican faith. "Do you think conducting this inquiry is useful? It seems to me an investigation at this point is futile. The eyewitnesses are dead. The ones who might know something are the two boys."

"Uh huh," Allerton agreed. "Well, the son of the man named Hen had the good sense to hide under the bed, so he probably didn't see anything. We could question the Dogue boy again."

"Mason told me the lad escaped," Washington said.

"Too bad," Allerton muttered, shaking his head. "I'm not sure what Berkeley expects us to achieve. Still, we're the justices of the peace, so I suppose anything we write and sign gives gravitas to his report to the king."

A grin spread over Washington's face and then he burst out laughing.

"What's so funny?"

"I believe you're right. Sir William can use our report to show he's taken action." He paused to expectorate the tobacco he was chewing into the grass. "Anyone in Stafford will tell you he hasn't done a damn thing."

Allerton rolled his eyes. "So, we waste our time giving the governor a report demonstrating to His Majesty that he's doing his job?"

Washington chuckled. "Ha! Don't forget we'll get paid. Maybe we should contact the Marylanders. The Susquehannock fort is on their side of the river. Let's see what they plan to do."

The same afternoon they wrote to Governor Calvert of Maryland. They explained Virginia's governor authorized them to look into the Dogue and Susquehannock matter and to raise a militia of five troops. They did not have to wait long for Calvert's reply. He sent Thomas Dent across the Potomac to meet them. Dent told them that since the Dogue violence, others had been attacked in Maryland. People assumed Seneca foraging parties committed the violence.

Nevertheless, Governor Calvert decided to revoke his treaty with the Susquehannocks and ask them to move out of Maryland. He would send two hundred-fifty mounted horsemen under the command of Major Thomas Truman to rendezvous with them at Chaptico Creek. It was located halfway between St. Mary's and the Susquehannock's fort. Truman's orders were to convince the Susquehannocks to move, and if they refused, to forcibly expel them.

Fort Piscataway, Maryland
Season of the Harvest Moon - September 1675

Wannis and Connawa left before sunrise to check on the traps they laid in several of the streams that emptied into the Potomac. When they returned, the last rays of the sun glistened on the water as their canoe glided back into Piscataway Creek. Cheena-wan stood waiting for them, her arm around someone about her height. Wannis started to wave but instead inhaled sharply when he realized who was standing next to her. He wanted to rub his eyes to be certain it really was Nansemond. The canoe ground into shore and he leapt out whooping with joy. He embraced Nansemond around the waist, hauling him off his feet. He released him, but grasped his shoulders with both hands as his face contorted and tears threatened to spill down it. "I thought you were dead."

"I escaped," Nansemond said.

"Did they torture you?" He still held his brother but leaned back to examine him.

"No. I expected them to kill me, but the redheaded man protected me from the one who killed our family. He took me home and his woman fed me and talked a lot. I wish you'd been there." Nansemond looked at Wannis. "I couldn't understand anything she said."

Wannis squeezed him again, then released him. "I wish I'd been there too." He understood how fortunate he was to be able to read and write English. His uncle, tayak, or paramount chief of the Piscataway on the Maryland shore, sent his daughter Mary Brent to study at St. Mary's with the Jesuits. After she married the white man, Giles Brent, and moved to Virginia, Kittamaqund tried again. This time, he sent his nephew, Wannis to study in her place. Wannis thanked the gods to have such a wonderful opportunity. It gave him insights into the foreigners' minds which proved useful to his tribe.

"Come," Connawa said. "I'm starved and Nansemond can tell us about his adventure while we eat."

Nansemond spoke of his capture and escape as they sat around the hearth. "At first, I was afraid to eat what they offered. I used my mind power to block them out and to focus on happy things. I thought about the summer you brought Matachacomoco to live with us. The dream was so real I felt you standing in front of me."

Wannis' eyes lit with recognition. His dream. His brother smiled knowingly. They named a baby squirrel who sat on his haunches, observing the world with dignity—just like their chieftains, Matachacomoco, or "great man." Wannis found the tiny, black ball of fur lying under a tree. Its mother was nowhere to be seen and it looked like it had fallen from high above. He took it home and it became the family pet. At night, Matachacomoco would curl up between Wannis and Nansemond.

"One night, as they slept, I escaped. I headed north, following the Potomac. The only place I could think to go was Chee-na-wan's." He looked at his sister. "This morning, I started to swim the river, but halfway across Connawa's war band saw me and picked me up."

⟫⟫⟪⟪

A week after Nansemond's return, Wannis perched on the bough of an ancient sycamore hanging out over the water. The brilliant shades of autumn gilded the trees across the cove but as the sun sank below the horizon, they became dark and violet-hued. It had been a beautiful warm day in the month the English called September.

With the sun gone, the air chilled rapidly and Wannis turned to climb down when he spotted what he awaited. A canoe glided around the curve in the river and into the bay. He scrambled down the limb. As it grounded, Connawa sprang from the prow, raising his arm in greeting. His dark eyes flashed and he said "They come," and without a pause, sprinted up the slope to the fort.

They sent out scouts each day to spy on their enemy since an ally in St. Mary's warned them Governor Calvert marched against them. His intention—to take back the land given them under the peace treaty. Wannis hurried after Connawa, entering the fort in time to hear that many English soldiers crossed the Potomac from Virginia and camped at Chaptico Creek.

He watched Tonna Hoorn, Connawa's father and the supreme leader of the Susquehannock people, raise his hands calling the Matachacomoco council. Then, accompanied by the four tribal chiefs, he turned and walked with great ceremony into the meetinghouse. Behind the chiefs came their war captains. Through the open door, Wannis saw the most senior men sitting on benches along the sides of the hall. The others sat on mats on the floor. Connawa entered last, fastening his wolf cape about his shoulders and closing the door behind him.

Hours into darkness, more scouts arrived and disappeared into the meetinghouse. Once they reemerged, Wannis discovered the enemy force grew larger as Virginia's invaders combined with Maryland's mounted troops. Much later still, a lone scout came with news that the Piscataway, Chopticos, Mattawoman, and Mangern joined the attackers. Wannis did the arithmetic he learned from the Jesuits: one thousand foes against two hundred fifty Susquehannocks, of which less than half were warriors. At almost ten to one, the odds had just worsened.

He crouched back down near the entrance to wait, joining several others. To his chagrin, they moved away from him and stared reproachfully, as though he was to blame for the Piscataway uniting with their enemies. He wanted to shout that only his mother was a Piscataway, the rest of his family were Dogues and they lay murdered.

Raising his chin, he gazed into the velvet night, ignoring them. He thought instead of Nansemond's miraculous homecoming. After he returned from the land of the Occoneechee and found his family slaughtered he was distraught, but now, with his brother alive, everything seemed brighter. He smiled to himself and muttered, "Thank you Okee." How ironic, Wannis reflected. After admiring the English and working hard to learn their language and adopt their ways, they massacred his family, and now turned on the very people who had given him refuge.

He must have dozed off, for when a hand clasped his shoulder, he jumped. Connawa reached down, pulling him to his feet. "Let's go. I could eat a bear."

Nansemond greeted them at Connawa's dwelling, while Chee-na-wan held out a bowl of water to wash their hands. Once settled on mats in front of the fire, Chee-na-wan nodded at Nansemond, who had remained standing. He chanted a prayer of thanks, and took a piece of meat from the serving pot, tossing it into the blaze as an offering. The blessing completed, Connawa raised his bowl and Chee-na-wan served him a hefty portion of venison. She first roasted the meat and then stewed it in broth thickened with ground corn flour and flavored with wild onions and berries. She passed the platter. Wannis took some and topped it with a ring of squash. From his pouch, he pulled out a handful of curtenemons, the seeds of the tuckahoe plant. He sprinkled the seeds on top.

Chee-na-wan smiled with affection as she watched him. "You should have been the cook," she chided and Wannis grinned.

They ate in silence. Finally, Connawa leaned back wiping his mouth on the back of his hand. "We decided to negotiate with the foreigners and try to stay here. Wadonhago wanted to attack them while they're moving. Everyone considers them treacherous and unreliable—offering us this land with one hand and taking it back with the other. However, my father argued we're outnumbered, we're all that remain of our people and we can't afford to lose a single warrior. We might take many with us, but once we're dead, who will protect our women and children?"

"Our first consideration must be survival," Wannis nodded, looking much older than his sixteen years. "We have everything to lose if we're forced to find shelter so late in the season. These walls are strong, so we can repel our enemies. But, if they bring their great guns, we need to go. I've seen them fired at St. Mary's and their destruction is like one hundred muskets discharged at a single target."

"Let's pray they don't." Connawa smiled. "We're well supplied for winter. Today, we gathered our crops and harvested the smallest squash and pumpkin to prevent our foes from finding anything edible. Our men have exhausted the hunting around us too." Connawa turned to him. "Wannis, my father asks you accompany the tribal leaders when the English arrive since you speak their language. Don't let them know you understand. Listen and report."

Wannis nodded, pleased to be asked to help, because it indicated they accepted him as a member of the tribe.

Chee-na-wan cleaned up the remnants of their meal and retired to the sleeping platform she shared with Connawa. Nansemond yawned and excused himself but Wannis stayed by the fire with his brother-in-law. A short time later, Shae-ee-kah poked his head through the entrance. Connawa gestured him to join them.

Wannis wanted to ask Connawa something, and now with Shae-ee-kah's arrival, the time seemed appropriate. "What about the "Blue Mountains?"

Some years back, Connawa and Shae-ee-kah travelled over the mountains into the vast wilderness to hunt and trap. The journey took many moons and after they lost their settlements on the Susquehanna River to the Seneca, Connawa argued they should move to this rich, new land beyond the blue mountains. It was far from the Seneca and the reach of the white man.

Shae-ee-kah smiled. "Many in the council tonight called Connawa sagacious in foreseeing the problems we would have here. They say we waste time trying to enchant these people. I think we should move where the sun sets, as Connawa proposed."

Before responding, Connawa pulled an unburned piece of wood from the fire's edge, then threw it on top. "Our first priority is to remain here for the winter. However, we need to prepare ourselves for the worst. If our talks don't succeed, my father asked me to plan for the alternative." He sounded unemotional, but his face was grim.

⟫⟪

Several days later, Wannis sat on the embankment. The sun was not up, but the sky was brightening so the remaining foggy wisps hovering over the water were cast in a pearly haze. Across the cove, the treetops appeared outlined in gold and the incoming tide, surging into the inlet from the Potomac, drove row upon row of waves hurtling into the shore. It looked so beautiful, he thought. It was hard to believe men were on their way to destroy them.

Wannis looked back at Nansemond, standing close to the water. Turning slowly in a circle, his younger brother intoned a prayer beseeching Okee to look after their adopted tribe. His right hand gently wafted smoke from what looked like dried plant matter. He finished, facing the direction where the sun would rise, and then cast the remains of his offering into the creek. He watched the waves claim it and then headed up the slope.

Wannis stood to meet him, draping his arm around his shoulder. "It's a good idea to ask our god to help our new brothers."

"I hope Okee listens."

They walked back to the fort in silence. Chee-na-wan handed each of them a warm bowl of boiled cornmeal mixed with chopped pohickery nuts. Wannis loved the chunky crunch of the nuts with the hot hominy. As he scraped the last bite from the bowl with a mussel shell, he remembered when he lived with the English at St. Mary's, they served a similar dish. It was considered a delicacy and made with grain, boiled in milk, and seasoned with a nut called almond, which came by ship from across the sea. His people ate hominy most days in the winter months, but they ate theirs only on special occasions. He had emulated the strange newcomers and wanted to be like them, until they took all that was important to him and ended his way of life.

CHAPTER 7
THE ENGLISH ARRIVE

Fort Piscataway, Maryland
Season of the Harvest Moon - September 1675

LATER THAT DAY, THE ENGLISH BEGAN TO ARRIVE. WANNIS watched as the mounted men filtered through the trees to the south. Although the midday sun shone brightly overhead, an eerie silence hung over the settlement. The birds stopped singing and the only sound was the occasional creak of leather.

The leader rode up to the fort with his men, raised his hand and brought them to a halt more than an arrow shot away. Leaning back in the saddle, he arched his back and then inclined forward, rolling his shoulders. His head swiveled, taking in the scene before him.

The stronghold occupied the top of a small hill, in the center of a clearing surrounded by cultivated fields. It looked like it could withstand a siege and shelter several hundred people behind its walls. Nansemond came up beside Wannis as the warrior on horseback glanced up toward the platform where they stood. As he did so, Nansemond gasped and jumped back.

"What is it?" Wannis looked at his brother.

Nansemond shook his head to clear it. "The leader—his eyes— they are like the eyes of a demon. I sense great evil in him. Those eyes saw me." Nansemond shuddered, taking another step away from the wall.

"Our spy in St. Mary's said the commander was hard and cruel. This must be the man."

The man they observed turned his horse and began to bark

commands. His men set up camp to the west. After pitching the tents, they allowed the horses to forage in the fields in front of the fort.

After a while, the leader approached with another man, who called out. "My name is Shankes and this is Major Truman. We want to speak with Chief Heriguera."

Wannis translated Shankes' words into Iroquoian. Tonna Hoorn replied in that language. "Chief Heriguera died in the time of the Snow Moon, but I'll send our chiefs to speak with you."

The man called Shankes thanked him in broken Iroquoian.

Within a short time, the five tribal elders emerged from the fort, led by Tonna Hoorn. His brother, Connawa Rocquaes, and Sawaheguh, Dahedaghesa, and Wadonhago accompanied him. They were richly dressed in intricately beaded tunics coming almost to the knee, and trousers decorated with fringe. Tonna Horn wore the lustrous pelt of a red fox. Wannis walked behind them with Connawa, carrying a pole with a white cloth tied at the top. He explained to the chiefs that the English honored this as a sign of peaceful intent which safeguarded the ones carrying it.

The elders stopped and the Susquehannock chief raised his hand, palm outward in greeting. "I am Tonna Hoorn, leader of all people of the great Susquehanna who have taken up this land at the invitation of your king. These lands belonged to my people long before you came. You forced us to leave them, but Governor Calvert recognized this as unjust and invited us to return."

"You ceded the lands between the Patuxent and Choptank rivers to us after your defeat in 1645," Truman muttered.

"These are my chiefs," Tonna Hoorn continued, introducing each one.

"I'm Major Truman and Governor Calvert sent me. You've murdered two settlers and you've broken the peace treaty. Now you must go back to where you came from."

Truman, a spare, ascetic man had a thin, hard face. When Wannis regarded his eyes, he tried to cover his shock. They were so pale—a shade of grey tinged with yellow—that they seemed inhuman, like the devil the English feared. Nansemond had somehow known

63

this even though he was too far away to see them. Fortunately, those demon eyes stared at Connawa, not him.

"We've killed no one. We've not broken our treaty," the Susquehannock chief said. "However, several days ago the Seneca stopped here on their way home. They bragged about killing a settler and offered to sell his gun to us."

"Show me the gun," Demon Eyes demanded.

Shankes translated and Tonna Hoorn drew himself up, visibly offended. "We would not trade for something belonging to our friends."

Truman rumbled something about the goodness of the English toward the Indians. His eyes kept flitting to Connawa. The Susquehannocks were taller than the English, but Connawa towered above everyone. He stood with legs wide apart, his left thumb hooked casually in his belt, with the tips of his fingers resting lightly near the handle of a long, brutally serrated hunting knife. Wannis considered he seemed unyielding and powerful. He tried not to grin at Demon Eyes' unease.

Shankes interpreted the remarks, while Truman's left hand moved to the hilt of his sword, striking the same pose as Connawa with his thumb in his belt. His strange eyes continued to stare.

Wannis took the measure of Shankes. He had on clean buckskin britches, and he noted he had adopted some of the ways of the Susquehannock: his body had little odor and his hair appeared clean under his floppy hat. Major Truman was another matter. His stench struck the Susquehannocks full in the face from four paces away.

Connawa whispered, "Skunk," and the elders and Wannis cracked a smile. He always wondered how Englishmen could wear the same sagging, dirty clothes day after day, not bothering to take out stains or wash their bodies. Demon Eyes could have some sparkle to his hair, but it hung in greasy, smelly tendrils of an unidentifiable color. He made a mental note to avoid standing too close to him for he might be teeming with vermin.

Connawa's uncle, Connawa Rocquaes stared at Truman. "My brother King Tonna Hoorn told you, the Seneca passed four days ago. My warriors followed them to make sure they left our lands. If you hurry, demon-eyed pale man, you can catch them."

Truman shifted his weight back and forth listening impatiently to Shankes' translation, which Wannis noted, omitted the insult. As if he had not heard, Truman glared at Shankes. "Ask them about the raids on our plantations and the murder of Randolph Hanson, who lived near here."

Shankes met his glower. "Major, what they say makes sense. Let's ask them to take us to the Seneca. Then we'll know whether they made up this story."

A voice of reason, Wannis thought. Shankes seemed clever; perhaps he could convince his companions. As Truman turned to walk away, he grabbed Shankes' arm and growled. "I think they're lying."

"Nope. I think it was the Seneca. Them canoes carrying the hogs the Virginians reported seeing could've belonged to the Seneca, too."

"Hmph," Truman said. "We'll see once Washington gets here."

⸎⸎⸎

Late in the afternoon, as the sun hovered in the west, John Lucas beheld the Susquehannock fortification on Piscataway Creek for the first time. He gazed up at it from the leeward side and noticed people on the rampart staring back at him in silence. With winter approaching, he wondered how eager the tribes would be to leave such impressive defenses. He would reiterate to Mason and Washington his suggestion that Virginia and Maryland should offer them land farther north as an incentive to abandon the fort.

The crew shouted orders, as they released and secured the sails, interrupting his thoughts. He was glad to be off the boat and watched it pole around and head back down the creek. He and the men set up their camp on the eastern side of the clearing. He was assigned to the tree removal brigade, while others dug trenches around their positions to create a breastwork in front of the fort.

Before the first tree fell, a messenger arrived from Colonel

Mason ordering him to take some men, make a reconnaissance around the stronghold, and map it out. Good. He always preferred drawing to chopping trees. When he reached the north side, he saw the marshy ground by the creek. He sent a man back with the news they could not totally surround the north side and suggested they anchor a ship or two in the creek.

Once he completed the survey, he returned to find Washington's tent up. Mason and Allerton stood in front of it.

"Take a seat, gentlemen." Washington motioned at the campstools. They sat outside under the awning of the tent.

"I asked Lucas to scout the defenses." Mason grinned. "He knows more about the Indians than most of us, and he can draw. Show us what you've found."

Lucas rolled out a piece of canvas showing his sketch of the fort's layout and the armies of Virginia and Maryland. He picked up a compass and a candlestick and set them on the corners of his drawing to keep it in position.

When Truman and Shankes arrived, they found Virginia's officers seated at the low camp table, leaning over the diagram.

Washington introduced them. "Sorry, we're short of chairs, but gather around the table."

Lucas pointed at the defenses on the hill. "You can see it's well situated on a rise and built up with high banks of earth." The officers looked at the south wall, now illuminated with the remains of the afternoon sun, and then back down at his drawing. "It's about seventy feet long. I found no low spots or weaknesses. They've surrounded the walls with a counterscarp, or outer wall with sloping ditch."

"And the walls themselves?" the colonel asked.

"The stockade's made of split and stripped logs. They're about twelve inches in diameter and are probably dug down into the earth three or four feet." Lucas gestured at the diagram. "They left some of the branches on at the tops of the trunks and twisted them together."

Washington turned to Mason. "What do you think, George?"

Mason looked back at the drawing. "We should try hard to convince them to leave, because if—"

"I say we rush the fort," Truman interrupted in his rasping voice. "They're surrounded and we greatly outnumber them. They couldn't have more than a couple hundred men."

"I would like to hear what Colonel Mason has to say." Washington's eyes narrowed as he clamped his teeth together clearly displeased with his subordinate's interruption.

"We've surrounded it and secured all the exits," Mason continued. "But you can see for yourself with the high walls and ditch, they can pick us off from the ramparts with ease." He turned to Lucas. "What did you tell me about how fast they fire their arrows?"

"I've seen it at a competition. They can release up to ten forty-five-inch arrows in the amount of time it takes us to uncork our powder horns and begin to ready a flintlock." He mimed the process of loading and firing the gun as he spoke. "We'd have heavy losses if we charge."

Mason nodded. "Perhaps we could siege it."

"That will take weeks," Washington said. "How about mining under it?"

"We don't have anyone with experience in sapping. Too much water, anyway," Mason said. "We've got the Potomac on the west and the creek to the north."

Shankes, the interpreter, cleared his throat and spat. "Colonel, if they won't leave, we still have an advantage. This time of year, the warriors hunt and fish, and the women gather berries, nuts and fruit to help them through winter. If we bottle them up in the fort, they won't be able to. It will force them to eat their winter stores and we can starve them out."

"I'm not so sure." Lucas looked around the table. "Notice the silence here: there aren't any chipmunks, squirrels or fowl of any kind. You can bet they killed anything that moved when they heard we were coming. It's more likely we'll starve first. Our best bet is to persuade them to go. If we pay them to do so, that will save many lives."

Truman scowled. "I still say rush the fort. They're bound to have a weak spot and we outnumber them."

Washington frowned. "Numbers aren't the only factor, Major.

Tomorrow I'll meet with the Susquehannock chiefs." He stood up, turned his back on them and walked into his tent, allowing the flap to fall behind him.

⇒⇒⇒⟫⟪⟪⟪

Throughout the night, the two sides observed each other. As the grey light of dawn filtered through the smoke hole, Wannis sensed, rather than heard, footfalls near his bed. Looking up, Connawa motioned him to get up.

He swung off the platform and followed Connawa outside. As the two walked toward the main gate, Connawa said, "My father wishes me to stay behind the walls when they go out to speak with the English today, in case something goes wrong. But he wishes you to go with them."

Connawa placed his hand on Wannis's shoulder and gave him a nudge toward Tonna Hoorn and the tribal leaders standing by the wall. The sun inched over the treetops and the gate swung opened. They stepped through it and paused as the light brightened their buckskin garments, and sparkled off the beading on their tunics. They strode down the slope and crossed the breastworks the English had started the day before. Wannis and two warriors walked behind them bearing gifts and the white cloth tied to a pole.

Tonna Hoorn raised his hand in greeting, palm outward, and once again introduced himself and the chiefs. Washington nodded and then introduced his officers.

The great chief motioned to Wannis, who handed him a magnificent three-foot-long pipe carved out of bone and engraved with cascading designs. He turned back to the white men.

"Many seasons have passed since we made a peace pact with your great leader. In remembrance of this peace, I offer the white chief this gift." The chief extended his hands to Washington who stepped forward and accepted it.

Looking down at the pipe, he admired its design and finally smiled. "Thank you, noble king of the Susquehannocks. I can tell from the beautiful designs on this pipe that your people are

68

highly skilled."

Shankes translated and Wannis noted he embellished Washington's words.

Tonna Hoorn smiled and replied, "We have several other gifts for you." He motioned to the warriors flanking Wannis, who stretched a deer hide on the ground. On it, they set ceramic bowls decorated with geometric designs etched with a stylus before firing. Then, there were audible intakes of breath as the warriors shook out and deposited a deep russet fur of an immense animal that once roamed Virginia, called a buffalo. The English assumed this animal was mythical, for they had never seen it.

Washington stood speechless, amazement written on his face. Wannis realized he had not expected such generosity. Before the colonel could recover, Demon Eyes kicked the edge of the hide with the tow of his boot and scowled at his superior. "Tell him why we're here."

Washington grimaced. He turned to the interpreter, ignoring his evil-tempered subordinate. "Thank the chief for these fine gifts." Shankes chose his words carefully, while Demon Eyes glared.

"Well?" Demon Eyes demanded, looking at his superior officer.

"Hold your tongue." Washington muttered. "Chief Tonna Hoorn, you have killed people on both the Maryland and the Virginia side of the Potomac. The leaders of our people have sent us here to insure these murders stop. We invited you here to live peaceably with us, but some of your warriors have broken this peace."

Tonna Horn stood without moving a muscle. "Leader of the English, we have not committed the crimes you accuse us of. We told you yesterday the Seneca came to trade with us and bragged of the attacks. They should be four days upriver." He waved his arm northward.

"Can you show us where they are?" Washington said.

Before Shankes could translate, Tonna Hoorn replied as though he understood the question. "My warriors will take you there." His dark eyes never left Washington's. "We don't dishonor the relationship we have with you. Look here." He pointed at

Connawa Rocquaes, whom his son, Connawa, was named after. "He bears the great seal of the White Father."

Connawa Rocquaes stepped forward, holding the rare silver medallion that hung around his neck. It bore the image and seal of Lord Baltimore. "This gift is a badge of safe passage on the lands held by your people. We've not killed the white men although you have wiped out our village with women, children and old men."

Washington tilted his head as Shankes translated.

Truman moved close and said under his breath, "Let me take them to see Hanson's place. I think I can convince them they should leave."

Washington frowned. He walked several paces away, motioning Truman to follow. "Do you really think you can persuade them?"

"We've brought gifts. They can never resist a musket or those woolen matchcoats they like better than their fur cloaks," Truman said.

Washington nodded. "That might work."

Wannis studied Truman and Washington, but could not hear what they said. Their body language told him that Demon Eyes was angry and Washington irritated. When they parted, both seemed to have relaxed.

Washington stopped in front of Tonna Hoorn. "We've brought gifts for you: muskets and matchcoats in many colors. Major Truman will take you to select the ones you want."

Shankes translated, and when he said the word "muskets," the chiefs smiled with pleasure, for they did not have the technology to create these wondrous weapons.

Wannis studied the facial expressions of Demon Eyes and the way his fingers stroked his baldric. He sized the man up the night before: he was a man whose word meant nothing. He inched closer to Tonna Hoorn. "Don't go, great chief," he whispered. "I don't trust the man called Truman. Demand they bring the gifts here."

Tonna Hoorn cocked his head. "Thank you for your offer, but please bring the gifts here." Tonna Hoorn gestured at the ground.

"There are far too many and the matchcoats are in many

colors," Truman said, pointing toward a large tent on the outer edge of their camp.

Shankes translated and Wadonhago leaned toward Tonna Hoorn. "Let's go with them. Your son and our war bands watch from the walls. What can they do? We came to them under a truce. It should be safe."

Demon Eyes motioned them to follow him and set out across the tent-filled field. Wannis implanted the pole in the soil and returned to the fort with the two warriors to explain what was happening. They joined Connawa on the parapet.

As Truman reached the large tent he had pointed to, he skirted it and continued down the slope to the Potomac. They could no longer see the fort.

"Where are our gifts?" Tonna Hoorn asked.

Truman looked at him with contempt and without uttering a word, raised his hand and slashed it downward. "Now." His men leapt forward and grabbed the chiefs, wrestling them to the ground. Tonna Hoorn and the others struggled but they were unarmed and outnumbered. Connawa Rocquaes grabbed at a musket but the man holding it slammed him on the side of the head with the butt. Stunned, he collapsed, blood oozing from the wound. Truman's men bound their arms and legs and once subdued, Truman pulled his sword from his shoulder baldric and raised it. "Kill them, but do it quietly."

The men did not move. His lip curled, and he snarled, "That's an order. Kill them."

"Major, they're unarmed and came under a flag of truce," a man said. "They can't fight back."

"How perceptive." Truman growled. "They'll be easier to kill that way, don't you think, you whoreson?"

The men shifted, making no move to obey him. Truman waved his sword under the neck of the nearest man. "Kill their leaders and their resolve will crumble."

At that moment, Tonna Hoorn managed to free his legs and lurched to his feet. He started back up the hill but Truman moved to intercept him. Swinging his sword, he buried it deeply into the chief's neck almost severing his head.

As Tonna Hoorn's body dropped to the ground, blood spurted covering the grass and earth in red. The remaining chiefs struggled to escape and butted their captors with their heads and shoulders. Twisting his body, Wadonhago tried to grab a musket from behind his back with his bound hands. But a second man clubbed him, cracking his skull. Truman's men did what he wanted. They bludgeoned to death the bound Susquehannock chiefs.

⬦⬦⬦

Wannis stood next to Connawa on the platform behind the walls surveying the enemy troops going about their duties and tending their fires. It looked peaceful. As they watched, Demon Eyes and his men returned alone. Demon Eyes walked over and uprooted the flag of truce before sauntering over to Washington. He threw it on the ground. They appeared to be arguing. Finally, Demon Eyes tossed back his head and laughed, then spat on the ground and stalked away.

Connawa shouted from the fort, "We have sent our tribal leaders to meet with you in peace. Return them to us." No answer. Connawa tried again. There was no reply.

"If anything has happened to them, I'll kill twenty English for each one of our great men," Connawa swore.

CHAPTER 8

THE SIEGE OF FORT PISCATAWAY

Fort Piscataway, Maryland
September 1675

THE MEN SLEPT IN THEIR TENTS UNTIL PIERCING CRIES AND gunfire dashed the predawn silence. Drawing swords from baldrics and grabbing muskets, they bolted half-dressed and unbooted out onto the frost-covered ground.

John Lucas dashed to Washington's tent to alert him. He collided with his commander as he came out of the entrance. "It's Truman. He ordered an attack on the fortification."

"What?" Washington growled, fumbling with the buckle of his baldric. They ran together to the perimeter where they found Truman, watching their Indian allies rushing the fort. They brandished war clubs and occasionally fired muskets, all the while making unearthly screams. However, before they got within twenty feet of the walls, they were shot by arrows.

Lucas surveyed the scene, grinding his teeth at the sight of so many of their allies lying motionless on the field. About a dozen of the survivors ran back toward the camp to escape the shooters on the walls. Finally, only two men remained and they came straight at him at a flat run. The farthest away seemed to pause in midair. He dropped his war club, spread his arms wide, and threw back his head before crashing to the earth. One of the infamous forty-five-inch arrows trembled where it lodged in his back.

The second man kept coming, his knees churning. Lucas held his breath for it seemed he would make it to safety. A musket roared, and he dropped like a rock about thirty feet away. A blood-curdling howl came from the rampart. Lucas looked at the warrior on the platform who pumped his musket overhead and wailed in triumph. From that distance, he seemed inhuman and like a giant wolf.

"Damn it! What the hell do you think you're doing?" Without waiting for a response, Washington shouted at him, "I thought you said we were at least fifty-feet beyond the reach of their arrows."

"For a moment there, I thought they would take the fort for us." Truman's eyes glistened as he grinned. "We promised them matchcoats. The same ones we promised to the Susquehannocks." He laughed, his strange eyes gleaming with malice. "They were eager to oblige us. Now we have the range of their weapons." He shrugged, turned his back on the head of the Virginia forces and his superior officer, and swaggered away.

Lucas thought his colonel would explode as he stared at the major's back. He outranked the man, but since each reported to his respective governor there was little he could do.

Later, Lucas went to check on the men charged with disabling the Susquehannock canoes. He found them chatting and laughing as they hacked up the last one. They stopped speaking when they saw him, but not before he heard them laughing at the massacre of their allies, which they called Truman's Trounce.

Over the next few days, they lost over thirty men to Susquehannock arrows. September became October. The days became shorter and colder but they could not breach the fort. Thinking the attack would be over in a day or two, they provisioned for a week. As the weeks went by, they sent out hunting parties in ever-widening circles. At last, they sent the boats back for more supplies.

Fort Piscataway, Maryland
Season of the Hunter's Moon - Mid-October 1675

Before sunrise, Wannis followed Connawa and Shae-ee-kah along the ramparts' walkway as they made their inspection. When it became clear that their chiefs had suffered a terrible fate, the people elected his brother-in-law leader of all the Susquehannock. Although unusual to choose someone so young—he was twenty-five—he led the war band of the strongest and largest tribe. They also selected new chiefs for the other tribes.

Connawa looked every bit the chief in his wolf cape with the animal's head snarling atop his own. These daily inspections gave him the opportunity to speak with the sentries and get to know those from other war bands. "How are our supplies?" he looked at Shae-ee-kah, who was charged with tracking food and material.

"We have one barrel of powder and two hundredweight of lead gifted to us by Maryland. Thanks to your father's foresight in sending us to the Occoneechee, we also have another two barrels of powder and shot. This should last us."

"Good. I want the men to keep using their bows and arrows. Save the powder. Tell them they're doing a great job." Connawa insisted the men of his war band use bow and arrows to keep up their skills. He endured many gripes over this because the musket took less exertion. But saving the white man's weapons for the most urgent of situations might prove a shrewd decision, now that they were at war and access to powder was limited.

Shae-ee-kah nodded. "Our grain supply will last through the winter if we're careful, but it's over a moon since we've had fresh fish or fowl."

"And meat?"

"Less than half a moon's supply." Shae-ee-kah shrugged.

"Damn!" Connawa grimaced. "If we can't hunt we'll eat through our winter provisions." With over two hundred people in the fort, he instituted rationing, but they needed an additional supply of food.

"Good thing we brought in all the late pumpkins when we learned they were coming. Otherwise, we would be feeding our enemies instead of ourselves. Look." Shae-ee-kah pointed at a sorrel horse that wandered toward them snuffling along the ground looking for fodder in the remains of their gardens. "Too bad we can't eat him." He pulled his right hand back to his ear, imitating a bowshot. "He'd feed more of us than a stag."

They watched as the horse ambled closer. Below them, children pushed their hands through the logs. One of them waved a handful of grass at the horse. Each time the children moved, the horse's ears went back, his head came up and he backed away.

Wannis jumped off the platform. "Here, not like that. Don't flap about and wave the grass at him. You need to hold still and speak to him reassuringly. Forget that razor grass." He took it from the boy and tossed it on the ground. "He won't eat that. Horses need tender grass, and they like fruit. Watch."

He put his hand through a space, palm up cradling the core of the apple he had eaten. "Look what I have for you, old boy. You see this?"

"But we don't speak his language," the boy said.

"It doesn't matter." Wannis spoke to the horse in Iroquoian. Its ears pricked forward as it moved closer. It nuzzled the log walls before gingerly reaching out and taking the core from his hand. The animal munched loudly, and then moved closer, allowing him to rub its nose. "That's all it takes. You need to be reassuring, keep your voice soothing and no jerky movements. See, he likes our language as well as the white man's."

Connawa listened from above and a wide grin spread over his face. He punched Shae-ee-kah's arm. "Perhaps we can eat him, old friend. Wannis, come up here."

Wannis climbed the steps and rejoined them on the platform. "You learned the ways of these animals when you lived with the English?" his brother-in-law asked.

"Yes."

"I'm thinking those horses could feed us for many moons. Could you get them to come through the gate?"

Wannis looked at Connawa's hard, handsome features, pleased his advice was being sought. He took a deep breath, hoping he did not sound too eager. "It's not much different from the way we attracted and kept the hogs quiet at Matthew's plantation. Feed them to get them accustomed to you and then harness them."

Connawa looked at him. "What's a harness?"

"It goes over the horse's head so you can guide him. I think the women could make them from braided leather and maybe reeds."

He wrinkled his forehead in concentration. "If I lead a horse across the field, their sentries will see me. I would need to ride at a gallop to make it. But if I do that, I could only bring one."

"Is it difficult to ride?" Connawa asked. "Maybe my warriors can ride them too."

Wannis remembered his first riding experience with Mary. She put her heels into her mount and cantered off. His horse tossed his head, snorted, put his ears back waiting for instructions, and receiving none, took off after her. He slid off the rear of the animal, landing with an impact that jarred his bones. Afterwards, he practiced so it would not happen again, but that experience indicated that untrained warriors could not ride easily.

He looked at his brother-in-law. "It's hard to ride a horse at a gallop. I don't think the warriors could do it."

A week later, on a moonless night, dressed in dark clothing and smeared with charcoal, Wannis stole out of the fort through the north gate. He edged around the wall to the field between the fort and their enemies' camp. Crouching, he dropped to his belly and inched toward the herd which was crudely fenced in with rope and brush barriers.

When he reached the makeshift corral, he started to stand, but a blond horse snorted, whirled and pranced back a few feet away. Wannis stood slowly so as not to alarm the herd. From the pouch he carried at his waist, he took a handful of corn. He held it in his palm, offering it to a plump mare. The blond horse crowded in extending his head and sniffing with interest.

"Not you old boy. You're much too fine." He gave the blond horse a pat on the neck, before shoving him away. He moved back to the mare. As she reached for his palm, he stroked her with his free hand. "Good girl." He slipped the reins over her head and then adjusted the halter. The blond horse threw up his head and whinnied, clearly unhappy that he was not going for a ride too. Wannis froze.

"Who goes there?" a sentry bellowed.

His partner joined him. "Something's disturbing the herd."

"Bet it's a rodent."

They listened for a moment. "Whatever it was, it's gone." His partner moved back to his position.

Wannis grinned. The English set their sentries in between their camp and the herd. It never occurred to them that their stock might be at risk. He quietly pulled away a section of brush enclosing the corral and guided the mare through the opening.

He shifted onto the balls of his feet, gripped the reins and pulled himself onto her back. With a kick, he got the mare moving and swatted her rump with a stick. He dug his heels in again and she surged forward. They crossed the first fifty feet of the field before the sentries became aware something was happening.

"Hey. What's going on there?" a voice yelled.

Someone cried, "Our horses are loose."

He heard pounding hooves behind him and knew without glancing back that the blond horse followed. He kicked his heels into the mare's flanks. The animal responded, breaking into a canter. He pressed his knees tightly and gripped the mane.

They neared the main gate and he allowed the blond horse to pull parallel. Leaning out he smacked it on the nose with the stick, which caused the animal to swerve away, bucking and kicking up his heels. He turned his mount into the wall. The gate opened and he guided the mare through, relieved they would not be eating the handsome blond horse.

The sentries did not get their first volley off before he disappeared behind the walls and the door slammed shut. Great whoops of laughter came from behind the stockade, while the enemy camp erupted into chaos. The English fired their guns blindly into the darkness.

"Cease fire," someone shouted, but the firing continued. "Cease fire, you imbeciles," the voice shouted again. "They're already behind the walls."

That week, the tantalizing aroma of roasted meat lingered in the crisp air. Wannis did not know how many people one horse could feed, but it turned out it lasted a week, after which he planned his next incursion into the herd.

The second time would be more difficult. Their adversaries redeployed their sentries in front of the herd. Remarkably, they did not move the horses. Wannis suggested he take several warriors with him to silence the guards and help him harness more horses. Connawa agreed.

They spent the day making harnesses. That night, they slithered across the ground on their bellies and slit the guards' throats. They harnessed five horses. Shae-ee-kah jumped on behind him the way they had practiced. One arm clutched him around the waist while the other hand gripped the lines leading the horses. They walked out of the corral before breaking into a trot. Once again, they made it back before their enemies could fire a shot.

They repeated their success time and again. They killed more sentries, and the English hardly had time to fire their weapons before Wannis and his companions reached the safety of their walls. The besiegers lost twenty percent of their mounts. The Marylanders grumbled and the Virginians made fun of them, laughingly telling them they might have to trot home on foot. After this, Truman ordered that they stake a few horses, including his, between the tents, and the rest he sent home with another urgent message to send food.

Fort Piscataway
Season of the Beaver Moon - November 1675

By the end of November, the siege was in its ninth week. Most of the English had never endured anything like this before. They tired of the monotony, the diet of dry corn and the icy ground they slept on. Good-natured and pliant men became fractious and quick to anger. The Susquehannocks, while eating well, continued to worry about their supplies.

Connawa called a council to discuss alternatives and invited Wannis. Under normal circumstances, Wannis would be considered too inexperienced to attend, but he proved himself a brave and resourceful provider of the people. When he walked into the warm longhouse, the aroma of tanned leather, sweat and burning tobacco washed over him. He joined the younger men seated on mats on the floor. He could not help but notice the empty spaces on the benches lining the wall, where the great men had once sat.

Connawa stood. "We've defended ourselves boldly. We owe a special thanks to the brave men who risked their lives to bring us food." He looked around meeting the gaze of his warriors. "You have all worked hard and our fathers would be proud of us. I would like to recognize an especially brave young man, Wannis." He gestured to his brother-in-law seated on the floor. "He has not been a Susquehannock since birth, but we are glad he's one of us, for he's introduced us to a new source of food."

Everyone laughed and those closest to Wannis clapped him on the back. Wannis smiled, trying not to show how much this tribute pleased him.

His brother-in-law lifted his arms for silence. "We must decide what we do next. Our enemies have been here since the season of the corn moon. If they bring reinforcements and more supplies, they can outlast us. I think that's their intention. If we attack head on we will kill many of them, but we risk our women and children. If we abandon this home and seek a new one there are also risks. I ask for your counsel on this important decision."

Shae-ee-kah stood. "I think we must escape from the fort to survive. Now, we are strong and able to fight. The meat Wannis has brought us has fortified us." He grinned and winked at Wannis. "But, eventually when our food runs out, we will weaken, or sickness may strike us."

Many worried about this and there were grunts of agreement.

"Where would we go?" Quaachow asked. "We can't go east toward the Patuxent River. If we go around or through their soldiers to the south, they would chase us into more settled areas around the place they call Maries."

"If we went north," Ex-undas growled, "it would be back into the arms of the Seneca."

Shae-ee-kah and Connawa discussed this many times. Last night, they included Wannis in their talk. They know where to go, but again the silence lengthened.

At last, Shae-ee-kah spoke up in his deep voice. "We should go west—beyond the blue mountains."

"But to go west," Quaachow said, "we must cross the river and they have destroyed our canoes. Winter is upon us. How many of our people would survive?"

"I say avenge our murdered great men before we leave this place." Tong-quas, the son of chief Wadonhago, had remained silent, but could not restrain himself.

"Our great men are worth twenty of the English, Tong-quas," Connawa said. "We have killed some of them over the past months but we owe them many more deaths. I promise you, we will settle this score. But, for now, the survival of our people is our main concern."

It became quiet and Shae-ee-kah finally broke the silence. "The journey is long. With our women, children and old ones, it will take several cycles of the moons. But there are vast grasslands and meadows, where great beasts and much game roam."

"Buffalo!" Sheehays grinned, punching the air with his arm for emphasis. "My grandfather said that in his boyhood they roamed the Susquehanna valley."

Connawa leaned forward. "The only option for us is westward past the vast forests and beyond the blue mountains, to the land the Shawnee call Kain-tuck-ee. It has a great advantage." He paused. "It's too hard a journey for these soft, white men. So, at last, we'll be rid of them."

"The swim," Ex-undas grumbled. "Many of our people will not make it across the river."

When they discussed this last evening, the greatest problem they grappled with was logistical. The water temperature had dropped steadily since the English arrived in September. Now, in November, thin icy fingers often rimmed the Potomac's shore. Some of the small children and older people might not make it.

"There's a way," Connawa said, standing and moving toward the fire, where he pulled out a half-burned branch.

He drew parallel lines and pointed with the stick. "This is the river." He then intersected the river at a right angle with two other parallel lines representing Piscataway Creek. "The creek empties into the river creating a small bay; at this point the river is widest. However, north of this, it narrows." He erased the upper part of the first lines and curved them to reduce the distance from shore to shore to show them what he meant. "If we swim across the creek and follow the coastline until it flows into the river, the distance across is not so far."

Warriors who had left their seats to get a better view of his drawing now muttered to each other.

"Wannis has made this swim. He'll tell you." Connawa nodded at him and he felt his face flush. At first, he thought his brother-in-law teased him because weeks before, Nansemond and some friends were playing in a canoe that drifted out into the bay. Wannis swam after it, but the incoming tide pushed him toward the creek's north bank, while the lighter canoe drifted out into the river. It seemed the faster he swam, the more he coasted north. Realizing this, he took advantage of the tide to get upriver of the canoe. By the time he caught up with it, he was on the Virginia side. He had to swim back hauling it because the boys had left the paddles on shore. Several warriors had just come in from hunting and were in fits of laughter as he struggled to drag the craft through the water behind him. For days, they teased him for not knowing you were supposed to sit and paddle, not swim in front of it.

Now, he looked at his brother-in-law's solemn expression and realized he was not making fun of him, but rather wanted him to tell his story and convince the others. He stood. "If we catch the incoming tide it will push us north." He pointed at the drawing. "Here, the distance across the river is shortest. The tide has a second purpose too. It creates waves that crash against the shore of the creek and that noise will help mask our escape."

There were murmurs of understanding.

"We'll leave at night." Connawa smiled and nodded at Wannis. "It will be cold but we'll send warriors ahead of the people with our supplies. That way, when we arrive, we'll have our weapons, food and warm, dry clothing."

It was settled. When the moon waned, the tribe would sneak out of the fort, make their way in darkness past the boats of their assailants and cross the Potomac River. In the meantime, Shae-ee-kah and his band would begin taking supplies across on small rafts they would make inside the fort. Once on the western shore, they would scout out a sheltered place for a base camp and begin to provision it in anticipation of the people's arrival.

Over the following nights, warriors crept out, well away from the sentries, carrying rafts and weapons, bundles of clothing, furs and food. They did not return. Their orders were to avoid the sentries. The nights were quiet, so they were confident the men had made it across.

By the end of the following week, the tribe packed up the remaining food and weapons. They dug a pit to hide the items they could not carry. They took only as much as they could swim with. Stealthily, like phantoms, they left the fort behind. Warriors crept ahead of them, silencing the sentries by slitting their throats.

Connawa assigned Wannis to the first party. As he reached Piscataway Creek, he made out the shape of a boat anchored near the north bank. He searched for a sentry and smiled: the pale men thought no one would be foolish enough to take a swim. The crescendo of the tides' successive waves as they swept into the bay, snapping at the shore, helped mask any noise they made.

Connawa divided the people into groups, including stronger swimmers in each group. They crept along the shore. Wannis removed his clothing and stuffed it along with Nansemond's in the bundle he strapped to his head. With hardly a sound, they slipped into the icy water, breast stroking past the boat, toward the north shore of the creek.

The tide reduced the amount of effort required to swim. Still, it was freezing and many did not have the stamina to make it in such cold water alone. Several foundered, but there was always a stronger swimmer to grasp and tow them.

He and his weary group of eight dragged themselves from the river's icy grasp and onto the frost-covered bank. They came ashore not far from Mary Brent's. If only they could stop to warm up. But, they could not chance being caught by their foes. Connawa had impressed upon them the need to evaporate into the forests before first light.

As Wannis pulled Nansemond from the water, he saw Shae-ee-kah and the other warriors of the advance party step out of their hiding places and help them into the forest. One of them handed out weapons and he received his bow. Wannis' fingers fumbled as he opened his bundle so he blew on them. He extracted his tunic and trousers. Suppressing a shiver as his wet hair sent icy fingers trailing down his back, he tugged on his clothes, which caught on his wet skin. He slipped into his damp moccasins, his feet crunching on the rime underfoot.

Removing a length of rawhide from the bundle, he restrung the bow. He turned to Nansemond, who stood shivering uncontrollably and was only half dressed. He rubbed his brother vigorously and helped pull a dry tunic over his head.

Shae-ee-kah and his men handed out cakes of bread made from ground corn and tobacco juice. It was a mixture every warrior carried with him into battle as it provided nourishment and a burst of vigor. He took one gratefully, stuffing it into his mouth. Even though his face and ears were numb, he imagined a surge of energy. Later in the day, the sun would warm them, but for now, they needed to move fast.

They had achieved the impossible. More than two hundred people escaped the grip of an insurmountably larger force of well-armed Englishmen sleeping in their tents. They had neutralized the sentries and crossed through the freezing river. While they had less food and warm clothing than they would need to survive the winter, at least they would be able to hunt and trap again.

They were a strong people. They would survive. They would have revenge on their enemies.

⇛Part II⇚

⇨ CHAPTER 9 ⇦
THE SUSQUEHANNOCKS' REVENGE

Potomac River
Season of the Beaver Moon Late—November 1675

G O. GO." WANNIS HEARD SHAE-EE-KAH'S DEEP, COMMANDING voice urging them into the cover of the woods.

Shivering, he knelt and pulled Tong-quas' young daughter, Koweenasee, onto his back. Glancing back at the river, he could just make out the next group nearing shore. Turning, he followed Shae-ee-kah, who set a brisk pace into the blackness of the forest, leading them away from the English settlements. He trod with care, for in the darkness he could only see the lightness of his friend's tunic and the pale bark of an occasional sycamore. They walked inland, crossing one hill after the next, the only sound, the steady cadence of their feet.

Sometime later, they reached the top of a particularly steep ridge and he felt the welcome tingle of warmth creeping through his frozen limbs. Unexpectedly, a thunderous crash in the woods ahead, ended his sense of well-being. He dropped to the ground, taking Koweenasee with him. Silence. He sniffed the air for gunpowder or human smells. Nothing. He sensed Shae-ee-kah's rigid body in front of him and felt Koweenasee's small heart beating a rhythm against his back.

"Deer?" he whispered.

"Tree," Shae-ee-kah breathed. He waited a few more minutes before continuing.

Almost immediately, they left the game trail to skirt the gigantic tulip poplar which had crashed across the path. As they stumbled through the undergrowth, the doves calling back and forth to welcome the dawn became silent. He could imagine they wondered what was blundering through their refuge.

Back on the trail, the forest sounds resumed, and somewhere deep in the woods, came the faint sound of a buck rubbing his antlers on a tree. They walked through the night into the day, crossing Accotink and Pohick creeks. Well after midday, they descended a slope to the pebbly banks of the Occoquan River. Some collapsed, too exhausted to remove their bundles for they made only short stops during the night. Koweenasee's mother lifted her off Wannis' back, thanking him.

Shae-ee-kah's men passed around jerky and he lay back, stretching his back and allowing the sun's warmth to flood his face. He turned his head and looked back up the path. He could just detect one of the watchmen Shae-ee-kah posted hidden in the undergrowth and facing the other direction. The man turned and made the all-clear sign.

Sometime later, the rest of the tribe began filtering down the trail and through the trees. Connawa led them into the clearing. He watched as his brother-in-law moved amongst them, checking on the families and the elderly. A few of the ancients stayed behind in the fort so they would not imperil the escape. Connawa spoke to an old woman clasping her hands in his. Her crippled husband was one who stayed.

Toward sunset, Tong-quas trotted down the slope with his warriors. He begged Connawa to accompany his family, in the first group across the Potomac. Connawa refused, instead assigning Tong-quas the task of protecting the tribe's retreat. His brother-in-law was wise, for he knew the man raged with anger over the murder of his father, Wadonhago. They could not take the chance that he might forget that sneaking out of the fort was more important than exacting revenge.

Tong-quas stopped in front of Connawa, out of breath, his chest heaving. The sides of his shaved head glistened with perspiration despite the cold. "I bring good news. Pandemonium broke out when the English awoke to discover we were gone."

Tong-quas' wife and daughter, Koweenasee, came close to give him a hug while others clapped his back and asked what had happened.

The Susquehannocks loved nothing better than a lively tale and the warrior warmed to the enthusiasm of his audience. "The English slept until the sun was high above the horizon." He dramatically pointed at the horizon and inched his arm upward. Wannis grinned and the people chortled, making scornful comments. This was the first laughter in days. It buoyed their spirits as they huddled together for warmth.

"The English found their dead sentries. They ran around chaotically and shouted at each other, confused as the blind vole." Tong-quas raised his knees high, imitating their frenzied behavior. They rewarded his pantomime with a chorus of laughter.

"Stupid whites. They act like *achonhaeffti*," a warrior with a smug expression said. The man's wife punched him in the side at the disparagement to women and the man yelped. This sent everyone into new peals of laughter.

"They sent their interpreter to the walls of our fort and he shouted, but no one answered him. It took them a long time to realize the fort was empty."

"What happened next?" someone asked.

"They dismantled their camp and then torched the fort," Tong-quas said. At this, many groaned.

Connawa listened without comment. "How far off are they?"

Tong-quas turned to Connawa. "We watched well into the morning. We were ready to send runners to you when the English crossed in pursuit. This never happened. They boarded their ships and sailed home."

Wannis saw the mixture of amazement and relief on the drawn, pinched faces. They anticipated relentless pursuit. Any good commander would attack them now. He caught Connawa's glance. At the vision of the English sailing homeward, the two burst out laughing. A hundred voices joined them.

Just as quickly, Wannis stopped laughing and clasped Connawa's arm. Connawa looked at him with tears streaming down his face, as the others continued to laugh.

"They won't come after us," Wannis yelled.

"What?" Connawa shouted back.

"They won't come after us," Wannis repeated. "I should have remembered. The English have a saying: For every path they know into the forest, we know ten more." He left out the part where they referred to them as "savages knowing the paths." The laughter and talk subsided as he spoke. "We know the wilderness in a way they never can. They say we can disappear among the trees quicker than they can ram powder and shot down their musket's barrel and fire at us. They're afraid to follow us into the woods."

Connawa's black eyes gleamed. "And they should be. We'll make them regret killing our great men."

The people cheered, punctuated by earsplitting war whoops. Wannis could not help but think these sounds were what the English called "hellish, barbaric noise." This was supposed to be insulting, for they feared this place they called "hell." In fact, it was revealing they did not always strike terror in the hearts of their enemies, for they yelled the name of a place or a person.

Minutes before, he saw his people weary, bedraggled and cold. The news they had eluded their tormentors bolstered their determination.

⧽⧽⧽⧸⧸⧸

They marched hard, falling exhausted to the ground every evening, only to awaken before dawn, retie their bundles and follow Connawa back onto the game trails. They traveled west, and on the fourth day reached a stream which flowed into the Occoquan. The waterway they followed narrowed so that no boats could reach them. The land was barren of settlement, for the English planted only where the big ships could get in to pick up their tobacco.

In the afternoon, they arrived at the summit of a sloping hill. The gap allowed them to see to the east and west. Wannis climbed a boulder for a better view and gazed westward where the terrain became mountainous. He breathed in and something in his chest tingled with happiness. These mountains were indeed blue and the low-lying fog added to their mystery. He paused, savoring the moment, before climbing back down.

"Look," Wannis said, pointing down the trail, where a rear guard loped up the slope.

Connawa called out to the man, who looked at them, and shouted the words they had hoped to hear. "No sign of pursuit."

His brother-in-law smiled and thanked the man, sending him down to get food and drink.

"You were right, little *issimus*: they're afraid of us." Connawa chuckled, throwing an arm around Wannis. "And, I think you've grown since we traveled south. You were almost to my shoulder. Now you're a hand over."

Wannis grinned back, thinking how much he liked it when Connawa called him "brother," and noticed that he was taller.

⟫⟩⟨⟪

The next day, their hunting parties returned with the usual game—rabbits, squirrels and turkeys—but also, the carcasses of several deer and a mountain lion. The larger animals had been gutted and tied to poles by their legs. Wannis contemplated the beauty of the mountain lion with its tawny fur and paws as big as a bear's. As word spread, people came to see it, for they were rare. They agreed to present the pelt to Connawa once blocked and tanned to commemorate bringing them to safety.

That evening, they ate their fill at the many hearths strung out under the leafless trees. Afterwards, their new leader called them together. The chiefs and war captains formed a circle in an open area. As Wannis took a seat, behind them, there was a terrifying roar. Out of the darkness, a huge bear lumbered into the circle, standing on its hind legs as people outside the circle screamed. Its immense snout had teeth as long as half an ear of corn and its out-stretched arms, with hideous four-inch claws, reached for those seated on the ground. Wannis tried to jump up, but Shae-ee-kah grabbed his arm, holding him down.

Then he noticed everyone laughing. Behind the bear, his brother Nansemond danced. The bear's huge hind claws rode on

91

top of a pair of moccasins. Wannis felt foolish as he inspected the creature. Its fur had been so cleverly stitched that the arms and legs appeared real. Wyoming's eyes peered out between the bear's snout and lower teeth.

Wyoming, *saccheman* or holy man of the Susquehannock, raised his arms and everyone became silent. They had seen this before and Wannis prayed no one noticed how he had reacted.

"The earth rests," Wyoming intoned. "The leaves have dropped from the trees and the season of the beaver moon has frozen our world and caused it to sleep. Our garden plots and the many animals that sustain us also rest as they prepare for the warm times to return."

When Wyoming learned Nansemond had begun training as a holy man and healer and that his god eyes divined the type of man Demon Eyes was, he invited the youth to train with him. Now, Nansemond stepped forward, holding a burning branch aloft, which he placed in Wyoming's hands. The *saccheman* wafted the smoke in the directions of the great ones, east and west, and handed the branch back to Nansemond. Wyoming looked overhead, throwing his hands upward and opening his fingers. "We bless this site, where soon we'll finish our meeting hall. Then we shall celebrate the Feast for the Dead, and remember those who left us this season to join our ancestors."

Wannis and the others followed his gaze skyward to commune with the thousands of stars in the clear, cold sky. The stars were the people who went before them. A wave of warmth enveloped him as the gaze of his beloved parents and brother Chinkotook looked down on him.

With the ceremony completed, Connawa stood in front of the fire, casting a gigantic, crooked shadow on the trees behind him. "Today, we learned the English are not pursuing us. So, we'll camp here for the winter."

Cheers of approval broke out and he continued. "This place is a good one. Shae-ee-kah and his warriors have chosen well." He nodded at his friend. "There are no tribes in the vicinity. There is water, a warm spring, the forest is filled with wood for our fires and there is plenty of game."

Tong-quas' raw voice broke the bonhomie. "And what of our great men?"

"I promised you we'll take at least twenty lives for every one they killed. There are many English settlements at the headwaters of the Potomac and Rappahannock Rivers just two and three days east of here. So, this will be a good place to stage our raids. In the coming days, we'll avenge our chiefs."

Rumbles of approval broke out and he held up his hand for silence. "My people, we have other matters to settle first. Shae-ee-kah."

Shae-ee-kah stood. "Tomorrow, all warriors will help build our winter camp and secure food to feed us. I need at least thirty warriors hunting every day." Most of the warriors volunteered for this duty. "The women will smoke the meat and prepare the pelts as you bring them in."

"We all need to share the work if we are to survive," Connawa turned slowly to look at everyone in the circle. "Providing shelter, food and clothing for our people before the water freezes is our challenge. So all of us need to pitch in." People murmured agreement, as most recognized that despite their successful escape their situation was still perilous.

"What about our homes?" Ex-undas asked.

Connawa motioned again to Shae-ee-kah.

"The men and women, including the children, will build our homes. We need twenty men to fell trees for our *wickŵmen*. Once we have the frames up, the women and children will take over and cover the sides and roof with bark. We'll not have the luxury of separate dwellings; families must share. Each chief will apportion the houses among his warriors and their families."

The thought of doubling up brought grumbles from some, but then their leader added what they wanted to hear. "After we see to our needs—food and shelter first—then the warriors will go east to settle our score with the pale ones."

"We could build war canoes and sweep down the rivers attacking every plantation we see," Ex-undas said. "Wipe them out, one after the other."

Connawa shook his head. "No. They are spread over four

rivers. If we send many warriors, it will be easier for them to track us here."

"Our leader is right," Shae-ee-kah growled in his low gruff voice. "Small groups attacking one plantation at a time have the greatest chance for success. We scatter our attacks on different rivers, for it will reduce their ability to find us. Each time a war party returns, they must cover their tracks well. And they must never take the straightest route back here."

"We will be wily like the *rahaughcums,*" Connawa said, for all knew raccoons were among the most cunning of creatures. "One party will strike in one location, while another party will attack at least a day's walk in another direction. That way they will never know where to guard, or which direction to follow us."

Wannis was again impressed with his brother-in-law's strategies which were always based on careful assessments. The people launched work on the shelters with enthusiasm, for the men wanted to finish the elementals and get on with what burned at them: revenge.

Rappahannock River, Virginia
Season of the Long Nights' Moon – Late December 1675

Wannis squatted next to Shae-ee-kah, watching the man and boy, bending over the hard frosted earth to collect the remaining pumpkins. They amassed them into a small pile. Scavengers had nibbled on them, so they were hardly worth collecting.

"Thank goodness we planted these," he heard the man say. His dirty, tattered clothes hung on his scrawny frame and when he removed his hat, Wannis saw he was bald.

"Da, will the merchant give your musket back?" the boy asked. He wore rags, exposing several inches of ankle and his scuffed shoes had no bindings. They were too tight, Wannis mused, for he hated wearing English shoes.

"Nope. Gave me grain for my gun, but said he wouldn't let me buy anything on credit until the tobacco ship returns next year." The man sighed. "Our neighbor Smyth told me he borrowed against his shipment, but when the ship came back, he learned his hogsheads had molded on the crossing. He still owed the ship for transport and ended up losing his fifty acres and having to indenture his family to pay off the debt."

"Da!" the boy yelled, looking down in horror as his father pitched forward a long arrow protruding from his back. He started to run for the house, but the warriors clubbed him to the ground and with swift efficiency took his scalp. They headed for the house, but the boy's yell alerted those inside and the doors and windows slammed shut.

Potomac River, Dogue Bay, Virginia
Late December 1675

John Lucas stood looking up the slope at Robert Rawlings' small, unpainted wooden house. The plantation included several acres of cleared riverfront where the stubby remnants of the tobacco harvest poked through the soil. Closer to the house he noticed the vegetable garden. Most small planters risked starvation by planting only tobacco.

The militia visited five plantations that week. They found forty butchered bodies. After each attack, they pursued, but quickly lost the trail. The terror of the attacks escalated alarmingly. Planters feared to venture forth to tend their livestock or their farms. They even went to the outhouse in armed groups. On larger properties, with numerous indentured laborers, they fortified their houses with palisades. In Westmoreland, hundreds were killed and the survivors either moved in with neighbors or flooded into Jamestown.

"There were two canoes." John Crabb pointed at the marks on the shore. "Must have happened after the rainstorm. Lots of moccasin prints." He looked at his booted feet that made no prints on the hard frozen ground. He started up the incline but stopped. "Looks like they dragged something bleeding from the top of the slope."

John Washington joined him and peered at the trail of blood before joining him as they followed it up the rise. As the ground leveled off, the trail of blood broadened. They stopped, staring down at a carcass and gruesome heap of entrails. The Susquehannocks gutted the animal and took it to the canoes.

"Strange," Lucas said. "They don't usually slaughter livestock. They kill people and take whatever is not nailed down, including the animals."

"Maybe their camp is too far away to take live animals." Washington bit his lower lip.

From where they stood, they could see Robert Rawlings' body outside the small, wooden cabin, an arrow protruding from his back. A section of his scalp had been hacked off, leaving a raw wound. Chopped wood lay scattered on the earth where he dropped it and his ax and musket were missing.

Crabb looked at the arrow. "Algonquian?"

Lucas shook his head. "Too long. It's Susquehannock." He turned and walked to the doorway of the house. What he saw, took his breath away. The savages butchered the woman and little girls inside the house. Emma's head was unrecognizable as she had been bludgeoned repeatedly and lay sprawled in the center of the cabin. One little girl lay beside an overturned bucket, the other near a pile of sewing. They had all been scalped. Hen's son, came to live with them after his father's murder, but this time, his luck ran out. An arrow pinned his small body to the wall.

"They didn't have a chance." Lucas shook his head.

Washington turned, pointing to the men outside. "You three dig graves. The rest of you, head up river and try to pick up their trail. They must have gone ashore somewhere."

"You'll need another hand digging," one of the men offered following the three diggers.

"Yeah, I'll help too," another man said, leaving only four men to track the Susquehannocks.

Washington growled, "No. The six of you get going and see if you can determine where the bastards went."

The men headed to the boats, grumbling. They returned so quickly that the burials were not completed.

"We searched, but there wasn't a trace of them," one of the men said. "These heathens evaporate like banshees."

Washington ran his hand through his reddish hair in frustration.

"You didn't go far enough, man. They attacked after the rain, so there's a much better chance that we can follow them if we know where they beached the canoes."

"Begging your pardon, John." Crabb pushed the brim of his hat back. He knew Washington well, for their plantations abutted. "The men are afraid. They won't go after them unless you put together a larger force."

Washington exhaled and turned his back on the men sent to track the Susquehannock. "The attacks are always the same. They slip out of the forest and melt back into it without a trace. They don't burn anything, just kill the planters and take anything edible."

"I'd wondered why they don't burn the plantations to the ground, and ruin the fields so they can't be worked," Crabb said. "After all, that's how we treat our enemies."

"Interesting, isn't it." Lucas stared back. "They stick scrupulously to their purpose: to kill as many of us as they can."

York River
Season of the Wolf Moon - January 1676

They arrived just before first light and hid in the woods on either side of the river. Wannis shifted to relieve the cramp in his leg, releasing dead leaves and twigs that crackled as they rolled down the slope. Shae-ee-kah frowned at him and jabbed his finger downriver where the prow of a boat rowed around the bend. It made its way to the fallen tree which formed a bridge across the water.

"Yu-hoo. Anyone there?" one of the men called, scratching at his unkempt, salt and pepper beard. "Guess they haven't arrived yet, Fock."

"Yeah, well, let's tie her up." The man named Fock scanned the shore, as the boat bobbed. Spying a bush hanging over the water, he levered his oar into its branches and pulled close enough so he could grasp and loop a line around it.

"Good thinking," Simmons spit a dark glob into the water as he scratched at his crotch. "That way if we need to leave, we just jerk hard on the rope."

Fock looked around uneasily, stroking the strands of hair attached to his belt as if to sooth himself.

"You're going to wear that boy's hair out."

"Shut your trap. Everyone thinks it's a savage." Fock scowled at his companion, revealing discolored teeth that disfigured his long saturnine face.

Simmons shook his head, scratching again. "If anyone looks too close, they'll see it belongs to the planter's boy. Hair's too light."

"If you hadn't seen me cut it off the planter's son after the attack, you wouldn't have known." He stopped stroking the hair and drew his long serrated hunting knife from his belt. He pointed it at Simmons and moved the tip in small, threatening circles.

"Put it up, you jackass." Simmons hawked, this time spitting close to Fock.

"Do ya think they'll show?" Fock stopped the movement of his knife, studying his hand and then began to clean the dirt out from under his jagged, grimy nails.

"Yep, they're already here and have an arrow knocked at us," Simmons said.

Fock sat up with a jerk. His pale green eyes flitted back and forth and his companion chortled.

⟫⟫⟪⟪

A short time later, the brothers Quaachow and Hy-ye-naes, moved like shadows through the forest, coming up behind Wannis and Shae-ee-kah.

"We searched downriver. They're alone," Hy-ye-naes confirmed.

"Let's get going then." Shae-ee-kah stood. Wannis gingerly shook his cramped leg and followed him over the top of the ridge and down the riverbank.

Simmons, still scratching his crotch almost fell out of the boat when he spotted them. He recovered and raised his hand in greeting. "*Wabi* great *werowance* Susquehannocks. I greet you," he said, partly in Algonquian.

Shae-ee-kah watched the man with the greasy grey beard, before glancing at Wannis, one eyebrow cocked. "I guess he thinks we all speak the same language."

Wannis grinned and replied in Iroquoian. "He says he sees us, great chief."

Shae-ee-kah grunted and folded his arms over his muscular chest. He turned back to the two white men, but offered them no greeting. Wannis could tell he found these two grubby men as distasteful as he did. They were the lowest of the scum, for they sold powder and guns they knew would be used to kill their own people.

The one called Simmons, climbed from the boat and lifted a barrel, placing it on the shore. Wannis watched as they bartered in sign language. Shae-ee-kah was not pleased with the single keg of powder. He indicated he would give them fewer furs.

Fock's gaunt frame leaned over the rail toward Simmons. "Tell these ignorant bastards we're taking a chance trading with them. Someone told me folks were suspicious about the furs."

Simmons snorted. "We could tell the authorities where they meet us and take the reward."

Fock smirked. "That's the smartest thing you've said all day."

They concluded the trade, and as Simmons climbed back into the boat, Wannis said quietly under his breath, "They intend to betray us. We can't let them go."

Without turning around, Shae-ee-kah growled in his deep voice, "Kill them!"

Quaachow knocked the gun from Fock's hand and delivered a skull-cracking blow to his head. He bludgeoned him with his war club, smashing through the skull and releasing slimy matter. He then swiped his knife left-handed across the man's throat. Fock slumped.

Simmons had grabbed the oars, but the warriors hidden in the brush on the opposite shore, released their arrows. One struck Simmons in the back, exiting through his chest with a spray of blood. He buckled over.

"Dump them in the boat and sink it," Shae-ee-kah ordered.

Within minutes, they had unloaded the guns and powder, weighted the bodies and sunk the boat, erasing any sign that men had stood on the spot. They melted into the woods, heading for their camp by a different route.

Winter Camp, West of the Occoquan River
Season of the Wolf Moon - January 1676

When they returned, Connawa called them to a meeting. As they entered the smoky darkness of the newly completed hall, Connawa rose to greet them. He wore the mountain lion cape for the first time. The animal's immense paws draped along his arms and its head perched on his own.

"You got the powder?" Connawa asked.

"Yes, but it's not much," Shae-ee-kah said pointing at the keg.

Connawa motioned them to be seated. "Sheehays is telling us about his meeting with the Queen of Pamunkey of the Powhatan tribes. They tried twice to expel the English from this land and almost succeeded. I sent him to ask them to ally with us. Together we might push them from our lands." All knew that Sheehays spoke Algonquian because his mother had been born a Powhatan.

"The queen received us with courtesy, but rejected our offer to form an alliance," Sheehays said. "She said her people suffered greatly and were diminished by wars with the English. When the whites arrived, they were several thousand souls. Today, they number two hundred. With the treaty, they are left alone. I spoke to some of her people too. They said they would never ally themselves with us because we are savage cannibals." This was greeted with laughter. "They have a bad impression of us."

Again, laughter, before a voice called out, "They have us confused with the Seneca. They're the ones who roasted our ambassador alive and ate him."

"That treaty is fine until it becomes inconvenient to the English. Then, they'll break it and push the Powhatan into the swamps." There were mutters of agreement.

"An alliance with the Pamunkey would have been good, because they are the most influential tribe west of the Chesapeake. They could have swayed other tribes to join us," Connawa shrugged. "Come, Shae-ee-kah, tell us of your trip."

Wannis watched Connawa's face as his friend, who was a great storyteller, embellished the story. He half listened until Connawa's face darkened in anger. Shae-ee-kah reached the part where they killed the whites.

Wannis spoke up. "When we concluded our trade, I heard one of the whites tell the other, they would turn us in for a reward. Shae-ee-kah thought it would not be wise to let them betray us."

Now, Connawa smiled. "Well done."

⟫⟫ CHAPTER 10 ⟪⟪
WANNIS SEEKS PEACE

Jamestown, Virginia
January 1676 of the Gregorian calendar

THROUGHOUT DECEMBER AND JANUARY, THE
Susquehannock exacted revenge on the planters living
along the Potomac and Rappahannock rivers. To the south,
people were terrified knowing the savages were working their
way down the bay to the York and James. They sent petition
after petition to the governor beseeching him to defend them.
Then, suddenly, things became worse. A trading vessel named
the *Young Prince*, arrived from the northern colonies with the
chilling news that King Phillip, a Wampanoag chieftain, had
wiped out six hundred colonists. New England was in chaos. The
merchantman, normally laden with grain, tar and lumber, had no
cargo to trade in Virginia.

That evening, the mood in the Snow Goose, was somber and
subdued. Thomas Swann pushed a piece of smoked ham around
on his plate trying to lap up as much gooseberry sauce as possible.
Lifting it to his mouth, he closed his eyes and chewed.

Lawrence broke the silence. "What did the governor want?"

He set his cutlery down and took a sip of ale. "He asked me if
I thought the Susquehannocks colluded with the tribes in New
England."

Drummond whistled. "What did you tell him?"

"That it was unlikely. King Phillip and his followers are
Algonquian; the Susquehannock are Iroquoian. They've fought
each other up and down the Atlantic seaboard forever and their

grudges go back so many generations no one can remember how they started.

"Do you think he'll raise the militia?" Drummond said.

Thomas smiled. His friend, Drummond had lived in Virginia for forty years, but his Scottish lilt had never diminished and his "r's" resonated above the other consonants.

He took another bite. "I don't think so. When I urged him to, he threw me out."

Lawrence looked around the room. "Look at these people. Everyone in this room has petitioned him to protect them. Most have lost their homes, not to mention their families."

Thomas sighed and shook his head. "He's convinced New England destroyed its colony because they attacked the Indians and upset the balance. He thinks pursuing them, when they disappear in the forests, is folly."

"He forgets we have men who know how to fight in these woods the way the Indians do." Drummond winked at his friend.

"True, but people like you and me are well past sixty. The governor mentioned young Nat Bacon keeps asking for a commission to pursue the Indians. He thinks he doesn't have the experience and will make a mess of it. Kill the wrong ones, like Mason and Allerton."

Lawrence leaned his elbows on the table. "He's protecting his own interests and his damn fur monopoly. He thinks if he attacks, the Indians won't provide him with furs."

Thomas was mystified that the governor would not lift a finger to protect the people he governed. Perhaps Lawrence was right. He stared at his cup as he swirled the ale around. "He told me he wants to control things, not place matters in the hands of thugs."

"Thugs? He must have been referring to me." Drummond chuckled and his dark eyes twinkled.

Thomas laughed. Once, Drummond and Sir William had been friends. Sir William even appointed Drummond as the governor of North Carolina. However, the Scotsman discovered that land was being granted based on patronage, sidestepping men, who had applied for patents years before. He became incensed and thought his patron was unaware of it. He wrote an official complaint. Sir William was not only aware of the grants, he authorized them and was furious his employee created a paper trail that could get back to the king. He explained the grants went to loyal friends, expecting him to retract his complaint. The explanation made Drummond even more intractable. Sir William, hurt by what he viewed as disloyalty, recalled and dismissed him. Now, Drummond took every opportunity to antagonize him. Thomas warned him not to cross Sir William, but his friend just laughed.

He had known the governor for over thirty years and served on his Council of Advisors for half that time. Sir William, once a vigorous man, had been concerned with Virginia's prosperity. They had gotten on well but things changed. He found it hard to interpret or predict his moods. The governor became spiteful. He preferred to be advised by men with their own interests at heart, who were incapable of acting for the common good—like defending the colonists. But Sir William was not just physically decrepit; his mental state seemed fragile too.

Green Spring, Virginia
January 1676

Thomas stumbled as he trudged along the snowy path that had all but disappeared under the drifts. The spiraling wind tugged at him, dislodging snow from the trees and his white hair whipped about his head.

He had not seen Sir William since they argued, but had received terrible news. So, wrapped in coat and scarf, he left his townhouse in such a hurry that he forgot his hat. He negotiated the icy staircase to the front door with care. By the time he reached it, his hair looked like a frozen cap of matted fleece.

The servant ushered him into the room, where Ludwell, Chicheley and Beverley lounged in front of the fire. The governor looking languid and flushed from the warmth, sat opposite in a large overstuffed chair. His foot rested on the ever-present stool.

"My dear Thomas, what brings you to see us on this wintry day?" The governor gestured to a chair. "Please have a seat and warm up."

"The Susquehannocks attacked Byrd's, on the Rappahannock. Thirty-six people slaughtered, including Tom Lucas and his family. Some were tortured and mutilated."

Chicheley hissed, "Infernal damnation. These ungodly heathens." He exchanged an alarmed look with Beverley. "The attacks are getting closer to our plantations in Gloucester."

"I fear the news is worse," Thomas said. "Of the seventy-one plantations along the river, our man reported that in Sittingbourne Parish, only eleven remain inhabited. A boat just docked with a dozen of its people."

Sir William's leaned forward, his relaxed expression gone. "We were just talking about this. I think forts are the answer—a fort at the headwaters of every river."

"They can avoid the forts." He tucked a strand of damp hair behind his ear. "I urge you to reach an agreement with them. Either that or annihilate them altogether and the only way to do that is to raise a militia which outnumbers them. Frankly, the people expect this of you."

Ludwell glared at him. "Come now, Thomas. These ignorant, small planters once their indenture is over, move into isolated places where they can't make a living. Then, when attacked, they want the full power of the Crown to come to their rescue."

Beverley, leaned back in his chair and stretched his legs toward the fire. "That's right. Why do they move so far away? They should never be released from their indentures. Me, I'd rather have slave labor. They don't get middle-class aspirations, like these recently-freed men do."

How out of touch Beverley was with the constituents he represented in the House of Burgesses. People moved far away because they could not afford land along the James. To them, remoteness was preferable to working someone else's land. And, both men were hypocrites: he seemed to remember that they started in Virginia as indentured servants.

He leaned forward, arms on his knees. "We must stop the attacks. Gloucester will be next, then the York, and then the James. Good Lord. If we twiddle our thumbs, the king will have no more settlements left to defend."

Sir William sat up abruptly, and dropped his foot to the floor, grimacing as he did so. "That's enough," he growled.

Chicheley broke the silence. "Pardon me for saying this, but sentiment does seem to be increasing regarding the Indian attacks, Sir William. Perhaps Swann is right. Some action beyond building forts might be in order."

The governor stared at him. "Are you volunteering, Henry?"

"It would be my honor, but I know Nat Bacon would also welcome the opportunity to lead the militia. He has some military background and would be a good choice."

Before Thomas could agree, Ludwell said. "Bacon doesn't give a damn about the people. He just wants to make a name for himself."

"The point is," the governor looked at Chicheley who had moved to stand near the fireplace, "he is inexperienced. If anyone goes, it is you, Henry. I authorize you to raise an army of three hundred. Either eliminate the Susquehannock or negotiate a truce. I will hear no more of this." He glowered at Thomas, who refrained from sighing with relief.

The governor turned to Ludwell. "Make it so. Draw up a commission." He motioned to his servant, who stood by the door. "We'll dine now. Four persons. We hadn't finished our business when you arrived, or I would invite you to join us."

Thomas ignored the slight and excused himself heading back into the frosty winds. Sir William invited these men to Green Spring when he wanted support. He arrived uninvited and irritated the governor. He'd need to be careful not to make him too angry. Still, thanks to Chicheley, it seems they now had a solution to their problem.

Jamestown, Virginia
February 1676

Several weeks after infuriating the governor, Thomas received a note instructing him to come to Jamestown in two days' time, armed and in formal attire. The request was a strange one and its wording carried no hint of the displeasure Sir William had shown in their last meeting.

He dressed in his best amber brocade waistcoat with wide buttonholes picked out in black silk. He added a silk cravat and fitted breeches gartered below the knee with satin bows. The last item was a baldric buckled over the right shoulder to which he fastened his sword below the hip.

When they reached the town dock, he shook his black velvet hat, noticing its plumy white feather, no longer curved; it bent at a right angle. God's blood, he hated hats. He tried to straighten it, gave up, and crammed it onto his head before heading up the incline.

As he closed the distance over the frozen ground, avoiding the patches of snow, he noticed a group of twenty warriors assembled under the giant leafless oak by the door. They wore long buckskin trousers and luxurious fur capes. Could they be the famous Susquehannocks? What were they doing here? One warrior, a bit shorter than the others stood watching him, a grin plastered on his face. Bloody hell! He had seen his frustration with the hat and was laughing at him.

Thomas shot him a wry look. The fellow's smile lit up his face, followed by a salute and a respectful bow. He had never seen a native bow and could not help himself from smiling back, and returning the salute before turning to climb the stone steps of the State House.

Inside, the governor sat at the end of the room on a throne-like chair. Ludwell leaned over him, one hand on his hip. He wore "petticoat breeches," the latest fashion which used as much cloth as a ladies' dress. Thomas tried to suppress a chortle, finding them ridiculous. The other council members sat in a circle. The only representative from the House of Burgesses was Beverley.

Sir William looked up and greeted him with a smile. "Thomas, we need your skills."

Thomas was surprised. The governor's sentiments ranged from delight to see him, to fury.

"I'm sure you noticed the Indian delegation outside. That cunning Cunkawa sent a messenger several days ago requesting

I receive his peace delegation to discuss a settlement. If we reach some sort of understanding, we can stop this nonsense."

Nathaniel Bacon cleared his throat. "They've killed too many people. The families will expect to be compensated." Several others muttered their agreement.

"That's not realistic, Nathaniel," Thomas said. "We've driven them from their home and forced them to live off of the land. Any goods they had would've been left behind when they escaped Piscataway."

"Then we should execute the leaders." Ludwell flicked back the tails of his pale blue juste-au-corps as he sat down.

Thomas' white brows came together in a frown. "Let me remind you, Phillip, we've already massacred their chiefs when they approached us under a flag of truce."

Sir William sighed. "If we agree to peace, then we need to decide where they would settle. Returning them north to the Susquehanna is my first preference."

"But, the Seneca drove them out," Thomas said. "I don't think they can go back unless we help them push the Seneca out."

"Well, I don't want to give up land in Virginia." Ludwell crossed his leg, swinging his foot. Thomas noticed his square-toed slippers were tied with large bows in the same fuchsia satin as his waistcoat. They must have cost several hogsheads of tobacco.

"Phillip's right. Land is scarce enough for honorable men like us." Beverley glared.

"Gentlemen! Plantations up and down the rivers lie abandoned." Thomas thought he saw greed reflected in the reactions of Ludwell, Hill and Beverley when he mentioned deserted land. "We need to choose whether we declare war or agree to provide both compensation and land to go with it. I think peace with no further loss of life is preferable."

"I agree," Nathaniel Bacon said. "Anyway, if we fight them, we'd have to raise taxes."

"Not necessarily," Nat, the younger Bacon, said. "Those of us in public office pay little tax and some of us are exempt altogether. If we remove our exemptions we should be able to finance an expedition against the Indians."

"I'm not giving up my exemptions," Ludwell said. "We run this colony and deserve to benefit. Without us, the small planters would be back in England's gutters."

Sir William raised his hand, examining the glittering red stone on his index finger. "Enough discussion. Thomas, please call them in and act as interpreter."

Thomas started to tell him that he spoke Algonquian and the men outside spoke Iroquoian, but changed his mind.

→»»«««

The man with the crooked feather walked down the steps and stopped in front of them. He raised his right palm and said in Algonquian, "I greet you in the name of our governor and invite you in to parley." He gestured with his left hand toward the State House.

Wannis considered answering him in the same language but spoke in Iroquoian instead, so Shae-ee-kah and Sheehays could follow the conversation. "I come in the name of our king, Connawa, to discuss peace with you."

The crooked feather man's eyes never left Wannis face. Finally, he inhaled and looked down muttering, "It seems we don't understand one another."

"Yes we do." Wannis replied in flawless English and proceeded to introduce his companions. He smiled at the dumbfounded look on crooked feather man's face.

"I'm Thomas Swann. If you would, please follow me."

Connawa sent Wannis on this mission with the understanding he would be in charge of talks with the white men. He turned to Shae-ee-kah and Shee-hays. "The discussions may be in English. You come with me, the rest stay here."

"I understand little brother," Shae-ee-kah said.

→»»«««

Inside, the man called Swann made the introductions. Wannis

sensed he intended to add that he spoke English, so before he could do so, he began to speak in Algonquian telling them why they had come. He noticed two men close to the governor whispering during his remarks.

The man called Thomas Swann translated. The governor nodded several times then asked them to be seated. Wannis sat down, but Shae-ee-kah and Shee-hays stood behind him.

"May I offer you some refreshment," the governor asked.

Wannis declined politely. Coming into Jamestown he commented the settlement seemed surrounded by swampy land. Shae-ee-kah replied, "I would never drink water from such an insalubrious site. Why would they locate where their waste could accumulate in the drinking water?"

The governor finally turned to the two men who had chatted through the introductions and silenced them. One said "We should remove the heads from these savages and send them back to that whoreson leader of theirs."

The other laughed. "They're so primitive, they probably wouldn't miss their heads."

Wood scraped as Wannis shoved his chair back and it clattered to the floor. He turned to glare at the man who had made the remark, his feet wide and arms crossed over his chest. "For many seasons, we have been at peace with you." He looked around the room, his eyes like hot coals. "You attacked us without provocation. My great chief Connawa asks, 'Why? Why did you join Maryland against us?'"

It took the others a moment to realize he spoke in flawless English.

"You murdered our chiefs even though they came at your invitation under truce. You act dishonorably." Wannis noted several of the men squirmed uncomfortably. Good. They deserved to feel bad about what they had done.

"You tried to starve us and drive us from our home. Our king, Connawa, said he would kill twenty of you for every one of our chiefs you murdered." Wannis made a slashing movement with his hands as though he held someone by the hair and hacked off the scalp.

"Our leader is a great man," Wannis said. "Despite your treachery, he is willing to offer you peace, but only if you accept conditions: you make good on our losses—our land, our crops and goods. In return, we will stop our attacks on your people and make a treaty to reinstate our friendship."

Everyone spoke. Wannis heard one call him an arrogant savage and say he had no right to imply they had no honor and to demand terms. He tried to suppress a smile.

The governor held up his hand for silence. "You've killed too many of our people. They clamor for revenge against you. There must be restitution for those families you killed. Your leaders must be turned over to us for punishment."

"No!" Wannis glared at their leader. "We didn't start this quarrel. You did. You murdered our chiefs in cold blood. I am authorized to promise that if you cede to us the land along the northern Potomac and as far west as one may travel, we will attack you no more. There will never be—what do you call it?—Restitution."

This brought the room into turmoil and everyone began to speak at once. Wannis' warriors, grouped behind him, moved closer to stand near him.

"Silence," the leader bellowed. He stared at Wannis without blinking. "I can't enter into a treaty without offering my people something in return. Leave out the lands."

"No," Wannis answered.

"But you ask too much," the governor held out his hands in supplication.

"So be it. Then we shall fight you to the last man." With that, Wannis turned and his silver fox cape ruffled as he strode to the door.

From behind him, the man called Swann said in Algonquian, "I'm sorry."

Wannis looked at him. This man's blue eyes were so much like Nansemond's, and he had treated him respectfully, not like most of the English who called him an ignorant savage.

"I know," he replied. "So am I." He motioned to Shae-ee-kah and Shee-hays. They walked away so quickly and silently, it was as though they had never been there.

111

Thomas sighed and closed the door. The young man who just walked out, was different from the good-humored person he greeted outside. He showed tough determination, something these people had displayed for months as they survived in the wilderness, attacking and disappearing as quickly as they materialized. He felt an immense sadness. His people caused this crisis but took no responsibility for it. Behind him everyone began to speak at once until Sir William stood, shouting for silence.

Beverley stepped toward him. "Let me go after them and give them what they deserve."

"They came under a truce for God's sake," Coles chided him.

"They're all savages. What's a truce to them?" Hill said.

→»》«««←

Late in the afternoon, the council deliberations continued. They discussed the Susquehannock's visit, worrying it this way and that unconstructively. Thomas dozed off as they yammered until the noise of a chair being thrust against the wall jarred him awake. The governor crushed a sheet of parchment in his fist and waved it angrily. "This is the third petition I've received this week."

"What does it say?" someone asked.

"Same as the others." Sir William frowned. "So and so's neighbor was attacked and send a military force to defend them."

"Why don't you issue a decree forbidding people from petitioning you?" Ludwell grinned.

The governor cocked his head and turned to Hartwell. "Draw up a proclamation that planters may no longer petition me for protection. The more I think of it, the more I like the idea of the forts."

"But, they will never solve the problem," Thomas said, now fully awake. "They'll be expensive to build and to maintain. They'll pull men from their homes, leaving their families unprotected. You heard what the Susquehannocks said. They'll fight us to the death."

The governor scowled, then turned to the others. "I'll call a General Assembly for March. We'll let the burgesses decide. Oh, and Henry, you are relieved of your appointment. No need for you to run off to pursue the Susquehannocks if the Assembly decides to build the forts."

»»«««

Thomas could not wait to leave. He walked to the dock, noting the wind blew from the east, so he asked his men to loft the canvas. He loved his pinnace and the lightest waft of a breeze gave him an excuse to raise the sail. He glanced up, admiring how the bleached canvas billowed against the cobalt sky. His hair tied back in a tidy queue, whipped out and competed enthusiastically with the sail. He inhaled the fresh air, greatly relieved to be away from the poisonous atmosphere of the Council.

Winter Camp
Season of the Cohonks Moon—February 1676

Wannis returned to winter camp in the second Moon of Cohonks, when the migratory geese had begun to return. They met with Connawa privately to tell him they had failed. Afterwards, he called the leaders together, entering the meetinghouse last.

Without preamble, he began. "We came to this place, as a temporary home. We have had our vengeance on the English. We killed more than twenty for every one of ours."

He outlined their situation. They had no cleared land for spring planting, they had to go farther to find game, and both the Powhatan and the English refused their offers. They must move on, and soon.

Men whispered. Most never believed they would ever move away from the salty bay and venture beyond the Blue Mountains.

"What of our boats?" Ex-undas said. "All of this walking is aging me."

The others laughed, but not to be side tracked, he grumbled on, "And, venison is fine, but what you suggest means we shall never eat oysters and salty fish again."

"That's not so," Sha-ee-kah said. "There are mighty rivers beyond the Blue Mountains. We'll build our boats again, and we'll fish and trap. We'll hunt the buffalo that used to roam the Susquehanna River in our grandfathers' time."

They smiled and some clapped their hands with delight.

Connawa described how they would split the tribe into three branches: Shae-ee-kah and his warriors would travel south to buy more powder from the Occoneechee; the major part of the tribe would stay close to the mountains; and, Ex-undas and his war band would continue to harass the English. At the first signs of spring they would all join forces and head west beyond the Blue Mountains.

⋙ CHAPTER 11 ⋘
THE GENERAL ASSEMBLY

Jamestown, Virginia
March 1676

WIND SWEPT ACROSS THE WATER, STINGING THOMAS' FACE and threatening to take the hat Mary insisted he wear. Overhead, a noisy, but much-loved sound competed with the wind. Looking up, about thirty geese followed their leader in a V-formation over the James. They flapped vigorously and seemed to try to out-honk each other. He wondered how they knew to fly south every autumn and return north while winter still lingered.

Smiling to himself, he continued down Front Street, past the State House and his town home, which formed its eastern end. He bought it to expand his business with Willy Drummond. They deepened the basement and used it to store imported goods, while the first floor rooms provided office and meeting space. When he reached the Snow Goose, he glanced down into the window of the basement. Trestle tables were already packed with people.

He stepped up to the front door and let the brass knocker fall. A servant ushered him in. "It's all right." He pointed. "I know the way." He walked through the central entry hall and rapped lightly on the door to the left. Without waiting for a reply, he entered.

"Welcome." Richard Lawrence crossed a handsome rust and indigo carpet to greet him. Giles Bland and Drummond sat by the roaring blaze of the room's fireplace. "Take a seat." He gestured at the chairs. "Nat should be here shortly. He's asking the governor again for authority to pursue the Susquehannocks."

Drummond looked up at the ceiling. "Please God; let him be successful this time."

Thomas settled into an ornate, carved chair. It looked rich, but the style introduced by their king when he regained his throne from Cromwell, was not made for comfort. He cast an admiring look around the room. Wainscoting, painted robin's egg blue covered the walls from floor to ceiling.

The brass knocker on the front door echoed through the house, and a few minutes later, Nat Bacon entered. His face was ruddy from the cold. He sat in the chair next to Thomas and stretched his legs toward the fire.

"Let me guess," Drummond said. "He turned you down again."

"He did." Nat exhaled rubbing his hands together. "He's all enthused about building forts to protect us." He scowled and his black brows practically touched.

"Forts," Thomas snorted in disgust. "The Indians will never go near them. Why should they, when they can pick us off plantation by plantation? Sending the troops out from the fortress after an attack will be about as useful as what's happening now."

"We're urging burgesses to vote against them." Drummond took a hefty swallow from his glass. "Many of them are with us."

Thomas tugged on his lower lip and shook his head slowly. "Let's face it. The burgesses may be sympathetic, but I'm not optimistic they'll vote against Sir William's forts."

"Besides," Lawrence said, "his cronies in the House want them because they'll get the contracts to build them."

His servant appeared in the doorway to announce supper and they moved to the adjoining room.

"This color turned out well." Thomas looked around the opalescent green room. "Did you know people are calling it 'Lawrence Green?'"

Their host laughed, clearly pleased with the compliment. "Our faint-hearted carpenter also did those." He pointed to the built-in cabinets on either side of the door, which had fluted columns, capped with graceful scallops. They had used the same master carpenter. The man had a great future but decided the harsh life of Virginia was not for him. After finishing Lawrence's house, he caught the next ship headed for the warmer climes of Barbados.

"The governor's financial hold on the colony," Nat said, "is starving us."

"Speaking of starving, this smells wonderful." Thomas raised his spoon of shellfish soup, made with oysters, clams, corn and cream.

"I almost feel guilty eating so well." Drummond grinned. "This is superb. What's it flavored with?"

"A dash of nutmeg," Lawrence said.

Drummond nodded. "I thought so. Heavenly spice."

Nat tried again. "The problem is, we have the only salaried jobs in Virginia. We are paid even if there's no business to conduct. So, the governor has most of us in his pocket: burgesses and councilors alike. New elections could help."

Lawrence placed his spoon in the bowl and patted his mouth with the linen napkin. "I guess you're impatient to discuss business."

"Sorry. The meal is delicious, but the injustices in this colony consume me," Nat said.

"All right." Lawrence said. "The governor called the Grand Assembly into session about the time I came to Virginia. It's been in session ever since. Twenty years with the same men running government, getting paid and doing nothing."

"I would love to receive one hundred fifty pounds of tobacco, to sit on my ass." Bland sat back and patted his belly. "They can't do their job and protect us from the Indians, but they never miss an opportunity to pass their own perquisites."

"It's not just they all have salaries." Nat leaned forward. "The legislators are exempt from paying taxes too. Newly freed men pay a poll tax of sixty pounds of tobacco per man, which includes sons over sixteen as well as servants and slaves. Larger planters have more servants, but if they're members of government, they pay nothing. Small planters pay more than their share."

"And the old goat has instructed the justices of the peace," Bland hit the table with his fist, "to value the tobacco paid as poll tax fifty percent below what they can sell it for."

"Planters must provide twice as much tobacco to pay their taxes. Sir William then turns around and sells it for what it's really worth." Drummond shook his head, staring into his glass. At last, he looked up. "He's getting rich on the backs of the poor."

"Virginians hate him for that poll tax," Nat said, with vehemence.

Thomas stared at his empty bowl, drumming his fingertips on the table. The poll tax financed a delegation to England to convince the king to reverse land patents granted to Lords Culpepper and Arlington, neither of whom had ever stepped foot in Virginia. As the colony grew, so did the pressure for land, but huge tracks of wilderness belonged to these lords. He voted for the tax, but began to see its unfairness.

While they talked, the servant took away the soup bowls and brought in two main courses, placing a leg of lamb before Lawrence and a roast of venison with garlic and berry sauce before Drummond at the opposite end of the table. They carved the meat, the others passed around the accompaniments: Indian corn pudding, leafy green vegetable tossed in bacon grease, and baked squash in butter with Jamaican molasses.

Lawrence passed the plates and Thomas inhaled the lamb's fragrance with a sigh. "Hmmm. Rosemary."

His host smiled. "Currants, mace, cloves, nutmeg and suet too. The dumplings are made with the stuffing."

He grinned at Lawrence's interest in cookery. He knew more about spices than their wives did.

"We still haven't solved our problem," Nat said, looking around the table. "If we can't get the assembly to vote against the forts, we're doomed. What can we do?"

No one spoke as Lawrence drummed the fingers of both hands on the polished table as though playing a keyboard. "One thing is clear," he said, "without elections, we can never hope to break the financial grip the governor and his cronies have.

"You're right. It's time to get rid of these nincompoops." Drummond made a face, adding, "Sorry, Thomas and Nat."

"If we can't persuade Sir William to go after the

Susquehannocks," Lawrence lifted his glass, "perhaps we can get something else from him."

"What?" Thomas said.

Lawrence leaned forward, elbows on the table. "You and Nat argue against building the forts. Maybe you'll succeed. More likely, you won't. But Sir William and his cronies won't be expecting a demonstration demanding elections. All these people we've spoken to—those who have fled their homes to escape the Indians—we invite them to State House to demand elections."

"Ha!" Thomas laughed and placed his glass down. "Ever since I've known Berkeley, he's feared an uprising. The threat of anarchy may motivate him."

Lawrence nodded with a grim smile. "We encourage them to shout their complaints to the burgesses and councilors as they enter the building. Berkeley may realize he's gone too far. And what is the least contentious thing he could give in on?" He looked at each man around the table.

Drummond answered. "Agree to call new elections."

Jamestown, Virginia
March 1676

Thomas awoke the following day, March seventh, but kept his eyes shut as he listened to the doves cooing. When he finally opened them, the room was still dark. It amazed him it could be dark and freezing outside, yet the birds sounded so jolly.

A short time later, dressed and fed he pulled on his heavy cloak and walked next door to State House. Although it was early, people milled about, most of them displaced by the Indian attacks. Lawrence and his friends had done a good job.

In the predawn light, he recognized John Lucas and a man named John Cotton, who lived on Queen's Creek, close to the elder Nathaniel Bacon. He greeted them and Cotton excused himself.

"I'm terribly sorry to hear of your cousin Tom and his family." Thomas patted his arm.

"Thank you. They came when my boy and I went for supplies, or we'd be dead too." He put his arm around the boy at his side and introduced his son.

"You look like a strong chap." Thomas tried to turn the conversation. "Your father must be proud to have you help him, and if you are as fine a shot as he, we'll welcome you in the militia."

Lucas' son grinned.

"My cousin paid almost seventy percent in taxes, and what did he get back?" Lucas said bitterly. "Nothing. No militia to defend him and no roads."

Thomas nodded. "Nat Bacon promises to pursue the Indians to hell if they kill another person, even if only twenty men follow him."

"The governor should just send him," Lucas said, "and I'll join him. We heard he's proposing to build fortresses instead. They won't hold back the Indians. For every way we know into the woods, the Indians know a thousand ways out, to kill us. They can do that without coming near the forts."

From the back of the crowd, someone shouted. Thomas turned and saw a coach pulling up. The governor leaned out the window and waved a gloved hand as though he gently stirred a pudding. Accustomed to adulation and groveling, it took a moment for him to realize the crowd stared at him in silence. They stepped back and a path opened before him. He walked as quickly as he could manage toward State House.

"Please, sir." A woman fell to her knees, clutching his coat. "They killed my man and children. I don't know what I'll do. Please stop these savages."

He stepped away, jerking his coat free. When he reached the steps, someone yelled, "Do your duty. Protect us."

"We don't want forts. They won't protect us," another person yelled.

Emboldened, the crowd began shouting, "No forts! No forts!"

Ludwell and Beverley stepped down to escort Sir William inside. He paused at the top of the stairway and turning back, scowled at the crowd before following Ludwell inside.

Sir William was normally a stickler for the manner in which a meeting was opened, but they barely had time to take their seats before he motioned to Augustine Warner, who called loudly, "Meeting will come to order. The Honorable Sir William Berkeley presiding."

The governor remained standing and held up his hands. "Today, I'm faced with demands to avenge the colony against the Susquehannocks. I appointed Sir Henry Chicheley to lead the militia, but then I received shocking news from the colony of New England which leads me to believe a military strategy is not the correct one. The Indians there complained the women and children starved because the colonists took all the fertile land. The Indians turned on them and killed hundreds."

He looked around the room. "I've sought to keep the war from those who would lead us down the same reckless path. From those who think of themselves first and not the good of our colony, from thugs and others, who would destroy it." He glared at Washington, Allerton, Mason and Brent, who were seated together and shifted uncomfortably.

He continued. "We won't search for the Indians recklessly, when they can disappear so easily. Instead, we'll show them our might." And with this, he launched into a homily on how building forts along the rivers would be the answer to everyone's prayer.

Thomas exchanged a look with Nat who rolled his eyes toward the ceiling. By now, many burgesses dozed, or if still alert, they fidgeted. The governor droned on, seeming not to notice. Yet, Thomas knew full well he did, for once, he explained to him that he gave his lessons like a spider: paralyze his victims so they would be unaware when he devoured them.

The heat from the fireplace warmed the room, but it also seemed to increase the odor from unwashed bodies. After an interminable time, Sir William concluded, "And, so, I ask that you vote for erecting fortresses." He eased himself into the chair.

Nat jumped up. "Give me authority to go after the Susquehannocks and I'll drive them out of Virginia. The forts won't protect us." Many burgesses stood, shouting their support.

Others, like Beverley booed.

The speaker of the Assembly shouted for order. When the room grew quiet, Sir William stood again, "I have explained to you why fortifications are important." He glared at Nat. "Some of you, who are new to the colony, don't understand what is at stake. You must behave responsibly, for if you don't, we are doomed."

"Well, at least he has the last part right," Nat muttered.

"We'll move upstairs and allow the burgesses to come up with a proposal." Sir William stood and the council followed. Twice Warner and Beverley came upstairs with a tie vote, which the governor refused to break, insisting they reach a majority. The hours wore by, and suppertime approached, but the governor refused to release them.

Finally, the burgesses reached the decision he wanted and sent the proposal upstairs: they would build the forts. Thomas felt like crying.

Nat shoved his chair back. "People won't tolerate much more. They think building forts is another scheme to take their tobacco. They are angry with us for raising taxes and keeping them in poverty. I'm afraid they'll revolt if they're asked to finance the forts."

"Nat is right," Thomas said. "You heard the people as you entered the building. If you don't defeat the Indians, then at the least, to prevent anarchy, you should call for elections. Let them elect new burgesses, if for nothing more than to make them feel you are listening to them."

Sir William glowered, his eyes darting between Thomas and Nat. "Nonsense. This is a majority decision."

They passed "An Act to Safeguard the Defense of the Country against Indians," which the Council endorsed; he and Nat abstained. The Act provided for the construction of seven fortifications at the heads of the rivers that would be manned by five hundred men. It also prohibited attacking the Indians without the governor's authorization and carrying arms to church and into the county courts. The prohibition on firearms was included in response to fear of an uprising.

Ludwell and Chicheley congratulated the governor as they

crowded around and ushered him toward the stairs. He paused at the first step and turned to stare at the two troublemakers, giving them his most sour look, full of the promise of bad things to come.

When he was gone, Thomas rose and stretched his cramped limbs. As he and Nat reached the stairs, they heard what they expected: boos and catcalls greeted Sir William and his entourage as they exited the building.

"Hey, hey, ho-ho the Burgesses must go,
Call elections or face your foes."
A woman bellowed, "The old toad has to go too."

They waited until the carriage drove away and then left to meet Lawrence and Drummond outside.

"It was a good strategy, Richard, but we were outvoted," Nat said.

"So I heard." Lawrence shook his head in sympathy. "I understand he has decreed the people can't petition him to defend them."

"Marvelous," Drummond murmured. "If we don't stop these Indian attacks before the growing season, planters won't make their crop. We can't afford another year like 1674. Too many people starved. Damn him."

Thomas shook his head, expelling a deep breath. "We won't have New England's grain to save us this year." He felt depressed: retracting Chicheley's commission; building forts; ignoring Wannis' threat; and, rescinding people's right to appeal. What next?

⫸ CHAPTER 12 ⫷
DEATH OF THE OVERSEER

Curles Neck on the James River
April 1, 1676

THE MIST CURLED ABOVE THE FIELD AS ROB CRADLED HIS flintlock and stepped aside to let the others pass. Now, when he ventured outside, because of the time required to reload, he carried multiple weapons. Today, a pistol and sword also hung at his side, and at his waist swung two leather bags: one filled with gunpowder; the other with round lead bullets.

He searched the hillside, studying the far edges of the tree line for movement or human form. The only thing out of context was the sound of clinking metal and creaking leather as the boy set the blade of the plow. A man and woman followed him in the first furrow, stooping to remove large rocks or pieces of wood left over from the burning and clearing last year. When they reached the end of the row, the lad clicked his tongue, snapped the reins and the horse plodded around the turn.

Along the path, Rob's son Jamie skidded before darting back into the trees. Rob smiled. Two summers ago, a Pamunkey stayed with them for several weeks. He taught Jamie to throw a knife and walk like the Indians, making no sound.

After the man departed, his favorite game became the pretense that he was a great warrior tracking enemies silently through the forest. He immersed himself in the game, stepping four feet off the path and concentrating how he placed his feet. A startled chipmunk darted away to safety. He squatted low to the ground, waiting and listening. The leaves rustled. Maybe his chipmunk returned. He stayed as still as a statue.

"Aaeeyea, yip, yip!" The terrifying screech and series of earsplitting howls broke the silence. He heard two gunshots and his father shouted, "Run!"

Jamie ran toward the field, now heedless of the noise he made. Reaching its edge, he crouched, down. Across from him, the woman fought as an Indian warrior grasped her hair. Swinging his war club, he caved in the side of her face and unsheathed his knife to take her scalp. Her companion raced in the other direction, pursued by three howling braves brandishing their war clubs. The boy plowing had looped the reins around his waist but his body now slumped over the plow riddled with arrows.

His father lay only ten feet away. An arrow protruded from his back but his hands made small movements as if trying to reach the tree line. Jamie inched forward. As he did so, his father saw him.

"Stop!" Rob whispered. "They haven't seen you. Go back. Warn your mother. Go!"

His son hesitated. He wanted to pull him into the brush.

"Damn it, go! Save the others." Rob's eyes closed.

Jamie backed into the underbrush, his eyes filled with tears. He stood up and scuttled back up the hill. Blackberry and nightshade pulled at his clothes, but he jerked away, oblivious to cuts and scratches. The whoops and bloodcurdling cries behind him spurred him on. He chanced a look back through the trees, before bursting out of the woods and onto the trail. He accelerated into a flat run.

><<

Nat Bacon's wife, Elizabeth stepped off the porch, her arms heaped high with laundry. Over the fire, heavy cauldrons of water bubbled releasing a halo of steam. Mary, their servant was up to her elbows in milky water scrubbing clothes.

At the bottom of the slope where the river bent northwards, Jamie burst into the clearing. His small legs pounded toward her. The rising sun blinded him and he almost ran into her. She shouted and seized him by the arms. Jamie tried to speak as he gulped air.

"Indians?" she asked.

His eyes wide and mouth open, he nodded.

"Quick. Get your mother." She pushed him in the direction of their house. Without a backward glance, he skirted the big house and raced to his home. She turned to Mary. "Quick. Get Andrew."

She grabbed her young daughter, Libby, by the hand and dragged her through the door. Turning, she slammed and bolted it, then hurried to secure the windows.

Mary and Andrew piled in through the front door, followed by Jamie and his mother. They banged the door shut and dropped the heavy bar into place. Elizabeth grabbed a musket from the wall and plunked bags of lead bullets and powder onto the table.

"Don't just stand there," she yelled. "Get the other gun. Mary, check and see what's happening."

Andrew reached up, grabbed the other musket and two long pistols, and began to load them.

"More shot and powder." Jamie's mother set two bags down.

Andrew nodded. "Good. Load."

The night before, Nat had drilled them in loading quickly. He could wrap a ball, ram it home, add powder and fire, in the time it took to breathe in and exhale. He insisted everyone on the plantation should be able to reload quickly. Now they would be tested.

Elizabeth tried to steady her hands as she poured powder down the muzzle and primed the pan.

"They're coming," Mary hissed.

Elizabeth moved to the window, pulled back the hammer and sighted.

"How many?" Andrew asked as he moved to join her.

"Six." Mary said.

"Take Libby to the cellar," Elizabeth called over her shoulder. "Jamie, go with your mother. Whatever happens, don't make a sound. Be quiet as mice."

Mary shoved the table back, revealing a trap door into the half cellar. She yanked it open and Jamie's mother headed down the stairs into the dark with the children. Mary grasped the handle, pushed it back into place and moved the table over it.

"Oh, no!" Elizabeth moaned. Thirty feet away, an immense warrior ran toward her. His angular face contorted in a snarl and he whooped an ungodly sound. In one hand, he hefted a deadly war club and, in the other, a hunting knife. Then he stepped into the shadow of the house. She watched terrified. He was twelve feet away.

She trembled. The gun discharged. The recoil rocked her and the explosion deafened her. Mary took the weapon from her and placed a pistol in her hands, giving her a small push back to her spot.

"Don't let them get so close," Andrew shouted, as he fired, set the gun down and grabbed a loaded pistol. Another thundering explosion followed by angry whoops.

Their fingers felt numb and their ears rang with the surrounding sounds. They kept reloading and firing, trying to block out the inhuman screeches.

Green Spring, Virginia
Later that morning

Nat left Curles Neck while it was still dark. As he neared Green Spring, the James River was bathed in the rosy glow of morning. He intended to ask the governor once more for permission to raise troops and defend Virginia.

He learned yesterday the Susquehannocks had reached the James and massacred an entire family a day upstream from his plantation. His friends and neighbors, William Crewes and William Byrd, asked him to join them in appointing military leaders to pursue them. He reminded them that taking up arms, even in self-defense, required the king's permission. They reluctantly agreed to wait for him to try again to convince their governor.

Nat entered Sir William's reception room and settled in an ornate chair. He had no sooner crossed one, hose-covered leg over the other, than Lady Frances Berkeley glided into the room.

Her farthingale, covered by a mauve satin skirt, swayed gently around her hips.

"Cousin," Frances cooed. She approached Nat, her head held high. She was one of the few women in Virginia who insisted on wearing satin and velvet, whether in the heat of summer or the coldest days of the winter. He stood and bowed over an extended leg as she bobbed a shallow curtsy in response before they exchanged airy kisses.

"What brings you so early in the morning?" she purred. "You must tell me about dear Elizabeth."

Of course, Frances wanted gossip about his wife, but she was more interested in information that helped her in the role she fancied for herself: advisor to her much-older husband.

"She's well, Frances, although worried about the new baby. It must be very difficult for you women in this hard environment."

Frances frowned but before she could reply, a servant said the governor would see him. Nat excused himself, but Frances announced she would accompany him. Together they entered his personal suite.

The governor sat facing away from them, but motioned at the chairs grouped around the empty fireplace. "Please, take a seat." He waved at the periwig adorning the wooden head on his vanity table. The servant removed the wig, positioned it and tugged downward at the edges. Sir William stood and turned around. With a smile, he tossed his head to settle the brown curls around his shoulders and then moved to his favorite chair.

Nat leaned forward. "The Susquehannocks have massacred four people at Smith's before going on to William Byrd's."

"Is Byrd all right?" Sir William said.

"He lost three of his indentured servants and his overseer. Two were tortured to death." He looked at Frances and was about to apologize, but her lips parted and she looked excited.

"I bet Byrd's servants were still alive but imprisoned in a room so there could be a great pretense of war against the Indians," she said.

Nat scowled and did not try to hide his irritation. "That's not true. Henry Isham confirmed their hands and feet had been hacked off while they were alive. They were scalped and hot coals placed on their raw scalps."

"Good heavens." The governor made a face. "How dreadful."

Nat fixed Sir William with his dark gaze. "They took hours to die."

Frances, with a loud intake of breath, sat up straighter. He looked at her husband. "I've come to ask, no, to beg you, to grant me the honor of leading the militia to rid ourselves of these wretched Indians."

"My intelligence says they are moving beyond our borders. They should be gone soon," the governor said.

"Damn it! They're still at Byrd's. We can't allow more people to be killed."

Sir William stared at him, his expression unreadable.

"If this continues, we won't be able to plant this spring." Nat lowered his voice. "That makes it unlikely we can send His Majesty the level of revenues Virginia normally provides."

Sir William pulled at his lower lip. The king counted on Virginia's wealth to keep his English nobles in line. Any decrease and the governor would be called to account. He might not be concerned for the people he governed, but he made sure his performance measured up at court. "I shall write the king. The Susquehannocks will be gone in time for the planting season. So, dear Nat, I can't grant you what you request. We have a treaty with the Indians, who for the most part are behaving. I can't risk offending the Pamunkey and other peoples with whom we live in harmony. I also can't raise taxes any more to bring a militia force of the size to tackle the Susquehannocks. They will move on. You'll see."

Nat stared at him, incredulity spread across his face. The governor seemed delusional. Did he really think calling up the militia would disrupt the peace with other Indian tribes? Or was he just concerned with the monopoly he held on the fur trade? Or that raising taxes would cause a revolt? Nat considered his next words carefully.

"We must act. Hundreds of people have been slaughtered by the Susquehannocks. Last year, Westmoreland County, contributed to our wealth. Now, its plantations are deserted. The Susquehannocks number a few hundred. You don't need to increase taxes. I know people will pay the cost of outfitting themselves to rid us of this curse." He stood and paced across the room. "You must defend the people, as you have been empowered by the king. No, as you have been mandated by the king." He swung his arm and almost knocked Frances over as she stood to confront him.

She trembled with rage. "How dare you accuse my husband of not doing his duty? Since you arrived in Virginia, you've sought to discredit him and take his position."

With effort, Nat kept his voice even. "I am pointing out a fact we need to recognize. People will not stand for more of this."

Her husband rose and walked across the room, his head down, mumbling. He reached the door and pulled it open. "I'm sorry to call this meeting to an end, Nat, but I have important business to attend to."

Nat hardly had a chance to wonder what business was more important than people's lives, before Sir William let the door slam behind him.

Curles Neck on the James
Early evening

Nat hurried back to Curles Neck. As he guided the sloop to its berth, the stillness was overwhelming. The house seemed deserted. No forest sounds, no children, no people. He slipped the line around a cleat and stepped onto the dock.

He knelt and unwrapped his pistols from the oilcloth. His eyes swept back and forth over the slope leading to the house. Checking his weapons, he eased back the hammers and strode across the yard.

When he was almost to the house, the front door flung open and Elizabeth tumbled out, crying as she ran toward him. The rest of the household followed her. Minutes passed before she calmed down enough to tell him that Rob, Aaron, Seth and Martha had been hacked to pieces.

Jordan's Point, James River
April 6, 1676

Several days later, John Lucas sailed with Nat, William Byrd and James Crewes across the James to Jordan's Point. It was a grim moment, and a meeting they prayed would not be necessary, but Nat's meeting with the governor failed. As they pulled into shore, Lucas saw many boats crammed into the harbor and rafted together. They put out their fenders, up rafted to the nearest boat and climbed over other craft to reach shore.

William Drummond waited for them. "Richard's in the church. He saved seats for us."

"I wasn't expecting so many people." Lucas surveyed the motley assortment of tents, wagons and temporary shelters cramming the space between the waterline and Merchant's Hope Church.

"Over three hundred." Drummond chuckled. "Most of the militia and civil leadership." He held out his hand to Crewes. "We haven't been introduced. I'm William Drummond. You're a captain in Henrico's militia, aren't you?"

"I am." Crewes smiled and clasped Drummond's hand. "I also have a seat on the bench, but I'm not part of the inner ring of the governor's friends. Too short in stature." He was a short man and touched his forehead with his hand palm down, chuckling at his own joke. Crewes had aqua eyes which contrasted with raven hair. Even when shaved, his face was dark with stubble. Lucas heard Nat's wife comment it gave him a roguish quality and ladies found it irresistible.

"All these people won't fit in the church," Nat said.

"They've elected their friends to represent them." Drummond jostled them across the yard. "Come on. The meeting's started."

As they pushed through the crowded doorway, Giles Bland spoke. Lucas went to stand next to him, while the others opened the gate to the private pew Lawrence occupied.

"They have massacred hundreds of people in the north. Now they're on our doorstep. Some of you know John Lucas from Sittingbourne Parish." He gestured to Lucas. "His plantation is on the south side of the Rappahannock River. John."

Lucas held up his left arm to be seen and someone cried out from the other side of the church, "I knew your uncle. He was a good man."

"Neighbors! Sittingbourne Parish is no more." He raised his voice. "I've lost my cousin and his family, my friends and every neighbor for miles around. My home became a fortification. We took in neighbors, until our house could hold no more. Now my family and I live in Jamestown on the charity of others."

A coin slipped from someone's pocket and hit the floor. It was so quiet that everyone heard it ping on the floorboards. "This slaughter must end now. We've been given a death warrant. The question is not when the Susquehannocks will strike next, but how many of us will be left."

Bland continued. "John is right. The governor sits and does nothing. What are we paying taxes for? They're supposed to finance the militia in times of war. Are our taxes being used for this?"

"No!" the shouts rang out around the room.

Lucas held up his arms again. "We're charged seventy percent in taxes on what we earn and the money goes to the governor and his friends, who don't pay taxes. It's time for this to stop."

"Right," someone shouted from the back. "I'm John Crabb from Westmoreland County. We're building these fine monuments across the countryside." Several people laughed. "These forts our governor thinks will defend us from the Indians. Well, they won't. I know it, and you know it too."

"My brother, Robert was killed with his whole family," Stephen Rawlings from Stafford County shouted. "I'm tired of waiting for our governor to defend us. I say, if he won't, we put together our own army and drive these savages out of Virginia."

People cheered, stamped their feet and banged on anything handy.

Lucas was amazed. When they invited him to the meeting, he thought it would be attended by local people. But farmers from as far away as Stafford sat around him. They spoke with one voice: the governor would have to listen.

Thomas Hansford, a militia colonel from York County, stood.

He raised his hands over his head and shouted to be heard. From the pew, Nat's deep baritone voice bellowed for order. He nodded for Hansford to continue.

"I would have raised the militia in York months ago, except for one thing." Hansford looked around. "If we take up arms to defend ourselves without the king's permission, it is an act of treason. You know the penalty for treason: death and forfeiture of estate. Our families would be left penniless."

Lawrence stood. "We have someone who graduated from Cambridge and practiced law at Gray's Inn. Let's ask him what he thinks. Nat."

Nat stood. "Hansford is correct. The penalty for treason is death and the estates of the traitor are forfeit to the Crown. While we might risk our lives and fortunes, we would also risk our families' survival, if we arm ourselves."

Someone shouted, "That's what the old goat is waiting for. His favorite pastime is taking what's not his, like our land."

Nat acknowledged the man with a wave of his hand. "There may be a way around the problem. I suggest we draft a petition to Sir William setting forth the situation, the numerous pleas we have sent for protection and the many murders. Once again, we beg him to defend us as the Indians are surrounding us. I shall take it to him myself. Giles will see a copy of this petition reaches the king. For those of you who don't know, his father-in-law is the king's Master of Requests."

Drummond stood, clearing his throat. "Aye, but this time we give him a deadline and tell him if he doesn't defend us we shall have to do so ourselves."

"Just so," Nat said, "and I'll deliver it to him personally."

The applause was deafening and it seemed it would never stop. Outside, the crowd demanded to know what had happened and a man near the back left to brief them. The church soon emptied but Nat, Lawrence, Crewes and Lucas stayed behind to draft the petition.

Once completed, Nat got to his feet. "I'll take this to Sir William now."

"Tom Wilsford's waiting for me," Lucas said. "I'm sure he'll take you too."

They found Wilsford outside. He was a captain in the York County militia and the son of a knight who lost everything in the civil war against the king. He escaped to Virginia, learned Algonquian and acted as an interpreter. Since he was on the wrong side of the civil war, Sir William despised him.

As they picked their way through the crowd to the boats, Lucas asked, "If it comes to forming our own army, who will lead us?"

"I would be willing," Crewes said.

"Let's see to the petition first." Nat nodded.

Someone overheard them and yelled, "We'll follow Bacon, if he will lead us." Before Nat could reply, the men around them shouted, "À Bacon, à Bacon."

He held up his hands for silence, but they only shouted louder. People thrust their hands out to shake his, while others patted his back. Lucas could see they regarded Nat highly.

Nat held up his arms for silence. "First, we formally petition. Then, if unsuccessful, I shall lead you. I promise you, the days of these Susquehannocks are limited."

After they climbed aboard Wilsford's ship, the shouts "à Bacon, à Bacon," started up again and followed them out into the current.

Nat turned to Wilsford. "You know these Indians. Do you think they've left Virginia?"

"No," Wilsford replied. "A fortnight ago, there were hundreds in their camp near the falls. Now there are about forty. The rest have dispersed. I think they've split their force."

"I wonder what they're up to." Lucas looked at Nat. "Have you noticed all the recent killings have one thing in common?"

"What?" Nat said.

"They aren't using guns. When they murdered along the Rappahannock, they shot people. Not now. That tells me they're out of powder, which makes sense because the governor prohibited its sale to Indians months ago. That means they need to replenish their supply."

"Hmm," Nat muttered. "If you couldn't get powder and shot from the colonists, where would you go?"

"To Occoneechee land," Wilsford replied. "They're merchants and have a trading post on an island in the Roanoke River. I'd look for them there."

For the rest of the trip, Nat plied him with questions about the logistics of marching to the Roanoke. When they docked in Jamestown, he went to speak with Sir William. The others headed for the Snow Goose. Later, Nat joined them.

"Well?" Lucas asked.

"He listened." Nat nodded his head. "He'll give us a reply by Friday, a week. If there's no word by then, we march."

No one spoke. They knew if the governor rejected their petition, they risked everything.

Green Spring, Virginia
April 8, 1676

Sir William slumped at his mahogany desk, enveloped in the silence of his sleeping household. The only sound was the scratching of his pen. He reread the opening lines of his report to the Lords of the Commission in England describing the Indian situation. Dipping the pen in the inkwell, he crossed out his last sentence. Mumbling, he replaced it with:

Virginia has now so strengthened her frontiers that there is no fear from the Indians even if they had ten times their present strength.

By the time, he finished his report, the sky had brightened and the household stirred. The brass door knocker resonated and soon Phillip Ludwell greeted him.

"You're early. I wanted to speak with you about another one of these infernal petitions. I'm worried about this one." He picked up the Jordan's Point petition Nat had delivered and handed it to Ludwell.

Ludwell read it, before looking up. "It appears to be just like the others, but with more signatures."

"This one is worse, Phillip. Nat insisted I reply by Friday. The petition is polite, but they want a commission to select their officers."

"Nat is behind this." Ludwell's eyes narrowed. "He and that old fart, Drummond, probably staged the whole meeting at Jordan's Point,"

"I don't think so, Phillip. Nat told me there were several hundred people at the meeting and they are angry. I can't get that many people to show up, even though I represent the Crown."

"The people love you." Ludwell smiled. "You led them through difficult times before."

"This may be different."

"Your strategy has worked so far." Ludwell examined his nails. "We keep a rein on the planters. If some get killed, that's in our interest. It makes land available for men of quality. I think these Indians have about spent their energies here. Just weather a couple of months and they should be gone."

The governor looked at him, and Ludwell added, "The people would never rise against you. But I did hear Bacon promise to lead an expedition against the Indians, if you don't answer. He is criticizing you behind your back, claiming you shirk your duties."

"He wouldn't do that. After all, we're related. He's Frances' cousin."

"I know," Ludwell said. "I am related to you too and have served you with the greatest loyalty, but Nat Bacon just arrived in Virginia. Actually, he's said he would be a good replacement for you, as you are up in years. I wouldn't put it past the arrogant pup to covet your job—as if he could ever replace you."

"What?" Sir William said. "He would never do that."

"There's a chance he might try." Ludwell smiled.

⋙ CHAPTER 13 ⋘
ATTACK ON THE OCCONEECHEE

Curles Neck, Virginia
Early May 1676

JOHN LUCAS SAT ON THE FRONT STEPS GAZING AT THE JAMES River and the lazy loop it made which gave the property the name "Curle's Neck. He insisted on returning with Nat, in part to see his plantation, but also because he thought their request to pursue the Susquehannocks would be rejected.

The day had been warm and now the sun skimmed over the water, illuminating the spars of Nat's sloop. The wooden hull creaked against the dock's fenders and the bees droned, completing their last tasks before sunset. He breathed in the peaceful beauty of the scene.

"It's wondrous, isn't it?" Nat sat down next to him.

"It is, and it's more reason why we must hang on to this land." Lucas smiled.

From the house, Nat's wife called out, "Supper's ready."

Lucas picked up his musket and followed his host inside, barring the door. Until recently, everyone left the doors open this time of year to cool the house.

They took their seats and Elizabeth served the plates, passing them around. "Still no word?"

Her husband shook his head. "No. he won't defend us. Henry Isham's man came over a while ago, and I told him the deadline had passed and to assemble the militias."

"I can't believe he ignores the prominent people from across the country who signed the petition." She shook her head.

"He has no morals. How can he allow so many innocents to be slaughtered?"

Lucas looked down at his plate, sighing. "You're right." He agonized over the knowledge that if the governor hung him and seized his property, men like Beverley would snap up his land without a thought for his family. What would become of them? Still, they abandoned their home because of the Indian attacks. What choice did he have?

>>><<<

By the end of the week, Giles Brent arrived bringing the Stafford County militia, as well as two of Lucas' friends, Stephen Rawlings and John Crabb from Westmoreland. Nat greeted them and showed them where to set up the tents and draw water.

Byrd and Crewes arrived later that morning. Both in their twenties, they became good friends when they shared the crowded space in the ship that brought them from England. They were officers in Henrico County's militia and brought the men they led. Henry Isham, a well-to-do Charles County planter in his forties, rode in on their heels. Volunteers from other counties poured in. Many held civil positions and had much to lose. Yet in the end, three hundred men followed Nat.

>>><<<

The next day, they crossed the James and headed south toward the Occoneechee trading post on the Roanoke River. They passed cultivated fields of pale green tobacco shoots, and Lucas compared it to the wilderness where he lived. Gradually, the terrain became more rugged with long tracts of thick woodland. It forced them to slow their pace and ride single file. The vast tree canopies filtered the sunlight before it reached the forest's floor. While along the James, most of these primordial trees with girths of ten feet had been cut to make way for tobacco, here, these centuries-old forest giants remained uncut.

After midday, they stopped along the Appomattox River to

eat. Nat sat with Lucas and they were deep in conversation when Wilsford joined them. He removed his hat and wiped his forehead on his sleeve. "It's hot as Hades."

"Yeah," Nat agreed. "I just told Lucas you accompanied Robert Fallam on the first expedition that explored the western slope of the Appalachian Mountains. Are there any tribes between here and the Occoneechee who might join us?"

"Hmm." Wilsford scratched his neck. "Most of the tribes are Meherrin. They're Iroquoian speaking, like the Susquehannocks. They used to live along the rivers but escaped Susquehannock raiding parties by moving inland. I'd say there's a good chance they hate the devils. I remember a settlement a bit southwest of here. It shouldn't take us more than a day to reach it."

After resting, they remounted and veered off their original course, heading southwest to the Meherrin settlement.

Henrico County along the James River
May 1676

They followed one of the trails which linked plantations along the river. Sir William dozed in the saddle until his horse stumbled, jerking him awake.

"Are you all right?" Coles rode behind him and urged his horse alongside.

The governor peered from unfocused eyes, his wig askew. "Yes, yes. Just a bit too hot." He pulled a silk handkerchief from his sleeve and mopped at his flushed face.

"We're close to the frontier," Coles said. "From here on, I suspect there are only game trails."

Thomas Ballard moved to the governor's other side. "I'm afraid we've lost him. It doesn't appear an army has passed through here and it's getting late. Perhaps we should turn back?"

"We could stay the night with William Randolph or Edward Hill," Coles said. "Although, I'm not sure whose side Randolph is on. He's married to Henry Isham's daughter, and Isham's with Bacon."

"I should have followed my instincts and replied to their

petition," the governor mumbled. "I wanted to warn Nat not to take matters into his own hands. Damn him!"

Coles looked at him with concern. "Let's go to Hill's then." He took the horse by the bridle and turned him around.

A few hours later, they reached their destination and the governor retired to his room to rest. Later, at supper, a messenger arrived. He reported that people were demonstrating against the forts and calling for new burgesses. When the man left, the governor pushed his plate aside and cradled his head in his hands. It pulled his jowls and cheeks down, making his eyes look misshapen. "The whole country is against me."

"You can't let them get away with this." Ludwell scowled, waving his fork. "You need to hang him, proclaim him a rebel and punish his followers. Otherwise, every indentured servant and slacker will think they can rebel against you."

"We've received petitions from every county in Virginia asking the governor for protection against the Indians. We've had almost as many petitions asking for new representatives," Ballard said. "If they aren't angry about one thing, then they are about the other. If we hang Bacon, you'll incite a revolution."

"You could announce elections," Coles said, "before you seize him. That would give them something they want and make it harder for them to object when you hang the bastard."

The governor looked at Chicheley. "What do you think, Henry?"

"You said you'd call elections in March and they were angry when they got the Act of War to build the forts, instead." Chicheley stared at his plate. "Calling for elections might just work."

"But you must dismiss the treasonous bastard from the Council of Virginia." Ludwell sneered. "And, from all other offices he holds, including justice of the peace."

Sir William hung his head. "I made him one of my councilors. I helped him obtain Curles Neck. I treated him like the son I never had. And what did he do?" He looked up from under his brows, his mouth tightening. "I shall declare him a traitor." He stood up from the table as though a weight had been lifted. "And yes, call the damn elections." He motioned to Hartwell, who sat at the table. "You and Ballard bring ink and paper to the drawing room and help me draft this.

They drafted the first proclamation charging Bacon with treason and removing him from the Council. It declared his followers would be forgiven if they returned home by the end of the month.

The second proclamation dissolved the Assembly. It required each county to elect two representatives and send them to Jamestown on June 5, 1676. As he paced back and forth, the governor could not resist adding he was surprised they did not like their representatives, since they chose them. "Oh, and Hartwell, add that the new burgesses should bring any grievances to the assembly. This includes complaints about me, in which event I'll join them in requesting I be removed. This would relieve me of the heavy responsibilities I have at my considerable age."

Ballard and Hartwell exchanged looks. They would never let him admit to being too old for the job. This was vintage Sir William—laying a paper trail to deflect criticism of his governorship. When they finished, they called the others to read the proclamations, after which, he dipped the quill and signed his name with a flourish: Sir William Berkeley, Knight.

Near The Roanoke River
May 1676

The day before they reached the island of the Occoneechee, they set up camp early and the men sprawled on a patch of grass. "We've veered off course to visit these Meherrin or Nottoway or whatever they're called," Crewes said.

"I don't understand why more warriors haven't joined us." Nat ran his thumb over the edge of the sword he honed. "At least we have that Meherrin warrior who speaks both Iroquois and English."

Lucas sat down next to Nat. "A messenger from Jamestown brought this." He handed him a leather pouch.

Nat lay the sword across his knees and broke the wax seal.

My Dear Friend,

Beware, for our Governor has declared you a traitor and removed you from the Council of Advisors. He offers clemency to your followers if they return to their plantations before the last day of May. The amnesty excludes you. He has agreed to call for elections. Please know Ludwell aims for your head.

Best regards,
Thomas Swann

"Bad news?" Lucas asked.

Nat looked up, frowning. "Disturbing news." He read the letter to them.

"We already had a handful of men turn back two days ago when their rations ran out and the terrain became more difficult. We'll lose more now," Lucas said.

"Can't blame them." Nat stood and returned the sword to its sheath.

"What should we do?" Crewes said.

"I'll tell them," Nat said. "They should have a choice."

The men were spread out in the woods, so they divided into small groups. Nat and his officers delivered the news and then the rations were brought to a clearing.

"It's not much." Nat looked at the mound. "If we divide it up we'll have food for at least four more days. We're close to the Roanoke. How many are leaving?"

"Forty," Lucas replied.

Isham overheard the remark. "Mostly they're the complainers who scrabble along grouching about the mosquitoes, their blisters and the heat. The fellows who are staying are good men."

Nat nodded. "Let's get some rest."

⇻⇺

The next day, they emerged from the woods and the Roanoke River stretched in both directions. The island lay directly in front of them. It had steep banks and on the top perched two wooden forts.

"That'd be hard to take," Crewes muttered, dropping the reins on his horse's neck and leaning forward, hands on the pommel.

"They'd pick us off before we even reached it." Lucas studied the fortifications, comparing them with Fort Piscataway. They did not wait long. A gate opened and a band of warriors strode out led by an older man. They strode down the slope to the water and motioned them to cross.

"Looks like we're invited," Nat said, but they continued to sit on their horses.

The leader said something to the man at his side who walked out several yards. The water was only ankle deep. He gestured with both hands showing the depth and again motioned them to cross.

"He's telling us we can cross with the horses." Crewes looked at Nat.

"Half of you with me," Nat said. "The others stay here." He urged his horse forward and at midstream, the river just covered its fetlocks.

Once on the island, they dismounted to greet the Occoneechee leader. Up close, the king appeared even older. He had a strong, straight body but one of his eyes was filmy and white, making the iris appear bluish. He spoke and their Meherrin interpreter translated. "King Posseclays of the Occoneechee people welcomes you to their island. He hopes you have brought many interesting things to trade."

"Did he say Persicles?" Byrd whispered.

"Sounded a bit like that," Wilsford replied. "But I think it's Posseclays. I've heard him called Roseechee, as well."

"Good thing you brought something to trade." Nat grinned at Wilsford before turning back to the Occoneechee. "King Posseclays, we bring you greetings." Nat introduced his officers and they presented gifts of blue glass beads and a metal knife. The king held up the knife, peering at it, as if to see his reflection. He beamed at them. This was a valuable gift.

He invited them to eat with him and motioned to women standing in the gateway of one fort. They marched out, spread mats to sit on, and began a fire. One woman held out a bowl of water. Nat was ready to take a drink when he saw Posseclays dip his hands in the bowl. They followed his example and the king motioned them to sit. Soon, the women brought steaming food piled on wooden boards and in hollowed gourds. The fragrance was mouthwatering. A stooped, disheveled old man stood, speaking in low tones. He turned to the four points of the compass, took a piece of roasted meat, said a blessing and tossed it into the fire as an offering.

Wilsford leaned toward Lucas and said, "He thanks the earth for feeding the people."

Lucas nodded. "It smells wonderful." The aroma of meat and corn wafted toward him. Once they began eating, conversation stopped and Lucas noted the Occoneechee wolfed down as much as he did.

Nat licked a fried, starchy substance from his fingers and looked at the king, pointing at the empty bowl. "This is wonderful."

Posseclays replied and their interpreter said, "It's called *Tockawhoughe*,"

"Tuckahoe." Wilsford repeated the word with a more English pronunciation and held up what looked like a muffin. "These little corn cakes are seasoned with curtenemons, the seeds of the tuckahoe plant. Funny thing is they're quite poisonous."

Byrd stopped chewing, his mouth open. Wilsford continued. "It's all right. You boil the curtenemons for half a day. That extracts the poison." He grinned and took another bite.

When they consumed the last of the food, Nat nodded at their interpreter and smiled. "King Posseclays, this meal is delicious. Seldom have we eaten so well and such unusual dishes."

As the interpreter translated, Posseclays smiled and his warriors nodded, looking pleased.

Nat leaned forward. "We've traveled far to see you, great king, but we didn't bring sufficient food with us. We'd like to buy supplies from you."

The king replied that he could provision them, but in exchange, for more of the wonderful metal implements. He looked at Nat expectantly, and when the interpreter had finished, Nat smiled and agreed.

"King Posseclays, we search for the Susquehannocks," Nat said. "Have you seen them?" Posseclays' face now became inscrutable. "They have killed many of our people and are our enemies. They are your enemies too. The Seneca ousted them from their homeland far to the north on the great Susquehanna River. For the past year, they've tried to take our lands. Now they're here looking at Occoneechee land as their new home."

Lucas watched as the king's already dark face seemed to grow even darker. His milky eye was devoid of expression, but his good eye narrowed. He turned to his warriors, speaking in urgent undertones.

Nat leaned forward. "We want to avenge our people and keep them from taking our land. If you join us, we can keep them from taking Occoneechee land too."

Posseclays' good eye shifted back and forth. He spoke, gesturing behind him and motioning overhead and then out toward where the Roanoke gurgled past them.

When he stopped speaking, the Meherrin interpreter said, "He says there are seven Susquehannocks, but Manakins and Annalecktons are with them."

"Who are they?" Nat asked.

"They're friendly tribes," the interpreter said, "that came to trade also. The king says they will kill the Susquehannocks, but not the Manakins and Annalecktons."

"Fair enough," Nat said.

Posseclays spoke to the warrior next to him. The man rose, and motioned to others to follow him. They entered the second fort.

Almost immediately, there were shouts from within the fort, followed by ear-piercing screams. Nat and his men eyed their weapons. More screams and then blood-chilling war whoops.

⇢⇢⇤⇤

Wannis and Nansemond swam on the other side of the island where the Roanoke's channel narrowed but ran deep. The river's current carried them downstream. Wannis drifted on his back, thinking they had reached a good barter with King Posseclays.

They had their gunpowder, and the king had the finest muskrat and beaver furs. Still, he could not wait to leave. Connawa was right: there was something devious about the Occoneechee. They planned a feast for tonight and Wannis had urged Shae-ee-kah to decline and leave, but he felt it would be bad manners and they might want to trade with the Occoneechee in the future.

Shots and screams coming from the island interrupted his thoughts. They seemed to be coming from the fort where Posseclays housed those who came to trade. He started to swim back to the island, but realized he had not even brought a knife with him. Instead, he and Nansemond swam to the opposite shore and pushed through the trees until they were across from it.

"See anything?" Nansemond asked.

The shouting ceased and they saw no movement at the fort. Wannis squeezed Nansemond's arm and whispered, "Stay here. If I don't return, make your way up river to find Connawa." Nansemond nodded.

Wannis slid into the river and swam underwater until he felt his lungs would burst. He surfaced carefully, taking several gulps of air and then continued. When he reached the island, he crawled through the waterweeds and up to the fort. He peered through the timbers and saw the Occoneechee warriors picking through bodies. What had happened?

The bodies of his people lay sprawled around cooking fires. They had been taken unaware. Close to him, a warrior held up a scalp with a fringe of deer hair, dyed red—Shae-ee-kah, Connawa's childhood friend and the tribe's great bard. There was a groan and the king's hatchet man kicked at a body before raising his war club and smashing it downward. Wannis heard the skull split from where he crouched. Then the warrior stooped over the body and hacked at the scalp. Yipping, as it came away, the warrior held up a bloody thing, mostly scalp, but with the remains of a dried human hand tied and woven into the hair. Wannis' stomach lurched and he swallowed rapidly. It was his uncle, Uwanno.

He slithered back down the embankment without so much as dislodging a pebble. Bundling their moccasins, knife and flint in the clothing they discarded to go swimming, he swam back to where Nansemond waited for him.

>>><<<

Posseclays' warriors returned to their king and spoke in low voices. Lucas wished he could understand them. Posseclays nodded and his warriors returned dragging a wounded Susquehannock warrior. The man's head hung on his chest and he had multiple wounds, including one on his head which bled, dripping onto the ground.

Posseclays pointed at him. "Six of the Susquehannock warriors have been killed. This one is our prisoner. Two boys got away, but we'll find them. For your entertainment, I invite you, my friends, to take part in torturing our enemy who would take our lands."

Lucas flinched and as he watched Nat, he noticed his mouth and nostrils tighten in distaste. As much as he hated the Susquehannocks for killing his cousin, torture sounded far from entertaining. He was relieved that Nat felt the same about it.

Nat turned to the interpreter. "Please explain to him that's not our way. We won't take part in it."

"No!" Wilsford thrust his arm out to stop the interpreter. "The torture of prisoners taken in battle is a great honor. To relinquish this to us is a token of his friendship and show of respect."

"Ye god's, man!" Nat spat. "We can't be a part of such a thing,"

Wilsford whispered to the interpreter, "Thank the king, but tell him our governor commands us to return home after our enemies are dead. We can't disobey his orders. If the king will give us the food supplies we discussed, we'll leave now."

Posseclays' face clouded with the translation. He spoke to the interpreter, gesturing and holding up both hands with some fingers held down. He then turned his back on them and motioned for his people to follow him. They pulled the dazed Susquehannock up by the rope around his neck. He fought back, but they punched him and dragged him back to the fort. The women and children followed. Some had knives and others sharpened sticks. They took turns lunging at the prisoner, slicing and stabbing at him. The gates to the fort slammed shut behind them.

Lucas and the others exchanged looks of surprise. Before they could question the interpreter, the man said, "The king is joining his wives. He invites us to stay six more days. That will give him time to put together the food he has promised."

Nat looked stunned. "He can't expect us to wait. He fed us well. He must have supplies he could sell to us."

The interpreter shrugged.

From the fort, they heard the howls and screams of the tortured captive. Nat and the others sat around the fire. They spoke in loud voices but could not block out the sounds. A sliver of moon rose in the sky and was joined by a companion star before the shrieks stopped. It took the Susquehannock a long time to die.

Lucas leaned forward and grasped a limb that had rolled away from the fire. He pushed it back into the blaze. When he looked up, he caught movement on the opposite bank and he pointed. "What's that?"

Byrd picked up his flintlock and readied it. "You don't suppose that old fox, Posseclays is attacking us from the other bank?"

A shot rang out.

"Take cover," someone yelled, as they moved away from the fire.

Lucas and several others dove behind a log. "Do you think they're Susquehannock?"

Crewes said. "They might be Occoneechee."

"One way to find out." Nat motioned to the Meherrin interpreter. "Go and get King Posseclays."

The interpreter shook his head but Wilsford grabbed him by the arm and pulled him toward the fort. They did not open the gate for them.

When they returned, Wilsford said, "The king says his people won't let him come out. He asks we leave his island."

"Why did he position men on the opposite bank then? That blocks our departure," Lucas said.

"Remember Needham?" Wilsford asked. "He traded with the Occoneechee for years before they turned on him."

Lucas nodded. He remembered the story of Needham, the wilderness explorer who went beyond the blue mountains to trade. Needham traded with the Occoneechee until they killed him three years earlier. He peered over the log and shouted, "Everything all right over there?"

A voice answered, "Yes. Someone shot a possum."

"Christ's sake," Nat yelled. "We thought we were under attack." He turned back to the others. "I don't trust Posseclays. He's up to something."

"We should burn the fort before they decide to attack us," Byrd said.

Soon after, they torched the first fort and heard panicked shouts and the screams of children. The fort brightened the night sky. The wailing stopped and all they heard was the crackling of the fire and an occasional crash. Every time they tried to fire the second fort, which Posseclays had entered, their men were kept away by gunfire.

When morning arrived, Posseclays led his warriors out a side door and ran for the field north of the fort. Instead of continuing to flee, the king, turned around and ran toward them firing his weapon. His warriors followed him, clustering around him to protect him. Someone's bullet found him and he fell to the ground. The others made their escape.

They ransacked the second fort and enslaved the women and children. They found a nice stash of muskrat and beaver pelts and food. Before leaving the island, they set fire to the fort.

Back across the Roanoke, Nat rode up beside Lucas. "We did it. We got the Susquehannocks."

"We only got seven of the Susquehannocks," Lucas said, "if Posseclays is to be believed. I wonder where the others are?"

"They traded and left before we got here. I'd say we've rid ourselves of one hundred heathens, including Occoneechee, Annalecktons and Manakins. At least, we've left the Indian nations, in civil war amongst themselves. That's no bad thing." Nat turned his horse onto the forest trail and urged it forward.

⫸CHAPTER 14⫷

BACON'S ARREST

Great Warriors' Trail, Virginia
Season of the Strawberry Moon

WANNIS FOLLOWED THE ROANOKE RIVER, LEADING Nansemond northwest. He debated striking overland to shorten the journey as Shae-ee-kah had planned to do, but he did not know this country. He knew the river eventually reached the rendezvous point. It was safer to keep to the river. Besides, the Occoneechee would not expect them to take the longer way.

For the first few days, they headed north. Every noise caused him to look over his shoulder and dive into the brush for cover. They ate dandelion leaves, snails, and anything they found along the way. At night, when the temperature dropped, he pulled Nansemond close and they huddled together for warmth, afraid to light a fire that would reveal their presence. He thanked *Okee* they both adopted Susquehannock attire or they would have been much colder.

After many days, the river turned to the west. With still no sign of pursuit, he decided to risk a fire. "Let's catch some fish for supper." Wannis pointed at the stream that fed into the Roanoke. He grinned, looking at his brother's wan little face.

They found a quiet pool overhung with flowering mountain laurel bushes and ferns. They stood in the water, hands dangling just below the surface. Wannis shifted his feet.

"Stop it. You're scaring them off." Nansemond frowned and moved upstream.

"I don't know how you can hold that position for so long."

Nansemond did not answer but suddenly his hands dived downward. "Got you." He tossed the fish on the bank.

Wannis tried again. Every once in a while, a fish would come close but when he tried to grab it, it darted away. "I give up. I'll start the fire." He took out his flint, occasionally looking up as his brother tossed another fish on the bank.

They skewered them on sticks and soon a mouth-watering smell accompanied the growls of their stomachs. Wannis thrust one in the flame to cook it more rapidly. He bit into it, curled his lips and blew out. It was burning hot. He finished it in several bites and picked up another. "This is the best fish I've ever tasted.

Nansemond looked at him and grunted his mouth too full to answer. It was the first meal since the massacre of their uncle and Shae-ee-kah.

Many days later, they reached a rise and Wannis sighed with relief. He pointed. "There. See the Blue Mountains in the distance." For some time, he worried he misunderstood the description of the route. Lying awake at night, he hoped he led his little brother in the right direction, and not toward danger or starvation.

⟫⟪

Finally, they reached their destination—a place the tribes called Big Lick—a well-known salt deposit. It spread across the game trail, which ran north and south, parallel to the Blue Mountains. The trail was a migration road where animals, and once the bison, roamed in huge herds. They named it the Warriors' Path because warriors of many tribes—the Tutelo, Monacan, Cherokee, Iroquois and Shawnee—used it when they made war.

He stood at the tree line where the salt deposit began, filling his lungs with air and feeling the tension drain from his body. He leaned his forearm on Nansemond's shoulder. The valley formed the start of a natural pass through the Blue Mountains and on to Great Meadow, or *Kaintuckee*. The river wandered through the valley at their feet. Although it was not late afternoon, deer, elk and families of opossum and raccoons meandered across Big Lick, ignoring each other.

"I'm hungry," Nansemond sighed. "I could eat a deer by myself."

Wannis' stomach rumbled. "Me too. Let's see what we can do for supper." At that moment, a buck, ambling up the incline, leapt into the air and crashed to the ground. His magnificent antlers dug into the dirt as he landed. Two arrows trembled from his side.

His brother started to shout, but Wannis clapped his hand over his mouth and pulled him back into the trees and the deep green growth of the laurels.

"Do you think they saw us?" Nansemond whispered from his prone position.

"I don't think so." He studied them as the band of warriors moved in on their kill.

"They don't look Algonquian," Nansemond whispered.

"Cherokee, maybe."

"I thought it was Connawa."

"I know. I did too, at first. We'd better find a place to wait for the tribe." Wannis pointed at spirals of smoke rising in the air at the other end of the field. "Someplace we won't run into enemies."

⋙⋘

Several hills away, he found what he needed: a cave whose hidden entrance faced east. It sat above a vale with a stream below. They could hunt and light a fire without detection.

He was uncertain when Connawa and the people would arrive. Since they left their winter site, the tribe split into smaller bands which moved from camp to camp and harassed the English. They could be anywhere. While they waited, he made a bow for hunting and their food supply improved.

Twice a day in the morning and evening, they approached Big Lick with caution to determine if there was any sign of Connawa and the others. He dreaded what he would say to Connawa about the death of his bosom friend, Shae-ee-kah. On top of this, they came empty-handed, without the powder and shot they had traded their furs for.

One evening, as they sat by the fire, Nansemond expressed the fears that Wannis tried to suppress since their flight from the island of the Occoneechee. "What if something happened to them?"

"Don't worry, little brother they'll come." He tried to sound confident.

"What if they left without us?" Nansemond's lip trembled.

"They won't leave without us. They're just killing more of the English. But if we missed them we'll go to Kaintuckee and find them." Wannis did not add he did not know the way.

Curles Neck, Virginia
End May 1676

Nat and his men marched homeward on a more direct route than the one they used to find the Occoneechee's island. They avoided the swamps that slowed them and arrived at the James River some days later.

After a bath and a cold meal, Nat closeted himself in his bedroom. He thought about his discussion with his friends on how he might reduce Sir William's rancor toward him. They decided the best course was to write a brief as though he reported to his superior officer. He had been composing it in his head since Thomas' letter. Now, the words flowed onto the page faster than he could keep the quill inked.

As he reached the closing, summarizing the results of the campaign, he wrote with a flourish:

> What we did in a short time and under difficult conditions was to destroy the kings of the Susquehannocks and the Occoneechee, and the Manakin king and his one hundred men. What we reckon is most important is we left all nations of Indians engaged in civil war amongst themselves. We hope to use this advantage to ruin and destroy them.

He signed the document, sealed it, and slumped back in his

chair. The emotional stress of keeping the men together, while negotiating with the wily Posseclays, and the worries of what could happen to his family if he could not repair matters with the governor, took its toll. He undressed, eased into bed and fell asleep. As he slept, wagon wheels rolled, chains clattered and voices whispered in the dark.

Much later, Elizabeth moved about the room picking up his discarded clothing. "Nat, you've slept like the dead. I was so afraid they would awaken you."

Nat peered at her and tried rummaging up a smile with his dry mouth.

"Come see," she smiled back.

He placed his feet on the carpet and hoisted the sheet to drape around his hips. Crossing to where she stood, he wrapped his arm around her waist, let the sheet drop and looked out the window.

He gasped. "My God! Who are all those people?" Wagons, horses, mules and people littered his front yard, and ships cluttered his waterfront.

"Oh, Nat, they've all come to beg you to represent them in government.

"What?"

"When the people heard Sir William removed you from his Council, they retaliated by electing you to the House of Burgesses. You and James Crewes are now the representatives of Henrico. Your friends are here to escort you to Jamestown and make sure the governor doesn't harm you."

Someone caught Nat's naked form at the window and the crowd turned toward him and began cheering. Nat waved back, holding Elizabeth in front of him as he backed away. "I better get some clothes on."

She picked up the sheet. "Eat first, and then go down to them. Since you went away, people have stopped by—even women from across the river. They brought jars of preserves, hominy, their best pies and flummeries, anything they can spare. Why one family from above the falls brought a puppy for Libby. They understand you risk everything to defend them, and they love you for it."

He tackled his undergarment one-handed, took a sweet bun

from the tray and stuffed it into his mouth. "What are those?" He pointed at the pile of papers she set on the table.

"Letters from all over the colony. They're expressions of solidarity. Oh, I almost forgot. There's a letter from Mr. Drummond. His man hand carried it with instructions to give it to no one but you. I saved it in the secret drawer." She reached the armoire and extracted Drummond's sealed message, handing it to him.

"I'll read it later." He placed it in his coat pocket and turned to go meet the people.

⟫⟩⟨⟪

John Lucas lounged on the front steps. When Nat stepped out, he jumped up and yelled, "Long live Burgess Bacon." People stopped whatever occupied them and joined in cheering and banging on any handy objects.

Nat had a dark complexion, but Lucas discerned he flushed with pleasure as people, shouted their support. Lucas took him by the arm and pulled him to the lawn. People crowded in, eager to grasp Nat's hand or clap his back.

"There's someone who would like to meet you." Lucas pulled him away.

A small, stooped woman, shuffled up to them. She appeared ancient, for her faded hair hung around her gaunt face, but when she looked up, her face was unlined, even young.

"This is my neighbor, Myra Paine. The Indians killed her husband and son."

The woman tried to straighten. She became no taller, but her kind grey eyes met his. "Thank you, Mr. Bacon." She pumped his hand. "God bless you for defending us. I haven't slept since my Joshua was butchered. I'll sleep now that I know you killed the savages that scalped my little boy." She turned and moved away.

Nat glanced at Lucas. "I saw poverty when I toured the continent. France's peasants lived in misery, but these people, our countrymen, are malnourished and wear threadbare clothing." He shook his head in disgust.

"It's hard to take when the governor and his friends make out so well."

⫸⫷

Later that evening, Nat remembered Drummond's letter. It cast a pall over the warmth of friendship which followed him throughout the day.

> Dear Nat,
> Thomas made the governor realize the wrongness of proclaiming you committed treason against the Crown, but then the man reversed himself. I've heard and rejoice at the news of your election to the lower house. Yet be cautious. Sir William's advisors are jealous of you. Even more so now that the country has risen in support of you. I expect the worse from them. Ludwell, Beverley and Coles argued vehemently you should be executed. Take care when you come. I suggest you anchor off Swann's Point so we might be able to apprise you of the latest developments before you enter town.
>
> Your affectionate friend,
> Willy Drummond

James River, west of Swann's Point
June 1676

Forty men accompanied Nat to Jamestown to take his seat in the House of Burgesses. They took two sloops: Nat's and the larger vessel of William Carver, a merchant and sheriff of lower Norfolk County, who participated in the Occoneechee expedition. They dropped anchor just off Swann's Point and sent a messenger requesting permission to enter the town.

They waited. Several hours later, Lucas pointed. "Our messenger's dinghy is still tied up at the wharf." They turned to look, just as an explosion and cloud of smoke came from the fort's walls. A cannonball splashed fifty feet from them.

"Raise anchor!" Carver bellowed from his ship as he moved

156

toward the tiller. On both ships, men bumped into each other as they jumped to get the sails up.

"Forget the sails," Carver shouted. "Row! Damn it! Row!"

Another loud explosion and a cannonball fell closer. By the time the third ball arrived, they had weighed anchor and moved the boats upstream.

⁂

Lucas awoke when it was still dark. The ship rocked as the water lapped its sides. Overhead, a loose line clinked rhythmically against the mast. He tried rolling over but sleeping bodies hemmed him in, and the sheet he shared with the man next to him cocooned them together. Lucas tugged at the sheet and Isham jerked and snorted a protest. Pulling forcefully, he dislodged it from the man's inert body and turned over to go back to sleep.

An explosion and crash overhead brought him fully awake. He kicked his legs over his bedmate and onto the floor, grabbed his sword and headed for the hatch. Lines and tackle dangled into the hold and a beam of wood barred their path. "It's the mast," someone shouted.

They emerged on deck. Debris cluttered it and the upper half of the mast leaned across it. Lucas looked around for their sentry and saw a shattered piece of wood jutting from the man's chest. His blood pumped into an expanding pool.

"Nat Bacon of Curles Neck, I arrest you in the name of the king's governor, Sir William Berkeley!" a voice boomed. It was Major Theophilus Hone, High Sheriff of Jamestown. Beside him stood the captain of the *Adam and Eve*, Thomas Gardner and Chicheley. Grappling hooks secured the larger ship to their vessel, and its sailors stood by the rail with weapons aimed at them. There was no sign of Carver's sloop.

By this time, more of his men came topside, their weapons at the ready.

"Tell your men to yield!" Hone barked.

"Stand down," Nat ordered. Weapons clattered to the deck.

"We have a warrant to arrest you all." Gardner waved his sword at them.

"On what charge?" demanded Nat.

Hone stepped over the railing and onto their boat. He pressed his sword point into Nat's chest. "For treason against the crown and attempting to overthrow His Majesty's government."

"That's ridiculous." Lucas made a face. "And, you know it."

"Arrest me, if you will," Nat said. "I demand to be taken to Sir William. These other gentlemen will stay onboard."

"You're not giving the orders. It's the dungeon for all of you." Gardner grinned.

"They've done nothing," Nat insisted.

"They keep company with you and followed you into rebellion. The governor begged you not to force him to take this action." Chicheley's voice rang out from the boat. They heard the clink of irons. "Chain them," Chicheley ordered.

≫≪

Thomas had made the trip across the river many times over the past weeks, and three times in the past twenty-four hours, summoned by Sir William. Yesterday, he learned they intended to arrest Nat, so he rowed over to speak with the governor before suppertime, to catch him alone—without his busybodies, Ludwell, Coles, Beverley and Chicheley. Thomas felt these men encouraged Sir William to act irrationally or at least in line with their agendas. He pointed out to the governor that people wanted the Indian situation dealt with and supported Nat in this. He urged him to embrace Nat and take credit for his success, an idea which seemed to appeal to the governor.

The rowboat bumped into the dock. Thomas grabbed an outstretched hand and hauled himself onto Jamestown's principal pier. "Thank you. My old knees make it difficult to get in and out of this contraption." He waved to his man who headed back to Swann's Point.

Straightening, he saw the man who had extended his hand. He had a swarthy complexion with black eyes. He could not place the face.

"I'm Tom Mathews, from Stafford County. I just got in myself. It took over a week to get here by boat. Long trip."

"Forgive me. Of course." Thomas smiled. "The trouble with the Dogues began on your plantation."

"Yes." Mathews winced. "I've suffered losses too. You remember George Mason, my co-burgess?"

"Did you come together?" Thomas extended his hand to Mason.

"No," Mason replied, his ruddy complexion creasing into many wrinkles as he smiled. "I came on horseback with some of the newly elected burgesses. It was faster than sailing." He shot Mathews a triumphant look.

"Well at least my rump is intact. We just heard they arrested young Nat Bacon. People are furious."

Thomas felt like someone hit him over the head with a hammer. Apparently, the minute he departed, the ill-motivated meddlers returned. God damn it! Sir William shifted back to the view that they took up arms against the king.

"Someone had the courage to go after the Indians, and this is how he's repaid," Mason grumbled.

"In Stafford, we heard rumors people rebelled against the government, but the rumors bore no resemblance with what in fact seems to have occurred here," Matthews said.

Not wanting to continue this conversation on the public pier, Thomas asked, "Has the assembly convened?"

"Yes. We've elected our new speaker, Godwin," Mason said. "I stepped out to get some air."

"I'd better get going." He bowed to them and turned to push his way through the crowd. Yesterday, people who turned out to protest packed the green; today, it was almost impassable. Folks who had nothing to do with the assembly came to support Nat Bacon. The looks on their faces, showed their determination and their anger.

Thomas entered the State House and joined Nat's cousin, Nathaniel and Henry Chicheley. After exchanging greetings, Chicheley gestured at the crowd. "I knew opening the vote to freemen was a mistake. Look at the dregs of society it has brought."

"What choice did we have?" Bacon shook his head. "People are enraged over the Indian attacks. The governor had to promise them something. Calling elections and allowing freemen the right to vote seemed a good idea."

Sir William joined them at the window. When the crowd saw him they booed. Across the square, a short stocky man in patched, homespun trousers and a filthy tattered jacket gesticulated, shaking his fist.

"My God! What an uncouth, filthy rabble." Sir William looked down his nose, his face rigid with displeasure.

"They're a gross lot," Chicheley sniffed. "Too ignorant to know the good we do them. If I had my way, we'd send them home after their indentures, not set them up to compete with us."

"Ignorant they may be," Thomas said, "but from their perspective, Nat avenged them from the Indian attacks. What have we done? We've seized their champion and imprisoned him. They're furious."

Chicheley seemed surprised, and Ludwell, who overheard the remark, said reproachfully, "You sound as though you approve of their egregious behavior, Thomas."

"I try to understand it." Thomas stared back at him.

Sir William gestured toward the table. "Let's get started,"

As they took their seats, Nathaniel Bacon leaned forward. "Thomas has a point. People are outraged we've seized Nat." Thomas noted he carefully used the plural, including himself and the advisors, while maintaining some space from his disgraced cousin. Survival tactics were important.

"The grumbles of discontent are louder and more frequent." Ballard sat next to Thomas. "This morning at the Snow Goose people said we don't do our job. We don't defend them against the Indians, and when brave Nat did so, we arrest him."

"I thought we agreed to take Bacon under cover of darkness so people wouldn't know," Coles grumbled. "What happened?"

The governor sighed, shifting in the chair. "It's impossible to keep anything a secret. It's almost as if we have a traitor in our midst." Frowning, he gazed around the table.

He does not understand the trouble he unleashes, Thomas thought. The day before, he saw people actually shunning Sir William when he strolled past them. They turned away, pretending not to see him. The heavy clunking of boots up the staircase interrupted Thomas' thoughts as Robert Beverley appeared.

"I asked Robert to join us," Sir William said, as Beverley made a deep bow. "He knows the mood of the lower house."

"Bacon and his gang need to be silenced. Permanently," Ludwell said. He sat next to Sir William. "It's the only solution. At first, he contented himself sending you petitions for a commission, but now he takes matters into his hands. He clearly thinks because of his kinship with Frances—"

"I'm not sure it's the best way to handle things," Thomas interrupted. "Young Nat never intended to defy you, he simply wanted to stop the Indian raids."

Ludwell snorted, but before he could counter, Thomas continued. "We need to focus on the future. The future is a strong Virginia, loyal to the king and to our governor."

Sir William nodded and motioned Thomas to continue. "He should make a public apology to you and promise never to go against you. We can do nothing about the Occoneechee. Young Nat may have settled this retched Susquehannock business for us."

"I say, hang him," Ludwell sputtered.

Next to him, Nathaniel Bacon became rigid. He found it horrifying every time someone encouraged Sir William to execute his cousin.

Sir William ignored Ludwell, looking instead at Thomas. "Will Nat recant?"

"He is most eager to do so," Bacon replied, his relief apparent. "Nat never would have gone against you if his people had not been massacred. His grief clouded his judgment."

"Well, let's see how pretty Nat can apologize." The governor nodded at Bacon. "Go to him and guide him." Bacon got up from the table and headed toward the jail to speak with his cousin.

They filed downstairs and called the assembly to order. Sir

William rose and faced them. "I'm pleased you arrived safely. I welcome you and know we can achieve many good things. But first, we have some unfinished business." He launched into a lecture about responsibility, explaining their actions affect their neighbors. He droned on and Thomas grew sleepy. He awoke with a start when Nathaniel Bacon returned from jail and sat heavily next to him.

Bacon nodded at the governor and whispered, "It's done. He has drafted an apology you will approve of." Sir William gave a slight nod of acknowledgement before continuing.

"There are scoundrels who jeopardize this colony by their recklessness. They are present today. Two of them crossed into another colony and attacked friendly Indians."

Ludwell shifted in his chair and Beverley seemed agitated. This is not going as planned. Thomas chuckled silently. They primed Sir William, but he rambled on about Mason, Brent, Washington and Allerton starting the mess with the Susquehannocks.

By this time, a red-faced Mason, appeared ready to rise to the challenge, but the others sat, gazing into the distance.

At last, the governor took a deep breath and sat down. Beverley stood up, gripping the speech that held the words he, Ludwell and Chicheley had crafted. "Honorable gentlemen, we have here today—"

Sir William rose to his feet, raising his fist in the air. "If there is happiness when one sinner repents, then we have joy now, for we have a repentant sinner!" he bellowed.

The assembly looked at him, astonishment written across their faces. Ludwell glowered and Beverley fanned himself with his speech.

"Bring in Mr. Bacon." Sir William lowered his voice, as the burgesses shifted in their seats, causing them to creak and grate on the floor.

"No!" Ludwell looked at Beverley in panic.

Nat entered, followed by Captain Gardner, and stood before the governor. He knelt.

"Do you ask to be forgiven?" Sir William said.

"Yes, I do. I ask God, our gracious king and most of all, you,

Sir William, to forgive me. Here is my written confession and repentance." Nat handed it to the governor.

Sir William took the written confession from Nat, nodding to himself several times as he scanned it. He turned to face the assembly, extending his arm, palm turned upward. "God and his gracious majesty forgive you, I forgive you. I forgive you. I forgive you," he intoned.

"And those who accompanied him?" Coles muttered.

The governor sat down and flicked imaginary lint off his cuff. "Yes, all of them."

The air hummed with the whispers of burgesses and councilors. They could not believe Nat was forgiven and they were astounded by Sir William's performance. The governor knew what the people wanted, after all, and tried to bridge the chasm separating them. The representative from York broke into applause and the others followed. Nat looked up, and Thomas saw the relief on his face.

Thomas leaned toward Nat's cousin. "It worked, thank God."

The man did not look at Thomas but nodded slightly. "It was a good confession."

Sir William stood a third time and held up his hands for silence. "Mr. Bacon, have you forgotten to be a gentleman?"

"No, may it please Your Honor," Nat replied, standing and making a low bow to Sir William.

"I'll take your word for it. If you live civilly until the next quarter session court, I promise to restore you to your place. There." Sir William pointed to Nat's now-empty council seat on the other side of Thomas.

Thomas found the way the governor's mind worked a mystery, for Nat was his heinous rebel in the morning and his favorite son by afternoon.

➤➤➤ CHAPTER 15 ◂◂◂

THE REFORM ASSEMBLY

The Snow Goose Ordinary, Jamestown
Early June 1676

THOMAS SMILED AS LAWRENCE STOOD AND SHOUTED, "Neighbors, friends. A toast." He raised his glass, looking around the room. "This is the first time in seventy years we have a popularly elected assembly. We have a voice in our governance. Down with tyranny!"

"Down with tyranny!" people cried, raising their drinks.

Thomas grimaced. He wished his friend had not yelled "tyranny." The governor was bound to hear of it.

Nat slapped his mug down and leaned back on the rear legs of his chair. He balanced carefully, placing his thumbs in his waistcoat. "He allowed freemen to vote and they chose reformers not his lackeys." His chair slapped the floor, and he grinned. "Only five of the thirty-one burgesses held positions gifted to them by the governor."

"What about the forts?" Lawrence asked.

"He agreed to abandon three forts: New Kent, Rappahannock and Henrico." Thomas took a sip. "He insisted we honor treaties with the Indians. That's a good thing."

Nat frowned. "But, those not settled on land in the last war, can be treated as our enemies. We can seize their land and sell it to defray the cost of the war."

That meant the Susquehannocks and small tribes who did not fight in the war of 1644. Thomas refrained from commenting, for many considered him a lover of the Indians.

"He's appointed me general of the army," Nat continued, "with authority to raise a thousand men, and provisions for two months."

"Who's going to pay for this?" Lawrence motioned for his glass to be refilled.

"He refused to give up the poll tax, so the poor will still pay more than the wealthy," Nat said. "I proposed to finance the war through estate taxes collected by our new single-term sheriffs, but he wouldn't agree to it. That would have spread the burden more equitably."

"Its quiet tonight," Drummond said, looking around the Snow Goose. "Nat's restored. People got the reforms they want, and now that the Assembly's over, they've gone home."

"And bizarrely, Sir William behaves as though he never threatened to hang me."

"When are you off to see Elizabeth?" Drummond asked.

"I wanted to go today, but when I asked Sir William, he begged me to stay a bit longer to discuss other matters with him." Nat sipped his drink.

Thomas frowned. Something about Nat's remark troubled him. In fact, the governor's erratic behavior mystified him. He yawned and stood. "Gentlemen, I'm to bed." He headed for the door just as Giles Bland stepped into the room.

"You're leaving?" Giles asked.

He nodded. "There's a warm chair." He gestured at the seat he had vacated. Giles held the door for him and then joined the others.

"I heard the old goat wouldn't allow an inspection of public revenues and the tax accounts." Drummond grimaced and gulped his drink.

"He sent a note downstairs telling us not to meddle in fiscal affairs until we resolved the Indian business." Nat stifled a yawn.

"Well, gentlemen, I'm off to bed, too."

They said goodnight and Nat climbed the backstairs to the bedroom he shared with five other men. He removed his baldric and sword, shrugged off his waistcoat and worked on his boots. Someone tapped on the door.

A boy stood in the doorway and handed him a scrap of paper.

As he held up his lantern to read it, he saw it was a warning from Thomas.

Nat wasted no time. He put everything back on, grabbed his money belt and juste-au-corps and dashed for the stairs. After slipping out the back door, he sprinted across the yard. When he reached the bushes, he heard feet crunching up the oyster shell path to Lawrence's front door. He stepped further into the shadows, just in time as men came around both sides of the house with torches. They pounded on the door, masking his steps as he ran for the stable on the outskirts of town. Shouts came from the Snow Goose as he bridled and saddled his horse. He edged out of town at a walk. After he cleared the last house, he broke into a gallop, heading up the causeway.

He rode hard. The sun was up by the time he reached Curles Neck, thirty miles up the James. He banged on the door and shouted waiting for someone to let him in. Andrew removed the bolt and Elizabeth stood on the darkened stairs.

"What's wrong" she asked.

"Sir William lulled me into thinking he would really allow reforms and waited until the men who came to support me returned home. Then he issued a warrant for my arrest. I barely escaped, and only because Swann warned me."

"The slimy scoundrel," Andrew muttered.

"But your letter said he restored you to the Council of Advisors," Elizabeth said.

"And so he did. He's more cunning and unstable than I thought. He forgave me publicly, embraced me as a son, but all along intended to imprison me and send me to England in chains."

Elizabeth sat down on the stairs.

"We must prepare ourselves. Andrew, go to Will Byrd's and tell him to muster the men in Charles County. I'll meet them there."

Green Spring Plantation, Virginia
June 1676

Thomas watched the governor clump back and forth, his face flushing red as his agitation increased.

"Damn it, man! How did he slip through your fingers?" he bellowed. "Of all the incompetent bunglers."

Hone shifted uncomfortably, not meeting the governor's stare. Chicheley examined his cuff while Ludwell scrutinized the mantelpiece. Thomas knew these brave fellows had gone to the Snow Goose to arrest Nat, but let Sheriff Hone shoulder the governor's wrath.

"We did arrest his servant for questioning." Hone offered. He received a contemptuous stare.

"And what good is that? Well, don't just stand there, man. Get out. Find him; and don't come back until you do, or I'll string you up by the neck."

Hone bowed and backed toward the door. As it closed, Chicheley looked at the governor. "We did put the fear of God into that scoundrel, Lawrence. I'm afraid the men damaged quite a few things in his home." He held up a fine mahogany box with an "L" inlaid in silver. Thomas winced, remembering his friend used it to hold tea.

The governor stopped pacing. "Dispatch messengers to the militia colonels on the lower James. Order them to assemble here."

"What about the upper James?" Ludwell ventured.

The governor stared. "Don't be as stupid as our sheriff. Those men are all in Bacon's camp. I need men loyal to me." He flicked his fingers at them as though shooing away flies. "Be gone. I have business to conduct. I'll ask the king's Office of Ordnance to send gunpowder, arms, shot and hand grenades as soon as possible to suppress these rebels." He turned his back on his advisors.

As Thomas headed to the Snow Goose, he noted several of the new burgesses leading their horses through town. He guessed they heard the news the governor again declared Bacon a traitor. When they reached the edge of town, and could be sure no one followed them, he could imagine they would mount and head away at a gallop to let others know.

><<

Several days later, the governor sat in an empty State House staring at the surface of the table. Despite the efforts of his acolytes, he felt despondent. His spirits had been low for weeks. In fact, since the first of June, when news filtered in that people credited Nat with a miracle—suppressing the fierce Susquehannocks and saving Virginia. If that was not enough, when he tried to punish Bacon, the people rebuffed him by electing the man to represent them in the House of Burgesses.

"Maybe I should leave with Frances," he muttered without looking up. "I asked the king to replace me with a younger man." He had placed Frances aboard the merchant ship *Rebecca*, with their silver and gold plate, along with letters to the king and to Secretary of State Henry Coventry, describing Bacon's treason and his revolt against the Crown. The ship rested at anchor off Sandy Bay.

Chicheley crossed to the window. "The scout we sent out yesterday should be back,"

"We've sent companies out by land and by water," Coles said, "but they can't find a trace of him. I think people are hiding him."

Sir William's mouth turned down and he did not look up. "Perhaps Swann was right all along; not pursuing and eliminating the Susquehannocks caused the people to turn against me."

"They love you," Ludwell said. "You were right not to go after them. They're leaving Virginia just as you predicted and after all, they've helped settle our land constraints."

The governor's scowl deepened. "They're writing sonnets about his bravery. Why there's even a ballad sung at Lawrence's public house praising him as the champion of the people." A tremendous commotion outside and the thundering of hooves, interrupted him. They stood and Ludwell helped him down the steps to the green.

The commander of one of the companies sent to locate Bacon slid from his horse. He attempted to bow, almost losing his balance. His horse, lathered and heaving, hung his head as though he would fall over too.

"What news?" Sir William asked.

"Sir. Bacon is marching on us at the head of a huge army."

The governor's tired face paled.

"How many men?" Ludwell demanded.

"Four, maybe five hundred," the commander replied.

They stood as motionless as statues.

"They say he didn't even need to issue a summons," the man added. "People flocked to Curles Neck the minute they heard you tried to arrest him."

"How far away are they?" Chicheley glared at the commander who seemed to show some sympathy to Bacon.

"A day, maybe two."

Without a word, Sir William went back into the State House. His men followed and he stopped so abruptly Ludwell bumped into him. The governor shoved him out of the way and walked back outside at a pace no one had seen him use for years. He headed for his carriage, muttering to himself, "If he can muster so many, it's hopeless. I'll ferry the rest of my treasure to the *Rebecca* and return to England with Frances. I could be well into the Atlantic by the time he arrives." Chortling, he turned around and climbed into the carriage. "Let them deal with him."

Another scout arrived, but the governor had boarded the *Rebecca*. The man reported the army would reach Jamestown the next day.

Later still, Coles returned saying the men from York answered the summons to defend Jamestown but were experiencing delays.

"What type of delays?" Chicheley asked.

"Truth be told, they aren't convinced of the cause." Coles looked at his colleague. "I've done everything I can, but the officers think Bacon is unjustly treated."

"But, they're coming?" Ludwell stood up and walked to the window.

"Yes, but not with dispatch," Coles said. "There are about one hundred men."

"One hundred! Bacon has five times as many." Ludwell turned around to face him. "If they don't get here soon, it'll be too late."

"He's gone for a fortnight and raises five hundred men, apparently without lifting a finger." Coles shook his head as if to clear it. "Why in the best of times, we could only raise a quarter of that, and we paid the militia. Bacon's men march for free."

Chicheley sent an urgent message to the governor begging him to return to town.

The State House, Jamestown

June 1676

At two in the afternoon on June twenty-second, Nat and his army arrived. Ships lingering just out of range of Jamestown's guns, sailed into port and began disgorging more Bacon men. They moved in smartly. His men disarmed people with politeness, promising they could retrieve their weapons later in the day.

Thomas watched from the window. Nat's men blocked and secured the streets. After they sealed off the town, Nat marched onto the green at the head of his men. He stopped in front of the State House, legs wide, arms akimbo. His fusiliers lined up behind him in several rows stretching the length of the building.

Thomas knew many of the officers. They were farmers and shopkeepers and quite a few were veterans of England's horrific civil wars who came to Virginia hoping to never again draw weapons against their own people. Today, they looked like a seasoned army. Nat's drummer began a slow syncopated roll.

"Prepare to fire," Nat bellowed, and the troops unshouldered their muskets and began loading. "Aim, but hold your fire."

They aimed at the State House as the crowd chanted in time with the drummer: "Bacon, Bacon."

Someone yelled, "Down with tyranny. Governor, go home." People took up the chant, their voices growing louder and more menacing.

"By God, they intend to fire on us," Chicheley said, incredulous.

In the next moment, the drum roll became softer, and Nat motioned to Hansford, who entered the building. Hansford, normally a shy man looked resolute as he bowed politely and said, "Your Honor, we request you come to speak with us."

Sir William ignored him and limped out the door followed by Thomas and the other council members. Nat ordered the fusiliers to stand down. They uncocked and lowered their weapons, standing still as statues. The drum crescendoed, and then stopped.

Sir William hobbled down the stairs, keeping the weight off his bad foot. Any pretense of dignity vanished. When he reached firm ground, he jerked open his shirt as though playing a role in one of his tragedies, for he was an acknowledged playwright. "Here, shoot me. I'm an easy shot for a traitor and a rebel."

Nat frowned, turned and walked past the governor, down the row of fusiliers. At the end of the row, he turned back, his hand on his sword hip. "No, sir." His baritone voice carried across the green. "We will not hurt a hair on your head, nor of any man here. I repeatedly asked you for a commission to protect the poor inhabitants of this colony."

"Then let's settle it." Sir William clumsily unsheathed his weapon with a rasp and waved it limply overhead.

"God damn it! Put your sword away, before you hurt yourself. I came for a commission, and you will give it to me. We won't leave without it." Nat's voice sounded as hard as metal.

The crowd chanted, "Commission. Commission." Nat held up his hand to silence them.

"I risked my life and my fortune to defend this colony. I want complete authority to engage with the enemy and thirty blank commissions for my officers." His dark eyes bored into the governor and then flicked over his councilors.

"No," Ludwell barked. "Only the governor can appoint officers."

"He can delegate," Nat spat. "I want men I can trust. I've had this discussion with you before. I don't intend to repeat myself."

Sir William's shoulders sagged and he muttered, "Very well."

"In addition, we shall have a letter to the king, signed by you." Nat pointed at the governor. "It will justify our actions against the Indians. You'll pardon all who serve with me. You and your cronies monopolized trade with the Indians for personal gain and sold guns and powder to them which enabled them to kill us. This will stop today."

People cheered. Some of the burgesses opened windows in State House and shouted their approval too. Thomas felt like joining in.

"We'll reform government. We want a law to displace certain parasitic persons from office."

Ludwell sputtered, "You can't do that."

"Be quiet," someone in the crowd growled and stepped forward menacingly, holding a club.

Nat held up his hands for silence. "There will be term limits for all public officers. They will pay taxes like everyone else, including your councilors. Oh, and I want restitution for my sloop, which Gardner and Hone destroyed. I suggest you and the council make yourselves comfortable. I shall work with the Assembly to finish the reforms and you'll sign them as we send them up."

The crowd roared, yelling and banging on anything that made noise.

Sir William bit his lower lip and his hands shook slightly. "Draft the damn things and submit them to me." Ludwell squeezed his arm, but Sir William jerked away. Without a word, he turned and hobbled back into the building.

State House, Jamestown
June 1676

Thomas shifted in his seat. For two days, while Nat worked below with the burgesses to draft reforms of the government, Sir William and the councilors sat upstairs maligning him. The rancor wearied him. When the commission naming Nat the General of the Virginia War was carried upstairs and the governor signed it, Thomas offered to take it back downstairs.

He found Nat standing over the burgesses as they drafted reforms. He handed the signed commission to Nat, made an elaborate salute and beaming walked outside.

"Well, do we have a commission?" Drummond's familiar voice rang out. He sat on a low brick wall with Lucas and Matthews.

"We do. Nat's authorized to impress men, horses and arms and to march in a week. Hopefully, this ends the problem with the Susquehannocks." He nodded at Mathews. "I heard you helped draft the letter to the king telling him of the terrible conditions we have endured."

"Yes." Matthews shifted uncomfortably. "I didn't want to. So many eyes are watching and it takes so little to fall from grace."

"You're right." Thomas studied him with interest. He lived far from the center of power, and yet he grasped the snares of involvement with government.

"One thing worries me," Matthews said. "Nat may concentrate his forces in the counties along the James. We're more exposed in the north. We hope he'll help us too."

"Most of the Indians seem to have moved south," Drummond said.

"Still, if we pay for this effort, we should benefit," Matthews said.

"Let's talk to Richard Lawrence about this." Lucas put his hand on Mathews' shoulder. "He's close to Nat. I'm headed that way. Come on."

>>><<<

Nat's men and the people crowding into Jamestown stayed close to the State House. They sent a clear message they supported Nat's reforms and expected a voice in their government.

Toward the end of the second day, with the work finished, people began to return to their plantations.

That evening, Thomas joined his friends at the Snow Goose. When their drinks arrived, Drummond raised his tankard. "Here's to a job well done."

"Hear! Hear!" George Mason sat across from them and sloshed his ale as he lifted his mug.

Thomas leaned toward Lucas. "What did Lawrence say about the defense of the remote counties, like Stafford?"

"He assured us the general intended to deal with the Susquehannocks throughout Virginia."

"I told you." Mason leaned his elbow on the table and wagged a finger at John Washington. "No, maybe it was you." He pointed at Lucas. "There's nothing to worry 'bout."

Thomas smiled and studied his ale. Mason had obviously arrived at the tavern early.

"Lawrence asked me for the names of persons fit to command, so I gave him your names and those of other county militia officers." Lucas nodded at Mason and Washington.

"It's in our interests to serve General Bacon," Washington said, compressing his thin lips. "If we refuse, he might appoint less qualified men."

"Lawrence also said something strange," Lucas said.

"What's that?" Thomas looked at him.

"He said although the commissions are signed, he wouldn't be surprised if he rescinded them. How could he not keep his word at this point?"

Thomas shook his head and Washington gave a dry laugh, shifting his lanky frame and stretching one leg in the aisle. "It wouldn't be the first time. Lawrence should know: he's suffered at the hands of our leader."

A commotion at the door caused them to look across the room. Nat and Lawrence walked toward them. Some men shoved their benches back and stood to greet Nat, while others patted his arm as he passed. Lawrence pulled out two chairs but Nat shook his head and looked around the table. "I wonder if I could impose upon one of you to write a few words for me."

"He writes a fair hand." Washington pointed at Mathews, who sat next to him.

"No, no. There are others who write well," Mathews protested, clearly reluctant.

Nat turned to him. "Sir, would you do me the honor to write a few lines for me?"

Mathews finally nodded, and they moved to an empty table.

"I'll get pen and ink," Lawrence said.

Nat placed the papers down and divided them into several stacks. Thomas leaned over, and saw blank commissions, bearing the governor's signature at the bottom of each page.

Nat picked up one as Lawrence placed quills and ink on the table. "This one will be for Captain William Carver of Lower Norfolk."

Mathews began filling in the commissions with specific orders for each officer. They worked into the night until the public area emptied.

Jamestown
Sunday, End June 1676

Thomas awoke when a rooster crowed somewhere across town, but dozed off again. Later, the sound of the bell pealing and the morning light streaming through the open window brought him fully awake. He swung the covers off, and eased out of bed, carefully unfurling his limbs until he stood upright. Stretching his arms overhead, he moved to the window.

The bell still clanged, while below, people shouted and ran toward the church. He had a bad feeling Nat had been arrested again. He dressed quickly and headed after them. When he saw Nat standing outside, he heaved a sigh of relief. "What's happening?"

"The Susquehannocks attacked again. This time in New Kent. They killed eight people."

Thomas frowned. "That's only twenty-three miles from here. Where's Sir William?"

"He returned to Green Spring last night."

"Did he sign the declaration to the king?" Thomas said.

"It's signed, sealed and safely aboard the *Adam and Eve*. It says the people disapproved of building forts and organized their own army to defend themselves. His first letter said I wanted to overthrow government." Nat raised his eyebrows and made a face. "But, the new one says I'm a loyal subject and acted in the best interests of the people."

"Thank goodness." Thomas exhaled.

"I'm off to New Kent. If things go well, I'll head straight for the rendezvous at the Falls of the James on the fifteenth."

"Good luck." Thomas gripped his hand.

Over the next few weeks, Thomas had news from Nat as he pursued the Susquehannocks in New Kent. To his surprise, Thomas Ballard, a member of the Council who had been dubious of Nat, was active in issuing warrants for him to press more men and secure provisions. In early July, Nat and his army moved into Gloucester County to meet Giles Brent, who arrived from the northern counties with several hundred men. Nat had raised

175

even more men from the south: six hundred infantry and seven hundred cavalry. With New Kent taken care of, Nat moved his army to the Falls.

PART III

⋙ CHAPTER 16 ⋘
THE ASSUMPTION OF GOVERNMENT

Green Spring, Virginia
July 1676

"GENTLEMEN, THANK YOU SO MUCH FOR COMING." FRANCES Berkeley smiled as she glided into the room, her farthingale swaying. Ludwell, Chicheley and Beverley stood to greet her.

"Please, please be seated." She gestured with her hand and smiled at Ludwell, who sat behind Sir William's desk. "I insisted Sir William stay in bed. He's exhausted and depressed that people have turned against him."

The three men nodded sympathetically as she took the chair next to the desk.

"With the rain making the day so dreary, it's a good time to stay abed," Chicheley said. "And the tobacco needs it. It's the first moisture we've seen for months."

"Yes, yes." She stroked the skirt of her lavender silk dress before folding her hands in her lap and smiling. "I understand Bacon's army has reached the Falls of the James and half the colony is with him."

"That's right. They may outnumber the savages ten to one," Beverley said. "I can't understand why they put him in charge."

"You know full well why. Because we failed to get him out of the away. Damn him!" Chicheley slapped his palm on his thigh. "He has no military experience. Others, like myself, do. I fought in the civil war for our king. Yet, the people choose him."

"I know, Sir Henry," she said. "Sir William recognized your talents and appointed you to go against the Indians, but he never wanted you to face the heathen. You're far too valuable to him."

Chicheley smiled at her.

"Well, what next?" She sat back. "My husband has been made ill by all of this upheaval. I should like to support you, however I can. We women are not without our means." She beamed at Beverley and then demurely lowered her eyes.

Beverley, short and stocky with lank liver-colored hair and not so attractive to the ladies, was a good candidate for her charms. Ludwell smirked.

"If only the good people of Gloucester would rise up." Frances studied her nails. "They are the most loyal county."

Chicheley, who was from Gloucester, responded. "Quite right. I told Sir William that very thing."

"But my husband needs encouragement." She fluttered her lashes. "He is devastated by what has happened. He needs some sign the people support him. If we had something in writing from them. A petition for his help, perhaps?"

"Maybe we should draft something for the people to sign..." Beverley's voice trailed off, unsure if he headed in the right direction.

Ludwell rubbed his finger over his cheek. "There isn't time. By the time everyone signs, it would be too late. Sir William needs to act now if we are to defeat this black-hearted weasel. It's up to us to convince him Virginia needs him."

"Let's draft it and sign it," said Chicheley. "After all, we represent Gloucester and Middlesex. I'm sure once we get there, the people will regret not having thought of it themselves."

Ludwell reached for paper stacked in its silver holder and picked up a quill. "I'll take a turn as our scrivener." He glanced at Frances and winked. Her mouth pursed into a smile.

"One place to start is with the confiscation of my slaves," Beverley said. "How am I supposed to run my place with my slaves off fighting with Bacon?" He was one of a few men who relied on slaves to run his plantation. "Oh, and we should mention the supplies he's taken from Gloucester. They far exceed what might be needed for a simple expedition."

They worked into the afternoon and when finished, they

departed.

The following day, they rode back to Green Spring with the petition, delivering it to the governor as a document written and endorsed by the county. Sir William became incensed when they told him Bacon rampaged through loyal Gloucester, pressing servants and slaves and making off with provisions. Ludwell pointed out Bacon seemed to be assembling provisions for something of longer duration than an attack on the Susquehannocks.

That was all it took. The governor ignored, or overlooked the fact, the signatures on the petition belonged to his three followers. He leapt to the conclusion Bacon intended to usurp the government. He sent urgent messages to the militias in Gloucester and Middlesex to meet him in two days' time.

Great Warriors' Trail, Virginia
Season of the Full Buck Moon - July 1676

His heart pounded as if it would jump out of his chest, but he ran on. Before first light, they hid in the underbrush by the water waiting for the family of deer to approach. His arrow hit the doe but did not bring her down. The herd bolted through the undergrowth before he could get off a second shot. He sprinted after them and could no longer hear Nansemond's feet behind him. At last, he saw her. She stood to the side of the trail, head drooping and sides heaving. The rest of the herd had left her. He drew the bowstring and released, bringing the doe to her knees. He moved in and slit its throat so it would not suffer. "Sorry, little one, but we need your sustenance."

Nansemond caught up with him as he gutted the deer and removed its organs. He helped him hoist the animal over his shoulders. They had traveled far from the cave chasing it and had to make frequent stops to shift the burden. By the time they reached their shelter, it was late afternoon. Wannis leaned back, closed his eyes and was asleep, before they had finished eating.

Exhaustion threatened to take him, but he ran on through the forest, its dappled sunlight failing to hide him. His pursuers were gaining. He leapt from the game trail to a massive flat boulder and turned to look over his shoulder. The Occoneechee warriors spread out to surround him. With a cry of defiance, he hurtled over the rock and dropped into the river far below. Down, down he went into blackness. His eyes opened and a light blinded him. The full moon shone at an angle into the mouth of the cave bathing him in light so bright, it was like the day.

From the darkness, came Nansemond's voice. "Nightmare, uh? That's why I moved my sleeping fur. Trying to sleep when the moon is full is hard enough without having it shine on your face."

He moved closer to his brother and at last slept. When the sky lightened, he tossed his cover aside and made his way to the stream where he splashed his face with the cold water. Back at the cave, he stoked the fire and skewered some of the venison for breakfast. Its aroma awoke Nansemond, who joined him. They ate in silence and then headed toward Big Lick and their morning check to determine if Connawa had arrived.

As they inched to the edge of the clearing on their stomachs, they saw the Cherokee camp was still there.

Nansemond exhaled noisily. "Why don't they leave," he complained. "You'd thing another tribe would kick them out of this hunting ground."

Wannis sighed. "You aren't tired of our well-appointed cave, are you?"

His brother gave him a sour look, but then grinned. "No, but I wish the others would get here."

Gloucester County
End July 1676

Sir William and his companions traveled by carriage, avoiding plantations they suspected supported Bacon. They crossed the York River at Queen's Creek and as they neared the meeting place, the governor stopped to mount his horse. When they rounded the next curve in the road, his spirits soared: hundreds of men answered his summons and stood in rows before them.

Colonel Francis Willis, co-head of the Gloucester militia with

Ludwell, rode up to meet them.

"It's good to see you, Sir William," Willis said.

"And you." The governor nodded. "How many men do we have?"

"Twelve hundred."

"Excellent. I'm gratified by the loyalty of you and your men. I shall address them." He heeled his horse to the midpoint of the line, on a slight elevation, and faced them.

"Men of Gloucester and Middlesex, it makes my heart glad to see so many of you today. I want to thank you for your loyal response to my call for assistance. All of us have suffered for over a year, from the terrible Indian attacks and murders. Today, we face a greater challenge, for one of us has revolted. Indeed, he rebels against the king we love so well."

The men stirred uneasily. Someone in the front row exclaimed, "What's he talking about?"

Sir William spread his arms for silence. "Nat Bacon, the younger, whom I elevated to my council and treated like a son, raises an army without my authorization and intends to usurp the government."

Willis turned to him, clearly startled, for he had been in Jamestown when Bacon received his signed commission. His men muttered.

"He's a traitor to the Crown and must be stopped. I ask that you join me in tracking him down."

A man in front bellowed, "You signed his commission."

The governor held up his hands. "I ask you, loyal men of Gloucester and Middlesex, to join me in capturing this rebel."

By this time, men were no longer at attention. One cried out, "You gave him the commission. I saw it with my own eyes." The shouting increased and men began to break ranks.

Ludwell spurred his horse alongside the governor's. "Tell them Nat's threatened to murder you."

One of the officers shouted, "Bacon's the only one who defends us. We won't attack him from the rear, when he's the only one helping us." They turned their backs and began walking off the field. Somewhere deep in the crowd, a voice shouted, "You're a liar and a coward."

Ludwell drew his sword and tried to surge through the men, but they grabbed his horse's bridle and refused to move out of the way. Their officers did nothing to stop them. They began to shout, "Á Bacon! à Bacon! Bacon!" Many brandished their weapons in the air.

Chicheley joined Ludwell. "For God sake man, put up your sword. We're outnumbered, in case you hadn't noticed."

Sir William's face turned ashen. Without a word, he tilted to the left and collapsed, falling from his horse in a dead faint.

Falls of the James River
Mid July 1676

Nat slumped on the edge of the camp bed, elbows resting on his knees. He cradled his head in his hands, fingers pressed to his forehead. When Lucas and the others entered his tent, he did not look up. His usually well-groomed glossy black hair hung in drab tendrils obscuring his face.

"Damn this rain. Hope it stops soon." Lucas shook out his hooded cloak.

Without looking up, Nat acknowledged the remark with a shiver, clutching a blanket more tightly around his shoulders. For almost two weeks, the rain beat a steady rhythm on their tents. Where the water found a frayed seam, it dripped into pans set on the floor with a metallic clink.

Lucas removed his shoes and stockings, holding them up to a brazier. "Let's hope it stops soon."

"We might have a chance at drying out these bloody tents, not to mention our hair." Byrd ran his hand over his wet hair.

"What hair?" Crewes laughed, pointing at the damp wispy strands on Byrd's head.

Nat peered through his fingers, attempting to smile.

Lucas grinned. "Do you think Giles Brent and his boys made it home before this started?"

Nat covered his face again. Byrd laughed.

"What's so funny?" Crewes asked.

Byrd sat down next to the leather map spread on the table and secured by two spluttering candles. "I remembered the look on Brent's face when he learned over twelve hundred men answered Nat's summons."

Crewes chuckled. "He brought the militia from Stafford and the northern counties and thought he and his men were the saviors of Virginia, eh Nat."

Nat did not look up.

"Too bad he left." Lucas draped his socks over the back of the chair and pulled his chair up to the table. "But, I guess there was no way we could feed so many."

"Our esteemed governor," Hansford said, "always complained he had trouble raising men for the militia. He'd be irate if he knew how easily we achieved it."

"People are afraid to leave their homes to join his militia." Lucas reached out and repositioned the candle so it would not drip on the map. "They know our government is corrupt and are fearful Sir William's cronies might strip the valuables from their farms." They laughed but then Nat jumped up.

"Damn," he grimaced. Clutching his abdomen, he dashed out the tent. A foul odor lingered.

"His stomach has been upset for weeks," Lucas nodded. "He's lost weight, too."

⟫⟪

When Nat returned, he apologized. "Sorry. I can't control my bowels. I no sooner eat than I must dash."

Lucas thought the circles under his eyes looked even darker in the flickering candlelight. "We'll be off tomorrow. Maybe you should take a break at Curles Neck and let Elizabeth nurse you back to health."

Before Nat could respond, someone tapped on the tent's leather. Wilsford's head appeared. "General, a messenger from Willy Drummond."

Behind Wilsford, Drummond's man, Martin, stood in the drizzle. "Come in, man, come in," Nat ran a hand through his dirty hair.

Martin removed his sodden hat, and tucked it under his arm, then stepped inside, water pooling around his feet as he fumbled with an oiled leather pouch.

"Sir, I bring a message from Mr. Drummond." He held it out.

Nat took the letter and broke the seal. His face darkened as he read. After folding the letter, he looked around at his friends. "The governor has declared me, and indeed all of us, traitors again."

Byrd chortled. "What did I tell you? He can't stay constant for a fortnight."

"There's more, sir," Martin said. "He waited until you reached the Falls of the James, then mustered the Gloucester militia. They answered, assuming they went to help you. But then he told them you were a traitor and ordered them to pursue and arrest you."

"What?" Lucas thumped the table causing the candles to flicker. "The man is mad! He commands us to subdue the Susquehannocks, all the while planning to sneak up and attack from behind."

"The militia refused to obey him," Martin said.

"He must have been furious." Nat shook his head in disgust.

"No, General. The Gloucester men were furious. They challenged him and chanted your name, drowning out what he tried to say."

Crewes gave a low whistle. "Did he arrest anyone?"

"He was outnumbered," Martin shook his head. "He went there with a handful of men, expecting the county to back him. When they told him they had seen your commission and they called him a liar, he swooned right off his horse."

Laughter resonated on the walls of the soggy tent.

"He fell off?" Lucas asked.

"Yes," Martin said. "Actually, he fainted, and then fell off. When they revived him, he told them they did not appreciate what he had done for them, so he would sail to England. Only a few people went to the wharf to say goodbye."

Nat's dark brows practically touched. "You mean he's abandoned government?"

"It seems so. That's why Mr. Drummond wanted me to find you, but he said to tell you there's a rumor that the governor stopped in Accomack and Custis is trying to raise an army."

Nat stared at the map. "If he's left, this changes everything."

"If we sent a ship today," Lucas said, "it will take five months for the king to appoint a governor and get him here."

"The wind isn't with us this time of year, so it's a four-month round-trip in the very best of circumstances." Nat looked at the others. "We won't have a reply from the king until after Christmas. We must put some form of administration in place. Some council members may help."

"I agree." Lucas looked at him. Someone needs to stay behind in Jamestown to provide leadership. We need to convene the counties as soon as possible."

"I suggest we invite them to meet in Middle Plantation," Hansford said. "It's closer for those living in the north."

"Good idea," Lucas said. "The king needs to hear this from us, so he doesn't accuse us of treason. We need to let His Majesty know we await his orders."

"Good point. Bland wrote to his father-in-law," Nat said. "He's the king's Master of Requests. He told him that since Sir William refused to defend us, a great many plantations lie deserted. He intends to take it to England personally. I'll speak to the men."

Nat had a basin of water brought to his tent. He shaved and wet his hair, tying it in a queue. Thirty minutes later, he emerged looking more energetic.

"Gentlemen and fellow soldiers. The news I have received may startle you, as it certainly has me. The governor has again declared us rebels and traitors."

His men jeered, and many insulted Sir William. Someone yelled, "This is the third time that old fart has called us rebels!"

Nat raised his arms for silence. "He rode to Gloucester to raise forces against us. But they refused to join him. It appears he has abandoned government and sailed back to England. We need to form an interim government until the king can send his representative."

"We're with you, General," a voice called out.

Afterward, Nat and his companions worked through the night. They drafted invitations to meet at Middle Plantation the following month to form an interim regime. Before the sky lightened and the rain stopped, messengers set off to every county.

Middle Plantation
Early August 1676

Nat and his men set up headquarters in the home of Captain Otho Thorp while they waited for the representatives of each of Virginia's nineteen counties. Angry men began to stream in to join them. They had suffered taxes so excessive that families starved. Those funds should have paid for their defense. Instead, they had to defend themselves, and after the governor at last agreed they could go after the Indians, he declared them traitors. Some spoke of evicting Sir William from the colony, while others proposed the king presided too far away to be helpful.

The day was pleasant but hot. A breeze intermittently wafted over the fields toward them. Lucas sat at one of the trestle tables under the chestnut trees. Bees hummed in the clover, birds chirped and the occasional crow broke the tranquility with piercing caws. It reminded him of that lazy summer day over a year ago when he sailed with George Mason to retrieve the stolen hogs. So much had happened since then.

About midday, a rider trotted up to the house and Thomas Swann swung down from his handsome bay gelding. Lucas and Nat strolled over to greet him.

"Sorry I'm late. Nat, you need to eat more."

"You know what campaigning is like. The food's bad." Nat smiled and extended his hand. The days and nights spent at Thorp's, out of the elements, in a decent bed and eating warm food, did much to improve his health. However, he was still too thin and the dark circles under his eyes accentuated this.

Thomas glanced around. James Bray and Thomas Beale, his fellow councilors saw him and waved.

"We have four councilors. How many burgesses came?" Thomas asked, keeping his eyes on Bray and Beale.

"Two from each county, except Accomack, and about twenty-five justices and other office holders." Nat grinned.

"Well done." Thomas sighed with relief, because most of the burgesses and half of the Council were present. "Only four officers and two council members, Ludwell and Coles, fled with the governor. Any actions we take now will be legal in the eyes of the law."

"You're right. To business then." Nat turned and stepped up on a bench. He waited as men gathered around him. "Gentlemen! The governor has abandoned us and we need someone to manage the day-to-day matters of Virginia. Our first priority is to establish a transitional government until the king can send a new governor."

Before anyone could respond, pounding hoofs beat up to the house. The rider leaned far out over the horse's neck, hands and reins practically behind the animal's ears. As he clattered into the yard raising a cloud of dust, men moved forward to find out what had happened. Only a fool or someone with dire news would lather a horse in such weather.

Lucas reached for the bridle as the rider swung his leg over the back of the saddle and sank to his knees. The horse hung his head, breathing like a bellows.

"The Susquehannocks," the man gasped, "they attacked us near Tindall's Point. Some of us made it to the fort but we had nothing to defend ourselves with except the muskets we brought."

"How can that be?" Drummond asked. "It's one of our best defended forts."

"Not any longer. A week ago, the governor arrived by ship and carried the arms and ammunition to his vessel. He stripped all of the forts." The man coughed trying to catch his breath and someone offered him a drink. After swallowing, he continued. "That's not all. Two days ago, he sent warships across from Accomack and attacked Wight. He raided several plantations, taking their food, livestock and valuables. John Custis was with him."

"By God!" Thomas swore. "The man has gone mad! He's fomented a civil war. We need to draft another declaration to His Majesty."

"He's made a mockery of the law," Lucas said. "He's bribed burgesses by making them county sheriffs and justices, and he's kept them in their jobs for decades."

"We should name Chicheley, Ludwell, Beverly, Lee, Coles, Sherwood, Spencer and Matthew Kemp for the parasites they are," Bland said.

"Don't forget his fur monopoly and how reluctant he's been to take on the Susquehannocks because it might upset his income," Byrd added. Byrd had a long involvement in trade with the tribes, and like the other colonists, the governor prevented him from trading furs, the most lucrative commodity.

By the end of the third day of August, they drafted a series of documents to the king, including the *Declaration of the People of Virginia*. They stated Sir William raised unjust taxes for the benefit of his favorites. He allowed his majesties subjects to be murdered by Indians and refused to defend them. They raised an army to defend themselves against the Indians, because he refused to. He abandoned the colony. He then attacked several plantations and started a civil war. Sixty-nine burgesses, council members and county representatives signed it, including Thomas.

Nat prepared an oath of loyalty, promising to support the army to remove the Indian threat. He insisted on an addition: if the governor raised an army, then they would oppose him, and if forces came from England, they would oppose those. Many did not agree with this last item, but consented when Nat threatened to resign as general. The full Assembly would meet on the fourth of September to elect a new government.

Later that evening, they sat under the trees discussing what they could do to deter Sir William. They decided to send Will Carver and Giles Bland after him.

"I want you to press the best ship you can find and pursue Sir William and Ludwell. Arrest them if you can, but otherwise, make sure they don't return to Virginia."

"There's still a merchant ship docked at Jamestown," Carver

Declaration of the people of Virginia

For having, on pretence of public works, raised unjust taxes for advancement of favourites; for during his long government not having advanced the Colony by fortifications, towns, or trade; for having abused and rendered justice contemptible by raising scandalous and ignorant favourites to places of judicature; for assuming the monopoly of the beaver trade contrary to his Majesty's prerogative and interest; for having for unjust gain bartered and sold the lives of his Majesty's subjects to the barbarous heathen; for having protected and emboldened the Indians against his Majesty's subjects; for having countermanded and sent back our army when just on the track of those Indians, who now burn, spoil, and murder, when they might have been destroyed; for having with the privity of favourites forged a Commission against the consent of the people for effecting civil war, which happily was prevented. Of all these articles we accuse Sir William Berkeley and the following persons, his wicked and pernicious councillors and assistants, viz.: Sir Henry Chicheley, Colonel Charles Wormeley, Phillip Dalowell, Robert Beverley, Robert Lee, Thomas Ballard, William Cole, Richard Whitacre, Nicholas Spencer, Jos. Bridger, William Claiborne, junior, Thos. Hawkins, William Sherwood, Jos. Page, clerk, Jo. Cliffe, clerk, Hubbert Farrell, John West, Thomas Reade, and Mat. Kemp. And further demand that Sir William Berkeley and all said persons surrender themselves within four days, otherwise we declare that the owners or inhabiters of places where said persons shall reside or hide to be confederates and traitors to the people, and their estates to be confiscated. These are in his Majesty's name to seize said persons as traitors to the King and country, and to bring them to the Middle Plantation, and secure them till further order.

Aug. 3. 1676.
Nath. Bacon,
General, by the consent of the people

Source: Calendar of State Papers. Colonial Papers, Vol. XXXVII, No. 41, 2 pp.

said. "We can use the guns on our barricade to convert it into a man-of-war,"

Nat nodded. "Make it so. I'm counting on you." He gripped Carver's arm. "I'm headed for Tindall tomorrow. Good hunting."

⫸CHAPTER 17⫷
THE SIEGE OF JAMESTOWN

Accomack County, Virginia
Late August 1676

SIR WILLIAM SLUMPED BACK INTO THE DARK WALNUT armchair, fanning himself with an ivory fan. "This is much cooler." He nodded at John Custis. Custis had moved everyone to his spacious entry hall. He propped both the front and back doors open with pearly pink conch shells, which a merchant in Barbados sent as a curiosity. This allowed the breeze to flow through the house.

The others removed their coats and vests but Sir William remained entombed in a silken shirt and satin vest. He wore the ever-present curly periwig. His wax-like face seemed to melt into his dense clothing. "If the tide's right, I want to be away early tomorrow. It will be wonderful to be back in England."

Beverley was cleaning the nails of his fleshy, white hands and looked up startled. "Sir William, stay a bit longer, I think we can make this our victory. When we raided the fort at Tindall and stopped in to see Goodman, you should have seen how quickly he denied Bacon. All I did was threaten his wife and children."

"Robert's right." Ludwell winked at him. "We can pick this rabble off on their plantations one at a time. That'll bring Bacon to his knees."

For days now, they had this conversation with the governor. They would convince him to raise troops in Accomack, and then he would change his mind and decide to sail for England.

"We could offer indentured servants and slaves their freedom."

Beverley tossed his head to settle his lank red hair over his shoulders. "Bacon's done it and two can play the game."

"The difference is," Ludwell snickered, "I think he means it."

A seaman from Custis' sloop appeared at the front door and tapped. "Sir, there's a ship in the harbor and it may not be friendly."

"What kind of ship?" Sir William fanned himself vigorously, before shifting his throbbing foot to a more comfortable position.

"Captain Larrimore's ship, the *Rebecca*." The seaman twisted his cap in his hands. "But when we rowed out and asked them what they wanted, they wouldn't let us aboard. Captain Larrimore stood on deck, but William Carver did the talking. He has orders to escort you to the mouth of the bay as you sail back to England."

"Bloody hell! What gall." Beverley jumped up, scraping his chair back and moved to the front door to take a look. His boots drubbed on the hardwood floor.

"That's not all. The *Rebecca* has been fitted with twenty guns and half of them are out and pointed at us. A seaman on the *Rebecca* slipped me this note."

The governor took the crumpled note, and Ludwell leaned close to him so he could see it too. They whispered. Sir William asked a question and Ludwell whispered a reply. He straightened and the governor nodded.

"Tell Carver, he's invited ashore under a truce to discuss the terms of my surrender." Sir William flicked his wrist, shooing the seaman away. "Go on then."

"You can't be serious," Beverley said. "You can't surrender to that scum."

Sir William smiled his tight smile. "It seems we have an ally on board the *Rebecca*—Captain Larrimore himself. He sent a note to me suggesting how we could retake the ship. Evidently, few of Carver's men are sailors, so they rely on Larrimore's men. They remain loyal to him, not to the Bacon scum."

He explained his plan. No one mentioned he had given his word Carver would not be harmed. He added, "In any event, I only promised Carver safe conduct while he met with us." A sly, almost feral smile touched the corners of his mouth and they laughed.

A short while later, the seaman returned. "He respectfully refused, Your Honor. He said he would come only if he's given your written word he wouldn't be harmed." The seaman stopped twisting his hat, to swipe his hand over his sweating face.

Ludwell leaned over and whispered. The governor turned to the others, "Very well. I'll give Carver a written safe passage. I pledge he shall not be harmed as long as he's my guest under Colonel Custis' roof. Phillip, handle it if you would."

Ludwell came back with the note, which the governor signed and the seaman returned to the ship. Sir William regarded Custis. "It's almost supper time. I'd like to invite Carver to dine with us." Custis nodded.

About an hour later, the dining table groaned with a feast of mouthwatering dishes: clams in their own juice, roasted game, thick slices of ham, small cakes of corn pone and warm bread, jellied fruits and a variety of vegetables.

When Carver arrived, he found them seated outside the dining room. Wonderful smells wafted toward him. Sir William waved his hand in greeting. "Good of you to come. I understand you have come to escort me, and just in time too, for I plan to sail tomorrow. I wish to avoid any further disturbance in Virginia. I asked the king to relieve me some months ago with a younger man."

Custis knew Carver through their business dealings, and he stepped forward to shake his hand. "We were going to have a bite and waited for you." They moved into the dining room.

Carver hesitated a moment, but decided since they were being so decent, it could not hurt to share their supper. They bantered about things such as trade and the weather, while the Barbados rum moved from the sideboard and around the table.

Toward the end of the meal, a message arrived. Sir William read it and passed it to Ludwell, who scanned it and then excused himself.

Later, Carver said his goodbyes, thanking Custis for the excellent meal. He weaved his way to the dock, but had difficulty throwing his leg over the side of the dinghy, a gesture he had made a thousand times before. It kept edging away from him. He tried again, heaving himself in and sprawling unceremoniously in the bottom. He crawled onto the plank seat and the men thrust the boat away, hoisted the sail and headed toward the *Rebecca*.

"What's the other boat doing, sir?" Talley, his servant pointed over the stern at a sloop racing from behind the point. It pulled hard to the open water where the *Rebecca* rocked at anchor.

Carver craned his neck. "Headed up the bay, maybe." He blinked several times to clear his head and watched as it disappeared behind the *Rebecca*.

Seconds later, Talley said, "I think it boarded the *Rebecca*. It didn't appear on the other side."

They drew closer and saw Bland standing at the rail with Captain Larrimore slightly behind him. Larrimore waved a handkerchief from his pocket as though dusting the air with it. Bland never moved.

"Something's not right," Carver said.

"Aye, it looks fishy. Mr. Bland is standing so straight that he looks like he's tied to a mast."

Carver barked, "Hard about. Out oars."

The men on the starboard backed their oars, while their mates began rowing forward. Carver glanced at the sail hanging limply at the mast as they entered the lee of the *Rebecca*. They urged their craft away, making it halfway around it's prow when the sloop they had watched came around the *Rebecca* and cut them off.

"Fire!" a voice thundered, and musket shots exploded. Talley and another seaman slumped over the rail, their oars flapping in their locks. As the smoke cleared, Ludwell and his men aimed their pistols.

"Yield or you're dead," Ludwell shouted.

"We yield," Carver yelled.

He was bound and taken aboard the *Rebecca*. They dumped Talley, whom he had served with in Tangiers, into the water.

On the *Rebecca's* deck, Ludwell swaggered up to Captain Larrimore, sweeping off his hat, and leaning far over his straightened leg. "Sir, we're in your debt. The governor expresses his deepest gratitude for the message you sent. He acknowledges you'll have your ship back; however, he asks your indulgence as he would like to use it to return to Jamestown."

Jamestown, Virginia
Early September 1676

John Lucas stood on the rampart of Jamestown's fort, hands clasped behind his back, staring down the James toward the bay. Earlier, two scouts arrived from Accomack with the news the governor had arrested Carver and Bland and prepared to sail with over one thousand men. He turned to Drummond. "I can't believe the old scoundrel promises tax relief for twenty-one years to the men who fight us."

Drummond puffed on his pipe. "What's worse, he's promising all of them part of the loot from our plantations."

"He's desperate. He'll promise anything," Lucas said. "Whether he honors his promises is another matter."

"They should be here by nightfall." Hansford drummed his fingers on the hilt of his sword. "I think we can hold until Nat gets here with the army."

Lucas shook his head. "Colonel, we need to be gone by then."

"Why?" Hansford asked.

"Look at them." Lucas pointed at the guards on the walls. "The governor's promises amount to more than these people could hope for in a lifetime of hard work. They love Nat, but the governor's offer must be tempting."

"Hmm." Drummond's black eyes met his. "You may be right. Let's abandon the town and find Nat."

"You go ahead. I'll come after I round up supplies. I'll take a few hostages too, to trade for Carver and Bland." Hansford made a half salute and headed for the stairs.

⊷⊶

It took them two days to find Nat in Henrico County. They

rode into his camp in the early morning, rain streaming off their greased cloaks. Lucas looked around, struck by the smallness of the encampment. "I thought he had a thousand men with him."

A man moved to take their horses and overheard the remark. "We did," he said, "but the general sent many home so it would be easier to feed everyone."

Drummond looked alarmed. "How many men do you have?"

"About a hundred," the man replied. "The general's tent is that one." He pointed to a large tent in the middle of the camp.

"Thanks." They turned toward the tent and saw Crewes.

"How goes it?" Drummond asked.

"We haven't found many Indians. We've taken some hostages, but most of them ran off into the woods. The largest settlement had twenty Pamunkeys." Crewes led them to the tent pitched next to an ancient sycamore whose girth exceeded the tent's perimeter by two times. The tree had been struck by lightning, creating a cavern-like space where Nat and his men sat eating. He waved them to the makeshift dining area.

They declined the invitation to eat and Drummond got to the point. "The governor has raised a large force and is approaching Jamestown. We came to get you."

"Damn that old weasel," Crewes said. "I'm running out of fingers to count how many times he declares us traitors."

"We need to get the men back to Jamestown." Lucas proceeded to tell them the governor had offered their plantations as payment for fighting. "If we can reach it before the governor..." Lucas winced as Drummond elbowed him.

Nat caught the movement. "What have you left out?"

Drummond exhaled slowly. "The governor captured Carver and Bland at Accomack and is threatening to hang them. They threw them into Custis' boat in chains. Hansford took hostages to exchange for them."

"There's no time to lose then." Nat turned to Crewes. "Send riders to catch the men headed for home. Tell them to meet us at Jamestown."

Crewes nodded and dashed out. Soon, the men dismantled the tents, as the rain pelted them and collected their belongings. They departed, marching about twenty-five miles through the woods.

The following day, Nat led his weary men out of the narrow forest path onto one of the colony's few rutted roads. A group of people with carts stood on the opposite side of the lane. An older woman reached into a cart and pulled out a smoked ham wrapped in gauze. She stepped in front of Nat and offered it to him.

"General, we thought you might need supplies." He thanked her and the others milled around with the provisions they brought the army.

Hansford walked up and saluted, taking the reins of Nat's horse. "They arrived three nights ago and anchored in the river. They sent a messenger offering to free the indentures and give them our estates. We didn't reply. We tied up his messenger, took what we could and came to meet you."

Nat swung down from the saddle and clapped Hansford on the shoulders. "Good job!" He turned to the woman with the ham, removed his hat with a flourish and bowed over his extended leg. "Thank you, ma'am and thank you all for the supplies you brought. Your generosity and goodwill will not be forgotten." He smiled and her wrinkled face beamed back at him.

Jamestown
Early September 1676

By the time they reached the road into Jamestown, the last rays of the sun flamed across the western sky. Nat's horse stopped, jarring him from his nap. He could not stay awake. His exhaustion worried his men who took turns riding beside him.

Lucas turned in the saddle to see the men on foot, forming up behind them. They looked almost as bad as Nat for they had lived in tents for weeks, and over recent days moved at a grueling pace without rest. He wanted to ask if they could fall out and eat a proper meal, but the pounding of hooves caused him to whip around.

About thirty riders beat toward them. Before Nat could issue orders, the party came to a halt so abruptly that the lead horse sank into its haunches, jerked sideways and bucked off the path before its rider regained control. In the blink of an eye, the leader yelled, "Back to the fort!" Taking advantage of being off the track, he dashed past his men, who followed in a hasty panic, shoving, bumping and swearing at each other.

Nat let out his breath and began to laugh, his exhaustion forgotten. "Did my eyes deceive me or was that the paragon of fine dress, Phillip Ludwell, in the lead?"

"Seems we scared them out of their wits." Lucas laughed too.

"Make sure they're not luring us into a trap." Nat motioned and Lucas turned his horse off the path and took several men to scout ahead. They wended their way through the trees until they came to the beach north of Jamestown, arriving in time to see the fort's gates slam shut behind Ludwell and his party.

He noticed that their young bugler, had joined them. "Sound a defiance, Burwell." The boy lifted the horn to his lips and blew several long clear notes.

As Lucas turned his mount back into the woods, a horn behind the fort's walls, answered, accompanied by canon fire. The shots fell short of the tree line but the thunderclap sent the horses moving smartly down the path and back to the road.

The men were setting up camp when Lucas rejoined Nat. They surveyed Jamestown's topography. A deep bay ran east to west bounding the north side of the peninsula. The James River formed the southern border, while to their west a narrow isthmus attached the peninsula to the mainland.

Nat pointed at the water, sweeping his arm from right to left. "We need to secure the entire neck that provides access to the mainland. Get the men started building a breastwork across the isthmus. I want them working until its finished. We'll use the chimney of the old glass factory as a watchtower. It's the highest point around and should give us a view of what the governor is doing and how he deploys."

Lucas saluted and Nat turned to Lawrence. "I would like you and Byrd to ride over to visit my cousin Bess Bacon. I want you to bring her back here, along with Angelica Bray, Elizabeth Page, Anna Ballard and Frances Thorpe. Be as polite as can be, but tell them their presence is required to help us avert a civil war."

"You don't mean arrest them, do you Nat?" Byrd made a face, clearly uncomfortable with the assignment.

"No. Don't threaten them. Use your charm, but make sure all the ladies are here by Sunday."

Before any of the men could ask about his intentions for the ladies, Nat turned to Crewes. "Take your scouts and assess the governor's position and strength."

Crewes returned minutes later.

"What is it? You look like the governor has more than a thousand men," Nat joked. Crewes grimaced and stared at the ground.

"It's Will Carver." Crewes did not look up. "When we reached the glass works we found his body hanging. I couldn't get him down. We were within shooting distance of the fort. I'd like to put my blade through the old toad."

Nat's face contorted in anger, for he and Carver were friends. "What about Giles Bland?"

"No sign of him. Just Will."

"People won't countenance this." Lucas voice trembled for he was also a friend of Carver's.

"We'll take him down after dark, and avenge him, don't worry." Nat put an arm around the shoulders of Lucas and Crewes. "I think you're right. Sir William steps over the edge of decency. Let's call the men together. I would like to address them."

Nat spoke words of encouragement and they spent the rest of the day building the breastwork. Later that evening, the noise of hammering and sawing competed with the noises of the night. Sometime later, it rained again. Lightly at first, but then increasing until it brought the work to a halt. At daybreak, ninety men arrived from surrounding counties to help with the siege. Construction began again and the blockade started to take shape across the isthmus.

➤➤➤◄◄◄

About midmorning, the governor sent Captain Gardner of the

Adam and Eve with several ships to the mouth of the creek on the northwest side of the peninsula. They began to fire at the men working on the defenses and disrupted their work. Nat ordered them to safety.

Lucas spoke to the men who arrived earlier that morning from Isle of Wight County. They salvaged and hauled several canons from the forts that Sir William had pilfered. He took them to see Nat.

"Nat, these men were gunners in the civil wars to reinstate King Charles," Lucas said. "They can hit those ships." He pointed at the bay.

"Make it so."

They pulled the guns into place and Lucas gave the order to open fire. The first shot fell about ten feet off the bow of the *Adam and Eve*. From shore they could hear the shouts of surprise, followed by bellowed orders to weigh anchor and move out of the canons' range.

"Any closer and you would have singed the captain's whiskers." Nat slapped the chief gunner on the shoulder. The man grinned.

Throughout the day, work on the barricade continued. By late afternoon, it grew high enough along its entire length so that men could walk behind it without crouching.

Jamestown's Battlements
September 1676

Sir William limped up the north stairs to Jamestown's battlements, cursing the intermittent drizzle. It had warmed up so the misty rain dripped steamily over the no-man's-land between the fort and Bacon's forces. The barricade now reached across the isthmus and blocked them from the mainland. Turning to the head gunner, he ordered them to begin firing the great guns. Nat had stationed men to protect the builders and they lay flat, muskets pointing over the top of the rampart.

After several rounds, the guns cleared a space in the barricade, damaging earth, shrubs and brush. Sir William turned and was about to call a cease-fire when the gunner fell backward, a black hole in the center of his forehead.

Horrified, he hastened to the stairs shouting for Ludwell. By the time the men assembled, he had worked himself into a frenzy. For days now, he tried to get them to commit to a pitched battle outside the gates to dislodge Bacon before the barricade grew higher. Every time he broached this, they had excuses.

"Damn it! You're all nothing but a bunch of cowards," he growled in disgust.

"Sir William, they can't reach us here. Let them sit out there. We can always sail away whenever we please." Ludwell repeated what he had been saying since they arrived in Jamestown.

"That's not the point," the governor barked. "They flaunt my authority. Why they have locked me out of my own country with that damned barricade."

"Perhaps tomorrow the weather will clear. The men can't keep their powder dry in this weather. If it would..." John Custis was cut short by the governor.

"Damn the weather too. Damn all of you," the governor said. "John, you have done me a great service by providing me with men and funds. The king shall know about it."

Custis responded with a smile and started to thank the governor, but before he could, Sir William cut him off. "But, what's the use of having eight hundred Accomack men assembled to fight, far outnumbering Bacon's motley crew I might add, when they are unwilling to do their duty? All they do is eat my rations as though it's a holiday."

The smile left Custis' face and he exchanged a worried look with Ludwell.

Seeing the governor's mood grow fouler by the moment, Ludwell finally conceded. "Why don't we send some men around to the beach side to see if we can outflank Bacon?"

"Make it so," the governor replied as he stalked away favoring his foot.

A short time later, a hundred troopers assembled before the gate. As it swung open, the grey clouds overhead opened, releasing a torrent. The troops slid forward at a snail's pace. From the rear, Beverley's voice shouted, "Head toward the spit of sand

203

on the left, you stupid bastards."

Lucas went to get Nat and let him know something was happening at the fort. They crawled to the top of the barricade in time to see the fort's gates swing open. He tried to shield his eyes from the rain. He saw the troops trudging out. Their lines were ragged and as a bolt of lightning made contact on the other side of the James River, followed by a boom of thunder, they jerked to a halt.

"Where are the officers?"

"Damn if I know," Nat said.

"Seems they're terrified of us." Lucas grinned. "Guess they don't know they outnumber us eight times over."

"Oh, I think they know. They're just smart to be afraid of us." Nat spat over the barricade. "There's the officer. Hiding way in the back and totally surrounded by his men. When they get within range, concentrate your fire in the middle. As long as they stay bunched up, we won't even need to target our shots."

They loaded their muskets and when the governor's men came within range, they fired. Dozens dropped in the first barrage. Within seconds, the formation disintegrated. Those in the rear turned and raced back to the fort. The men in front, realizing they had been abandoned, sprinted after them.

CHAPTER 18

THE REVOLUTION FALTERS

Bacon's Camp
Mid-September 1676

IN THE THIRD WEEK OF SEPTEMBER, JOHN LUCAS LAY IN
bed listening, hoping the seams would withstand the rain
pounding on his tent. He had just left Nat who again suffered
from stomach cramps and loose bowels. While they stayed at
Thorp's, his general's health improved, for a clean bed and good
food made all the difference. He knew the Powhatan had a way
of ridding themselves of enemies by grinding the root of the
water hemlock and using it on arrowheads or in food. As he
drifted off to sleep, he wondered again if Nat had been poisoned.

He awoke to the lament of mourning doves as they cooed
back and forth. By the time he emerged from the tent, the
mockingbirds and house wrens greeted him too. Most of the
camp still slept, so he claimed a bush where he could spread his
blankets and clothing in the sun to dry.

He headed for the project, Nat assigned him to: a wooden
structure sitting atop the rampart. The general admired the chess
pieces he carved from wood in his spare time and decided he
had artistic talents. The next thing he knew, he was in charge of
building a pavilion. He had the men frame it yesterday and by
midday, it was finished. Before Nat could inspect it, the ladies—
wives of Sir William's supporters in the fort—arrived.

Lucas watched the general walk forward to meet them,
sweeping off his hat and bowing over an extended leg. Nat
never forgot his manners and he wondered if he learned them at

Cambridge University. Lucas would give anything to have such a fine education.

Bess Bacon, the wife of Nat's cousin, pushed forward. She clasped her small plump hands over her ample girth and peered up at him. "Cousin, what are you up to? You send your men with orders to bring us here to see our husbands. Are they harmed?"

"Of course not. You know the love I have for you and Nathaniel. If any of my men so much as displayed the least bit of disrespect, you must tell me, for I'll punish them."

"No, but they left us very worried and would say nothing except they're safe, and they needed us to stop a civil war."

"Just so." Nat smiled. "Please, this way, ladies." He gestured to the newly-constructed pavilion on top of the barricade, gallantly offering Bess his arm to help her up the stairs. Silk in rich shades of tangerine, ochre and lavender hung from bars under the roof and formed the six walls. A gentle breeze wafted and caught the light fabric, which swirled and billowed upward before settling straight. It gave the pavilion an exotic air, totally incongruous with the hot, marshy peninsula that marked the entrance to Jamestown.

They gasped. Bess, who had a sharp eye, rubbed the silk between her fingers. Turning to Nat, she pointed. "This looks remarkably like the shade that Frances Berkeley wore to the last fete at Green Spring." When Nat laughed, her eyebrows lifted giving her an owl-like expression, offset by her dimples as she struggled not to smile back and show her missing teeth.

"You have an extraordinary memory." Nat grinned.

Lucas drew the fabric back on one side, tying it with cords to the pavilion's pillars to reveal an excellent view of the fort. Nat gave up his camp chairs, table and carpet to lend the place a comfortable feeling. He looked around examining the work and nodded at Lucas in approval. Lucas gave a sigh of relief, for based on Nat's description his men had converted the platform into a Middle Eastern sultan's abode. None of them had ever seen such a thing.

A man arrived with a tray of fruit drinks, and Nat excused himself, stepping off the stairs and heading farther down the barricade. Lucas trotted after him. "I hope we aren't making a mistake. That old buzzard might turn his canon on the women."

"He won't dare," Nat replied. "Most of the influential men of this colony are with us. He has only a handful of supporters; the rest are paid troops and he's bought them with extravagant promises. If he fires on the women, he will lose the few followers he has, and he knows it."

They walked to a point where their defensive wall made a turn and so could not be seen from the ladies' platform. Here, a second undecorated wooden platform stood. The captured Pamunkey knelt on it with ropes around their necks and hands tied behind their backs. They nodded to the men who guarded them.

Lucas spat on the ground for he hated them after his cousin's murder. "Do you think they get the message?"

"Maybe not the governor, but the men on the walls remember he never lifted a finger to defend them against Indian attacks. Let's get back to the ladies." Nat winked.

They reached the pavilion just as the cooks climbed the stairs with supper. "Mmm, smells delicious."

Nat guided Bess to the head of the table set with linen and pewter cutlery taken from the governor's home at Green Spring. He held her chair and motioned to the men to serve the food.

Throughout supper, Nat entertained them, but ate little. Lucas turned to look toward Jamestown as their laughter carried out and over its walls and noted with satisfaction they were being watched. After supper, several men who had musical skills played. The sun sank low in the western sky and crickets chirped and somewhere an owl hooted.

The next morning, light flooded across the James River and over the walls of the town, glistening off the metal on their defenses. During the night, Nat had the men reposition the great guns used to chase off the *Adam and Eve* and point them at the fort. Lucas grinned. His general was an exceptional tactician.

During the day, they entertained the ladies on the platform. One of them had an excellent voice, and her bright soprano song carried to the fort. In the afternoon, they played cards. Their laughter floated toward Jamestown. Just as Nat intended, the governor did not fire his canons nor send out his troops.

Before dawn, the following day, the sentries on the barricade changed and Lucas took over. "Anything to report?"

"Nothing, sir." The man snapped a salute. "It's quiet over there. There was banging two hours ago, but since then it's like a graveyard."

Lucas stared at the fort. "There should be some sounds of them awakening. Take some men and scout around the waterside to see what they're up to."

What they found astounded them and they hurried back. "The ships are gone."

"All of them?" Lucas said.

"Every last one. The fort appears deserted."

"Get the general," Lucas ordered.

After a reconnaissance team searched the grounds of Jamestown and found it empty, Nat entered the town. The governor had spiked the guns and fled sometime during the night. The town was stripped of everything of value: food, livestock and home furnishings.

Nat executed a brilliant strategy. He seized Jamestown with little effort and loss of life. Lucas thought once again how lucky they were to have Nat as their leader.

Great Warriors' Trail, Virginia
Season of the Full Corn Moon - September 1676

Several tense weeks passed for Wannis and Nansemond as they watched the Cherokees at Big Lick each day, and waited for the tribe to arrive. Finally, one morning they reached the edge of Big Lick's vast meadow to discover the Cherokee gone. On the opposite slope, they spotted what they had waited for. With a whoop, they raced down the slope where Connawa and the others were setting up camp.

The first evening, by the campfires, Wannis told the story of how they had escaped and made their way to Big Lick. He felt relieved no one blamed him for his failure to come back with the gunpowder. Everyone seemed interested in their tale of survival.

"We had some adventure, too." Connawa pointed at Hy-ye-naes. "We went far down the Powhatan River and harried the settlers around the falls after you left. Show them your prize."

Hy-ye-naes reached behind him and drew out a long slender bundle bound with rawhide. Opening it, he drew the weapon out of its covering with care. "A long knife."

Wannis nodded. "It's what the English call a sword."

"Swoord," Hy-ye-naes pointed the blade at Wannis who fingered its edge, then turned it away with his forefinger.

"Very sharp and lethal." He grinned at Hy-ye-naes, who balanced the weapon in his palm.

"Afterwards," Connawa said, "we followed the river west until we reached the mountains. When we turned south, we saw the most wondrous sight: the giant archway built by the sky god."

"Was it as tall as they say?" Nansemond asked, for the sky god's arch was a well-known landmark.

"At least four men tall." Nicotagsen laughed and squeezed his brother's shoulder. "Maybe we'll come back this way some day, and you can see it."

Jamestown
Mid-September 1676

Thomas Swann slept deeply until he heard the pounding on the door of his cell. The governor had returned, placed him in chains, and thrown him in this dungeon. As he fumbled in the darkness, he realized he was in bed, in his Jamestown home, and had experienced yet another bizarre nightmare. Lately, these unsettling dreams came to him every night. The events of the past days had been stressful. He backed Nat when Sir William abandoned government, but the governor's reappearance in Jamestown disconcerted him. If Sir William was restored, Thomas would be a dead man. Sir William's retreat down the James after an ignominious psychological defeat by Nat was a triumph, but it still had not soothed his unease.

The pounding on the door came again and he realized it was the front door. He hurried downstairs to open it.

"Thomas, you need to get dressed. We're burning the town," Drummond said.

For an instant, Thomas thought he had misheard, and then Lawrence, standing at the bottom of the steps, confirmed it. "It's the only thing to do. The governor's anchored at the mouth of the Chesapeake, hopefully waiting for a southeasterly to take him back to England. We've seized the plantations of the men with him, but Jamestown must be destroyed, so they have no place to regroup."

Thomas shook his head as though trying to clear it and stared at Drummond. He contributed to the colony throughout his life to see Jamestown became a proper English town. Now they wanted to destroy it.

Finally, he noticed that Drummond struggled with a large box which rested on the handrail. All he could think to say was, "What are you carrying?"

"Records: court records and those of the assembly. I've removed them from the State House for safekeeping. Meet us at the Snow Goose."

"Let me help you carry that." Lawrence took the other end of the box.

Late in the afternoon, Bacon moved his men to Green Spring. In the east, the smoke from the church and Jamestown's other buildings billowed above the treetops, marring the perfect blue of the sky. Drummond and Lawrence both set fire to their own homes, but Thomas could not bring himself to burn his house. Too much, and too many years went into building a proper State House, changing Jamestown from a bunch of shacks around a fort, to a town. He returned to Swann's Point and let others do the deed.

Green Spring, Virginia
End September 1676

Thomas climbed out of the boat onto the pier. He had made this trip hundreds of times over the past thirty years. However, this time Sir William did not summon him: Drummond and Nat did.

Drummond threw his arm around his shoulders, squeezing. "Thanks for coming so quickly. Come up to the house."

They strolled up the shell path to the governor's mansion. The army set up their tents on either side of it and Thomas frowned at the clutter littering the once beautiful gardens. The general sat behind the desk in the library.

Nat stood up to greet him. He smiled, but his face looked drawn and thin, with dark hollows framing his eyes. "Gloucester County never took the oath of allegiance. I'd like to try to win them over. William Coles is there. You know him well. Will you come with us and try to persuade him?"

Before he could answer, Nat excused himself and dashed for the door.

"Is he all right?" Thomas' eyes followed his exit. "I thought he felt better now that he has a roof over his head."

Lucas shook his head. "He still has terrible cramps and food doesn't stay put long. Could be the water. When the ladies were here, he gave them his tent and slept on the barricade for a week. Several of the men tried to give him their tents, but he wouldn't hear of it."

They sent a note to the county government of Gloucester, requesting they summon their men and meet them across from Tindal Point.

Two days later on a crisp autumn morning, Thomas stood on the steps, eating bacon and sausage between two pieces of bread and watched the men saddle up. The sky was cloudless, and toward the river, the sun shone on the trees, casting them in a blaze of yellows and reds.

He noticed Nat coming around the edge of the house. His face looked pinched and his hands pressed his abdomen. When he saw Thomas, he dropped his hands and managed a smile that did not disguise his discomfort.

They rode out with the army and crossed the river at Tindal's Point, where the men from Gloucester County waited for them. William Coles spoke for them.

"We know you're here to get us to take the oath of allegiance. First off, we don't want it forced on us."

Thomas had known Coles for most of his life. "We don't want to force it on you. We ask that you stay neutral, but if we are attacked while we are subduing the Indians, then we want your support."

"Very well. Let me see it then," Coles said. Thomas handed him the document. When Coles finished reading, he looked up frowning. "But this also promises we'll take up arms against any troops sent from England. That's treason. It's one thing for us to defend ourselves, but quite another to battle our king."

Nat had remained silent until now. "Sir William has sent for troops, but our grievances against him will arrive in England at the same time as his request for help. After the king learns the facts, I know he'll side with us. In the meantime, we need to hold out. We probably won't even exchange fire for we can keep him penned up in Accomack. That's the only base he has. We can keep the troops occupied on the ships and make it hard for them to find food and shelter on the western shore."

Most of them finally took the oath of allegiance, and by the end of the day, their general retired looking pale and exhausted. During supper that evening, he pushed his food around his plate as the others discussed how to win Accomack to their cause. Finally, he looked up. "The decision needs to be unanimous, and Accomack is the only county which hasn't joined us."

"What do you suggest?" Drummond asked.

Nat shivered. "Would you draft an appeal? I'll take it in person."

He left Drummond and Thomas to draft it. It stated that General Bacon had a valid commission from Sir William who illegally raised troops in Accomack without invoking the Assembly. They pointed out that if they convened the Assembly, it would not side with him, for everyone supported General Bacon. They asked the people of Accomack to turn the governor over to them to be sent to England for trial.

The next morning, they prepared to sail to Accomack, but a scout arrived from Rappahannock with news that Giles Brent marched from Stafford County at the head of a thousand men. "He intends to fight us," the man said.

"What?" Thomas looked dumbfounded. "Brent's with us. He

told me so himself just weeks ago at Middle Plantation. He found the orderliness and restraint of Nat's army impressive."

"He had a change of heart when he learned the governor hadn't departed for England and held Jamestown. The rumors from Maryland are that his father got on the bad side of Charles Calvert, their governor, and had to move to Virginia. Now he thinks the governor will win, so he doesn't want to be on the losing side."

They changed their plans and moved to intercept Brent. As they closed on his camp, a guide returned and stopped in front of the general.

"Sir, Colonel Brent's men have abandoned him."

"What?" Nat asked wearily, as though he did not understand.

The scout repeated his message, adding, "They learned from some of the locals that you had defeated the governor at Jamestown with only one hundred men and drove him down the Chesapeake. They told Brent they should follow any general who could achieve this, not oppose him."

Gloucester County, Thomas Pate's House
Mid-October 1676

The march to intercept Brent exhausted Nat. He slumped in the saddle and Lucas and Crewes crowded in on either side to prevent him from falling. When the army stopped for the night, the men dismounted and unsaddled their horses without conversation. Thomas watched as his men surrounded him, lifted him carefully from his horse and carried him into the house. He gasped when he saw the saddle slick with blood.

They set up camp. Their officers silenced any noise, for they all wanted to let their general rest. The men's stillness was deafening, and he wondered how many of them knew what he had learned in the last few days. Their beloved leader was gravely ill.

The following day, Nat tossed restlessly and moaned pathetically.

"He seems to be in terrible pain." Thomas stood by the bed "I wish we could make him more comfortable. The medicine the doctor gave him doesn't seem to do any good."

"He said the cramps were terrible: like snakes in the bowels." Drummond grimaced. "The doctor said poppy syrup would help, but he couldn't get it until the next ship arrives."

"He's lost a lot of blood," Lawrence said.

Nat would sit up with a start, but then slump back into the pillow. He seemed completely unaware of his surroundings. Shortly after midnight, he awakened, clutching his abdomen with one hand while struggling to sit up. By the one candle on the table, his bright eyes appeared unfocused. "Elizabeth?" he called out.

Drummond took his hand, cradling it in both of his own. "It's alright, Nat. I'm here."

"Willy? I can't see you. It's so dark. We won. Didn't we? The people are free. Berkeley's gone?"

"Yes, we won Nat, thanks to you. The proclamation we sent to Accomack has..."

Nat's head dropped, a look of surprise on his face as he stared sightlessly. Thomas reached for his pulse but then looked up and shook his head.

Drummond stood and leaning over, closed his eyes.

⫸ CHAPTER 19 ⫷
CHAOS

Great Warriors' Trail
Season of the Full Harvest Moon-October 1676

THEY STAYED IN A VALE BY GREAT LICK LONGER THAN THEY should. The cold season was closing in and they needed to be at the warm springs beyond the blue mountains before winter. The time had allowed them to hunt, fish and provision for their journey.

Wannis thought they would never break camp, but at last, they did and headed in the direction where the sun dropped off the edge of the world. His skin prickled as they passed through the first low hills, and then followed a series of hollows that paralleled the blue mountains. They traveled southwest for many days, following a branch of the Warriors' Trail through the valleys in between the ridges. Some days, they made adequate progress, but traveling with so many women and children slowed them.

Finally, after almost a complete cycle of the moon, they forded a mighty river and swung north, traversing narrow ravines that led to a gap in the foothills. That evening they camped by the water surrounded by peaks, which blocked out the last rays of sunshine. Connawa motioned to Wannis to follow him. They climbed a steep slope and did not reach its summit until the sun had almost gone from the valley where they camped.

Crossing the flat place at its peak, Connawa led him to look down the other side of the mountain. Wannis gasped. "What a wonderful sky." The land dropped steeply and in the distance, the golden air shimmered in the late afternoon sun. Far above, countless fluffy pink clouds drifted, their edges seemed outlined in golden light.

"Look!" Connawa pointed. Wannis' focus shifted downwards.

The valley, also gilded, spread out to the horizon. Wannis inhaled sharply, overwhelmed by the hundreds of animals drifting unhurriedly about: flocks of elk and deer, but above all a herd of bison stirring up dust with their hooves. They stood in silence, Connawa's arm around Wannis' shoulders, both unable to speak as they gazed at their new home.

Chesapeake Bay near Accomack County
End-October 1676

The Berkeleys said their goodbyes two evenings ago after supper at John Custis' house in Accomack. They intended to sail to England on the *Concord* but the small wind prevented their departure. Last night, in a second farewell dinner, the captain predicted strong, steady winds that would sweep them across the Atlantic in record time.

Sir William stood at the *Concord's* railing. The rising sun behind him radiated over the Chesapeake Bay and the land beyond—a territory he administered for over twenty-four years. His eyes brimmed with tears running unchecked down his sagging cheeks.

"How did it come to this? I governed well, firmly, but with concern for the colony. Why did the people turn on me?" He groaned, causing Frances Berkeley to look at him. She tucked her arm into his, her gloved fingers patting him soothingly. Thomas Ludwell, stood behind her and gave her elbow a squeeze.

"But what cuts me to the core is Nat's defection. I nurtured him. Only I recognized him as the brilliant strategist the next generation will need. I placed him on the Council, to the highest office in the land against the protests of much older men. Yet, he turned on me, and he poisoned the whole country against me. Why did they side with him?"

Suddenly Frances' fingers were no longer soothing, but dug into his arm. She took her other hand out of the beaver muff and pointed. "Look!" A ship tacked toward them from the direction of Wight. Catching a wind and heeling over, it headed straight at them. It seemed it would crash into them, but at the last moment, in an elegant move, it tacked to port, dropped sail and nestled about a hundred feet away.

They watched the flurry of activity on board, as anchor and sails were secured, and a dinghy hoisted over the side. A portly, bewhiskered man saluted them before turning his back and climbing down the rope ladder into the boat.

"Who can that be?" she said.

Robert Beverley and Thomas Grantham, captain of the *Concord*, joined them at the rail. Grantham supplied the answer. "It's Larrimore and the *Rebecca*."

Within minutes, two gloved hands appeared on the railing, followed by the bulk of Captain Larrimore.

Grasping his hat, Larrimore swept it from his head as he extended his right stockinged leg, bowing low. "Sir William, I bring tidings of the greatest joy." He recovered gracefully for such a large man. "The rebel Bacon is dead."

The creaking of the rigging could be clearly heard in the stunned silence that followed. Grantham broke the spell. "By God!"

Sir William stood as though glued to the spot. "Who..? When did this happen? Did the Indians kill him?"

"No. He died of the bloody flux," Larrimore said. "They said he became ill from living out-of-doors in the damp. They had to burn all his clothes because he was so covered in lice."

Beverley spat. "Now is our chance. Give me a commission, and I'll take care of the traitors."

Sir William turned his back on them, gazing back over the rail toward the mainland. "I must think, I must think." He turned around slowly, looking at Beverley, then Ludwell, the two men who had always remained steadfast. "We're still too few to defeat them."

"Maybe not if we strike quickly," Larrimore said. "Ingram named himself General of the Army, but the men split up after Bacon died. Many went home."

Ludwell moved closer to Frances and gave her a nudge toward Sir William. Frances reacted smoothly. "This is the opportunity we prayed for, darling. We must seize the moment. The people will never follow that rogue Ingram."

"Frances is right. We need to strike now." Ludwell punched his fist into his right hand for emphasis. "Don't give those bastards a chance to regroup."

"Give me a commission," Beverley raised his voice. "I'll not rest until all the traitors are captured and executed."

"Perhaps, you're right. This could be very fortuitous. Robert," he looked at Beverley. "I command you to sail for the York and apprehend the ringleaders and as many men as you can."

"And what of their estates?" Beverley stood, one hand at his hip, examining the nails of the other in an attempt to appear indifferent.

"Why, seize them of course: their estates, their tobacco and their worldly goods." The governor rubbed his hands together. "They'll have no use for them where they're going."

Beverley made a sweeping bow. Unable to hide his wolfish grin, he slapped Larrimore on the shoulder. "How soon can we sail?"

"As long as it takes for you to get aboard and transfer some of the troops from the Concord." Larrimore looked at Sir William one eyebrow raised.

Sir William turned to Grantham. "Captain? Will you lend us some men?"

For a moment, it looked like Grantham might refuse. "Certainly," he finally agreed.

After they departed to pursue the rebels, the Berkeleys returned to shore and resettled in front of the cozy fire in John Custis' library. Sir William shifted his foot on the ever-present stool.

"In the long term, when Nat's army reassembles, it outnumbers us." Ludwell contemplated the jewel-like color of the port in his glass, before finishing it. "If we're to succeed, we'll need more men and I know how to get them." He waited for everyone to lean forward in anticipation. "We press the private merchant ships and their crews into service. That makes the odds more even."

Sir William sank back in his chair. "I don't control them."

"You're the governor, appointed by King Charles, and his representative in this colony." Ludwell stood and moved to the mantle, setting his empty glass on it. "If there's a revolt against his authority, then the merchants must help you or be perceived as undermining the Crown."

"You forget one thing." Berkeley scowled. "They are revolting against us. Me! Not the king."

"More reason we need to convince them this is a revolt against His Majesty and it is their duty to help suppress it." Ludwell looked at Sir William and smiled. "Many of the merchant captains have strong commercial ties with the rebels. We'll need to provide them with incentives. We could reward them out of the proceeds of the sale of the traitors' properties."

"Brilliant," Custis stood in his enthusiasm and moved to join Ludwell closer to the fire. "You could hint that the rebels intend to change the terms of trade in their favor and are threatening to burn all the tobacco and send the ships home empty."

"That would be a disastrous loss," Sir William said, already half believing it himself.

◆》》》◀◀◀◆

Two days later, they invited the captains to supper. Things went as planned. Robert Morris of the *Young Prince*, John Consett of the *Mary*, Nicholas Prynne of the *Richard and Elizabeth*, Thomas Grantham of the *Concord*, and Thomas Gardner of the *Adam and Eve*, eagerly agreed to help suppress the rebels for a share of their estates.

◆》》》◀◀◀◆

Several weeks later, Beverley and Larrimore returned with two prisoners. One man walked, but two seamen dragged the other who looked unconscious, for his head hung and his feet trailed through the grass.

Beverley bowed to the governor. "I bring you the traitor, Thomas Hansford. I caught him in York. Show the governor his face, lads."

A seamen grabbed Hansford by the hair and jerked his head

upright. He hung limply between the two men, dried blood matting his hair and covering his face. His eyes were swollen shut and his clothes were torn and stained. One hand was wrapped in once white gauze, now a bright red as blood dripped onto the cold earth.

"Well, Hansford, I propose to hang you as a traitor for taking up weapons and revolting against the Crown."

Hansford appeared unconscious, until a low rumble issued from the bloody ruin that had been his mouth. "I'm no traitor. You gave me a commission to fight the Indians."

"Shut up!" One of the seamen punched him in the stomach and he slumped forward.

Sir William looked at the other man who had walked on his own feet. At the scrutiny, the man straightened and stared back. "I had nothing to do with Bacon. I demand you release me."

"He's a liar," Beverley said. "He took Bacon's bloody oath."

"I'm loyal to my king. Your men forced their way into my home, pocketed my silver and coins, took my winter supplies and my servants. That's four hundred pounds worth of goods. That shallop you see out there," he said turning and jerking his chin toward the trim ship anchored beside the *Rebecca*, "that's mine too. Your men stole it."

The governor looked at Beverley, a slight smile on his lips. "Mr. Beverley has done me a great service. No one forced you to take the oath."

Hansford groaned, drawing attention back to him. "What happened to his hand?" Ludwell asked noticing the bloody bandage.

Beverley smirked. "Allow me to present Captain William Diggs. He removed several of his fingers."

Diggs, a man with closely set eyes, stepped forward beaming. The governor eyed him without smiling, then instead addressed Beverley. "Did you find out where the army is?"

"It split up for the winter. Ingram took two hundred men to West Point. Three groups went to Bacon's on King's Creek, Warraseoyack Bay and Green Spring. Drummond and Lawrence are at the brick house in New Kent."

"Well, well. That's news indeed."

Just then, Hansford began to cough up blood, which spattered onto Sir William's soft shoes, stockings and satin breeches.

"God, man! Take him to the dungeon. We'll execute him later," Sir William said. "You know, I think he will be the first native-born Virginian to be executed on a gallows."

"What about the other one?" Beverley asked.

"Put him with the others. I'll think about his sentence later, but Hansford we execute shortly. In fact, before we dine."

⸻⸻⸻

That evening over supper, they discussed how to go after the five dispersed groups of Bacon supporters. Grantham proposed a partial solution. "I can be of service with this man, Ingram. I know him. He came to Virginia on my ship as an indentured servant and we spoke many times. I'm sure I can persuade him to surrender."

"Good." Sir William took a sip of his wine. "Let's start with York and Gloucester. The men in those counties are loyal to me." He turned to Grantham. "Captain you mentioned Richard Lawrence wrote to you."

"Yes. He stated they armed themselves to defend against Indian attacks and that no one should accuse them of treason." The governor started to rebuke him, but Grantham held up his hand. "He urged me to convince the other captains to remain neutral in this conflict and threatened to burn the tobacco if we didn't. I told him the only thing that might save him would be to surrender."

"Well done." The governor raised his glass and nodded at the captain.

Whitehall, City of London
Early November 1676

Sir Thomas Povey, Giles Bland's father-in-law and the king's Master of Requests, entered the spacious hall. "You sent for me,

Your Majesty." He bowed deeply.

The king wore a magnificent dark green velvet coat with gold brocade and a long curling wig. "Yes, sit." He motioned to a chair at the end of the table. Without glancing at the others already seated, the king raised his left hand in the air and snapped his fingers at one of the clerks standing against the wall across the room. "The letters patent?"

Responding instantly, the man walked around the table and stood at the king's elbow placing the document on the tabletop. "This one, Your Majesty, appoints the three commissioners to look into the uprising in Virginia, determine its causes and take any action needed to stop it and restore order."

The king examined the document. "This man, Moryson." He placed his finger on one of the names and looked at Povey. "We seem to recall he recommended that the grievances of the citizens should be heard, because he suspected they had reason to complain."

"Yes, Your Majesty," Povey said. "Moryson fled to Virginia in 1650 after the murder of your father, rather than remain here under Cromwell. He did well in Virginia and became speaker of the House of Burgesses. He's a man who stays on good terms with both sides."

"That could be a bad thing if he has no backbone." The king shook his head and the twenty-two-inch curls of his wig swayed. He nodded to the clerk, who dipped the gold-encased quill into ink. Carefully removing the excess he handed it to the king, who scrawled his name across the bottom. The clerk picked up the letter and handed it to a man beside him responsible for blotting the signature.

"Have you delivered the proclamation granting full pardons to my subjects provided they swear their allegiance?"

"Yes, Your Majesty," Povey said. "I personally, gave it to the commissioners this morning, along with the acts ordering the salaries of the Virginia Assembly be reduced straightaway."

"Excellent." The king paused and pursed his lips. "It does appear Sir William Berkeley milked my subjects dry. What about our letter to him?" he asked.

The clerk stepped forward. "Here is the letter relieving Sir William of his duties, Your Majesty." He placed the document in front of the king, who glanced at it, then signed his name.

"And, the letter to Berkeley pardoning Giles Bland?" The king nodded at Povey, smiling slightly at him. "It's along the lines we discussed?"

"Yes, Your Majesty. It's been made clear to Sir William he's not to interfere with the settlement of the Bland estate and the properties confiscated by the Ludwells are to be returned immediately to the Bland family." He positioned the letter on the table. The king signed again.

"Good," the king muttered, leaning back in the heavy chair. "We cannot imagine what Berkeley was thinking of, doling out so many perquisites to so few men and bankrupting the rest of my subjects. He seems to have taken leave of his senses."

"Well, he did ask to be relieved, Your Majesty, and I suspect his age plays a role. He served you well until now," Povey said.

The king snorted and raised his left arm in the air again. "Make sure Berkeley's letter goes out right away," he said to no one in particular.

The clerk shifted uncomfortably beside the king's chair. "Your Majesty, you placed an embargo on all ships to Virginia."

The king looked surprised but recovered quickly. "Yes, yes, so we did. Well let's lift the embargo so they can sail straight away. See to that personally. The letter to Sir William will have to go with the commissioners. That's awkward, but I can't see a solution. How long will it take them to get there?"

"This time of year, with the prevailing winds and tides, about ten weeks, Your Majesty," Povey said.

The king dismissed the senior clerk and his assistants, but the man did not move. He stood by the king's chair and cleared his throat. "Sire?"

Charles looked peeved. "What is it?"

"Your Majesty requested warrants for the Master of the Ordnance to send certain items to Virginia." The man paused, pulling another scroll from the large pockets in his justecorps. "Five hundred firearms, several thousand lanterns, and candles, fifteen drums, five tents of double canvas for the five captains commanding the forces—"

"Yes, yes," the king interrupted. "Do you have it?"

"Right here, Your Majesty." He stepped forward and placed the document before the king, who signed it.

"Anything else?" the king asked.

"I've also prepared the warrant to the Master of the King's Great Wardrobe, to prepare two colors for each of the five companies going to Virginia: one will be white waved with lemon, equally mixed with the red cross quite through with J. D. Y. for Your Majesty's brother, James, Duke of York, in—"

"We know who my brother is," the king scowled and grabbed the document, letting out an immense sigh of exasperation before scrawling his signature across the bottom: *Charles Rex*.

⋙ CHAPTER 20 ⋘
BERKELEY'S REVENGE

Swann's Point, Virginia
December 1676

THOMAS REACHED TO DIP HIS QUILL INTO THE INKWELL JUST as the wild geese, which had made a temporary home around his dock, honked noisily. It was almost dark, but glancing out the window, he could just make out a large gander flapping his great wings to make a running start over the choppy waters of the river. The others in the flock followed. One of his domesticated white geese, flapped furiously to join the V-formation. He lost a goose each year to the call of the wild. Smiling to himself, he dipped his pen, tapped off the excess and finished the letter to Edward.

He leaned back, examining his estate room. The yellow ochre walls—a popular color from Venice—set off the burled elm of the fireplace and bookshelves. The shelves on the right contained the plantation records and those on the left the export and import bills of lading. The latter had many empty spaces, for as his import and export business with Drummond grew, he transferred most of the paperwork to the office in Jamestown— the office that was now a burned shell.

After Nat's death, he maintained a low profile and expected to be arrested any day. The governor was furious with him for his role in forming a government. How much longer would he be enjoying this room? Could he do anything to save himself and his family?

"Thomas!" His wife's voice jarred him. "I've called you three times. He's waiting. Here, take your fur coat."

"Sorry, my dear." He stood and reached for the garment, then leaned to kiss her cheek.

Drummond's man rowed him across the river, and they landed north of Jamestown where two horses waited. Thomas settled into the saddle, his thick coat enveloping him in warmth. They followed the bridle path that skirted the charred remains of the town and headed toward the York River.

"We're here, Mr. Swann." Thomas awoke with a start and found Drummond's man leading both of their horses by the reins. When had that happened? He wondered if he could dismount, for it felt as if his bones had fused together. To his relief, the problem resolved when two men helped him, holding him under both armpits until he had taken a few steps and verified his legs still worked.

When he looked up, he saw Drummond. "Thanks for coming in the dead of night." His friend smiled. "It's safer. Are you hungry?"

Drummond escorted him through the door of the house and headed to the fireplace, while he greeted Lawrence and Lucas. Drummond swung the spit away from the hearth and removed the lid of a simmering metal pot. "We saved some for you." He ladled the meat stew into a bowl, which he handed to Thomas.

They reclaimed their seats around the fire as Thomas ate. "It's not bad, considering you cooked it," he said.

Drummond pulled on his pipe. "As you can see, we live very simply, but we do try to eat well. Our chef," he pointed at Lawrence, "prepared that dish."

"Excellent." Thomas nodded at Lawrence in appreciation.

Drummond puffed again and continued. "I'll get right to business. We wanted to discuss with you where we go from here. When Sir William abandoned the colony, we were right to form a provisional government. But now, he hasn't left. Worse, he's executing people and seizing their estates. The families of people like Tom Hansford and Will Carver are living in the woods. That scoundrel Beverley stole everything that wasn't nailed down."

Thomas shook his head. "Did you know the merchant captains

are helping? That brother of Hartwell's arrested a fellow and took his tobacco and household goods, down to the last pot. The man never even served in Nat's army, but he took the oath like all of us."

"Those captains are traitors! They're already making enough profit off us. Some more?" Drummond waved at the pot over the fire, but Thomas shook his head.

"Beverley has good intelligence," Lawrence said. "Never has a large force with him but plans well and strikes when everyone is abed. He's picking us off one by one. The question is, what can we do?"

"Probably nothing," Thomas sighed. "They've adopted the Indian's tactics—attack and disappear. It's hard to defend against that. Our present strategy of remaining scattered throughout several counties is the most we can do."

"Did you know Ingram's made himself General of the Army?" Drummond said.

Thomas nodded. "I know. With Nat dead, someone must lead them. Is he up to the task?"

"He's not the man Nat was." Drummond's bushy black brows drew together in a grimace. "He doesn't have the men's loyalty. We want to reassemble the army once winter's over, but we need a leader."

Thomas leaned forward, elbows on his knees and his blue eyes looked around at the others. "Our best hope is that His Majesty reads our reports on Sir William's treachery. We sent letters in August, so they should have arrived by now. He will be displeased his governor is misappropriating funds and fomenting civil war against his subjects. I figure the king's men should be here by the end of January or February. So, we need to hold until then."

Drummond scowled. "He might send troops to kill us, instead of help us."

"I think the number and quality of people who have written King Charles will have an impact," Thomas said. "I can't believe the king would decide against us in this."

They talked until late that night. Thomas learned that Lawrence buried Nat's body in the forest where Berkeley and his cronies could not find and desecrate it. When there was nothing left to say, they trudged off to bed.

The next morning came far too soon and Thomas felt stiff and exhausted. He climbed out of bed reluctantly and went downstairs. Lawrence had prepared warm porridge and after they broke their fast, Thomas reached into the valise and handed Drummond a hefty bag of coin.

"I'll pay you back," Drummond said.

"Don't worry about it." He reached into his justecorps and pulled out the letter he had written at Swann's Point. "Willy, if everything falls apart, you are at the top of the governor's list. You'll receive no mercy from him, you know."

"I know that too well. He wants my head." Drummond frowned.

"If things get worse, go to my friend Edward in Maryland. I've written to him," Thomas said, handing Drummond the letter.

"Thomas, I can't do that. I have my wife and the children to think of."

"Your wife's a strong woman." Thomas put his arm around his friend and patted him. "Don't worry about her. She's moved in with your daughter and my son Samuel. He'll take care of them."

"You'll be useless to her, if you let the governor stretch your neck," Lawrence said. "Thomas is right; our first priority is to survive until help arrives. Even if the governor wins, our struggle isn't finished. We've suffered intolerable exploitation. And we are far from England. Someday we won't need England."

Thomas looked startled, but recovering, continued. "This letter explains everything to Edward. He will help you and anyone who goes with you. He lives not far from St. Mary's City, but it's isolated. There are no roads so people reach his plantation from the waterside. I reckon he can hide you there for some time. If the worst comes, move to the frontier."

"I understand the frontier is lovely in the spring," Lawrence chuckled, poking Drummond with an elbow.

Drummond frowned, but took the letter. "What about you?"

"I've expected the governor to pull up to my dock any day to arrest me, but so far people closer to Accomack are his target.

The important thing for us is to stay alive. Especially you. He's set a price on your head. You can always disappear on the frontier. It's supposed to be not so different from the highlands of Scotland that you are always extolling." Thomas' mouth quirked as Drummond looked at him suspiciously. Thomas burst out laughing. Drummond slapped Thomas hard on the shoulder and then grabbed him close. When he dropped his arms, he turned his head to hide his tears.

The York River
December 1676

The mist hung like a blanket over the river just before daybreak. Beverley, Sir William, and their men rowed to shore, the whiteness so complete they failed to see the trees until the boats ran aground. The men piled over the sides into the icy December waters, while Sir William remained seated. Beverley ordered the men up the embankment, sending two parties in opposite directions to surround the house. He took the third group with him and headed to the front door.

Upstairs, Thomas Wilsford placed his stockinged feet on the floor. It was as cold as stone. The room he occupied with five other men faced west and would not warm up until afternoon. Inching off the bed so he would not waken his two snoring companions, he reached for his pants and struggled into them. He peered out the window at the back garden. The dawn haze was so heavy that he barely made out the jumble of beige stalks and weeds. Then something moved, and what he saw took his breath away even more than the cold—twenty or more men creeped through the trees and brush, taking up positions around the house.

"Get up!" he yelled, as he vaulted across the room to grab his weapons. "The house is being surrounded."

By the time the others were moving, Wilsford had drawn on his coat and buckled the baldric across his chest. Below, someone pounded on the front door. It sounded as though it was hammered with a battering ram. Wilsford poured gunpowder down the barrel of his musket, rammed a ball down, and drizzled a small amount of powder in the flintlock's pan. He repeated the process for his pistol as the other men loaded their weapons.

"Can we make it out the window?" one asked.

"We're surrounded," Wilsford shouted over the sound of the hinges giving way and the door crashing to the floor below them.

Through the shouting, they heard boots pounding up the stairs. Wilsford opened the bedroom door with the others crowding behind him. Just as a man reached the landing, Wilsford fired. His ball caught the first man full in the chest. The man tumbled backward into his comrade, his gun discharging into the ceiling. Bits of plaster fell on them as the others fired their weapons.

William Diggs raised his pistol, aiming at Wilsford. His gun exploded, and the man on Wilsford's right screamed and pitched over the banister. The landing was chaotic, filled with smoke, plaster dust and the acrid smell of gunpowder. Someone behind Wilsford fired a flintlock close to his head, deafening him and leaving him stunned. Within heartbeats, both sides discharged their weapons and then drew their swords. Wilsford and the others pressed back into the room.

Once the shooting subsided, Beverley took the stairs two at a time moving behind his men. Reaching the bedroom, he shoved a man aside, a pistol in each hand. Holding one to Wilsford's head, he thundered, "Drop your weapons or you're dead."

Once they complied, Beverley ordered them bound. As they secured Wilsford's arms behind his back, Diggs leaning close, sneered in his face. Wilsford spat in it.

Enraged, Diggs wiped the saliva off with the back of his hand. "You won't be feeling so good once I raid your plantation," he taunted.

Wilsford lunged at him but the man behind him jerked on the rope securing him.

Diggs laughed. "I intend to rape your wife. Maybe your little girl too. She's a sweet little thing."

Infuriated, Wilsford lunged at Diggs, headfirst, pulling the man holding his arm with him. Diggs flicked his sword down, slicing into Wilsford's cheek. Wilsford roared, tried to stagger away from the blade and keeled over sideways.

The man holding him fell too. "Damn, Diggs, you nearly got me."

"You've cut his ear off," another man said with excitement.

"Get up, or I'll relieve you of the other ear, you rebel scum," Diggs snarled, kicking at Wilsford's back.

"Enough. You've had your fun," Beverley bellowed. "Move them. The governor will be here."

They herded the men down the stairs to the main room, where they joined a man and his wife who had been asleep on the first floor. Wilsford foot caught on the last step and he pitched forward onto the floor.

"On your feet, you dog," one of the seamen said kicking at Wilsford as the governor walked through the space where the door had hung.

"Well, well, what have we here? Seems your face has taken a turn for the better," Sir William said. Wilsford did not acknowledge the barb, for blood streamed down his neck and torso, pooling on the floorboards. "Well, I have good news for you all. For having plotted against your sovereign, our king, I intend to execute you."

Sir William strolled to the center of the room and noticed one of the captured men, who scribed for him. "Cheeseman! Whatever caused you to follow the rebel Bacon? I thought you were a studious fellow."

"Your Honor, the Indians were annihilating us. I tried to protect us. I never raised a hand against you, and certainly not our king," the man said.

"Rubbish," Sir William said.

The man's wife, a young woman with a fresh honest face hurled herself at Sir William's feet, and on her knees, looked up at him, tears streaming down her cheeks. "Please, Your Honor. Not my husband. He had no part in this. You know he's a scholar. He handles all the legal matters and records of the county. He never would've joined the army had I not provoked him into it. I'm guilty. Please take me, instead."

Sir William stood looking down at her, his lip curling up slightly in contempt. "Then you must live with it, you lying slut."

"No, no," she shouted, clasping Sir William's booted leg. He responded with a kick, while his men grabbed her by the arms, pulling her away.

"Tie her, too," Sir William said.

"You devil," one of the condemned growled, lunging at Sir William. They yanked him roughly back by his bound arms. He struggled to free himself but one of Beverley's men punched him in the kidney.

"The executions will be carried out in Accomack. As for you," he spat at one of the men, "you're a Cromwell man. I spent years fighting scum like you. If I had my way, you would have been evicted from this colony long ago. Instead, I get to hang you." Sir William sneered and moved to the doorway, stopping with his boots atop the shattered door. "Good work, Robert."

West Point, York River
December 1676

"So Ingram defeated this Major Lawrence Smith without firing a shot?" Drummond raised his voice to carry over the howling wind. The windows and doors shook but held, for Rooking's stone house, possibly the oldest in Virginia, was skillfully built so that the winter winds could be heard but not felt.

"Appears so," Lucas uncrossed his legs and leaned forward as he watched Drummond take a stick from the fire to relight his pipe. "The major seized a plantation and split his force. He took half with him to chase one of our armies and left the remainder under the command of a minister of the cloth. Ingram shows up at this plantation and convinces the minister to lay down their weapons. When Major Smith returns, Ingram noticed his men looked fresh and unbloodied. Apparently, when the army Smith pursued turned to give battle, Smith turned around and ran."

"Hah!" Drummond chuckled.

"There's more." Lucas grinned. "While Ingram and Smith's forces lined up and eyed each other," "one of Smith's men, proposed to settle the matter by duel. Ingram accepted the challenge but the men argued. As they discussed the terms of the duel, Smith found his horse and rode off."

Drummond slapped the pewter cup on the table, splashing its contents as he roared with laughter.

⁂

Weeks passed. Then, on the seventeenth of January, they received news, although it was not what they wanted to hear. Ingram, who had the largest part of Bacon's army, surrendered two hundred and fifty men to merchant captain, Grantham on the York River.

"Damn, Grantham. How could he do it?" Drummond angrily stalked down the path to the river. "I've traded with him for years. We both benefited."

"He's a man who thinks about his own economic interests first." Lucas kicked at the oyster shells on the path. "The governor offered the merchant captains part of our estates. To a man like him, that's more important than friendships."

"He's dined with my family. We've sent presents to his wife." Drummond stopped.

"But why did Ingram surrender? Why?"

Lucas looked at him appraisingly. "Grantham told him Sir William granted amnesty. Freedmen could continue in arms against the Indians, but would be reimbursed on terms set by the Assembly.

"You jest?" Drummond said in disbelief.

"No," Lucas said. "But, you haven't heard the worst. He also promised indentured servants they would be freed and their owners compensated, and," he stressed this last point by slicing his hand downward, "they believed him. They relinquished their arms and sailed with him to Tindal's Point to swear allegiance to the governor. When they arrived, the governor sent the servants and slaves home to their masters, but the rest were put in chains!"

"Damn!" Drummond stopped and stared at Lucas.

"We need to move." Lucas said. "We're too vulnerable here. Splitting the men up into five groups seemed like a good idea, but it's made it easier for the governor to pick us off. We need to get the army back together."

"How do we solve the supply problem if we bring all the men

together?" Drummond said. "If we can last another month, we should have news from England."

"Why don't we at least get the men at Nathaniel Bacons to join us here," Lucas said. "They're sitting ducks at King's Creek. That should give us about three hundred men more than the governor."

They discussed their plan with Lawrence and the others. They agreed they should move farther up the river. A day later, the army at King's Creek moved to meet them, towing two groaning wagons heaped with Nathaniel Bacon's food stores and furnishings.

Gloucester County
December 1676

Robert Beverley carefully extended his feet closer to the hearth and beamed at the warmth. He raised his cup to Diggs in a toast of the fine port they had taken from one of the plantations they had pilfered, "Here's to good hunting tomorrow." His neighbor gave him information that one of Nat's officers, hid nearby. Apparently, the man left his regiment and took refuge in the house of his wife's father. The house was not far from Beverley's own.

The next day, he awoke well before daylight and roused his men. It was a short sail and Diggs sat on the plank of the boat shivering uncontrollably. He pulled his hat down over his ears, a wool scarf obscuring his lower face.

"Don't look so grumpy," Beverley grinned.

Digg's growled back, "You don't need to look so chipper,"

"Damn! I've never felt so alive," Beverley said. "For over a year now, Bacon completely confounded the governor, but now we're getting even. Every day I awaken charged and ready to face new challenges."

"That's because you're becoming a rich man with all the plunder you've taken." Diggs pulled the scarf up to his eyes.

"What's that?" Beverley leaned toward the man who was so muffled up that his words were unintelligible. Diggs shook his head.

They reached their destination and stilled their oars, allowing the boat to drift to shore on the tide.

"Are you sure this is the right spot?" Diggs asked. "I don't see any light."

"It's the right place. I think we've caught them asleep."

They crept across the yard and a dog barked. Moments passed before a candle flickered in a window. Seconds later, one of Beverley's men, slipped through the back and unbolted the front door. The men split into groups and some clambered up the stairs. They burst through the doors of the upstairs rooms where a man stood in his nightclothes and cap. His wife began screaming. The couple in the other room threw open the door when they heard her screams.

"Shut up woman," Beverley warned her, "or we'll tie you up and gag you." He nodded at his men, who bound the two men and hustled them downstairs.

"What's the meaning of this?" the man sputtered as they jostled him along.

"You've committed treason against the crown," Beverley said, pointing his pistol at John Harris, the man who was one of Nat's officers. "I'm taking your goods in the name of the king."

The men he'd left downstairs to round up anything of value, lumbered toward the front door carrying a wooden box. One of the women lunged at the man, screeching and pounding him with her fists.

"Stop that woman," Diggs ordered, and one of the men jerked her backward, preventing her from following the man outside.

"You lout!" the woman shouted, shaking her fist at Beverley. "That's my sterling. It has nothing to do with this."

"On the contrary, madam," Beverley replied tightly. "I am under orders from Sir William to seize all the possessions of those harboring traitors." He pointed his weapon at her, waving her away from the door as two of his men staggered down the stairs carrying armloads of what appeared to be gowns and petticoats.

One of the men pushed his head around some crinkly material and grinned up at Beverley, "These will fetch a fine price by match and pin auction, Major."

"My clothes," the woman protested in dismay. "Surely, sir, you don't need those?" She fixed her gaze on him pleadingly, hoping to shame him or evoke some pity, but Beverley was resolute, motioning his men to carry on.

Beverley tilted his head toward the woman. "It's necessary, madam. You see, I can't allow you goods to sell that will enable you to harbor rebels in your home."

"That's absurd," her husband said. "You're even taking the warm clothes that will keep my wife and daughter alive in the winter. You're leaving us destitute."

"You should thank me. After all, I'm leaving the roof over their heads." Beverley shoved the man out the door and toward the dock. "Be glad I didn't burn your home."

The woman looked in despair as her clothes disappeared. Then she saw a burly seaman towing her young servant by the arm. The girl struggled to get away and he finally lost patience and struck her a stunning blow across the face. He threw her now limp form over his shoulder.

"Put that girl down!" yelled the woman. Just as she said this, more of Beverley's men filed past her on the way to the dock prodding farm stock and three more indentured servants, who were tied together in a line.

A short time later, the woman and her daughter stood at the water's edge clinging to each other in the cold pale light. They watched as Beverley and his men weighed anchor and headed out into the York River with their husbands, servants, livestock, clothes and food.

⋙ CHAPTER 21 ⋘
THE KING'S MEN ARRIVE

Nathaniel Bacon's Plantation, King's Creek
January 1677 of the Gregorian Calendar

L ET'S GO, MY DEAR OR WE'LL BE LATE," SIR WILLIAM CALLED down into the captain's cabin.

"Coming." Frances appeared at the bottom of the ladder and carefully gathered her skirt to avoid stepping on it. She emerged on deck, sunlight falling on her dark auburn wig. Its curls bobbed, making her appear younger than her thirty plus years. Her gown, a rich mauve satin with bows down the front, peeked through her navy velvet cloak with red fox trim. She wore a matching hat and carried a fox muff which hung around her neck suspended on a silk cord.

"You're ravishing, my dear." Her husband stepped forward, placing her gloved hand on his forearm and guiding her to the *Concord's* railing.

Captain Grantham helped Frances to the ladder, while a burly seaman stood at the bottom ready to assist. She took the seat next to Ludwell. Nearby, a second vessel filled with armed men rocked on the choppy waters.

Once on shore, Nathaniel Bacon stepped forward to greet them, followed by Thomas Ballard, Edward Hill and John West. Hill swept off his hat with a flourish and gave the Berkeleys a deep bow. Frances gave the man a brilliant smile, her greenish eyes seeming almost feline.

"Who are those people?" Frances looked down her nose, pointing at the shabbily dressed people standing at the edge of the lawn.

"Relatives of the condemned," Hill said, as they climbed the steps to the front door.

They spent several hours inside by the warmth of the fire, drinking and toasting their success in apprehending rebels. Sir William stood, stretching. "Well now, for the grand finale."

The others laughed as they put on their cloaks and headed outside. A makeshift scaffold had been constructed under a leafless oak tree and three nooses hung from one of its sturdy limbs.

The six condemned men were brought from the cellar, their arms tied behind them. The crowd yelled and pushed forward, trying to reach the men. A woman succeeded and threw her arms around Hall Clarke before being yanked away by the soldiers. She cursed them.

Ignoring her, the governor opened the proceedings. "You've been found guilty of rebelling against His Majesty, King Charles the Second of England. You are sentenced to death by hanging."

All of the doomed men stared at him. None avoided his gaze. Finally, one of them, a man named Henry Gouge, shouted, "We've done nothing but defend ourselves against the Indians. You signed the commission yourself."

"Nonsense!" Phillip Ludwell pointed a finger. "You bore arms against our king."

"That's a lie," Hall Clarke said. "I never served in any army. You know that for a fact, Phillip."

"Hmpg," Ludwell cleared his throat. "Do you remember your inquiries into the appropriation of public goods?" Malice gleamed in his eyes. "Well, Sir William remembers and you will hang for that."

"I backed General Bacon's army." James Wilson glared at Sir William, who laughed at something Frances said. "I'm proud of it, and you signed my commission."

The governor looked up and stared at him with a bored expression. "Execute Wilson, Clarke and Gouge first." He turned back to Francis.

The guards shoved the three men up the steps to the scaffold.

"Noooo," the woman who had hugged Clarke, screamed. She lunged at Sir William but the guards restrained her.

The nooses were placed around the necks of the condemned men and tugged to make sure, they would hold. At a nod from the governor, the bolts on the trap doors were released. Their necks broke from the jolt caused by the rapid release. Their legs jerked spasmodically. Sir William and his entourage watched until the bodies ceased to sway, then resumed their conversation.

The observers stared at them with hatred. Clarke's wife sat huddled on the ground crying uncontrollably. Her tears did not move those in the Berkeley party. For most of his time in Virginia, people greeted the governor warmly, or at least respectfully, but no longer.

Henry Page, Thomas Young and John Harris were hanged next. While their bodies still shuddered, the governor turned abruptly. "Supper will be waiting aboard the Concord, and we don't want to miss any of that excellent port we took from Gouge's house, do we?" He laughed as he led his party back to the ship. The people at the edge of the lawn said nothing but stood in the same spot, watching as the Berkeleys left.

≫≫≪≪

Several days later, the *Concord* still rocked at its anchor in the bay in front of Nathaniel Bacon's plantation. The late afternoon sun glinted off the water, casting glittering patches of light across the ceiling. Philip Ludwell pulled the last card from his sleeve and Frances laughed with delight at the trick.

"Begging your pardon, My Lord," A seaman peered around the door, "but you didn't answer."

"Come in, man," Ludwell replied.

He twisted his cap nervously. When he saw he had the governor's attention, he pulled at his forelock. "Your Honor, Captain Grantham requests your presence. He has a prisoner you will be interested in."

Sir William yawned and hoisted himself from the cushions on the banquette and followed the seaman. Arriving on deck, he inhaled sharply and a feral smile spread over his face. The filthy man before him wore boots so caked with mud it was hard to see where they ended and his legs began. Muck also encrusted the hem of his fur coat. His head was uncovered and his dark hair, normally kept in a tidy tail, dangled in matted clumps. Still, he stood straight, his black eyes never leaving Sir William's.

"Mr. Drummond, I am gladder to see you than any man in Virginia. I propose to hang you." He laughed, clasping his arms around his chest and hugging himself in congratulations.

"We caught him yesterday in the Chickahominy Swamp." William Hartwell, brother of the clerk to the Council explained.

Sir William looked at him. "And what of Lawrence?"

"No sign of him, but my men expanded their search in all directions. They should be reporting back soon."

The governor pulled on one of his curls, stretching it out and brushing his nose with it. He glowered at his nemesis. "You'll walk to Bray's."

He turned to Hartwell. "You've done well. Take him away." He turned his back on them and returned to the warmth of the cabin.

They took Drummond ashore and chained him in Nathaniel Bacon's cellar. The beam they pinned him to, was directly under the dining room. They did not give him water to wash, not that it would have helped much. He was filthy from tramping through the swamp to evade capture. In the morning, they gave him boiled hominy then took him outside.

He blinked in the brightness, even though the sun had not yet burned through the milky winter sky. In front of him, Ludwell stood talking with Nathaniel Bacon, Ballard, Hill, West and Hartwell. Drummond looked at Bacon but the man would not meet his gaze.

Ludwell motioned to the hangman and smith and pointed at Drummond. "Chain him."

The hangman stepped forward. "Off with the fine coat. You won't need it where you're going." He smirked. "I'll take it as part of my fee."

The hangman took off his own coat, tossing it at his prisoner.

"Here, you can have mine." The man wrapped himself in the once luxuriant fur, running his grimy hands down its length and smiling at the feel of it. Drummond recoiled from the smell of the hangman's garment but reluctantly put it on.

As the blacksmith fitted the metal collar around Drummond's neck, Ludwell and the others mounted up and headed out the yard. The carriage followed them and a tinkle of laughter floated out its window as it rumbled down the driveway.

The blacksmith added wrist bracelets and connected neck to arms with one long length of chain. Once secured, the captain of the guards stepped forward and regarded the disappearing carriage. He pointed at one of the horses. "You may take that bay, Mr. Drummond."

"That is kind of you, Lieutenant, but I'll walk. The governor intended that, and I wouldn't like to get you in trouble."

It was a good five miles to James Bray's and they stopped to rest. Drummond sat heavily. Despite his exertions, he was cold. He watched the lieutenant as he leaned his back against a tree, and busied himself filling and tamping down his pipe. "Lieutenant, I wonder if I could get my coat back."

The lieutenant eyed the hangman, who shook his head and truculently pulled the fur closer. "It's mine now."

"I can offer you a smoke," the lieutenant said holding out his pipe.

"I wouldn't want to deprive you."

"I insist. I can smoke any…" his voice trailed off as he realized the implication that the prisoner's chances of a future smoke were non-existent.

Drummond smiled wryly and accepted the pipe, nodding his thanks. He took several puffs, allowing the haze to slowly spiral from his mouth. "Thank you, Lieutenant. This is very kind."

They set off again and soon arrived at Bray's place near Middle Plantation. The dining room was converted into a courtroom by turning the table parallel to the windows and arranging the chairs in a semi-circle behind it. Nicholas Spencer, Charles Moryson, Edward Ramsey and Robert Page joined the others and sat with Sir William presiding from the center. A guard shoved Drummond to his knees. With a wave of his hand, the governor gestured for Nicholas Spencer to open the session.

Spencer stood and stepped around the table, one hand tucked into his waistcoat. "On this twentieth day of January in the year 1677, we convene this courts-martial to judge one William Drummond, charged with rebelling against His Majesty and inciting people to revolt. He has committed numerous treasonous acts, including forming a counterfeit government to replace His Majesty's and raising arms with the intent of usurping the governor."

"William Drummond, how do you plead?" the governor asked.

"Not guilty." The prisoner tried unsuccessfully to stand. "I haven't taken up arms, so this courts-martial is illegal. In fact, I have loyally served in the king's militia with the rank of colonel."

"It's well known you're one of the ring leaders," someone said.

Sir William regarded Drummond. "Is that all?"

"No." Drummond glared back. "You once were an honorable man with the best interests of Virginia at heart. But somewhere you changed and allowed these spineless lackeys to sway you to rule like a tyrant, with no regard for the people. Now, you totally lack ethics and integrity."

Ludwell jumped up and started to bound around the table when Sir William placed a hand on his arm. "I think we've heard enough. Gentlemen, I would ask for your vote. All who find this man guilty, say 'Aye.'" He glanced around the table as they voted yes. "It's unanimous then. William Drummond, I sentence you to death. You will be hanged by the neck until dead."

That evening, the Berkeleys and the others sat in Bray's dining room, drinking Portuguese wine and congratulating themselves on the day's events. The sound of hoof beats interrupted them as a rider galloped into the yard. He brought news that Bacon's army at Tindal's Point surrendered and declared for the king. The next day they learned the men holding Green Spring would surrender to Sir William if he would come in person.

Green Spring, Virginia
January 1677

Sir William and his entourage headed for Green Spring and received its surrender. While Frances supervised the servants in cleaning the house and removing the barricades and debris from the approaches to the house, Sir William cloistered himself in the library with his followers. Over the next few days, they busied themselves with courts-martials and executions.

"Damn, I wish we could capture Lawrence. Where did they see him last?" Sir William asked.

Ludwell cleared his throat and looked down, for he had already answered this question several times. "In Stafford, trudging along the Potomac, in deep snow. He had four men with him and one was probably John Lucas."

"We'll catch him," Ballard said. "Meanwhile, we still have more rebels to execute."

⬦⬦⬦⬦⬦

That afternoon, they hanged James Crewes, William Cookson, John Digby, William Rookings and William West. This left them in such a cheery mood they held another courts-martial. At this one, they banished two men, John Turner and Henry West for seven years. They never served in Bacon's army, but offended Sir William on other matters. Their lands, homes, furnishings, crops and workers were confiscated and divided amongst Sir William's small group of supporters.

Spencer commented that fortune smiled on Turner and West for they received five pounds to pay passage to the destination of choice: England, Barbados or Jamaica. The others laughed.

Later in the day, they relaxed in the library. A rap sounded on the door and the estate administrator entered.

"Sir." The man bowed. "I delivered your instructions to Sheriff Swann." The year before, Thomas Swann's son, Samuel, became sheriff of Surry County.

"And he read them?" Sir William said.

"Yes, and I reiterated that he must seize Robert Kay's possessions and send the sheep to Green Spring at once. Also, your men are back from Drummond's plantation. They left not a grain for the widow and children."

"Well done. That will be all." The governor turned to the others chuckling. "Tomorrow, we'll enjoy a nice leg of mutton."

The governor excused himself, but Ludwell and Beverley stayed with Frances.

"So, tell us about the Drummond woman." Ludwell leaned toward her with a grin.

Frances smiled back. "Well, I arrived and she tried to assert herself. I informed her that her husband was dead and his entire estate forfeit. I put her in her place."

"And you do that superbly," Beverley said, sitting on the edge of his chair. "I would love to have seen you in action." Beverley worked hard to be agreeable and he almost fell from the chair when Frances rewarded him with a disarming smile and a flutter of eyelashes.

"We took her entire crop of tobacco," she continued. "It took so many carts to load it that I had to send my servants back to collect the corn crop."

"Didn't they have anything else of value?" Ludwell asked, knowing full well that she had already taken their silver service, jewelry and expensive kitchen implements.

Frances just smiled seductively at Ludwell and laughed.

Jamestown Harbor
End of January 1677

On a crisp winter day, an English man-of-war, heeling hard against the wind, sailed into the Chesapeake Bay and sped across to the western shore. When it reached the mouth of the James River, the wind dropped, forcing it to disgorge its small fleet of rowboats, whose lines tightened as oarsmen pulled upstream, hauling the ship behind them. It was HMS *Bristol* and billeted two of the three commissioners sent by King Charles to investigate both the situation of anarchy pronounced by

Berkeley, and Berkeley's corruption described by so many others. The remainder of the convoy consisted of two other ships of war, the *Ross* and *Dartmouth*, and eight hired merchantmen carrying over a thousand soldiers. A storm separated them, but hopefully they would arrive soon.

After they dropped anchor across from what used to be Jamestown, the Admiral of the Fleet, John Berry, wrote to Sir William. He requested a meeting and informed him the king appointed himself, Colonels Francis Moryson and Herbert Jeffreys, Commander-in-Chief of the Land Forces, to investigate the rebellion and report back. He also asked the governor to provide a place for them to stay, adding that they had been in tight quarters for ten weeks and greatly looked forward to being on land.

Green Spring, Virginia
Later that day

Sir William sat in his library, studying the carpet, his eyebrows pinched together in a scowl, the letter dangling from his fingers. He had just read it to the others.

Finally, Frances broke the silence. "I can't believe, after what I've suffered, my life in turmoil, my house turned upside down by rebel scum, and living in the tiny cabin on-board the *Concord*, that Berry has the nerve to ask us to accommodate him. Let them stay on their ship." She rose slightly out of her chair to rearrange her skirts. "Who accommodated us?"

Ludwell laughed at her venom. "Frances is right. They can fend for themselves. You didn't request their intervention. Meanwhile, we need to work out a strategy."

The governor did not look up. In the days since they arrived back at Green Spring, he regained some of his faculties but was still not the confidant person whom others once respected. He often seemed lost in a world of his own. Now, if someone showed him deference, it was from fear, not respect, for too many had experienced his vindictiveness.

"Write and tell them you're ill and will come to them when

you're better," Beverley said. "We must stall them so we can finish the executions. I want to catch a few more rebels to send a clear message to these pathetic people."

"Robert's right," Ludwell added. "We need to delay them as long as we can and wrap up the loose ends before the king's lackeys become involved."

Sir William at last looked up and nodded agreement. "Hmm. Kindly summon my secretary so I might dictate a note about my ill health." His thin mouth curved in a smile.

Frances stood, shaking out her skirt. "We'll celebrate this evening, my dear, by having some of the nice mutton the sheriff sent you."

The HMS *Bristol*, Jamestown Harbor
January 1677

"I'm speechless," Admiral John Berry said, hand flat on the letter spread on the chart table in his cabin. "He says he can't see us as he is indisposed. He hopes in three or four days he will be recovered. We've spent three months on this wretched ship, and he expects us to wait to go ashore because he's indisposed? He wrote the king urgently asking for help. Well, the help is here."

The admiral turned and paced back and forth, his ruddy face flushed with anger. "And that's not all." He pivoted shaking a fist. "He says he has no place to quarter us now that Jamestown has been burned. The nerve of the man. Who does he think he is?"

Francis Moryson's elbows rested on the table, fingers steepled in front of his face. He looked up peeking through his fingers. "The brother of Lord John Berkeley, that's who. The king's decorated companion."

Berry shook his head as though to deny it. "We're all decorated. That's no reason. We can't just sit here until Berkeley feels like seeing us."

"I have an idea." Moryson pushed away from the table. "We're anchored between Jamestown and Thomas Swann's place. He may be able to help us. If nothing else, he'll be a good source of information on what's happening."

246

"Isn't he one of the treasonous rebels Berkeley mentioned in his letter to His Majesty? One he vowed to hang?" Berry raised his eyebrows at his own question.

"Just so, but I think he's a reasonable man. We served in the militia together for a decade—also in the House of Burgesses. He's been on the Council of Advisors longer than any man."

"What about this charge of treason?" Berry asked.

"I don't believe it." Moryson shook his head. "For one thing, he must be close to eighty. I can't see him riding around the countryside fomenting rebellion, not to mention sleeping in anything less than a featherbed. He's wealthy with a fine house. The governor's charge is spurious. We should invite him for a chat."

Several hours later, Thomas Swann sat at the admiral's table and told the commissioners about the events leading up to the rebellion, from the mistreatment of the friendly Dogues and Susquehannocks, to the year of violence. He concluded, "and, despite hundreds of English killed, the governor refused to defend the people. Then to make matters worse he began these vindictive executions after Bacon's death and the illegal seizure of properties."

Berry shifted in his chair. "That's quite different from Sir William's report to His Majesty."

"I don't doubt it. But there are many other reports from reputable citizens of Virginia that will confirm what I've just told you. The governor has few supporters."

"Who are the men on his side?" Moryson asked.

"Aside from the merchant ship captains who help him, his supporters are Ludwell, Beverley, Hill, Coles, Spencer and Chicheley. You'll find the population loathes these men." Thomas paused and looked out the wide windows of the ship's stern. "These men are falling over themselves to get the estates of those executed. You should know they are seizing estates without trial and sentence of death. The governor has become so brazen that he places his own private mark on the hogsheads of tobacco he confiscates."

"This must stop," Berry said. "His Majesty pardoned every one, except Nat Bacon, provided they swear loyalty to him. We have his proclamation and he ordered us to publish it." He went on to describe for Thomas why the king had sent them and that they were under orders to hear the colonists' grievances.

"By the way, His Majesty has also rescinded the grant of territory to the lords Arlington and Fairfax. That land will now be available to men willing to settle it," Moryson said.

"People will be grateful to His Majesty because there is a shortage of good land here," Thomas smiled, then looked back at the admiral. "Sir William will try to neutralize you and keep you away from the people. I suggest the first thing you do is publish His Majesty's decrees pardoning his subjects and invite them to meet with you."

"Hmm," Berry studied his hand before looking back at Thomas. "There is another matter I wanted to raise with you. We have brought a pardon for a man named Giles Bland. Do you know where we might find him?"

"That's good news," Thomas said. "Giles' sins have been blown out of proportion."

"You know him?"

"Indeed, I do." Thomas proceeded to tell them about Bland's discovery of theft by the governor and Thomas Ludwell, Phillip's brother. "The governor imprisoned him months ago and threatens to hang him. They tortured him, so it might be wise to show the governor the king's pardon right away."

"Thank you again for your candor. Your insights are most helpful," Berry smiled for the first time. "Might I suggest we conclude our discussion with some fine port?"

"I am at your service, sir," Thomas said.

It was dark by the time Thomas rowed back to Swann's Point. Meeting the commissioners was a blessing. The governor refused to lodge them so he offered his home and suggested others who could house the troops.

As he walked slowly up the crushed shell path, his step felt like that of a much younger man. He and his family had lived under a cloud for months now, never knowing when Sir William might send his men to hang him and seize his plantation. Mary would be greatly relieved when she heard the news. Then he chuckled to himself. She would be furious at first that he promised to put the commissioners up at Swann's Point, for it would be a huge drain on their stores and much extra work for her.

Still, it could be their salvation, he thought, as he hastened up the steps to his home.

CHAPTER 22

THE KING'S REACTION

HMS *Bristol*, Jamestown Harbor
Early February 1677

A WEEK AFTER SIR WILLIAM WROTE TO THE COMMISSIONERS saying he was too ill to receive them, he sent a message saying he felt better. He intended to visit them aboard ship to learn why they were here and how he could help them.

When the seaman arrived to tell them the governor's boat was on the way, John Berry Admiral of the Fleet, stood hands behind his back, in the sunlight of the *Bristol's* ample aft window. "We'll be right there," he said, dismissing the seaman, and turning back to Moryson. "I don't see why I need to explain to him why we're here. He wrote the king and asked for support. Well, here we are."

Moryson exhaled noisily. "He's accustomed to having people defer to him like a king because after all, his monarch is a three-month sail over a rough sea."

"I suppose we can show some sensitivity to his feelings," the admiral said, putting on his hat and holding the door for his companion. They headed topside in time to greet Sir William and usher him to the warmth of the captain's cabin. Samuel Wiseman, the official secretary for the commission sat at the table, paper and quill ready.

"His Majesty was alarmed with the situation you described in your letter," Berry began. "He attaches a high priority to the well-being of this colony. Thus, he has sent three men-of-war and one thousand soldiers to quell the revolt."

The governor sat immobile in his chair, scarcely seeming to breathe during the admiral's introduction. The corner of his thin mouth twitched. "My dear sirs, the rebellion is over. I acted immediately and crushed the traitor Bacon. He is dead and I executed fourteen of his officers and twenty of the ringleaders. The remainder of the traitors have disbanded and gone home."

Berry cleared his throat but the governor continued. "I have called the General Assembly of burgesses and councilors for the twentieth of this month. I intend to repeal the laws that Bacon forced upon us. So, as you can see, everything is in hand. You needn't envision a long stay here."

The admiral frowned. "That's good news, indeed. As you requested, His Majesty accepts your retirement from service. He has appointed Colonel Herbert Jeffreys as governor and commander of the ground forces to relieve you. A storm separated us, but I expect him any day. I see no reason why the transfer of government to him shouldn't be as smooth as possible. Do you, Moryson?"

His fellow commissioner bobbed his head and smiled at Sir William, who returned his look with a cold stare.

"By the way," Berry continued, "speaking of the assembly, you should know that the king has reduced their salaries, as well as the frequency with which they meet."

If the governor had been stiff before, now he became rigid, his lip curling. "His Majesty delegated the governance of Virginia to me. I shouldn't think he would concern himself with how often we meet or what I pay my staff, and I can't see you have any expertise in this area, sir."

The admiral inhaled. He straightened his shoulders and plowed ahead. "The king sends you several communications. The first, pardons the colonists provided they take the oath of allegiance to him. The second asks all men to come forward and state their grievances. His Majesty wants a thorough vetting of complaints, so we can put this matter behind us. He wants you to publish these announcements." He stood, picked up the packet of documents and held them out.

Sir William stared at his hand, making no attempt to take

them. Flicking his hand at them, he said, "I wrote to him months ago. Frankly, the situation has changed since His Majesty penned these. I think it would be improper to publish a pardon now considering all that has occurred in between."

"What do you mean?" Berry asked.

"I received new intelligence on some of the traitors." The governor leaned forward. "We've executed quite a few, but there are others who must not be forgiven. I'm sure he would agree, for they have long caused trouble in his realm."

"Sir!" the admiral brought the flat of his hand down on the table for emphasis. "The king makes it clear he wants a general pardon of all people."

"You are simply unfamiliar with the situation here," Sir William said. "I'll issue my own proclamation and call the country forward to state their complaints."

"So you'll describe his pardon to the people?" Berry barely concealed his irritation.

"Certainly." The governor stood. "I shall work on it as soon as I'm back in my bed."

"The king also pardons Giles Bland." The admiral slid the sealed document across the table, this time without leaving his seat.

"Bland?" The governor sniffed, then reached for it and the stack of papers. "I shall read this acquittal with interest." He took Bland's pardon and stuffed it into the pocket of his waistcoat. He nodded to them, causing the locks of his periwig to sway, and turned his back, moving toward the door.

"Excellent. Now that's taken care of," Moryson rushed to open the door, "we haven't found quarters for ourselves and the men. We are quite desperate to get off this ship. Any day now, Jeffreys will arrive with a thousand soldiers. Where are we to put them?"

"That's a grave problem," the governor said, staring at Moryson. "As you can see," he pointed at the window in the direction of Jamestown, "our city is no more, or they could stay there. They may have to be split up and accommodated in several counties, but I shall make inquiries on your behalf." He turned and smiled tightly. "I must say I believed a frigate, or perhaps two, would have sufficed. I never desired so many ships with over a thousand soldiers. This will startle the people."

He limped up the stairs to the deck, where an icy wind blew. He handed the documents to his man, and used both hands to prevent his hair from departing overboard. He settled into his launch, with his back to the *Bristol*, but waved a handkerchief edged in lace in slow circles over his head in farewell.

The commissioners returned to the cabin in silence.

"He didn't look ill to me," Berry snorted.

Swann's Point, Virginia
Mid-February 1677

Jeffreys' ship arrived two weeks after their meeting, and the commissioners accepted Thomas' offer and moved to Swann's Point. The three commissioners sat with him in his estate room. Jeffreys sat on the other side of the polished desk, chin in hand, staring at the pages spread before him.

Finally, he leaned back, his lips compressed in a grimace. "In reply to our request for his assistance to quarter troops, the governor writes we shouldn't ask him to do the impossible because he's so ill. He's already feeding two hundred men at Green Spring and had to borrow to do so. He's gratified our communications are now in writing so the king can see them."

Thomas snickered. "I know for a fact he and his friends aren't paying for their food."

Moryson looked at him quizzically and he explained. "After executing Robert May, Sir William declared his estate forfeit and ordered his two hundred sheep driven to Green Spring. His cook is hard-pressed to invent new ways to prepare mutton. He could easily share with your troops." He handed Jeffreys a paper. "I've prepared the list you asked for with those who might lodge the men."

⇶⇇

Later that afternoon, they sailed down river to see the planters on Thomas' list. They could see men chopping wood and smoke drifting from chimneys, but when they dropped anchor and launched the dinghy, people fled. In one empty house, a partially eaten and still warm meal, graced the table. They returned from their useless trip, greatly frustrated.

"You were right, Thomas," Berry said. "You warned us folks were frightened after the months of terror they've suffered."

Thomas nodded. "From their perspective, they see a man-of-war from England and think you are here to confiscate their property and execute them. They're unaware the king pardoned them." Thomas paused, considering his next words carefully. "I think you shouldn't wait any longer for the governor to issue the king's pardons. Do it yourself. It will do much to settle people's nerves."

After some deliberation, they decided to publish it and send it to all counties. They also issued a statement that the king sent them to report on affairs in Virginia. They invited all the inhabitants to meet with them to provide their insights into why the rebellion occurred and state their grievances.

⋙⋘

Thomas accompanied the commissioners to Isle of Wight County some days later. Several hundred people showed up to complain about exorbitant taxes and lack of defense. They also criticized the large salaries their government paid itself and the seizure of properties without cause.

He ran into Sam Pressley, a burgess from Stafford, who traveled home due to illness in his family.

"The governor seems intent on hanging every decent man in Virginia," Pressley said. "He has executed eight burgesses including Anthony Arnold and Richard Pomfrey. Lucky William Hatcher: they only censured and fined him ten thousand pounds of tobacco and eight thousand pounds of dressed pork. He and his family will starve."

He knew them all. They were honorable men and certainly not guilty of treason. Pressley went on to tell how the governor and his men threw their wives and children out of their homes, confiscated their estates, and divided the spoils among themselves.

"We're terrified we'll be next," Pressley said. "We've petitioned Sir William not to kill any more people with honest reputations and handsome estates. Those who escaped execution did so only because they had done nothing to offend the governor. Still he had a rope placed around their necks and forced them to their knees to beg his forgiveness. He allowed them to live, but commandeered everything they owned."

Thomas scowled, shaking his mane of white hair in disgust. "He banished others to Jamaica, Barbados or England for periods of seven years or even life. And of course took all their assets so they were destitute when they disembarked."

⋙⋘

Several days later, Jeffreys handed him Sir William's version of the king's absolution. It contained a list of those not pardoned—that included everyone he executed, still held in prison or hoped to apprehend. As he scanned the list, Thomas spirits fell. "All of these men have lucrative estates and disagreed with or provoked the governor."

"I can't believe he's countermanded a direct order from His Majesty pardoning his subjects," Berry snorted. "Only the king has authority to exempt people from pardon."

"You instructed him not to execute people since they're pardoned?" Thomas asked.

"Yes. We've written him repeatedly." Moryson said. "We've also asked for a list of those he's put to death and a tally of the estates he's grabbed so we could give the king an idea of the property accruing to him."

"He wrote back," Berry said sarcastically:

'Thank you for admonishing me in so weighty an affair, but confiscations are a customary part of war.'

"He reminded us that he served with King Charles and personally witnessed his appropriation of the estates of lords Essex and Roberts."

"We also told him not to place his personal mark on seized property, such as tobacco hogsheads," Jeffreys said, his clear gray eyes narrowing. "He's accumulated quite a hoard that makes him a very rich man. He wrote back saying he's never marked one hogshead."

"There are twenty people who will swear to the contrary," Thomas said. "Instead of writing to Sir William, why don't you issue a decree stating the governor's property seizures are illegal. This formulaic writing back and forth is too deferential to him. You're the ones with troops to back you."

"That's an excellent suggestion," Jeffreys said. "Then he can't claim he thought it was legal."

⤜⤛

Two days later, the commissioners asked Thomas to join them again. Papers, representing the latest correspondence between the commissioners and the governor, covered the desk in what used to be his estate room.

"The governor sent us a note saying he would sail to England to consult with His Majesty," Berry said, "and he would leave the government, during his absence, in Jeffreys' hands. We thought we'd better clarify he is removed from service at his own request."

"All the councilors were there, except you, Thomas," Moryson added.

"Well, I'm not likely to be on the Council again," Thomas shrugged.

"We read the king's appointment of me as the new governor of Virginia," Jeffreys said. "The appointment states I shall take over when Berkeley conveniently departs."

"The idiotic council began to argue over what the word 'conveniently' meant," Berry said. "Was it the king's convenience or the governor's? Was the governor being recalled permanently or temporarily?"

Thomas tried to suppress a laugh. He participated in many such meetings with no agenda, much posturing and nothing decided. This was exactly what Nat Bacon felt held Virginia back.

"The Council interpreted," Jeffreys said, "the word 'conveniently' as being the governor's convenience and that he would leave when his affairs were in order. He advised us he would let us know when it was convenient for him to temporarily step down."

"I think our hope rests with the General Assembly," Thomas said. "You can address them. Explain His Majesty pardons them and removes Berkeley."

"I'm afraid not," Berry said. "Sir William announced in front of everyone that it would be inappropriate for us to attend the assembly because he was not stepping down as governor."

"What?" Thomas finally looked shocked, reached for the arm of a chair and sat down heavily. "The old fox will justify his murders and the properties he snatched."

"What do you mean?" Moryson asked.

"By keeping you out of the assembly, he'll legislate to cover his tracks. Pass acts to exempt people from the king's pardon." Thomas leaned forward, resting his forearms on his knees, looking at the three men. "He'll pass an act of attainder justifying all the properties they've stolen."

"Will the burgesses vote for these things?" Jeffreys said. "I thought you said most supported Bacon's reform and raising a force for defense?"

"They did. Of forty thousand men in Virginia, less than three percent support Sir William. For a brief period, most hoped Virginia would be a fairer place to live and one where everyone could have a good life if they worked hard. But they've now experienced his vindictiveness. They'll vote the way he tells them too."

Green Spring, Virginia
February - March 1677

Sir William convened the assembly at Green Spring on the twentieth of February. As Thomas predicted, they passed twenty acts justifying the executions and the appropriation of land and possessions. They also repealed the reforms they passed nine months earlier.

The assembly ignored the questions put to them by the commissioners, who responded by demanding Beverley turn over their minutes going back to the reforms under Bacon. The man refused. They requested a list of estates seized and their value and received the same reply the governor had given them. Sir William outmaneuvered the commissioners at every opportunity and undermined Jeffreys by claiming he was his deputy, not the king's legally appointed governor.

>>><<<

Thomas sat at a desk squeezed between the staircase and the dormer window in his attic. Since the commissioners published the king's pardon and invited the citizens of Virginia to voice their grievances, his estate room was never empty so he moved his business upstairs. People came from all counties and parishes, bringing lengthy written protests. They described how the Indians terrorized them for a year, while Berkeley stood by and did nothing. They complained bitterly of the reign of terror he instituted after they suppressed the Indians, executing their friends and becoming wealthy from the appropriations. Thomas knew the steady stream of grievances prompted the commissioners to write His Majesty that peace could not exist until Berkeley, and his cronies who called themselves the Loyal Party, were removed.

"My dear." Mary interrupted Thomas' thoughts. She stood on the landing peering up at him. "John and Herbert would appreciate your presence." Thomas stood and headed down the stairs, patting Mary's arm as he passed. He knocked on the door and entered.

Berry waved him to a seat. "The governor summoned us to Green Spring to bid him farewell. He's sailing, or at least he says he is."

"He wasn't in the least cordial," Jeffreys said. "Offered us no refreshment. His councilors stood around looking officious."

Thomas tried to repress a sigh. What did they expect?

"He really called us," Jeffreys continued, "to tell us he wouldn't answer any of the questions we asked concerning the revolt. He was sailing to England and would tell the king when they are face-to-face.

"Oh," Berry said, "and you were right about Beverley. He told us he had not plundered enough and that the rebellion ended far too soon for his purposes. He bragged he became rich taking the goods of others." Berry shook his head in disgust. "When we left, the governor said he would call his coach for us."

Jeffreys snorted. "They slammed the door on us. We went to get into the coach and saw it was a hearse driven by the hangman. I could see Lady Berkeley peering out from the library window, laughing."

"We refused the ride," Berry scowled, "and walked the mile or so to the dock. We sent him a note of protest on our surly treatment. Do you know that he had the affront to write back? He says he is innocent as the blessed angels."

"He also said," Moryson added, "that Jesus was accused, but not guilty, and so was King Charles' father. Imagine comparing yourself to Jesus Christ and His Majesty's father?"

Thomas exhaled slowly and pressed his fingers to his forehead. The rancor that existed between the governor and the commissioners staggered him. However, they brought it on themselves for they could not seem to find their backbone.

"My God!" Jeffreys raised his voice. "The king named me governor and here we are foiled at every step. I intend to remove Beverley and Ludwell the first chance I get."

"Don't forget Edward Hill," Moryson said. "Sir William made him president of Charles City County. We've had so many complaints of that insolent, turbulent fellow and his greed that it is taking up a shelf to store the grievances."

"And that bitch, Lady Berkeley," Berry said. "I think sending the hangman to drive us was her doing. It's much more the spiteful thing a woman would do."

The governor did not depart and the executions increased. The commissioners again asked him to stop. He replied by executing Giles Bland. One of Bland's jailers had been indentured to

Thomas. Thomas paid the man to inform Bland of the king's pardon and that they hoped to have him released soon. He felt terrible for having given Giles a glimmer of hope.

Whitehall, City of London
May 15, 1677

At last, the dispatches sent by the commissioners in February reached England aboard the *Concord*. The king was furious.

"My, God!" he waved his fist and brought it crashing down on the table. "That old goat has killed more of my subjects in his petty revenge than we did in retaliation for the murder of my father." He shoved his chair back violently and stood hands on his hips, glaring at his advisors, who also stood up. His master of requests, Sir Thomas Povey, watched as the king stormed down the great hall. He knew better than to speak.

"Do you think Berkeley could have warned us of this?" he raged. "No! We receive pages and pages of complaints and letters from people all over Virginia, whom we've never heard of." He whirled around and stormed back. "See that he is instructed to report fully on this incident."

The king pivoted and began to stride away again, waving one fist to underline his points. "We are deeply troubled that Berkeley, who for so many years served my father and me through the worst of times, would have the affront to withhold my proclamation and put out one of his own in its place." He turned and strode back to them. "The impudence of the man to exempt persons whom we have pardoned. Is he insane?" He stopped in front of one of his advisors and stood staring at him.

The man decided he wanted an answer. "Much of this sounds like the acts of deranged men. Sir William, Sir Henry Chicheley, everyone, but especially Sir William."

His Majesty turned again, the tails of his justecorps swaying around his frame despite being stiff with the embroidery of heavy golden thread. He glared at them. "We want you to write Sir William immediately and in no uncertain terms, tell him to put the government in the hands of Jeffreys without further delay.

Make it clear to him he is to repair to my presence straightaway. And tell Jeffreys that if Berkeley refuses, he is to be physically carried on board any convenient vessel and transported to England."

⋙ CHAPTER 23 ⋘

EPILOGUE

Swann's Point
Three years later, September 1680

THOMAS SAT IN HIS ESTATE ROOM ENJOYING ONE OF HIS favorite panoramas: the spread of his lawn, the golden sycamores just beginning to shed a few leaves, and in the distance, Jamestown, or what had once been Jamestown. From this very window, he watched Sir William sail down the James River for the last time. Months afterwards, it became common knowledge the king was furious with his governor for executing so many of his subjects and for refusing to relinquish power to Jeffreys as instructed.

He stared at the paper, dipped his quill in the inkwell and continued his history. *The governor died about a month after he returned to England. He never got his audience with his sovereign. His brother, John, Lord Berkeley, employed a Mr. Culpepper to go through the Colonial Records and make copies of those pertaining to his deceased brother.*

Thomas paused, moving the quill to the side so that it would not drip on his work and spoil his efforts to put the true story on paper. He felt certain the intention of John, Lord Berkeley, was to whitewash his brother's sordid performance. He wondered if any of the records had been altered, or even removed altogether. He dipped the pen again.

Sir William's brother seems to have won because the Lords of Trade and Plantations issued a statement saying they hoped Sir William would be vindicated when more information emerged. Shortly after, the king decided not to take a decision on the matter of William Berkeley at all. He quietly dismissed the Commissioners and ordered his Chamber of Council to bury the Commissioners' report.

"Thomas. Your physic." Mary stood at the door with a tray in her hands, which contained the medicine prescribed by the doctor. He knew it would not cure him, but he took it to please his family.

He picked up the cup and saucer. His hand shook causing the china to rattle. He steadied the saucer with his right hand. Taking a sip, he regarded his wife. "I promise I'll take it when this palsy stops."

She sighed, rolled her eyes and closed the door. He shoved the cup aside and dipped his quill again.

The reports the Commissioners sent back to England condemned Sir William's handling of the Indian situation, his failure to defend the people, his misappropriation of taxes and other abuses of his office. Nevertheless, the final report itself was more of a narrative. It didn't actually blame Bacon, although it depicted him in a poor light, which was grossly unfair. Bacon was a genuine hero of the people of Virginia and they loved him. Unfortunately, the victorious write the histories, not the vanquished, and who knows what the Beverley's and Ludwells will write and what will be believed and remembered many years from now.

Once our new governor, Herbert Jeffreys, took over, he restored order and immediately reinstated me to the council. We concluded a peace treaty with the Algonquian Pamunkey, Wyeanoke, Nottoways and Nansemond at Middle Plantation. Of course, the Algonquian tribes didn't cause the terror in the years 1675 and 1676. We were at peace with them when conflict broke out with the Susquehannocks.

As for the Susquehannocks and Dogues, I heard that a few of them escaped to Kentucky. I hope the young man, Wannis, was among them for he seemed extremely able. One terrible result of our troubled times is we no longer try to live in harmony with native peoples. Our new policy is to shove them west and out of the lands we covet.

Philip Ludwell, Edward Hill and Robert Beverley continued their efforts to undermine Jeffreys' authority. Fortunately, the king removed and excluded Ballard, Bray and Ludwell from ever serving on the council again due to their "unworthy behavior." He also removed Robert Beverley and Edward Hill from all employment or position of trust and called them "evil characters."

In the coming months, we overturned many of Berkeley's policies. The king came to the conclusion, that freed indentured servants and small planters—our rising middle class—were a voice to be reckoned with. The king seemed to side with the small planters against the great planters. We eliminated the hated poll tax and reduced the salaries and terms of office for burgesses, justices and other officials.

One result of this was that the large planters decided not to import indentured labor who could challenge them in the future. Instead, they import slaves and the number of putrid ships sailing into Jamestown has greatly increased.

Thomas leaned back in his chair and stared at the unappealing, brownish physic. He lifted the cup in both hands and took a sip, making a face. Setting it down, he went back to his history.

Some of the survivors of Sir William's butchery reclaimed part of their estates. Samuel, my son, helped Willy Drummond's widow recover some of their property. She and her children hid in the forest for weeks. Samuel wanted to take them into his home, but he feared, as did all the colonists, that he would be punished for helping the family of one of the rebels. He provided food and shelter in a small hovel in the woods. Of course, Sara Drummond's silver and valuable assets went with Frances Culpepper Berkeley to England and never reappeared.

Somewhere, a door slammed, causing him to look up. Hearing nothing further, he looked back down and continued.

William Byrd distanced himself from Bacon adroitly. He stayed on his plantation high on the James and as a result maintained his neck and his property. With time, he expanded his holdings by buying the Bland's estate at a bargain price: the same estate Giles tried to restore to his family. Byrd has done so well that there is discussion of appointing him to the council when an opening appears.

Thomas Ballard, who at first supported our reformed government when Berkeley fled to the eastern shore, redeemed himself by enthusiastically participating in the courts-martial and executions. He was always adept at being on two sides at once. People who are able to do this, often do surprisingly well in life.

Robert Beverley, the governor's excessive supporter and one of the worst scoundrels in the country, managed to keep most of the wealth he stole from his fellow citizens.

Phillip Ludwell came out best of all, for when his brother Thomas Ludwell died, he inherited his properties in Virginia. Later, he married Frances Culpepper Berkeley and is now nicely ensconced as the lord of Green Spring, Virginia's finest plantation. This year, his new brother-in-law, Lord Culpepper, became our governor. When Charles II died, Ludwell managed to get himself reinstated on the Council.

Thomas paused to take a new quill, turning it slowly in his fingers to examine it before dipping it in ink.

Hardly a day passes that I do think about speaking to William Drummond, that doughty Scotsman. Sometimes, I have a conversation with him and we discuss what I shall include in the next order to England. Then, I realize again, he is gone. I paid the hangman a good sum to recover his body and buried him in an unmarked grave in the Swann's Point family cemetery. One day I will place a proper headstone on his grave. He was one of the finest men I have known.

And Richard Lawrence? They confiscated his estates—Nathaniel Bacon got a good part of his assets—but he escaped and kept his life. I think John Lucas went with him.

Almost a year after Sir William departed I received a long letter from my friend Edward near St. Mary's. He reported that my goods had arrived safely and he sent them on to the frontier. The goods were used to open a small school with six pupils from neighboring farms. Eventually, when more people settle there, a public house would be opened. My friend described what I had sent to him in a guarded way, but then he should for Lawrence and his companions are still remembered here.

Thomas stared out the window, smiling inwardly and wondering how Lawrence got along without his cook and shelf of spices, and if Lucas still delighted people with his woodcarvings.

As for me, I am very fortunate, I think. Sir William promised me death and refused to pardon me, yet no one ever came to Swann's Point to arrest me. I believe that the presence of the commissioners in my home had everything to do with this. Thank heavens Berkeley's arrogance and his need to intimidate the king's commissioners left them with no housing. The governor probably thought he punished me by shoving all of these people into my home to feed. In the final analysis, having dodged his vindictiveness, it became my salvation.

Thomas exhaled loudly as he closed his eyes. It was becoming dark for being yet early afternoon. He felt pleased with his history of what really happened in Virginia. Perhaps someday, it would see the light of day.

⟫⟫ Author's Note ⟪⟪

THE FIRST POPULAR INSURGENCY IN AMERICA OCCURRED in Virginia in 1675-1676, a century before the American Revolution. The outcome shaped the country's development in three ways. First, the emerging middle class made up of freemen (former indentured servants) rebelled against disproportionate taxes, a harsh political and economic monopoly, and the failure of their corrupt government to defend them against Indian attacks. They discovered that by standing together their voices were heard. Second, large planters stopped using indentured labor which might challenge them, and instead imported African slaves, who would never have a voice. Third, while colonists tried to live peaceably with Native Americans, the aftermath of the uprising resulted in a strategy of driving them from their lands into the west or hunting them down.

Despite these far-reaching impacts on the nation's future, history books seldom emphasize the 1675-1676 rebellion. The reasons could be twofold. First, King Charles II was angry and embarrassed by his corrupt governor, Sir William Berkeley. The governor was the brother of the king's closest companion, which may explain why he initially ordered an investigation into the causes of the rebellion, and then subsequently ordered that the matter be closed. The report of the Royal Commissioners sent to Virginia to investigate was placed in the British Colonial Records' archives where it remained buried for over a century.

Second, from Virginia's perspective, many of its foremost families—Washington, Mason, Lee, Ludwell, Beverley, Custis, Kemp and Spencer—are on the immoral side of the uprising. The governor, and his cronies executed many innocent people for disobeying orders forbidding them to take up arms to defend themselves against the Susquehannocks. After executing their fellow citizens, these officials became rich men by evicting widows and orphans and dividing up the estates of the deceased. Robert Beverley, son of one of the most corrupt officials, wrote *The History of Virginia in Four Parts*. It misrepresented the rebellion and what took place, and yet for centuries, people read it and accepted its accuracy. As historians remind us, the vanquished do not write histories, the victors do.

It wasn't until after the American Revolution, around 1803, that the facts began to emerge when Thomas Jefferson received a copy of one of three first-hand accounts. Written by Thomas Matthews and entitled *The Beginning, Progress, and Conclusion of Bacon's Rebellion, 1675-1676*, Jefferson willed it to the Library of Congress. A second account, *History of Bacon and Ingram's Rebellion* was among the family papers of Virginia Congressman, William Burwell. He permitted the Massachusetts Historical Society to print his document in 1814. The Royal Commissioners sent to investigate the causes of the revolt compiled the third record of events, *A True Narrative of the Late Rebellion in Virginia*. In addition to these chronicles, we now have access to letters, proceedings and proclamations describing the events as they unfolded. Many may be accessed on-line through the archives of the United Kingdom (British Public Records, Colonial Office America and West Indies), and in the archives of Virginia and Maryland and their historical societies.

For the most part, I have used primary source material and endeavored to adhere to actual events. The dates occurring at the beginning of our year in January through March have been altered to reflect the Gregorian calendar. England only adopted this more familiar calendar in the eighteenth century.

While I have relied on primary sources as much as possible, I have taken some liberties in developing the personalities of

268

several colonial leaders who opposed the governor. Although they formed the majority of people in Virginia, little was written about them. For instance, it is uncontestable that Thomas Swann a Council member, helped form a new government, hosted the Commissioners in his home and had a deep friendship with William Drummond. Whether he supported native peoples, is the author's conception. I have also opted not to accept the Royal Commissioners portrait of Nat Bacon as arrogant and looking down at his neighbors. The governor openly praised Bacon and appointed him to his Council of Advisors at a young age. Bacon's neighbors supported this view, for when they learned the governor removed him from the Council, they voiced their displeasure by electing him to represent them as their Burgess.

The personalities of the small contingent of the governor's supporters are well documented in primary sources. Many people filed "grievances" against them to the king. To quote the Royal Commissioners:

"But soe great was the Cowardize and Basenesse of the Generality of Sir William Berkeley's Party being most of them men intent onely upon plunder or compell'd and hired into his service that of all, at last there were onely some 20 Gentlemen willing to stand by him..."

That so few men supported Governor Berkeley is revealing indeed.

Finally, in the List of Characters, an asterisk denotes fictional characters. This includes most of the Native Americans, for no one recorded their names. Further, there are scant first hand records documenting customs and language of the Susquehannocks and Dogues, who played a pivotal role in the uprising. The Susquehannocks inhabited a fort on Piscataway Creek and escaped in the dead of winter swimming the Potomac River to safety, a feat of extraordinary bravery and perseverance. I have given Wannis and Connawa names derived from the research of experts on the Dogue and Susquehannock people. The Select Bibliography cites a few of these authorities. Whether the Susquehannocks escaped to the west is speculation. Yet, I found no record that the 250 souls that fled were killed, and one would like to think they retreated to a better life, away from the treachery of the colonists.

⇒ LIST OF CHARACTERS ⇐

Isaac Allerton – Major in Stafford County militia, Justice of the Peace and one of six big slave owners in 1675.

Nat Bacon – A brilliant, Cambridge-educated lawyer and a member of the governor's Council of Advisors.

Nathaniel Bacon (Senior) – Older cousin of Nat Bacon and also a member of the Council of Advisors.

Thomas Ballard – Colonel in militia and a member of the Council of Advisors.

Frances Culpepper Berkeley – The governor's wife and cousin to Nat Bacon.

Sir William Berkeley – Governor of Virginia who overtaxed small planters and refused to defend them against Indian attacks. His patronage system made his associates wealthy.

Robert Beverley – Burgess from Middlesex County and one of six big slave owners. Charles II banned him from holding any public office.

Giles Bland – Collector of Customs who uncovered government corruption.

James Bray – Member of the Council of Advisors.

George Brent – Captain of Stafford County militia, cousin of Giles Brent and one of six big slave owners.

Giles Brent – Officer in Stafford County militia and son of Mary, daughter of the Piscataway king.

Joseph Bridger - Colonel of Isle of Wight County militia and a member of the Council of Advisors.

William Byrd – Officer in Henrico County militia who managed to survive Governor Berkeley's wrath.

William Carver – Captain of Norfolk County militia and High Sheriff.

Charles Calvert – Governor of Maryland.

Sir Henry Chicheley – Burgess from Lancaster County and member of the Council of Advisors, who inherited property (Rosegil) through marriage to a wealthy widow.

Charles II – King of England, who regained his throne from Oliver Cromwell.

William Coles – Colonel of Warwick County militia and member of the Council of Advisors.

John Crabb – Planter with property next to John Washington's in Westmoreland County.

James Crewes – Officer of Henrico County militia and Justice of the Peace.

William Diggs – Son of Governor Edward Digges who tortured Thomas Hansford and removed his fingers.

William Drummond – A Scotsman who arrived in Virginia in 1637 as an indentured servant and later accumulated wealth and property.

John Gerrard – Planter from Westmoreland County who participated in the siege of Fort Piscataway and later testified that Maryland murdered the Susquehannock chiefs.

Thomas Hansford – Captain in York County militia.

Henry Hartwell – Clerk to the Council of Advisors and Sir William Berkeley and one of six big slave owners.

William Hartwell – Captain and brother of Henry who seized and kept the property of his fellow-citizens.

Robert Hen – Thomas Mathews' herdsman in Stafford County who cheated the Dogues which led to over a year of violence.

*Tobey Hen – Robert Hen had a boy with him when he was killed and this narrative portrays him as Hen's son.

Edward Hill – Lieutenant Colonel of Charles County militia and Burgess. The commissioners characterized him as "a most notable coward and insolent turbulent fellow."

Henry Isham – Charles County planter.

Richard Lawrence – Burgess with hundreds of acres and a common house in Jamestown, herein named the Snow Goose.

John Lucas – Captain of Westmoreland County militia and nephew of Thomas Lucas, one of the original settlers of Rappahannock County.

Tom Lucas – John Lucas' cousin.

Philip Ludwell – Brother of Thomas and member of the Council of Advisors who Charles II banned from holding any public office.

Thomas Ludwell – Came to Virginia in 1646 as an indentured servant and appointed to the Council of Advisors. With his brother, Phillip, took the property of the Bland family.

George Mason – Burgess of Stafford County and Colonel of the militia. His plantation on Pohick Creek passed to his descendant who contributed to the Constitution and Bill of Rights.

Thomas Matthews – Burgess from Stafford County whose herdsman cheated the Dogues and set in motion the rebellion of 1676. He wrote one of three first-hand accounts of the event.

William Pressley – Burgess from Stafford County.

Robert Rawlings – Planter from Stafford County.

Stephen Rawlings – Brother of Robert Rawlings.

Thomas Swann – Colonel of Surry County militia, veteran of Indian Wars of 1644 and member of the Council of Advisors, who managed to survive Governor Berkeley's wrath.

John Shankes – Accompanied Thomas Truman in the siege on Ft. Piscataway.

Thomas Truman – Sent by Governor Calvert to convince the Susquehannocks to move away.

John Washington – Colonel of Stafford County militia whose property on Little Hunting Creek would one day pass to

List of Characters

President George Washington.

Captain Thomas Wilford – Captain of York County militia who accompanied Robert Fallam on the first expedition to the unexplored western slope of the Appalachian Mountains.

The Commissioners Sent to Investigate the Rebellion

Francis Moryson – Sent to England with Thomas Ludwell to secure repeal of land grant to Arlington and Culpeper. Charles II appointed him to return to Virginia as one of the Commissioners.

Sir John Berry – Admiral of the Fleet who served in the West Indies and in the Mediterranean against Barbary pirates.

Col. Herbert Jeffreys – Appointed by Charles II to command the land troops and to replace Sir William Berkeley as governor.

Samuel Wiseman – Recording secretary of the Commission.

Native Americans

Mary Brent – Daughter of a Piscataway chief and married to Giles Brent, Sr.

*Chee-ne-wan – Connawa's Dogue wife.

*Chinkotook – A Dogue and brother of Wannis.

*Connawa – War captain of the Susquehannock's most powerful tribe and later its leader.

*Connawa Rocquaes – Connawa's uncle who was murdered by Thomas Truman.

*Dahedaghesa – Susquehannock tribal chief murdered by

275

Thomas Truman.

*Ex-undas – Member of Connawa's war band.

*Koweenasee – Quaachow's daughter.

*Nansemond – A Dogue and younger brother of Wannis.

*Nicotagsen – A Dogue and brother of Wannis.

*Quaachow – Member of Connawa's war band.

*Sawaheguh – Susquehannock tribal chief murdered by Thomas Truman.

*Shae-ee-kah – Member of Connawa's war band and his best friend.

*Sheehays – Member of Connawa's war band.

*Tong-quas – Member of Connawa's war band.

*Tonna Hoorn – Connawa's father and Susquehannock tribal chief of the largest tribe murdered by Thomas Truman.

*Wadonhago – Susquehannock tribal chief murdered by Thomas Truman.

*Wannis – Dogue warrior whose Algonquian-speaking people are massacred by Mason and Brent. He is adopted by the Susquehannocks.

*Uwanno – Wannis' uncle and war captain of their tribe

Merchant Captains who Supported
the Governor for Profit

John Consett – Captain of the *Mary*

Thomas Gardner – Captain of the *Adam and Eve*

Thomas Grantham – Captain of the *Concord* who wrote an account

Thomas Larrimore – Captain of the *Rebecca*

Robert Morris – Captain of the *Young Prince*

Nicholas Prynne - Captain of the *Richard and Elizabeth*

* Those marked with an asterisk are fictional characters.

⋙ SELECT BIBLIOGRAPHY ⋘

Primary Sources

Andrews, Charles M., Ed., *Narratives of the Insurrection, 1675–1690*. (Reproduces three first-hand accounts), New York: Charles Scribner and Sons, 1915.

Bacon, Nathaniel. "Bacon's Appeal to the People of Accomack," July 1676, and "Declaration of the People of Virginia," August 3, 1676, British Public Records, Colonial Office America and West Indies, Calendar of State Papers (BPR). "Account of their troubles in Virginia with the Indians, June 18th, 1676," William and Mary College Quarterly, Vol IX, No. 1. "Manifesto concerning the present troubles in Virginia, August 1676," Virginia Magazine of History and Biography , Vol. 1, No. 1.

Berkeley, Sir William. "Letter to Secretary Coventry," Feb 2, 1677. William and Mary College Quarterly, Vol. , No. 3.

Bland, Giles. "Letter to Thomas Povey, Master of Requests to Charles II," July 8, 1676, BPR, Vol. XXXVII., Nos. 27, 27 I.

Campanius Holm, Thomas. "A Vocabulary of Susquehannock," American Language Reprints Series, 2nd Edition, from "Vocabularium Barbaero- Virgineorum," Stockholm, 1696.

Gerrard, John, interview by Nicholas Spencer and Richard Lee. "Gerard's Account of Ft Piscataway," William and Mary College Quarterly, Vol. 11 No. 1.

Ludwell, Philip. "Letter to Secretary Sir Joseph Williamson: an account of the distressed condition of this poor country." June 28, 1676. BPR, Vol. XXXVII., No. 16.

Morris, Robert. "Journal of the ship *Young Prince*, Robert Morris, Commander, during the time she was in the King's service in James River, September 19, 1676 to January 29, 1677." BPR, Vol. XXXVII, No. 52.

Secondary Sources

Billings, Warren M., Ed., *Papers of Sir William Berkeley*. Richmond: Library of Virginia, 2007.

Billings, Warren M. *The Old Dominion in the seventeenth century: documentary history of Virginia, 1606-1689*. Chapel Hill: University of North Carolina Press, 1976.

Engerman, Stanley L. and Robert L. Gallman, Editors. *The Cambridge Economic History of the United States: Colonial Era*, Vol 1. Cambridge: Cambridge University Press, 1996.

Eshleman, H. Frank. *Lancaster County Indians: Annals of the Susquehannocks and other Indian Tribes of the Susquehanna Territory from about 1500 to 1763, the Date of their Extinction*. Lewisburg: Wennawood Publishing, 2000.

McIlwaine, H.R., Editor. *General Court of Colonial Virginia*. 2nd edition, Richmond: Virginia State Library Press, 1979.

Neville, John Davenport. *Bacon's Rebellion: Abstracts of materials in the Colonial Records Project*. Jamestown, Va: The Jamestown Foundation, 1976.

Rountree, Helen. *Pocahontas's People: The Powhatan Indians of Virginia through Four Centuries*. Norman: University of

Oklahoma, 1990.

Rountree, Helen. *The Powhatan Indians of Virginia: Their Traditional Culture.* Vol. 193 of Civilization of American Indians. Norman: University of Oklahoma Press, 1989.

Tate, Thad, and David Ammerman. *The Chesapeake in the Seventeenth Century: Essays on Anglo-American Society.* Chapel Hill: University of North Carolina Press, 1979.

Webb, Stephen Saunders. *1676: The end of American Independence.* New York: Knopf Publishing, 1984.

Wertenbaker, Thomas J. *Bacon's Rebellion, 1676.* Baltimore: Genealogical Publishing Company, 1957.

⋙ ABOUT THE AUTHOR ⋘

CAROLIN A. CRABBE is a
development economist who
worked in over forty countries
during her career, providing
essential projects and services
to low income groups. Upon
retiring, she returns to one of
her primary loves: American
history and the historical novel.
Although published in the field
of finance and economics, this
work is her first in the genre of
historical fiction. She lives in
Washington DC and knows the
Chesapeake Bay and the sites
where the action of this story
takes place extremely well.